THE CASE
OF THE MISSING
GAME WARDEN

THE CASE
OF THE MISSING
GAME WARDEN

STEVEN T. CALLAN

coffeetownpress

Kenmore, WA

A Coffeetown Press book published by Epicenter Press

Epicenter Press
6524 NE 181st St.
Suite 2
Kenmore, WA 98028

For more information go to:
www.Camelpress.com
www.Coffeetownpress.com
www.Epicenterpress.com
www.steventcallan.com

This is a work of fiction. Names, characters, places, brands, media, and incidents are either the product of the author's imagination or are used fictitiously.

Cover design by Scott Book
Cover photo by Steven T. Callan
Back cover photo of Glenn County Courthouse by Steven T. Callan
Design by Melissa Vail Coffman

The Case of the Missing Game Warden

ISBN: 978-1-60381-306-8 (Trade Paper)
ISBN: 978-1-60381-307-5 (eBook)

Printed in the United States of America

For Kathy

ACKNOWLEDGMENTS

M Y FIRST NOVEL, *THE CASE OF the Missing Game Warden*, is the product of hard work, life experience, and persistence. It could never have come to fruition without help from these people I call my friends.

To Phil Garrett at Epicenter Press and Jennifer McCord at Coffeetown Press, I owe my most sincere thanks for the confidence you've shown in my writing and for your continued support.

Kathy Callan's encouragement, incredible editing skills, and advice played an indispensable role in bringing *The Case of the Missing Game Warden* to life. I couldn't have done it without you, sweetheart.

Thank you to Professors Brunella Windsor and Gerardo Mireles at California State University, Chico, for their generosity in sharing their expertise in the Italian and Spanish languages.

One of the highlights of doing research for this book was learning about the Glenn County Courthouse—built in 1894 and still in use. I'm indebted to former Glenn County Superior Court Executive Officer and current Tehama County Superior Court Executive Officer Kevin Harrigan, Glenn County Superior Court Administrative Assistant Karen Dura, Glenn County Deputy Sheriff Dan Perry, and current Glenn County Superior Court Executive Officer Sharif Elmallah for sharing their knowledge of this historic treasure.

Kathy and I spent a glorious day at the University of California, Berkeley, libraries while I was doing research for this book. I would like to thank Monica Alarcon (Bancroft Library), James Eason (Bancroft

Library), Dean Smith (Bancroft Library), Iris Donovan (Bancroft Library), Natalia Estrada (Doe Library), and Desirae Mendoza (Doe Library) for all of your help and for the gracious way we were treated.

A special thanks to all the people who have followed my writing since 2013. Your kind words inspired me to write this book.

PART ONE

PART ONE

ONE

IT WAS LATE AFTERNOON, in early December 1956, when twenty-five-year-old Blake Gastineau walked out of the two-room guesthouse on his father's rice farm northwest of Gridley, California. Wearing faded Levi jeans, a dark-green army fatigue jacket, and PF Flyers tennis shoes, Gastineau loaded his Remington Model 11-48, semiautomatic 12-gauge shotgun and four boxes of number 4, high-base shotgun shells into the trunk of his dark-gray, 1949 Ford coupe. Elvis was belting out his latest hit, "Don't Be Cruel," when the former Gridley High School quarterback flipped on the radio and cruised out the long gravel driveway toward the county road. Passing under a wrought-iron archway reading GASTINEAU FARMS, Blake turned right, stomped on the gas, and roared westward toward the highway.

Clouds from an earlier storm were breaking up over the Sutter Buttes when Gastineau reached the Sacramento Valley farm town of Gridley, turned up a side street, and pulled into the Shady Rest Trailer Park. Down at the end of the park lived two ne'er-do-wells: Hollis Bogar and Richie Stillwell. Both men performed menial tasks for Blake's father during the growing season but "lived off the land," as Bogar was often heard saying, during the winter months.

"Living off the land, my ass!" local game warden Norman Bettis would respond. "Those two no-good sonsabitches are the worst duck poachers in Butte County." Bettis had once been a hard-charging game warden, but chasing duck hunters through the tules for thirty-two years had taken its toll. Now his knees yelped with pain every time he donned his hip boots and tried to hike across a muddy rice field. Overweight and out of shape, the sixty-two-year-old veteran game warden did most of his enforcement work from the seat of his 1954 Ford sedan patrol car. If he wasn't on patrol, you could usually find Warden Bettis drinking coffee and swapping stories with the old-timers at Pearl's Roadside Diner out on Highway 99.

Norm Bettis had been a warden for the California Department of Fish and Game for so long that he proudly wore Badge Number One above the pocket of his immaculate uniform shirt. A day didn't go by without him hearing the same query from one of his elderly coffee-shop companions: "Hey, Norm, when ya gonna retire?"

Bettis's answer was always the same. "What would I do if I retired— sit here bullshittin' with you guys? I can do that now and get paid for it."

HOLLIS BOGAR KICKED THE TRAILER DOOR open with his size-fifteen tennis shoe and stepped outside carrying a 12-gauge shotgun in one hand and a six-pack of Burgermeister beer in the other. "Hey, man," he said, "did ya bring me a box a shells?"

"Yeah, I brought one for each of you," said Gastineau. "The trunk's open. Throw your shotgun in back, and let me have one of those. Where's that crazy little cousin of yours?"

"He's tryin' ta find his tennis shoe. I think the dog next door drug it off the porch last night."

"Looks like we got lots of birds down from up north," said Gastineau, popping open his beer. "I wanna get out there before dark and see if we can figure out where they're gonna feed tonight."

"Here he comes," said Bogar. "Richie, I see ya found your shoe."

"Yeah, that stupid mutt chewed it up."

"You can climb in back. I got shotgun."

"You always get shotgun."

"That's 'cause I'm way bigger than you."

"Uglier too," said Stillwell. "Hey, Blake, did that contact of yours pay us for all them ducks we killed the other night?"

"Yeah, I've got some dough in my pocket for you guys."

"Wha'd we get?" said Stillwell, removing a brass lighter from his front pocket and lighting a cigarette.

"Same as always: five dollars for mallards, four for pintails, and three for teal, wigeons, and everything else."

"What about all them gadwalls we killed a couple weeks ago?" said Bogar.

"He said the fancy restaurants won't take gadwalls anymore. They won't take wigeons either, if they been feedin' on alfalfa. The restaurants in Chinatown will take whatever he brings 'em, but they won't pay more than two bucks for anything but mallards, sprig, and cans."

"We ain't shot a canvasback in two years," said Bogar, chugging his second beer. "Baste them gadwalls in wine and a little melted butter, and those rich bastards in San Francisco won't know the difference."

"You got that right," said Stillwell. "Hey, I'll take one a them brewskis."

"Not unless you give me a cigarette first," said Bogar.

Stillwell reached over the front seat of the parked coupe and handed Bogar a cigarette. "I'm waiting."

"First you gotta say the magic word."

"I got your magic word. Give me a beer or I'll wrap the butt of my shotgun across the back of your giant head!"

"You're probably crazy enough to do that," said Bogar, handing Stillwell a beer.

"You're damn right I am. Now, how am I gonna open this without a church key?"

"Hand him the damn can opener so he'll shut up," said Gastineau, pulling a wad of cash and some change from his pocket and counting out $95.17. With the car still idling, Gastineau handed Bogar his cut.

"What about me?" said Stillwell.

"You ain't gettin' any," said Bogar.

"I'm gonna climb over this seat and take yours. You owe me for your share of the rent, anyway."

"Here, hand this back to him," said Gastineau. Bogar reached over the seat and handed the money to Stillwell.

"Ninety-five-seventeen?" said Stillwell. "How much did you get, Blake?"

"Yeah, Blake," said Bogar, "how much did you get?"

"Okay, here's the deal, and I'm not gonna explain it to you two halfwits again. The other day I delivered 101 ducks. He paid me $423. Divided four ways, that's a hundred and five dollars and seventy-five cents apiece, but I took ten percent out of each of your cuts."

"How come you did that?" said Bogar.

"Because I run the risk of getting caught driving down the highway with all those ducks in my trunk. If I get busted and thrown in jail, my old man will disinherit me and I won't get my share of the farm when he kicks the bucket."

"What about that connection of yours?" said Stillwell. "What's he get outta this?"

"He gets whatever the big-city restaurants pay him, and that depends on how badly their rich customers want roast duck for dinner."

"What big cities are we talkin' about?" said Bogar, cutting loose with a gigantic belch.

"I know he delivers to San Francisco, Oakland, and Sacramento. After that, I'm not sure."

"How come you won't tell us who this connection of yours is?" said Stillwell.

"I told you guys not to ask me that," said Gastineau, angered and visibly shaken by the question. "Jimmy's expectin' us at 3:30, so we better get goin.'"

Jimmy Riddle lived with his mother and grandparents at the southeast corner of a run-down, hundred-acre almond orchard, three miles west of Gridley. At the northwest corner of the property was a corrugated metal packing shed with a cement slab floor. Since the trees were no longer productive, the shed had become a convenient place for Jeb Riddle, Jimmy's eighty-four-year-old grandfather, to store farm equipment and old furniture his wife no longer wanted. Everything in the shed was draped in fifteen years of dust and cobwebs.

The neglected orchard gradually became overgrown with weeds and high grass—ideal cover for the multitudes of ring-necked pheasants that lived in the area. Every November, on opening weekend of pheasant season, hunters would fire away at pheasants in the corn and grain fields surrounding Jeb Riddle's property. Like lambs to the slaughter, those pheasants that survived the initial onslaught would set their wings and glide into Riddle's orchard, where Jimmy Riddle and his high-school buddies were lying in wait. There was nothing illegal about ambushing pheasants, but the boys got carried away and killed considerably more than the law allowed. That went on for three seasons, until someone at school overheard Gastineau and Bogar bragging about their good fortune. Tipped off, Warden Norm Bettis showed up on a Sunday evening and caught Jimmy Riddle, Blake Gastineau, and Hollis Bogar picking and cleaning a giant pile of pheasants in Jeb Riddle's packing shed.

Bogar was already on probation for punching out the assistant football coach, so he spent thirty days in juvenile hall. The other two junior outlaws received a tongue lashing and six months' probation from the juvenile-court judge in Oroville. Ralph Gastineau, Blake's father, told

Blake if he ever embarrassed him like that again, he would will the entire farm to Blake's younger brother and Blake could spend the rest of his life digging dock weed in the fields.

Blake Gastineau turned off the county road onto a well-traveled dirt road between two rows of almond trees. Two hundred yards farther, he turned left and followed a path leading from Jeb Riddle's house straight to the old packing shed. "It's about time," said Jimmy Riddle, dressed in blue jeans, a white T-shirt, and a shiny new black leather jacket. A cigarette dangling from the side of his mouth, Riddle stood next to a lime-green, 1952 Rocket 88 Oldsmobile with a primer-gray left front fender. "I was beginnin' ta wonder if you guys were gonna show up."

"These two idiots were givin' me a hard time about their cut for the ducks we killed the other night," said Gastineau.

"Oh, yeah?" said Riddle, pulling a plastic comb from his back pocket and combing his shiny-black, ducktail hairdo. "How much did we get?"

"You get the full hundred and five bucks, since you're providing the shed and transportation."

"That's good, because my boss at the body shop keeps buggin' me about makin' a payment on this gas guzzler he sold me."

"Hey, Jimmy," said Bogar, sneaking up behind Riddle and messing his hair. "I think ya need a little more grease."

"If you weren't so big, I'd teach you a lesson," said Riddle, recombing his hair.

"I'd like to see that," said Bogar, climbing into the back seat.

"Me too," said Stillwell, attempting to slip into the front passenger seat without being noticed.

"Nice try, Richie," said Gastineau. "Now get in back. I need to ride up front to tell Jimmy where to go."

"I'll be happy to tell Jimmy where to go," said Stillwell.

TWO

CLARK MATHEWSON WAS THE QUINTESSENTIAL young Republican before anyone at the University of California, Berkeley, ever thought of forming an organization by that name. Gregarious, good-looking, and exuding confidence, he majored in business, with the career goal of becoming a real-estate tycoon and making his first million before he turned thirty.

With war raging during the early 1940s, Mathewson joined UC Berkeley's Reserve Officers' Training Corps (ROTC) and was eventually commissioned as a second lieutenant in the U.S. Army. Clark would serve briefly overseas, but upon being promoted to first lieutenant, he managed to secure a cushy company commander's post at Fort Ord, near Monterey, California, where he spent the remainder of his military career.

At twenty-six, Mathewson resumed his original career path and became a Bay Area real-estate broker. Within three years, he was listing and regularly selling six- and seven-figure properties. Clark made his first million on April 16, 1953, a week before his thirtieth birthday and two days before his marriage to Barbara Cleary, the beautiful daughter of a prominent San Francisco businessman. Soon after, Clark and Barbara Mathewson bought their dream home in the Berkeley Hills and assumed their position amongst the Bay Area's post-war nouveau riche.

AT EIGHTY-SIX, VALENTINO VANNUCCI STILL LIKED to drop in unannounced and check on the family business. After all, Vannucci's had made a name for itself in San Francisco's historic Embarcadero District, and its original owner wanted to keep it that way. "What's going on here?" the eccentric, gray-haired old man would bellow, as he stormed through the back entrance, scaring the kitchen crew half to death and causing his son Victor considerable consternation.

Sixty-year-old Victor Vannucci managed the day-to-day operation of the restaurant and acted as maître d' every evening, except Monday and Tuesday. Vannucci's was closed on Mondays, and Carlo Vannucci, Victor's fifty-two-year-old cousin, would fill in on Tuesday evenings. Carlo also served as Vannucci's lunch-hour maître d'.

"Vannucci's," answered Carlo, one Saturday afternoon in mid-December 1955. "How may I help you?"

"Hello, Carlo. This is Clark Mathewson."

"Mr. Mathewson! How nice to hear your voice."

"How's business?"

"Business is good. We always have our regulars, and this time of year the holiday-tourist crowd spills over from Fisherman's Wharf."

"That's great. I wanted to make a reservation for tonight."

"Of course. What time and for how many?"

"There will be four of us, and this is a special occasion, so I'd like to order a wild-duck dinner."

"Un momento per favore," said Carlo. He reached under his podium and retrieved a maroon-colored binder with VANNUCCI'S emblazoned across the front cover. Carlo opened the binder to a page reading "Clienti di Riguardo." Seeing Clark Mathewson's name on the list, he ran back to the kitchen and discretely asked his cousin Lorenzo, the afternoon chef, if their weekly supply of wild ducks had come in.

Lorenzo Vannucci was Valentino Vannucci's second son. Lacking the business acumen of his father and his older brother, Lorenzo had been blessed with an extra helping of empathy and good humor. Tall, thin, and exceedingly handsome for a man in his late fifties, Lorenzo was Vannucci's go-to guy if anyone had a work-related problem he or she wanted to talk about. The female employees loved him, and all the male employees, except one, looked upon Lorenzo as a close friend and confidant.

Lorenzo advised Carlo that their supplier had made a delivery that morning and he would check to make sure the requested items were available.

"Mr. Mathewson, I'm sorry for the wait," said Carlo. "The afternoon chef is checking on our supply. May I call you back in just a few minutes?"

"Sure," said Clark, providing Carlo with his phone number.

"Very good."

Lorenzo walked into the cooler and inspected eight freshly pro-cessed turkeys, all placed in a row on a waist-high, stainless-steel shelf. Six of the turkeys weighed over twenty pounds, and two were in the ten-pound class. Lorenzo reached inside the body cavity of the first tur-key and pulled out a two-and-a-half-pound duck, neatly wrapped in cellophane. Removing the cellophane, Lorenzo noticed that the duck had been professionally picked and cleaned, with not a single pinfeath-er left on the bird's supple, fat-laden body. A small section of orange skin had been left at the heel joints, allowing Lorenzo to easily identify the duck as a mallard.

"Nice and plump, just the way we like 'em," mumbled Lorenzo. "This one's definitely been feeding on rice."

One by one, Lorenzo retrieved a single duck from the body cavity of each turkey. Based on size, shape, and skin color, he confirmed that four mallards, two pintails, and two green-winged teal had been delivered that morning.

Wearing a traditional white toque, white coat, and white apron, Lorenzo walked into the dining room and whispered to Carlo, "Ne ab-biamo sei grandi e due piccole."

"Excellent," said Carlo. Carlo understood that grandi generally indi-cated mallard or pintail and piccole meant green-winged teal. Vannucci's had been one of San Francisco's top-rated eating establishments since it first opened many years before. As such, they refused to offer any-thing but the highest quality and most sought-after variety of wild ducks to their "special" customers. Mallards, pintails, and teal were the ducks of choice. Canvasbacks had been popular during the restaurant's early years, but since numbers of this once-coveted species had plummeted, they were no longer a reliable alternate-menu item.

"Be sure to ask if they want them roasted with skins on or skins off," said Lorenzo, walking back to the kitchen.

THE TELEPHONE RANG AT THE REAL-ESTATE brokerage office of Clark Mathewson.

"Mathewson Real Estate Group," answered the receptionist. "Dorothy speaking."

"Yes, this is Carlo at Vannucci's Restaurant. May I speak to Mr. Mathewson, please?"

"Yes, Carlo. He's been eagerly awaiting your call."

"Carlo, my man! Thanks for getting back to me."

"You're in luck, Mr. Mathewson. We will have no problem completing your order."

"That's great!"

"I have a couple questions so we can make this a perfect evening for you and your guests."

"Sure, go ahead."

"Will there be ladies present?"

"Yes. My wife and our friend's wife."

"Sometimes the ladies prefer a smaller bird. Will that be the case with your party?"

"I think the ladies would prefer the smaller birds. I know Barbara is always watching her weight. Don't tell her I said that."

"I won't," said Carlo, chuckling. "Would members of your party prefer the birds roasted with the skins on or skins off?"

"With skins on. That's the best part. My mouth is watering already."

"We usually serve this special meal with wild rice and vegetables. Will that be satisfactory?"

"Absolutely."

"The reason I'm asking these questions is because the items you've chosen take ninety minutes or more to prepare. Giovanni wants your meal to be perfect in every way. It will be necessary to begin your order long before you arrive at seven o'clock."

"Everything sounds wonderful," said Clark. "We'll be looking forward to this evening."

Hanging up the phone, Carlo rushed back to the kitchen and advised Lorenzo of the customers' preferences. Lorenzo walked into a small corner office and wrote down instructions for Giovanni Sabatini, Vannucci's head chef. Giovanni usually arrived about 3:00 p.m. to begin preparations for the evening's meals.

Fifty-six-year-old Giovanni Sabatini enjoyed the well-earned reputation of being one of the Bay Area's finest chefs. Feasting on one of his exquisitely prepared wild ducks was a culinary delight that kept most of Vannucci's "special" customers coming back again and again.

Giovanni's exemplary cooking skills were exceeded only by his exaggerated opinion of himself. Loud, brash, and unapologetic, Giovanni showed little or no concern for the feelings of others. One afternoon he had arrived early to prepare a duck dinner for some important political figures when Frank, a bright young chef's apprentice, said, "Giovanni, are you ever concerned about getting caught?" The buying or selling of wild ducks was a violation of state and federal law, and everyone at Vannucci's knew it.

Without so much as an explanation, Giovanni burst into a rage, lambasted Frank with a tongue lashing in Italian, then turned and walked away.

Lorenzo, who happened to overhear the conversation, patted Frank on the shoulder and said, "Follow me." Both men walked outside, where two dishwashers were leaning against the back wall, smoking.

"Larry," said Frank, still reeling from Giovanni's rant, "what did Giovanni say?"

"Before I tell you, let me explain a few things."

"Sure," said Frank.

"I know you are my nephew and used to calling me Larry, but inside the restaurant, it's better you call me Lorenzo. It goes with the ambiance of this fine old Italian restaurant, and the customers love it. Outside the restaurant, you may call me Larry or Uncle—anything you want. That goes for just about anyone who works here, except Giovanni: being the arrogant asshole that Giovanni is, he prefers to be called Chef Giovanni by his kitchen staff."

"What are they laughing about?" said Frank, looking in the direction of the dishwashers.

"Never mind," said Lorenzo, waving at the dishwashers to go back inside and get to work. "You're gonna make a fine chef someday. Everyone likes you, and Victor and I are impressed by how quickly you've learned. If you have questions about anything that goes on here at the restaurant, come to me first."

"I will," said Frank, smiling and feeling much better. "But you still haven't told me what Giovanni said."

"Oh, let me think," said Lorenzo. "As best as I can recall, Giovanni said, 'My grandfather was a duck poacher, my father was a duck poacher, and my brother still poaches ducks. I don't kill ducks, I don't sell ducks, I just cook them.'"

"Is that all he said?"

"No, he also told you to wash the pans and stop asking stupid questions. I think Giovanni is sensitive about the duck thing and doesn't want to talk about it."

"Is it true what Giovanni said?"

"Is what true?"

"That his family was a bunch of duck poachers?"

"We have some time before the rest of the crew gets here, so I'll tell you a little story. You must promise not to breathe a word of it to anyone."

"I promise," said Frank.

"First, his real name isn't Giovanni."

"What's his real name?"

"It's Ed."

"Ed?"

"Yes," said Lorenzo, chuckling. "When the person we know as Giovanni was born, his mother wanted him to have a genuine American name, so she named him Ed. Not Edmondo, not Edward, just Ed."

"How did you find that out?"

"A couple years ago, we were closing up after a busy Sunday evening. People had been partying heavily and left half-empty wine bottles all over the dining-room tables. It was customary for the clean-up crew to bring the leftover bottles into the kitchen, stack them next to the sink, and pour them out before tossing them into the dumpster outside. 'Hey, someone forgot to take care of all these wine bottles,' Carlo said, after everyone except Giovanni and I had gone home. 'I'll take care of them,' I said, 'but before I do, why don't we have ourselves a drink?' 'Good idea,' said Carlo. 'Tomorrow's our day off, so we should all relax a little.' I poured Carlo and me a glass of Chianti from one of the bottles. 'Hey, Giovanni, come and have a drink with us,' said Carlo. Giovanni was in his office doing something. 'I'm busy,' said Giovanni. 'Come on,' I said. 'You're never too busy to have a drink with your friends. Get your stuck-up Italian ass in here!' 'Okay,' said Giovanni, 'but only one, then I have to go home.'

"So, did Giovanni have a drink with you?" said Frank.

"The three of us drank Chianti, Brunello, Barolo, Frascati—you name it. By the time we had finished off four or five bottles, Giovanni was feeling no pain. A few more drinks and he wanted to tell us his life's story."

"What did he tell you?"

"First, he told us his real name was Ed. He said he chose the name Giovanni because it had a better ring to it than Ed Sabatini, famous Italian chef. I thought Carlo was going to hurt himself, he began laughing so hard. I told Giovanni I could see his point. Ed was better suited for some shithole coffee shop out on Highway 80. That's when we all started laughing and didn't stop until almost daylight."

"Did he mention his family and all the duck poachers?" said Frank.

"Yes, before the night was over, Giovanni told us his entire family history. His grandfather had lived on the East Coast and was what Giovanni called a market hunter. These market hunters slaughtered ducks by the thousands, stuffed them into barrels, and shipped them off to big cities like Chicago and New York."

"What else did he tell you?"

"He said the market hunters eventually killed off all the canvasbacks, making it difficult for his grandfather to earn a living."

"So, what did Giovanni's grandfather do?"

"Apparently, Giovanni's grandfather had some cousins who lived here in the Bay Area. They wrote and told old man Sabatini that hunting was great in the Delta. He could move out here, join them, and take up where he left off."

"What year was this?"

"I think it was just after the turn of the century. Anyway, all Giovanni's grandfather knew how to do was kill ducks, so he packed up the family and came out to California. Giovanni's father would eventually learn the family business and teach it to Giovanni's older brother."

"What about Giovanni? Did he become a duck poacher too?"

"No. He said he had no interest in guns and chose to look away when his father and his older brother arrived home with a load of ducks and geese. Giovanni loved to cook. Even as a child, he dreamed of being a famous chef."

"That's a great story," said Frank. "Do you mind if I ask you one more question?"

"Go ahead. Then we better go inside."

"How do you feel about illegally selling wild ducks? Aren't you worried about getting caught?"

"You're a very inquisitive young man. Where are all these questions coming from?"

"We're studying conservation in one of my college classes. Last week, the professor took us on a field trip to the Suisun Marsh and spoke to us about waterfowl conservation."

"Anything that goes on here at the restaurant, you must keep to yourself," said Lorenzo. "Your father worked here for many years, and it's because of his loyalty and hard work that Victor gave you this job."

"I understand. You don't have to worry about me saying anything."

"That's good. Here's the way I look it. Valentino Vannucci, my father, has probably had ducks on the alternate menu off and on for the last thirty years. When I say alternate menu, I'm talking about the one we show only to customers we know and trust. Most of those customers are wealthy businessmen or important government officials. We are able to charge exorbitant prices for Giovanni's duck dinners because, for these people, money is no object."

"Like the couple who pulled up in a limo last week?"

"Exactly. I don't think we sell more than a hundred duck dinners a year. It's only during November, December, and early January that our supplier has them available. I know of at least five other restaurants here in the Bay Area that sell several times that many."

"Who is our supplier?"

"Haven't you seen that refrigerator truck out back on Thursday mornings?"

"You mean the one with the chubby kid on the side eating a drumstick?"

"That's the one. Sometimes they deliver more than just turkeys."

"What if you get caught?"

"If we get caught, we'll pay the fine and say we're sorry. About fifteen years ago, several restaurants got caught. Their fines were minimal, and they wrote it off to the cost of doing business."

"I guess it's worth the risk, huh?"

"Business is about making money, young man. If there's enough money to be made and we can make a few special customers happy, it's worth the risk. Now let's go to work. You still need to wash those pans Giovanni left for you."

THREE

ARDIS "DUD" BOGAR HAD ENGAGED IN the dirty business of duck dragging since its heyday in the 1930s. Still actively poaching ducks in his fifties, Dud taught his then eighteen-year-old son, Hollis, and Hollis's high-school buddies Blake Gastineau and Jimmy Riddle everything they needed to know about creeping up on thousands of feeding ducks in the middle of the night and killing hundreds of the vulnerable birds at the same time. "Pick up the dead ones, especially the mallards and sprig, and don't waste time chasin' after all them wounded birds," Dud would tell the boys. "You'll need a driver you can count on. He'll drop you off, pick you up, and act as a lookout. Ain't no way the game warden's gonna catch ya if you make the pick-up spot a mile or two from where ya done the shootin'. If ya see the game warden a-comin', just start a-runnin'. Game wardens ain't gonna catch nobody in them heavy rubber boots they wear. And whatever ya do, don't get caught with all them ducks. Hide 'em in a ditch or someplace safe, and come back later when the coast is clear."

Five months before succumbing to a combination of serious lung and liver ailments, Dud Bogar asked Blake Gastineau to meet him in the King's Market parking lot in Gridley on a hot morning in July 1954. Once an imposing hulk of a man, Dud had been reduced to a mere shadow of his former self by his illnesses. His dark, leathery skin had turned white as a sheet, and his booming voice was now weak and raspy.

"What's this all about?" said Gastineau, pulling up in one of his father's flatbed trucks.

"Hop in, and we'll take a little ride," said Dud, coughing heavily.

"Man, you look like shit," said Gastineau, climbing into the passenger seat of Dud's 1947 Studebaker sedan. "You still driving this old junker?"

"It gets me where I wanna go. Besides, I don't want people thinkin' I got lots a money."

"You don't have to worry about that. Are you gonna tell me where we're goin'?"

"I might not be around much longer," said Dud, interrupted by a coughing spasm.

"Hey, man, I didn't catch that."

"I said I wasn't gonna be around much longer," repeated Dud.

"Oh. I kinda figured you weren't feelin' too good."

"I want ya ta meet my connection."

"Your connection?"

"Yeah, did ya think I been sellin' all them ducks we killed myself?"

"I guess I never thought about it."

"Well, it's time ya did."

"Why me? Why not Hollis?"

"Hollis is my boy and all, but let's face it, he ain't the sharpest tool in the shed. If I leave Hollis in charge, you'll all end up in jail."

Bogar and Gastineau continued into Yuba City and east, through Marysville. Passing the Bryant Baseball Stadium, Dud asked Gastineau if he'd ever played ball there. Gastineau said he hadn't played much baseball but had been recruited to play football at Yuba College.

"What happened with that? I ain't seen you play football since you and Hollis won the league championship your senior year in high school."

"Duck draggin' happened. My first year at Yuba College was the same year the entire Butte Sink was swarmin' with ducks. Instead of goin' ta football practice, I was out scoutin' the rice fields with you and Hollis. After killing ducks all night, I didn't feel much like goin' ta class or football practice the next day."

"Yeah, but we made a potful a money. You boys are gonna make even more when I set you up with my connection."

"Whad'd you say his name was?"

"I don't think I ever mentioned his name. I done business with his pappy for almost twenty years. When old Clyde Butler bit the big one about five years ago, I started sellin' to his kid."

"So, what's his kid's name?"

"He ain't really a kid no more. I'm guessin' Pinky's pushin' forty."

"Pinky?"

"His real name's Clarence. His pappy used ta call him Pinky 'cause he's got this freckly, white skin that turns pink when he gets mad."

"Can we trust this Pinky?"

"Let me tell ya a little story. I've probably sold ten thousand ducks to the old man and a few thousand more to his kid over the years. When the feds busted all them poor bastards back in 1939, me and the old man were about the only ones that didn't get roped inta that mess."

"Wha'd ya do?"

"We kept our mouths closed and shut down our business for four or five years until the whole thing blew over."

"Were ya scared they'd come after ya?"

"Maybe once or twice, when we'd hear a rumor or read somethin' in the paper. As it turned out, the fines them guys paid weren't much at all. The old man and me made more money off one night's kill than all the fines put together. I think a few a the dumber sonsabitches did time in jail, but it weren't much, considerin' all the time and money them federal game wardens spent tryin' ta catch us."

"How long did this go on?"

"I ain't exactly sure. I know some a them federal game wardens was workin' in plain clothes and managed ta buy a few ducks from fellers I know over in Willows. I can't believe them boys was that stupid. Why, I can spot a game warden a mile away, don't matter what he's wearin'. He could be wearin' skivvies and I'd—"

"Yeah, I get the picture. What else is this Pinky into?"

"Let's just say they's a whole lotta ways ta stuff a turkey."

"What's that supposed to mean?"

"I already done said too much. You'll see when we get there."

Leaving Marysville, Bogar and Gastineau traveled southeast for seventeen miles before turning east on Coon Creek Road. Entering a vast landscape of undisturbed grasslands, five-hundred-year-old valley oaks, and meandering wetlands, Gastineau said, "What do they call this area?"

"I'm not sure what they call it," said Bogar. "I know Lincoln's up ahead a few miles, and Sacramento's over thataway. I kinda like bein' able ta see a long ways without any buildings spoilin' the view."

"Seems like a waste ta me. All that land just sittin' out there doin' nothin'."

"It ain't gonna be that way forever," said Dud, glancing at his young protégé. "The way Sacramento's growin', I expect this'll all be houses someday." Gastineau didn't respond, but Dud could tell from the look in his eyes that the wheels were turning.

Several minutes had passed when Gastineau began thinking out loud. "If I had the money, I'd buy up as much of this land as I could."

"What would ya do with it?"

"I'd just hold onto it for now. When the time's right, I'd bulldoze it all flat and build those houses you were talkin' about. Lots and lots of houses. Before ya know it, I'd be richer than my old man."

"What about your old man? With all that farmland he owns, Ralph Gastineau must have more money than Carter's got pills."

"Yeah, but he might not be givin' any of it to me. The other day, he told me if I get in trouble one more time, he's gonna throw me outta the guesthouse."

Bogar and Gastineau drove another two miles on Coon Creek Road before turning north onto a well-traveled dirt road toward Coon Creek. Crossing under a wooden archway reading BUTLER FARMS, Dud said, "Ya better roll up your winda. It's gonna get a little dusty from here on in."

About the time Gastineau finished rolling up his window, a refrigerated delivery truck roared by, headed in the opposite direction. "Damn!" he said. "That guy almost ran us over."

"We'll sit here a minute or two and let the dust clear," said Dud, coughing again. "Ya gotta watch for them delivery trucks when you're drivin' in and outta this place. They don't slow down for nobody."

"What was that picture I saw on the side of the truck? It looked like a chubby kid with grease all over his face, holdin' a drumstick."

"That chubby kid was Pinky."

"Oh yeah?" said Gastineau, laughing.

"His old man put that pitcher on the side of all his trucks back when Pinky was about sixteen years old. It became their trademark. Look! It's even plastered on the side a that turkey shed up ahead."

"I can't wait to meet this Pinky character," said Gastineau, chuckling.

"Ya best not be makin' fun of Pinky if ya know what's good for ya. He's the friendliest guy you'd ever wanna meet if he likes ya, but he can turn mean in a hurry if he don't. I walked inta one a them turkey sheds last winter while Pinky was teachin' one a his braceros a lesson."

"A lesson for what?"

"The way I understood it, Hector was talkin' to some a the other farmhands about joinin' together and askin' Pinky for mas dinero. Trouble was, Pinky overheard the conversation."

"So what happened?"

"I'll tell ya what happened. Pinky beat the hell outta him with his bare hands. Pinky told that poor sonofabitch if he ever caused trouble or even thought about askin' for more money again, he'd throw him in the meat grinder. I think that's Hector over there, wavin' to us."

"He looks happy enough now."

"You damn right he's happy. He's happy he ain't been turned inta turkey food."

"How big's this Pinky?"

"He's about your height, maybe six-one or six-two, but he must weigh 300 pounds."

"What's Pinky's last name?"

"It's Butler, you dadgum moron. Didn't ya read the sign we just passed? It was on the side a that truck too. Before I forget, don't ask Pinky how you're gonna get paid. When it's time ta pay ya for the ducks you brung him, he'll just pull a big wad a cash outta his pocket and hand it to ya."

"Wow! I've never seen so many turkeys."

"What?" shouted Dud, opening his car door and stepping outside. "I can't hear ya over all this noise."

"I said, 'Have a few turkeys,'" shouted Gastineau.

"I told ya this was a big place. Make sure ya roll up your winda and close the door. I don't want the inside a my car smellin' like turkey shit."

Pinky was sitting behind a wooden desk piled with scattered bills, a half-eaten baloney sandwich, and two empty beer bottles when Dud Bogar and Blake Gastineau entered the small office near the farm's entrance. The zipper on Pinky's blood-spattered, white overalls had given way to pressure, partially exposing his enormous belly. Hanging on the wall behind Pinky's desk was a framed photograph of an older, baldheaded gentleman bearing a striking resemblance to Pinky. Under the photograph hung a wooden plaque inscribed with the words HEAD TURKEY.

"Where the hell ya been?" boomed Pinky. "I thought you said you'd be here by ten."

"Pinky, this here's Blake Gastineau, the young man I told ya about. Come this winter, he'll be the one deliverin' the goods."

"Is that so?" said Pinky. "How do I know this pimple-faced punk ain't some kinda cop, or worse yet, a damn game warden?"

"Your old man and me done business together for twenty years," said Dud, pointing to the photograph on the wall. "Ain't it enough that I'm vouchin' for him?"

"Yeah, I'm just givin' ya a hard time," said Pinky, standing and extending his hand to Gastineau. "Welcome aboard, partner."

Gastineau extended his own hand and found it quickly engulfed in the vice-like grip of Pinky's massive paw. "Thanks," said Gastineau, grimacing as Pinky stared into his eyes and continued to apply pressure.

"You kill 'em, gut 'em, and deliver 'em to me. If you keep your mouth shut and nobody else finds out about our arrangement, we'll get along just fine."

"Do ya want anything besides ducks?" said Gastineau.

"Whaddaya have in mind?"

"I don't know—quail, pheasants, deer?"

"Sure," said Pinky, finally releasing Gastineau's hand. "I've got customers who'll pay good money for quail and pheasants. If I can't sell the venison, I'll throw it in the grinder and feed it to the turkeys."

"Turkeys eat deer meat?" said Gastineau, flexing the fingers of his right hand.

"Turkeys will eat damn near anything, as long as it's small enough to slide down that long gullet a theirs. I've seen 'em fightin' over frogs, mice, even snakes."

"I didn't know that," said Gastineau, feeling more comfortable in the company of his new business partner.

"My super-duper grinder crushes everything I toss in the hopper, even bones. Whatever comes out, my birds eat. They don't call 'em gobblers for nothin'."

"We better be goin'," said Dud.

"Yeah," said Gastineau, "my old man's gonna wonder where I went with his flatbed."

"Pinky, if I don't see ya again, it's been good doin' business with ya," said Dud.

"Yeah, sure," said Pinky, ignoring Dud's gesture and grasping Gastineau by the back of his neck. "I'll be seein' you this fall, young fella. Make sure you remember what I said about keepin' your mouth shut."

Driving out through the gate, Gastineau asked Dud where Pinky lived. Dud stopped and pointed in a northeasterly direction, toward Coon Creek. "See that two-story house sittin' under the big oak tree? Pinky's old man built it years ago. As far as I know, Pinky and his wife still live there."

"You mean Pinky's married?"

"He got married to Tina shortly after his pappy kicked the bucket. I think Pinky was lonely in that big old house all by himself."

"I can't imagine any woman wanting to marry that guy."

"Neither can I. Did ya see the way that sonofabitch gave me the brush-off when I tried to shake his hand? Why, I'd sooner be married to a razorback hog than Pinky Butler."

"What's she like?"

"She's a mousy little gal. Usually stays up at the house. I was bringin' Pinky a trunkful a ducks early one morning when I heard him cussin' her up one side and down the other: 'Tina, get your ass back in this house and make me breakfast!'"

"Do you ever deal with her when you're deliverin' the ducks?"

"No, and, come ta think of it, I ain't seen Tina in quite a while. Pinky don't talk about her much anymore neither. Is you thinkin' what I'm thinkin'?"

"I don't know; those turkeys all look fat and happy to me," said Gastineau, chuckling.

FOUR

THE SUN WAS GOING DOWN as Jimmy Riddle, Blake Gastineau, Hollis Bogar, and Richie Stillwell proceeded north on Pennington Road, past several miles of wetlands, riparian forests, and farmlands—most of it recently designated as a state wildlife area by the California Fish and Game Commission. With all four windows rolled down, the foursome turned west onto Old Colusa Highway. "See anything yet?" said Riddle, concentrating on a fast-moving truck headed in the opposite direction.

"A few small flocks circling," said Gastineau, "but nothin' big."

"Here we go!" said Bogar, from the back seat. "Must be ten thousand birds gettin' up right now."

Riddle swerved the car to the side of the highway and cut the engine. As if engrossed in a drive-in movie, all four men sat quietly in their seats and watched as an enormous congregation of over 10,000 ducks rose from the wetland, circled overhead, and disappeared into the night sky.

"Looks like they're headed into Colusa County," said Riddle.

"I think I know right where they're goin'," said Gastineau. "There's an entire section of harvested rice stubble about five miles northwest of here. Keep headin' this way, and I'll tell you when to turn."

Minutes after crossing the Colusa County line, Jimmy Riddle turned north onto a one-lane county road, slowed the car to a turtle's pace, and cut his headlights. With no traffic visible in either direction, all four men remained silent and listened for any sign of nearby waterfowl activity.

Familiar with every county road, rice field, dirt road, ditch bank, and levee within twenty miles, Riddle had no problem navigating in the light of a full moon.

Riddle and company had traveled another mile or so when Gastineau said, "Stop!" Riddle complied, pulling the car to the east side of the road. Gastineau opened the front passenger door and stepped out into the cold night air. The dome-light bulb in Riddle's car had been removed so there was no chance of a light coming on and alerting any state or federal game wardens who might be lurking in the area. Walking to the front of the car, Gastineau cocked his head toward the northwest and listened.

The group repeated the drill several times throughout the evening. Each time, Riddle would bring the car to a stop and Gastineau would climb out and listen for the tell-tale chatter of feeding ducks. Three hours had passed when the gang of outlaws turned west onto an unpaved levee road that led into one of the largest rice-stubble fields in the valley.

"Whose place are we on now?" said Bogar.

"What difference does it make?" snickered Stillwell. "You think the game warden's gonna care whose place we're on if he catches us out here poaching ducks in the middle of the night?"

"What a joke," said Bogar. "Bettis ain't caught nobody poachin' ducks or anything else in years. Every time I drive by that coffee shop south of town, I see his game-warden car parked in back."

"I seem to remember him catchin' you with a giant pile a pheasants a few years back," said Stillwell. "And didn't you have ta serve thirty days in juvie?"

"That happened eight years ago, when I was a dumb-ass kid," said Bogar.

"Well you ain't no kid anymore," said Riddle and Gastineau simultaneously.

Stillwell finally caught on to the joke. "But you're still a dumb ass," he said, laughing so hard he fell against the back door, causing it to fly open.

"Richie, we need to get serious and find those ducks," said Gastineau. "Besides, that's a sore subject for me and Jimmy."

"I forgot you and Jimmy were involved in that too," said Stillwell.

"Yeah. I never knew for sure who snitched us off, but I have a good idea."

"Quiet!" said Riddle, cutting the engine. "Do ya hear that?"

"Whaddya hear?" said Gastineau.

"Listen," whispered Riddle, pointing to the west. "They're right out there."

"I hear 'em," said Bogar. "A bunch just got up and landed again."

"There must be ten or fifteen thousand birds," said Gastineau, stepping from the car. "I think they're about a half mile out, movin' southwest. Let's turn this thing around and head back toward the main road."

Riddle turned right at the county road and slowly headed west toward Colusa. Every quarter mile, he pulled to the side of the road and turned off the engine. Each time, Gastineau climbed out of the car and listened for the *tic-a-tic* of feeding ducks.

It was approaching 2:00 a.m. when Gastineau finally heard the sound he'd been waiting for. "Boys, I think we hit the jackpot," he muttered. "It's time to pull a drag."

FIVE

WITH THE PRECISION OF A MILITARY DRILL TEAM, Blake Gastineau, Hollis Bogar, and Richie Stillwell walked to the trunk of Riddle's car and began loading their respective 12-gauge, semiautomatic shotguns, each equipped with an extender capable of holding eleven live rounds. When the shotguns were loaded, each man filled his pockets with just enough extra shotgun shells to serve his purpose, but not so many as to restrict his running ability. Three army surplus canvas bags, all bearing shoulder straps, lay at the back of the trunk. Each bag was stuffed with individual, two-foot lengths of twine.

"Okay, the three of us are gonna head northwest and intercept the feedin' ducks," said Gastineau, pointing in that direction. "Jimmy, I want you to check out the area for any sign of game wardens and pick us up in three hours on the levee road where we first heard the ducks. If any of us get split up, just remember to head toward the levee road and wait for Jimmy's signal. Jimmy, if you see anything that looks suspicious, give us two quick honks, wait thirty seconds, then honk once more. Now get the hell out of here."

Riddle hopped in the driver's seat, lit up a cigarette, and slowly headed west. When he'd gone a half mile, he flipped on his headlights and began searching every county road within five miles for any sign of a game warden.

Gastineau, Bogar, and Stillwell crouched forward and began a slow trudge through the recently rained-on rice stubble. Every time they came to a rice check, they ducked into the weeds and listened to the distant *tic-a-tic-a-tic-a-tic* of feeding ducks. Once they were within a hundred yards of the oncoming birds, Gastineau motioned with his hand for the others to drop to their knees and begin a tedious belly crawl up to the anticipated firing line. With knees and elbows caked in mud, all three men crept forward, stopping at fifteen-yard intervals to rest and listen.

Like a massive harvesting combine, the ravenous ducks ate their way across the field. In a continuous effort to store nutrients and maintain muscle mass for the long migration back to the breeding grounds, they played a game of avian leapfrog—jumping into the air, flying a hundred feet or more, then landing again and feeding at the front of the line.

The roar of wingbeats and constant chatter had become almost deafening by the time Gastineau, Bogar, and Stillwell reached a point directly in the path of the approaching flock. Gastineau pointed at Stillwell and gestured for him to take the left flank. Stillwell slowly backed away and crawled forty yards to his designated shooting location. Bogar, who had engaged in this exercise countless times before, already had assumed his position forty yards to Gastineau's right.

The first wave of ducks, for some unknown reason, veered to the west and avoided coming within range of the poachers' shotguns. All three men remained perfectly still, lying on the wet ground while peering through the three-foot-high weeds and matted grass that occupied each rice check.

The avian symphony grew louder and louder until it reached a crescendo and suddenly stopped. The night had become deathly quiet and Blake Gastineau knew why. Either he or one of his fellow duck poachers had snapped a twig or accidentally bumped the magazine of his shotgun. They had been discovered.

Up they rose, the flock of ten thousand ducks producing an ear-shattering clamor so loud, their distress calls could be heard from miles away. In the midst of the pandemonium came a volley of shotgun blasts in rapid succession. *BOOM, BOOM-BOOM-BOOM*. Ducks fell from the sky like rain. Unable to identify their targets, Gastineau and company fired into the panicked throng. *BOOM-BOOM-BOOM*. Some victims folded their wings and tumbled to the ground while others fluttered for a distance before succumbing to their wounds. *BOOM-BOOM-BOOM*. The stench of exploding gunpowder fouled the cold night air and smoke engulfed the shooters as they continued their merciless onslaught. *BOOM, BOOM-BOOM-BOOM-BOOM, BOOM-BOOM*.

"Looks like we did good!" said Gastineau when the shooting finally stopped. "We're not gonna be able to carry all these ducks, so grab all the mallards and sprig you can, and leave the rest." The shooters placed their shotguns on the ground and began retrieving dead birds, all the time ignoring the wounded ones that flapped and flopped desperately in the sticky mud. Reaching into their canvas bags, each man removed individual sections of twine and began tying every mallard and pintail he could find into batches of ten birds. By 4:00 a.m., Gastineau, Bogar, and Stillwell had gathered over a hundred ducks and were hightailing it back to the levee road.

Moving at a brisk pace, Gastineau's gang of three trudged and sloshed their way through a mile and a half of rice stubble to their predetermined pick-up site. Once they were within fifty yards of the levee road, they hid the ducks and their shotguns in a nearby irrigation ditch and covered them with weeds. "We'll leave 'em here for now," whispered Gastineau.

In second gear and with his right foot light on the gas pedal, Jimmy Riddle began working his way back north on the levee road. Headlights off, he rolled his window down and flipped on the radio.

Gastineau, Bogar, and Stillwell scurried over the remaining distance up to the levee road, ducked into a patch of tules, and waited. "Damn!" said Stillwell. "My toes are frozen in these wet tennis shoes."

"Stop your bellyachin'," said Bogar.

"Quiet!" said Gastineau. "I think I hear a car comin'."

"How we gonna know it's Jimmy and not the game warden?" said Stillwell.

"I'll know," said Gastineau.

"How ya gonna know?"

"Just shut up and listen."

"Gooood mornin'!" came a familiar voice over Riddle's car radio. "It's five o'clock here at the KVLY studios in beautiful downtown Chico. Time for the *Dallas Stovall Mornin' Show*. I'm your host, Dallas Stovall."

Riddle reached down and turned up the volume.

"I hear somebody talkin'," said Stillwell. "Sounds like he's gettin' closer."

"We've got lots of your favorite country tunes comin' up on this cold, Northern California mornin'," said Stovall, "but first, me and the boys have a special treat for all you fans out there in radioland. We're gonna sing a popular little ditty that the Ames Brothers rode to number nineteen on the charts a few years back ..."

"I thought that was somebody talkin'," said Stillwell, laughing. "It's that cornball Dallas Stovall on the radio."

Gastineau stepped out of the tules and onto the road, followed by Bogar and Stillwell.

"Here's one of today's country hits by the Tennessee Plowboy himself," said Stovall. "This one's goin' out to Bonnie, over in Hamilton City. It's called—"

"Turn that shit off," said Gastineau, as Riddle pulled up and stopped. "Did ya see anything we need to be worried about?"

"No," said Riddle. "The coast is clear for a mile each way."

"Normally, we'd leave and come back for the ducks and our shotguns later," said Gastineau, "but this field is full of rats. I almost stepped on one a mile back and don't want those toothy bastards chewin' up all our profits."

"I hate rats!" said Bogar. "Let's go get the ducks right now."

"Open the trunk, Jimmy," said Gastineau. "We'll be right back."

SIX

"I HATE TO TELL YOU THIS," said Riddle, "but we're not gonna make it to the packing shed unless I stop for gas."

"Now you tell us!" said Gastineau. "Why didn't you fill up yesterday, before we got to your place?"

"I didn't have any money until you paid me. Besides, I figured half a tank would be plenty. How was I ta know we'd be drivin' all over two counties tryin' ta find those ducks?"

"I think the only station open this early is Bill's," said Bogar.

"Looks like we don't have any choice," said Gastineau. "Let's put some gas in this thing so we can get started guttin' and hangin' these ducks."

"I'm almost out of cigarettes anyway," said Riddle.

Ding-ding. It was just after 6:00 a.m. when Jimmy Riddle, Blake Gastineau, Hollis Bogar, and Richie Stillwell pulled up to the ethyl gas pump at Bill's Friendly Service. Stillwell and Bogar were sitting in the back seat, arguing over who was the better singer, Elvis or Pat Boone. A minute or two had gone by when Gastineau turned the radio down and shouted out the window, "Hey, what do we have to do to get some service around here?"

"He just opened the station," said Riddle. "I don't think the pumps are even on yet. Besides, those duck hunters in the pickup were here first."

Bill Oliver had owned and operated the tiny, two-pump filling station on the outskirts of Gridley since retiring from the U.S. Navy at the end of World War II. A former chief petty officer, Oliver insisted on running a tight ship. Every gas-station attendant who ever worked for Bill had undergone the same orientation: The repair bay shall remain shipshape unless there's a lube job in progress or the attendant is fixing a flat tire. The office shall remain free of clutter; that means empty oil cans, gas receipts, rags, and assorted waste will be stowed in their proper receptacles. The restrooms out back must be checked at least three times daily and shall remain clean and presentable at all times. And at no time shall anyone other than the attendant be allowed in the back room where surplus sales items are stored. Bill kept a detailed inventory of every sales item in the station, including oil cans, windshield wipers, cigarette cartons, soda pop, and candy. "One last thing," Bill would say. "If you hear the bell ring out front, you'll run—not walk—to meet the customer."

"Hey, wasn't that Peachy Keane?" said Bogar.

"It sure looked like him," said Riddle, "but he musta gained fifty pounds since we saw him last. I remember him bein' skinny as a rail and too clumsy to get outta his own way."

"What happened to Dennis Deaver?" said Gastineau. "I thought he worked here in the mornings."

"I heard he got canned," said Bogar. "Somebody told me he was drinkin' all the Orange Nehis in the back room and not puttin' money in the till."

Just then, the office door flew open and twenty-five-year-old Elwood Keane came running out to the gas pumps. On leave from the Navy, Keane had volunteered to help his former employer out for a few days. "Sorry for the wait, guys," said Keane. "I've got one car ahead of you, so I'll be just a couple minutes."

"Screw those duck hunters," said Bogar, slugging down the last swallow of his stale beer.

Two duck hunters with a dog and a gunny sack full of decoys in their pickup bed were parked on the other side of the gas pumps, facing in the same direction. They had been waiting for the station to open since before daylight. As Keane began filling the duck hunters' gas tank, he noticed that the black Labrador in back was shivering and making whimpering noises. "What's the matter with your dog?" said Keane.

"I've been watching her in the rearview mirror," said the driver. "She started acting like that right after that other car pulled in."

"Strange," said Keane, pressing down on the nozzle trigger so the gas would pump more quickly.

"Yeah, I've seen her do that before, usually when I've shot a duck and she's waiting for my retrieve signal."

Everyone in Riddle's car was still laughing about Dennis Deaver and his legendary eating habits when Gastineau slapped the car's roof liner with the back of his hand. "Hey, be careful what you say around this guy. I think he's the one who snitched us off to the game warden."

"What makes you think it was him?" said Riddle, snuffing out his cigarette in the overloaded ashtray and lighting another.

"It had to be him," said Gastineau, having rolled up his window so Keane couldn't hear. "He was standin' right behind Hollis and me in the gym when we were bragging about killin' all those pheasants the year before and stashin' 'em in your grandpa's packing shed."

"What'll it be, fellas?" said Keane, suddenly standing at the driver's-side window. "Regular or ethyl?"

"Here," said Gastineau, handing Riddle a five-dollar bill.

"Five dollars' worth of ethyl," said Riddle.

"Would you like me to check the oil?"

"Just pump the damn gas so we can get the hell outta here," said Gastineau.

"Yeah," chimed Stillwell, from the back seat. "Pump the damn gas, and make it snappy."

"Aren't you bein' a little hard on the guy?" said Riddle, rolling up his window.

"He was a pain in the ass in high school, and he's a pain in the ass now," said Gastineau.

"Let me outta here," said Bogar. "I can't hold it any longer."

"Here's two bits," said Riddle. "Buy me a pack of cigarettes while you're at it."

While Keane pumped gas at the rear of the car, Hollis Bogar pushed the seat forward and climbed out the passenger-side door. In doing so, he accidentally kicked a half-full beer can out onto the gas lane. "Hey, Peachy, is the head unlocked?" said Bogar, not bothering to pick up the beer can.

"It's around back. The key's hanging just inside the office door. Don't worry about the can. I'll take care of it."

"Damn right you will," said Bogar.

Keane couldn't help noticing that Bogar's tennis shoes and pant legs were splattered with mud. Glancing downward to avoid Bogar's scornful gaze, the attendant spotted fresh blood and what appeared to be tiny down feathers sticking to the rear bumper. *So that's what that dog was excited about*, thought Keane. *Here it is forty minutes before legal shooting time, and they already have ducks in their trunk.* Still deep in thought, Keane suddenly felt Hollis Bogar's hand resting on his right shoulder. "Huh?" said Elwood. "I didn't see you come back from the restroom."

"Peachy," said Bogar, his beer breath strong enough to kill a horse, "I ain't seen ya since high school. Where ya been?"

"I joined the Navy right after graduation."

"Me and Blake have missed ya. You gonna be around town for a while?"

Turning away, Keane said, "No, I'll be leaving again tomorrow."

"That's too bad. We got somethin' we wanna talk to you about."

Keane remembered Bogar as the classic bully. He'd egg some poor kid into a fight, wrestle him to the ground, then beat him senseless with his fists and incredibly hard head. Having risen to the rank of petty officer first class and in line for another promotion, the last thing Elwood needed was to let someone like Bogar goad him into a fight.

"Hey! Hurry it up back there," shouted Gastineau.

"Did ya get my cigarettes?" said Riddle, as Bogar climbed back in the car.

"Yeah, I got 'em," said Bogar. "Peachy said he was leavin' town tomorrow."

"That's too bad," said Gastineau. "If we weren't gonna be so busy with those ducks, I'd suggest we give him a send-off."

Ding-ding. Gastineau and company drove away. Elwood had intended to disregard what he'd just witnessed, but something told him to pull a pen from his shirt pocket and scribble Jimmy Riddle's license number on the palm of his left hand.

SEVEN

HAVING WAITED ON A DOZEN CUSTOMERS, patched a flat tire, and swept the repair-bay floor since Gastineau and his gang left the station, Elwood Keane still couldn't shake the thought of his former schoolmates hiding illegal ducks in the trunk of Riddle's car. Two hours had gone by, but the blood on Riddle's bumper and the indignity of Bogar's subtle threat still haunted him. "It's been eight years since high school," mumbled Keene, "and those no-goods haven't changed a bit."

The office telephone rang. "Bill's Friendly Service. May I help you?"

"Elwood, this is Bill. I really appreciate you filling in these last few days. What's your schedule for the rest of the week?"

"Early tomorrow morning, I take the Greyhound to San Diego. Friday, I ship out."

"Okay, I'll come by before your shift is over and pay you. When do you think you'll be back this way again?"

"I doubt if I'll ever be back," said Keane. "Since my mother passed away and I sold her house, there's really nothing to keep me here. Besides, I'm in the Seabees now, and I heard they're sending us to Antarctica."

"Antarctica! Why would they send you to a place like that?"

"We're buildin' bases down there so the scientists can conduct studies."

"Well, good luck, and try to stay warm," said Oliver. "Be sure to write once in a while and let me know where you are."

"I will," said Keane, hearing the bell. "I've got a customer. See you this afternoon."

Elwood ran out to the gas lane, only to receive the surprise of his life. There before him was a dark-green, 1954 Ford sedan with a ten-foot-high radio antenna attached to the rear bumper. "I don't believe it," mumbled Keane, shuffling around the rear of the car and up to the driver's window.

"Fill 'er up with regular," said the driver, handing Keane a credit card.

It's him, thought Keane, turning on the pump and popping the nozzle into the gas-tank receptacle. *He was supposed to retire years ago, after I turned Gastineau, Bogar, and Riddle in for poaching pheasants.*

"Would you like me to check the oil?"

"Sure, go ahead," said Warden Bettis, jotting down figures in a green, hardbound diary. "Could I get you to wash the windshield while you're at it?"

"You bet." While washing Bettis's windshield and checking the oil, Keane pondered his options. *Should I bring up what I saw or just let it go? He obviously doesn't remember me, so he'll probably think I'm making a big deal out of nothing. Looks like Warden Bettis has lost most of his hair and put on about twenty pounds since I saw him last.* "Your oil looks good," said Keane, displaying the dipstick. "Only a half quart down."

"Okay, thanks."

Keane replaced the dipstick, closed the hood, and walked past the driver's window. "I'll be right back," he said.

"The man has no idea who I am," mumbled Keane, as he placed Bettis's credit card in the machine and pushed the slider forward. "Maybe I should let him sign the slip and go on his way. It'll be less complicated for me that way."

"Thanks for cleaning the windshield," said Bettis, reaching for the gas-receipt tray.

"No problem. The sky's getting dark. Looks like another storm's comin' in."

"Yeah, it sure does." Bettis signed the gas receipt and placed his copy into a flat, aluminum case that sat on the passenger seat next to him.

"We're giving away these styrofoam balls, if you'd like one."

"What are they for?"

"They stick on the end of your antenna. It's kind of a promotional thing."

"Yeah, sure, go ahead and stick it on there."

Keane walked to the rear of the car and pulled down the ten-foot antenna. Placing the bright orange ball on the end, he released the antenna and let it spring back to its lofty position. "Thank you," said Keane. "Please come again."

Elwood was disappointed that Warden Bettis had not recognized him. Had Bettis broken the ice by engaging in conversation, Keane might have found the courage to come forth and tell the veteran warden what he'd seen. *That bunch has gotten away with murder for years,* thought Keane, watching Bettis's patrol car pull away from the station. *Now they're gonna get away with this too, all because I don't have the guts to say something.* "Like hell I don't," blurted Keane, bolting out of the station and sprinting after Bettis's car. "Hey, stop!"

Bettis had already pulled onto the highway and was headed south when he glanced into his rearview mirror. Seeing Keane, he swung the patrol car around and headed back toward the station. "Whad ya do, forget to replace my gas cap?"

"No," said Keane, catching his breath. "I've got somethin' important I want to tell you. Would you mind parking behind the station?"

"Yeah, sure. Do you want to talk back there, or should I meet you in your office?"

"Let's talk in the office. Business is slow right now, so that shouldn't be a problem."

Pushing some binders aside and finding a seat on top of a cabinet at the back of the office, Bettis said, "What's this all about?"

Keane sat down in Bill's desk chair. "Don't you remember me?"

"No, can't say that I do."

"It was eight or nine years ago. You checked my hunting license when I was out pheasant hunting near Biggs."

"I contact a lot of people, son. I can't remember all of them."

"I told you about those guys killing overlimits of pheasants on old man Riddle's place and hiding 'em in the packing shed. The next day at school, everyone was talkin' about them getting busted, so you must have done something."

"Oh, yeah! Was that you who tipped me off?"

"It sure was. They were never sure it was me who turned 'em in, but that big Neanderthal Hollis Bogar has given me a hard time ever since."

"Bogar. It's all coming back to me now. I chased old Dud Bogar around the rice country for years. I remember him drivin' through the rice fields in that beat-up Studebaker of his. I knew what he was up to but could never catch him in the act."

"What about Hollis Bogar? Have you run into him since the pheasant incident?"

"Oh yeah. Hollis is a chip off the ol' block. Big like his old man and always up to no good. He's usually got that sneaky little cousin of his with him. Just this past summer, I ran into those two out west of Stony Gorge Reservoir."

"What were you doing way over there?"

"Mike Prescott, the Willows warden, was off on vacation for a couple weeks, so I thought I'd sneak over into his district for a change of scenery. He does the same thing when I'm on vacation. Anyway, I left the pavement and headed up one of those dusty Forest Service roads. If I'm boring you, let me know and I'll shut up so you can tell me your story."

"Not at all. I want to hear what happened, and we're not busy this early anyway."

"I had driven three or four miles when I came to an old logging spur heading off to the west. There was a locked Forest Service gate in front of it, with a sign that said ROAD WASHED OUT. I probably would have driven right on by, but I figured it was a good place to stop and take a leak."

"Never want to pass up a good place to take a leak," said Keane, laughing.

"I'm standin' there by the gate, takin' care of business, when I see these fresh vehicle tracks leading through the gate and up the hill. With nothing better to do, I decided to drive in and find out what was up."

"Did you have a key?"

"I've got a key chain in my patrol car with a couple hundred keys on it."

"Where'd ya get 'em?"

"Just collected 'em over the years. Some I inherited from the warden I replaced twenty-five years ago. If ya don't let me finish my story, we'll never get to yours."

"I'm sorry. Please continue."

"I started up this steep canyon on a dirt road not much wider than my patrol car. Nothing but chamise and buckbrush on the north side of the road and a sheer cliff on the south. I had gone a mile or two when I came to this rusted-out, forty-one Chevy pickup—tires bald and the back window busted out. At first, I thought it had been abandoned, but I felt the hood and it was still warm."

"So, it wasn't the Forest Service?"

"No, it sure wasn't. I found two sets of foot tracks leading away from the pickup and farther up the road. It would have been better to follow the tracks on foot, but my sciatica was killing me, so I decided to drive.

That turned out to be a mistake. I hadn't driven another half mile when here they come—Hollis Bogar and that smartass little cousin of his—walking down the road in my direction."

"What were they doing up there?"

"That's what I asked 'em. They swore up and down they were just out for a walk and hadn't been hunting. I knew that was hogwash, but they claimed they didn't have any weapons or ammunition, so there wasn't much I could do. I asked for identification. Bogar said he'd left his wallet at home. His cousin showed me an Oklahoma driver's license. I wish I could remember his name. Anyway, I asked 'em to empty their pockets so I could see if they had any ammunition on 'em. No ammunition, but whaddaya think dropped out of Bogar's pocket?"

"What?"

"A Forest Service key. They're larger than most other keys and easy to identify. I asked Bogar where he got the key. He said he'd worked on a fire crew a few years back and forgot to turn it in."

"Did you take it?"

"You bet I did. Then I checked their hands and clothes for blood and hair. They were clean as a whistle. I made 'em sit on the side of the road while I looked around for twenty minutes or so. The whole time I'm lookin' around, Bogar's smartass cousin was harping at me and makin' wisecracks."

"What do you think they were doing up there?"

"I know damn well what they were doin'. They were lookin' for a deer to kill. I figured they musta heard my car comin' up the road and hid their rifles."

"So wha'd ya do?"

"First I walked 'em back to my patrol car. When we got there, I made 'em stand there and watch me take out that key I confiscated and add it to my key collection. Then I told 'em to start walkin'. When we got to their pickup, I made 'em drive it back to the gate. I let 'em out and sent 'em on their way."

"Were they upset?"

"Upset ain't the word for it. That cousin of Bogar's was cussin' and swearin' to beat the band. I knew they'd hidden their guns somewhere and planned to come back and get 'em later."

"What did you do?"

"I drove back up the road and spent the next two hours lookin' for their guns."

"Did you find 'em?"

"I found one. They had run up this deer trail and stashed it behind a manzanita bush. It was a nice little lever action .30-30 with fancy engraving. Lying next to the rifle were a buck knife and a canvas bag containing a rag and a half-dozen .30-30 rounds."

"Were you able to make a case against them?"

"Knowin' full well they'd be back to get their rifle, I wrote out this note and tacked it to the manzanita bush. The note said to call the Sacramento Department of Fish and Game office and I'd arrange to meet 'em and give 'em their rifle. In exchange for their rifle, I'd issue 'em a citation for huntin' deer out of season and failure to show on demand."

"Failure to show on demand?"

"Yeah, there's this neat little section in the *Fish and Game Code* that says they gotta produce their weapons if a game warden asks for 'em. If they refuse, it's a violation."

"So, did you ever hear from them?"

"No, never heard a word. That rifle is still sittin' in the evidence locker in Sacramento. Now, what was it you wanted to talk to me about?"

"This morning, a little after 6:00, a green Oldsmobile with a primer-gray left front fender pulled into the station. Jimmy Riddle was behind the wheel, and three other men were riding with him." Keane handed Bettis a grease-smudged envelope with the Oldsmobile's license number written on it.

"I haven't heard that name mentioned in a while. Wasn't Riddle one of the boys I caught with all the pheasants?"

"Yes. They were picking and gutting the pheasants in Jimmy's grandpa's packing shed."

"That's right. Now I remember. It was out at the end of that old almond orchard. There were three of 'em: Riddle, Bogar, and that arrogant kid of Ralph Gastineau's."

"Blake."

"What's that?"

"Ralph Gastineau's kid. His name is Blake."

"Yeah, too bad they were all under eighteen, otherwise, old Judge Rubin would have thrown the book at 'em. As it was, I had to take 'em into juvenile court. What a pain in the ass that was. I don't think any of 'em received more than a slap on the wrist. I remember Gastineau's old man getting involved. He pulls a lot a weight in this county, ya know."

"Besides Jimmy Riddle, the other three in the car this morning were

Blake Gastineau, Hollis Bogar, and some greasy little punk with a big mouth. I heard Gastineau call him Richie."

"That's it. His name is Richie Stillwell. Don't ever turn your back on that guy. He's a psycho if there ever was one."

"It's starting to rain," said Keane, looking out the window at the gas lane.

"I better run back and make sure I didn't leave my window down," said Bettis. A few minutes later, the warden returned. "Where were we?"

"These four guys showed up just after I opened the station. Bogar got out of the car to use the restroom, and I saw that his pant legs and tennis shoes were soaking wet and covered with mud."

"That's interesting. Kinda early to be out sloshing through the mud."

"Wait until you hear the rest. While I was pumping gas, I noticed fresh blood all over their rear bumper and little white feathers sticking to the blood."

"That could have been from yesterday. The nights have been pretty cold lately."

"I thought that, too, until I ran my finger through it. The blood was still wet."

"Anything else?" said Bettis, looking at his watch.

"Yes," said Keane, beginning to think that Bettis was losing interest and wanted to leave. "These two duck hunters were parked on the opposite side of the gas pumps from Riddle's car. The black Lab in the bed of their pickup was going crazy."

"Whaddaya mean, goin' crazy?"

"She was whimpering and bouncing up and down like she wanted to jump out of the pickup, with her eyes trained on the trunk of Riddle's car the entire time."

"I've seen dogs do that before, usually when someone's got a deer in the trunk."

"There's one more thing," said Keane.

"What's that?"

"Every time I came close to their car this morning, these guys would clam up and stop talking. I did overhear Bogar mentioning the packing shed. He had to be talking about old man Riddle's shed, where you busted 'em before."

"That's good information," said Bettis. "Is there a number where I can reach you?"

"After today, you won't be able to reach me at all."

"Why's that?"

"I'm shipping out for the South Pole."

"The South Pole! Why are you going to the South Pole?"

"It's a long story," said Keane, running out the office door. "I have to wait on this customer."

"Well, thanks for the information. I'll see what I can come up with."

EIGHT

IT WAS RAINING CATS AND DOGS when Norm Bettis hurried back to the patrol car after his conversation with Elwood Keane. While contemplating his next move, he wrote a few notes in his diary and listened to the pounding rain bouncing off the rooftop. *I had my heart set on a cup of coffee and a slice of Pearl's apple pie,* thought Bettis. *Martha was too busy to cook this morning, and we were out of eggs. That bowl of cornflakes didn't last long.*

Bettis slowly pulled out onto the highway and instinctively headed south. *It's almost nine o'clock and those guys left the gas station over three hours ago. They're probably long gone by now. Damn, my stomach's growling somethin' awful. I guess I could check this out, but more than likely, it'll be a waste of time.*

He could see his coffee-drinking buddies Earl Glenn and Winston Maxwell sitting at the counter when he pulled into Pearl's gravel parking lot and drove around back. As he was about to climb out of his patrol car and run through the pouring rain, Norm's conscience overpowered his appetite. *What am I doing? Twenty years ago, I would have already been down at that packing shed rousting those outlaws. Am I still a game warden or nothin' but a washed-up old fool, wasting the last years of my career sitting in this coffee shop?*

Three heads turned in unison as Bettis's patrol car raced back across the parking lot and out to the highway. "I say," said Winston, "where is our gendarme going in such a hurry?"

"He'll be back," said Earl. "Pearl, this is damn good pie. How 'bout cuttin' me another slice?"

"That was kinda strange," said Pearl. "I hope everything's all right."

"Pearl, I'd like another slice of apple pie."

"Earl, if you say that one more time, you'll get the whole pie on top a that shiny, bald head of yours."

Bettis had a hunch that if Gastineau and his gang did have illegal ducks, they'd be foolish enough to draw and hang them at the packing shed where he had made the big pheasant-poaching case against Gastineau, Riddle, and Bogar several years before. Driving north on the highway, he turned west and continued another three miles to what was left of Jeb Riddle's almond orchard. *I'm not sure if that shed is even here anymore*, thought Bettis. *As hard as it's been raining, I'll probably sink up to my axles if I try to drive out there.*

Parking in a wide spot at the north side of the county road, Bettis quickly changed into his rubber hip boots and a full-length, camouflage rain parka. *Let's check this out and get it over with so I can go back and get a slice a Pearl's apple pie. She should be taking a fresh one outta the oven right about now.*

Not bothering to radio the dispatcher to report his location, Bettis locked the patrol car and began sloshing his way across the orchard. Two hundred yards in, he came to the unpaved road that led from the farmhouse to the packing shed. "Looks like somebody's driven on this road recently," mumbled Bettis, "and the tracks are headed in one direction."

Encouraged by the tire tracks, Bettis ducked into the adjacent trees and proceeded on a parallel path toward what he hoped would be the packing shed. He had trudged through the mud another hundred yards or so when the distant echo of male voices caught the veteran warden's attention. Stopping to listen and catch his breath, he turned to his right and slowly crept out onto the road. "They're here!" he whispered, jumping back into the cover of the trees. He'd seen the front end of the green Oldsmobile Keane had described earlier and an older-model, gray Ford coupe parked nearby. *I'm finally gonna catch that bunch of no-good duck poachers in the act. This will be a fitting end to my career, and I can retire feeling good about myself.*

Step by heavy, mud-encumbered step, Warden Bettis edged closer to the packing shed. As if on cue, the drenching rain suddenly turned to a drizzle and a patch of blue appeared overhead. Seconds later, a beam of sunlight shone through the parted clouds and was reflected by the packing shed's corrugated metal roof. Temporarily blinded by the glare, Bettis stopped, shielded his eyes, and listened.

"One more night like this, and I'll be able to pay off my Oldsmobile," said a voice coming from the shed.

"Yeah, maybe that penny-pinching boss of yours will get off your ass," said another.

Approaching the packing shed, Bettis found Jimmy Riddle's Oldsmobile backed halfway inside the front entrance. Scurrying around back, he came to a sliding metal door that was secured by a chain and padlock but cracked open slightly. Trying desperately to slow his racing heartbeat and control his heavy breathing, Bettis leaned against the building's back wall and eavesdropped on the conversation inside.

"This is the last of 'em. We'll let 'em hang here until tomorrow morning, then I'll run 'em down to Lincoln."

That must be Gastineau, thought Bettis. *Based on what the kid told me, Gastineau's the ringleader of this den of thieves.*

"What are we gonna do with this barrel of duck guts? My mom sold the backhoe last week, so we can't use it to dig holes anymore."

Bettis was unable to positively identify the last voice he'd heard, but based on the conversation, he figured it had to be Jimmy Riddle's. Riddle's grandparents had both passed away, leaving the house and property to Jimmy's mother.

"We'll worry about the duck guts later. Hollis, how about gettin' off your lazy ass and helping Jimmy with the rest of those ducks."

"Keep your pants on, Blake. I was just takin' a breather."

That makes three, thought Bettis. *I'd recognize Bogar's voice anywhere. He sounds just like his old man.*

Peering through the four-inch opening between the sliding metal door and the building, Warden Bettis couldn't believe his eyes. *My God, look at all those ducks. There must be over a hundred mallards and pintails hanging from one wall to the other. I've seen enough!*

Removing his parka and hanging it over a rusted tractor seat, Bettis marched around the north side of the shed and made a beeline for the west entrance. Without stopping to survey the situation or confirm the number of people inside, he proceeded to the center of the cement floor and stood with his forearms crossed in front of his chest.

Oblivious to Bettis's presence, Hollis Bogar continued to hang ducks on a section of heavy twine stretched across the width of the structure. Meanwhile, Blake Gastineau was sitting on a moth-eaten old couch in the corner of the shed, tallying figures on a pocket-sized notepad.

"Apparently, you boys didn't learn your lesson the first time,"

announced Bettis, his stern, authoritative voice echoing through the brutally cold, dimly lit building. Gastineau was so surprised by the sound
of Bettis's voice, he dropped his pencil and watched it slip through the
crack between the couch pad and frame. The first thing that crossed his
mind was the likelihood of his father finding out what he'd been up to
and the certainty of losing his inheritance.

Jimmy Riddle, who had a bloody pocketknife in his right hand and
the backside of a hen pintail firmly clutched in his left, continued with
what he was doing. Without looking up, he said, "Hollis, I'm tired of gutting ducks, and my fingers are numb. I don't have time for your stupid
games."

"Jimmy," said Bogar.

"Hollis, I'm warning you."

"I'm not kidding, Jimmy. We've got company."

Riddle looked up to find Warden Bettis staring back at him from the
center of the room.

"Here's what I want you gentlemen to do," said Bettis. "One at a time,
beginning with Mr. Riddle, I want you to take out your identification
and your car keys, place them on the table in front of me, and sit down
on that bench over there."

"Do you mind if I wipe the blood off my hands first?" said Riddle.

"Go ahead, and be quick about it." After wiping his hands on a rag
caked with dried blood, Riddle removed the driver's license from his
wallet and placed it on the table in front of Bettis. "That's good. Now
your hunting license and your car keys."

"I don't have a hunting license," said Riddle, "and I didn't shoot any
of these ducks."

"Shut up, Jimmy," said Gastineau.

"Just put your car keys on the table and sit down on that bench over
there," ordered Bettis.

"I don't have my car keys."

"Where are they?"

"I left 'em in the car."

"All right, go over there and sit down. Now you, Mr. Bogar."

"I don't have no car keys."

"Then remove your driver's license and place it on the table."

"I ain't got no driver's license neither."

"I think his driver's license was suspended," offered Riddle.

"Jimmy, I told you to shut up," said Gastineau.

"What form of identification do you have, Mr. Bogar?"

"I got a huntin' license and a duck stamp, but I think they're both last year's. This one's got a picture of some flyin' geese on it."

"You're right—that's last year's. Just leave what you have on the table and sit down. Mr. Gastineau, that leaves you." Gastineau failed to respond, his eyes transfixed on the uniformed officer. "Mr. Gastineau, I'm ordering you to take out your identification and your car keys and place them on this table in front of me."

Gastineau didn't hear a word the warden was saying. Rising to his feet, he continued to direct his eyes in Bettis's direction.

Shifting his attention to Bogar and Riddle, Bettis noticed that they, too, had stood up and were intently watching something directly to his rear. "Hey, I thought I told you . . . what the—"

PART TWO

NINE

LAND BETWEEN THE CITY OF RIVERSIDE and the Old West-style town of Temecula remained mostly undeveloped during the 1950s and 1960s. In the days before Riverside became the fastest-growing county in California, communities like Temecula, Murrieta, Lake Elsinore, Winchester, Perris, and San Jacinto were thought of as rural and out in the country. With lakes, farm ponds, fields, hillsides, and endless open space for Henry Glance and Larry Jansen to explore, it was like growing up in paradise.

Henry Glance and Larry Jansen met for the first time in 1955, as students in Mrs. Scott's second-grade class. Born a few days apart, Henry and Larry were both natural athletes and shared a penchant for outdoor adventure. The two obvious differences between the boys were their sizes and their personalities: Larry was twice the size of every other kid in class, while Henry was of average height and weight for a seven-year-old. Larry was loquacious and outgoing, while Henry was quiet and shy.

With an insatiable interest in nature and gifted with a photographic memory, young Henry Glance buried himself in every book he could find about birds, mammals, reptiles, amphibians, fish, butterflies—even plants. If Henry and Larry weren't at school or playing baseball, they were usually looking for snakes and lizards on the rocky hillsides overlooking Temecula or fishing in one of the nearby lakes. One of the most memorable events in their young lives happened on Saturday morning, April 18, 1959. Henry and Larry were soon to turn twelve and couldn't wait to try out their newfound independence.

Henry lived with his parents, Will and Mary Glance, on a ten-acre farm two miles east of Temecula. Larry Jansen and his parents lived in town. Since the boys planned on going fishing early the next morning, Will and Mary invited their son's best friend to spend Friday night at their home. That evening, Mary made Henry's favorite dinner: fried chicken, mashed potatoes, and corn fritters.

"Hey, Larry, how do you like those corn fritters?" said Henry, watching Larry finish off his third helping.

"They're so good, I can't stop eatin' 'em," said Larry.

"Eleven years old and he weighs more than I do," mumbled Will. Hearing his father's offhanded wisecrack, Henry burst into laughter, sending a gulp of milk up his nose.

"Henry, don't encourage your father," said Mary, handing her son a cloth napkin. "Larry can eat all he wants, and there's plenty more where that came from."

After dinner, Larry walked into the living room, flopped down on the carpet in front of the TV, and began moaning.

"Larry, are you all right?" said Mary. "Would you like something to help your stomach?"

"I'll be okay if I can just lie here for a few minutes." As Larry closed his eyes and began to doze off, the Glance's golden retriever walked over and gave him a slurp across the mouth.

"Yuck," said Larry, wiping the slobber on his shirt sleeve.

"Aw, sweet Daisy," said Mary. "She was just trying to make you feel better."

The sun was peeking over the San Jacinto Mountains when Henry and Larry heard a knock on the bedroom door. "You boys better get up if you're going fishing," said Mary.

"Okay, Mom," said Henry, throwing a pillow across the room and hitting his houseguest in the face. "We're up."

As the boys walked into the kitchen, Henry asked where his father was. "He's out feeding the chickens," said Mary. "What would you boys like for breakfast?"

"I don't care, Mom. Whatever Larry wants is fine with me."

"Larry, what would you like?"

"I don't know. What do you have?"

"We have eggs, pancakes, waffles, French toast, cereal—"

"That sounds good," said Larry.

Henry laughed. "Mom, he's not kidding."

The kitchen was still in an uproar when Will walked in through the back door. "I hope you left your muddy boots out on the porch," said Mary.

"I did. What's everybody laughing about?"

"Sit down, and we'll tell you. Would you like a cup of coffee?"

"Is the pope Catholic? Where's the morning paper? I wanna find out how the Dodgers did last night."

"They lost to the Cubs, nine to four," said Henry.

"Thanks, Hank. Have you already read the paper this morning?"

"No. It says right there on top of the front page: Dodgers lose to Cubs, nine to four."

"I was going to ask you who pitched for the Dodgers, but—"

"Stan Williams."

"I thought you said you hadn't read the paper."

"I read yesterday's paper. It said Stan Williams was going to pitch last night."

"I'm glad we cleared that up," said Will. "It's so nice to have a walking encyclopedia in the family."

"Will, how do you want your eggs?"

"Over easy. So, you boys are planning to ride your bikes all the way to Vail Lake this morning?"

"Yeah, Dad. Do you mind if I take your binoculars?"

"Go ahead, but make sure you don't lose 'em."

Everything the boys needed for the day's adventure was stuffed inside their backpacks: two-piece fishing rods, reels, hooks, sinkers, bobbers, stringers, lunch, water, and a makeshift butterfly net to catch grasshoppers if they ran out of worms. With that, Henry and Larry climbed on their bikes. Henry would ride the same twenty-six-inch Schwinn Spitfire he'd been pedaling back and forth to school since he was eight. Larry's transportation for the day was a three-speed Raleigh he inherited from his older brother, Ron.

"You boys be careful now," said Mary, waving goodbye.

"We will," said Henry, looking back and seeing Daisy running alongside. "Mom, would you call Daisy?"

"Daisy, you can't go, sweetheart."

The plan was to pedal four miles to Vail Lake by way of the back roads. Once there, Henry and Larry would hide their bikes in the bushes and walk a narrow trail to their secret fishing spot. If everything went well and the fish were biting, the boys would return before dark with a couple of nice bullhead catfish and a stringer of bluegill.

"Did you remember to bring the nightcrawlers?" said Henry, doing his best to keep up with his speedier sidekick.

"I did. What did your mom make us for lunch?"

"Don't worry, you aren't gonna starve."

"Did she include those cookies I saw on the counter?"

"I don't know. I was doing my chores while Mom made our lunch."

"I hope she did."

The boys were halfway to their destination when they stopped to rest at the top of a hill. While taking a healthy slug of water from his canteen, Larry couldn't help noticing a slow-moving car approaching the intersection below. "Hey, that's a fifty-six Chevy, just like my brother's, except Ron's is cherry red and that one's gray."

"Is Ron's jacked up in back like that?"

"No, but it's got this neat little steering wheel and a piston for a gear-shift knob."

The car below turned right at the intersection, cruised another fifty yards in the same direction the boys were headed, and came to a sudden stop at the side of the road.

"I wonder what they stopped for," said Larry.

"Let's find out," said Henry, reaching into his backpack for his father's binoculars.

"I forgot you had those."

"Yeah, I brought 'em along in case we see an eagle or something."

"What do you see?"

"On the other side of the fence, there's a pair of honkers and eight or ten little goslings."

"Can I look?"

"Here, they're lined up along the bank of that irrigation ditch, just beyond the car."

"I see 'em now. Wait a minute, there's something sticking out the car window."

BOOM!

"Quick, let me have the binoculars," said Henry. "They just shot that big gander. See him flopping around in the pasture?"

"What happened to the goslings?"

"The hen is swimming downstream in the ditch, and they're right behind her."

"Hank, they're getting out of the car."

"I see 'em. It looks like they're gonna climb the fence and go after that goose. The short guy is crawling under the fence, and the taller guy is stepping over it. Wait a minute, the short guy just tore the back of his shirt, and he's yellin' at the other guy to come and help him."

"Unbelievable!" said Larry. "I see a house and a barn just up the road."

"Here, take these binoculars and my backpack."

"Where ya goin?"

"You'll see."

Larry watched his friend coast down the hill as the two goose poachers ignored the no-trespassing signs and began chasing the wounded goose across the field. Reaching the poachers' car, Henry laid his bike on the pavement and peered through the driver's open window. Seeing that the keys were still in the ignition, he reached in, took the keys, and placed them in his pocket.

"Hey, what the hell are you doing?" shouted the driver.

When Larry saw the two poachers running back to their car, he tossed the backpacks aside and dashed down the hill to help his friend.

"If that kid did anything to my car, I'm gonna kick his ass," said the driver, a short, stocky, twenty-plus-year-old with a flattop haircut.

As the two goose poachers approached the fence, Henry reached into his pocket, grabbed the keys in his left hand, and tossed them into the weeds on the opposite side of the road.

"Chuck, the kid took your keys," shouted the shooter, about the same age as his partner and wearing a grease-stained, foam-rubber baseball cap.

"Ray, now my pants are hooked on the fence. I need your help."

"Why didn't you crawl under, like you did before?"

"Why don't you shut up and give me a hand here."

"Did you hear me say the kid took your keys?"

"I heard ya. Be careful you don't tear my pants. Ouch! Now look what you've done."

"I'm right here, Hank," said Larry, dropping his bicycle on the pavement and running to Henry's side.

"All right, you miserable little punks," said Chuck, "hand over the keys."

"Little punks?" said Larry, supercharged with adrenaline after his dash down the hill. "You're the one who's a punk. My friend and I are bigger than you and we're only eleven years old."

Henry nudged Larry with his elbow.

"How would you like a smack in the mouth?" said Chuck, doubling his fist. "If I don't get those keys back in two minutes, you're gonna get one."

"I had your keys in my pocket a minute ago," said Henry. "They musta fallen out here on the ground somewhere."

"He's lying," said Ray, searching the immediate area around the car. "That kid knows where the keys are."

"You guys are in big trouble for shooting that goose," said Henry.

"I tell you what," said Chuck, dropping to his knees and searching under the car, "Ray will give you each a dollar if you show us where the keys are."

"How 'bout we show the game warden where the keys are instead?" said Henry. "Here he comes now."

"The kid's right," said Ray. "I think we're screwed."

"You just keep your mouth shut and let me do the talking," said Chuck, coming to his feet. "Who's he gonna believe, us or these two kids?"

"Looks like there's someone following him in a pickup," said Larry. "I bet it's the farmer who owns this property."

The Fish and Game patrol car came to a stop directly in front of the poachers' 1956 Chevy. Right behind the warden was a gray Ford pickup with two bales of hay in back. "This is where the shot came from, Ned," said landowner Lester Tibbets, climbing from the cab of his pickup and running up to meet the officer.

Warden Ned McCullough had been around the mountain a few times and preferred to take his time and size up the situation before charging in. He grabbed his Stetson from the front seat and covered his neatly combed gray hair.

"Just last week, I found one of my mouflons right out there, shot in the head," said Tibbets. "When I heard a shot this morning, I called your dispatcher right away. Luckily for me, you were in the area."

Henry and Larry had never encountered a real game warden before and were immediately impressed with McCullough's stately appearance in the standard field uniform of the day: work boots, khaki pants, and a short-sleeved khaki shirt with a star-shaped badge pinned just above the left pocket. Holstered at his right hip was a .38-caliber Smith and Wesson revolver. A blue-and-gold patch reading RESOURCES AGENCY—CALIFORNIA DEPARTMENT FISH & GAME was stitched to McCullough's left shoulder.

Warden McCullough checked out the poachers' Chevy sedan, making sure there were no other people inside. He noticed a double-barreled .410 shotgun lying across the front seat and a bolt-action .22 rifle on the floorboard in back. Opening the passenger door, McCullough picked up the shotgun, broke open the breech, and removed two shotgun shells—one expended and one live. He laid the shotgun across the hood of his patrol car, with the breech still open. The .22 rifle held a clip containing live rounds, but the firing chamber was empty.

Walking over to the four individuals standing at the rear of the poachers' car, McCullough noticed two bicycles lying on their sides in the middle of the road. "Let me take a stab at this," he said. "The bikes belong to you two boys, and you gentlemen are connected to this car in some way."

"The car belongs to me," said Chuck, later identified as Charles Sloan, a steelworker out of Fontana.

"And the shotgun?" said McCullough. "Who does it belong to?"

"The shotgun's mine," said Ray, later identified as Raymond Beacham, "but I ain't shot no mouflon, whatever that is." Beacham was also a laborer at the Fontana steel mill.

"It's a sheep," said Tibbets.

"Well, I ain't shot no sheep neither."

"What did you shoot?" said McCullough.

Beacham started to answer, when Sloan interrupted. "He shot at a ground squirrel, but he missed."

"Yeah," said Beacham, "I shot at a ground squirrel."

Henry and Larry had watched the entire episode without saying a word. They figured the warden would get to the bottom of the situation and the poachers would eventually confess to their deed. It soon became clear that Sloan and Beacham were consummate liars, intent on telling one whopper after another until the warden gave up and sent them on their way.

"Excuse me," said Henry, walking up to the warden and examining the gold name tag pinned above his left pocket. "Warden McCullo?"

"It's McCullough," said the warden.

"Like Flint McCullough on *Wagon Train*?" said Larry.

"That's right, except I'm better looking than Robert Horton."

"What the hell?" quipped Sloan. "If you're gonna stand around here talking about TV shows, me and Ray would like to leave."

"Warden McCullough, Larry and I saw the whole thing from the top of that hill up there."

"What's your name, son?"

"My name is Henry Glance, but everybody, except my mom, calls me Hank."

"Well, Hank, tell me what you saw."

"There was this family of Canada geese standing on the edge of that ditch over there." Henry pointed toward the bank of a narrow irrigation flume that ran the length of the pasture.

"How many geese were there?"

"At least eight or ten: a hen, a gander, and several goslings."

"You seem to know something about geese," said McCullough, smiling.

"He's always reading about animals," said Larry.

"The kid is makin' this crap up," said Sloan. "There's no way he could tell what Ray was shooting at from way up there."

"He saw 'em with his dad's binoculars," said Larry.

"What?" said McCullough.

"Hank saw the geese with his dad's binoculars. They're still up on the hill with our backpacks."

"Ned," said Tibbets, "there has been a family of wild geese around here lately. I saw 'em just yesterday."

"Thanks, Les."

"Warden McCullough, me and Larry can probably find the goose they shot. Do you mind if we go look for it?"

"Okay," said McCullough. "While you boys look for the goose, I'll get some information from these two gentlemen."

"What for?" said Sloan. "That kid ain't proved nothin'."

"To start with, there's a matter of the loaded shotgun I found in your car."

"Ray, you dumb sonofabitch, I told you to make sure that gun was unloaded."

"I thought it was," said Beacham.

Henry and Larry searched for the next half hour but were unable to find any trace of the goose. "I'm sorry, Warden McCullough," said Henry. "We've looked everywhere."

"That's okay, boys. You did your best. These fellas say you took their car keys."

"I took 'em so they wouldn't get away," said Henry.

"Would you please give them to me."

"I'll have to go find 'em," said Henry, pointing to the opposite side of the road. "Before I find the keys, I wanted to tell you one more thing."

"Sure, go ahead."

"Hey, warden," said Sloan. "They didn't find the goose because there ain't no goose. Those two kids made the whole thing up. If you're gonna write my friend a ticket for havin' his shotgun loaded, then do it so we can get the hell outta here. I have to be at work by three o'clock."

"You guys hold your horses until I hear what this young man has to say."

"I saw something that looked like blood on the back bumper of their car," said Henry.

"You're a very observant young man," said McCullough. "Maybe someday you'll decide to be a game warden yourself."

"I'm gonna be a major-league baseball player when I grow up."

"And I'm gonna be president of the United States," said Sloan. "The kid's got quite an imagination."

"What position do you play?" said McCullough.

"Pitcher."

"You must be pretty good."

"He's really good," said Larry, watching Henry cross the road to search for the keys. "Hank threw two no-hitters last year and one already this season."

"How much more of this crap do we have to listen to?" scoffed Sloan.

"Found 'em!" shouted Henry, from the other side of the road.

"It's a good thing," said Sloan. "We got better things to do than hang around here all day. You ain't got no right to keep us here any longer."

Ignoring Sloan's latest outburst, McCullough walked over to the Chevy sedan, inserted the key, and popped open the trunk. Inside, he found seven cottontail rabbits, a hen mallard, and a great horned owl.

"We didn't shoot that owl," said Beacham. "We found it lyin' dead on the side of the road."

McCullough reached inside the trunk and picked up the owl. It was still warm to the touch and fell limp in his hand. Running his fingers through the breast feathers, McCullough found a tiny hole where a .22-caliber bullet had penetrated. Laying the owl on the hood of his patrol car, McCullough gathered the duck and all seven rabbits. As Sloan and Beacham watched, McCullough reached into the back seat and retrieved the .22 rifle he had examined earlier. After removing the clip, he placed the rifle on the hood of his patrol car.

"So what's gonna happen?" said Sloan.

"The owl, the duck, the rabbits, and both of your weapons are being seized into evidence," said McCullough. "I'll be filing a criminal complaint with the Riverside County District Attorney, charging you both with unlawful possession of a protected owl, a mallard duck during closed season, and seven cottontail rabbits during closed season. You also had a loaded shotgun in your car on a public road and were hunting without hunting licenses."

"That's tellin' 'em," blurted Larry, grinning from ear to ear.

Henry gave Larry a nudge.

"Will we be able to get our guns back?" said Beacham.

"Don't press your luck," said McCullough. "I'm not going to charge you with shooting the goose, only because we couldn't find it and I don't want to have to pull the boys out of school to testify. Based on what I found in the trunk of your car, I have no doubt that everything the boys said is true. I should book you both into the county jail, but since you have valid IDs, I'm going to let you go on your way. You'll be notified when to appear in court. It won't bother me one bit to come down to that slag heap where you two work and slap the cuffs on you, so make sure you show up. Now you're free to leave."

McCullough stayed and chatted with Lester Tibbetts and the two boys after Sloan and Beacham had left. "I want to thank you boys for the fine job you did helping me apprehend those two violators. That took a lot of courage, but I feel I need to caution you about reaching into someone's car and taking their keys."

"Was that wrong?" said Henry.

"It wasn't really wrong, but you could have been hurt. Those two men weren't exactly model citizens, and they could have pulled a knife or even a gun on you. In the future, you may want to just take down the license number and get to a phone as soon as possible. Does that make sense?"

"Yes," said Henry, "but I was so mad about 'em shooting that goose, I wanted to make sure they didn't get away."

"I understand, but some of these poachers can be dangerous and unpredictable."

"Speakin' of dangerous," said Tibbets, "I been meanin' ta ask you about a story I read three or four years back. It was in the Riverside paper."

"I'm all ears," said McCullough.

"It was about a game warden up north somewhere who disappeared. I forgot his name. Apparently, they never found him or his car."

"I know what you're referring to," said McCullough. "The warden's name was Norman Bettis. I met him many years ago at a training conference. Norm's patrol district was north of Sacramento, near a little town called Gridley."

"Did they ever find out what happened to him?"

"No, they never found him or his car. There were plenty of theories floating around the department, but none of them ever panned out."

"What were the theories?"

"His neighboring wardens figured old Norm had stumbled into something he wasn't capable of handling. Bettis was in his sixties and not in very good physical shape. He was one of those old-timers who refused to retire."

"Look where it got him," said Tibbets. "You guys have a dangerous job."

"It can be, at times," said McCullough. "We've lost a few good officers over the years. Some of those market hunters who hunted the rice fields up north would have just as soon shot a game warden as looked at him."

"Is that kind of thing still goin' on?"

"Any time there's money to be made, there's potential for someone to get killed or badly hurt. I've known outlaws who would kill the last wild animal on Earth to make an easy buck."

"I hope they eventually catch the dirty bastards who did it," said Tibbets. "Excuse my language, boys. I forgot you were still here."

"That's okay," said Larry. "My pop talks like that all the time."

"I need to take care of all this evidence," said McCullough, "so I best be running along."

"Warden McCullough," said Henry.

"Yeah, son?"

"If we can find the goose after you leave, would it be okay if I take it home and try to save it?"

"Sure," said McCullough, loading evidence into the trunk of his car. "You boys are welcome to try. If the goose only has a broken wing and isn't wounded internally, it might survive. Here, I'll give you a card with my phone number on it. Call and let me know if you find it." McCullough and Tibbets climbed into their cars and drove away.

With the landowner's permission, Henry and Larry climbed the fence and began searching the high grass for the wounded goose. It wasn't until Larry almost stepped on it that the bird jumped up and furiously flapped its uninjured wing.

"Grab him," shouted Henry. "Don't let him go." Henry removed his gray sweatshirt and placed it over the goose's head and body. "This will keep him still until we get to our backpacks," he said.

The boys walked their bikes up the hill, Henry pushing with one arm and cradling the goose in the other. Reaching the top, Henry emptied his own backpack and jammed all his belongings into Larry's. It took the strength and agility of both boys to slip the goose inside Henry's backpack, feet first. Only the gander's neck and head were sticking out when Henry pressed a couple of snaps and secured the agitated bird inside.

"I wonder if anyone will ever find him," said Henry on the three-mile ride home.

Who?" said Larry.

"The game warden who disappeared. What are you laughing about?"

"I'm laughing at the goose. He's trying to peck you on the back of the neck."

"They haven't even been able to find his car," said Henry. "Don't you find that strange?"

"What car?"

"The game warden's car. Weren't you listening when Warden McCullough told us that story?"

TEN

"I'D LIKE TO THANK EVERYONE FOR COMIN' OUT to the ballpark on this warm August afternoon," said the announcer. "This is the last game of the 1967 summer season here at beautiful Evans Field in downtown Riverside. It's turned out to be a classic pitchers' duel between right-hander Gary Miller of Redlands and the big left-hander from Riverside, Hank Glance. Going into the bottom of the eighth inning, the score remains Redlands nothing and Riverside nothing. Leading off for Riverside is shortstop Don Hartline."

"Hank, whaddaya hear from Stanford?" said catcher Larry Jansen, sitting on the bench next to his best friend.

"The coach said I could finish up my last semester at Riverside City College and enroll in time for baseball season next spring."

"Do ya think you'll make the team?"

"He seemed to think so," said Henry, trying to concentrate on the game. "They need a good left-handed pitcher."

"That's the first walk given up by Miller," said the announcer. "Batting for Riverside is third baseman Dale Bagley."

"Come on Bags, you can hit this guy," shouted Coach Ron Carroll from the bench. "Keep that left shoulder in." Bagley hit Miller's first pitch for a single up the middle.

"What if you don't make the team?" said Larry.

"Then I'll probably have to find another school. Stanford is more than I can afford without a scholarship."

"Do you have anything in mind?"

"I was thinking about Chico State, up north."

"My cousin went to Chico State," interjected center fielder Mitch Rider.

"How'd he like it?" said Larry.

"He said it was the best four years of his life. It's a beautiful old school with ivy-covered walls, just like the traditional schools back East. And a trout stream runs right through the middle of campus. Every spring, they have this event called Pioneer Week, when the fraternities and sororities build a Western town and throw keggers."

"What's a kegger?" said Larry.

"It's a party, usually outdoors, where everyone drinks beer out of a giant keg. Fred said it gets pretty wild sometimes. Last year there was a party on just about every corner for several blocks."

"What about girls?" said Larry.

"According to my cousin, the girls outnumber the guys three to one. Chico State has this outdoor quad and rose garden in the center of campus where all the jocks sit on benches and watch the babes walk by on their way to class."

"Chico State sounds like my kind of school," said Larry. "What about you, Hank?"

"Sounds pretty good," said Henry, watching the ball game and not really engaged in the conversation.

"Now batting for Riverside, catcher Larry Jansen."

"Jansen!" shouted Coach Carroll. "Where's Jansen?"

One of the players pointed toward the far end of the dugout.

"Jansen!"

"Yeah, coach."

"Leave Hank alone and get your ass out there. You're up."

Larry Jansen hit a line shot that almost tore Miller's glove off, but the skillful Redlands pitcher snagged it for the first out. Jansen was followed by second baseman Pete Moran. Moran hit a weak fly ball that fell in just out of the second baseman's reach, allowing Hartline to advance to third and Bagley to slide into second. With bases loaded, right fielder Darryl Weeks flew out to center field, allowing Hartline to tag up and score Riverside's first and only run. Left fielder Tim Erskine grounded out to shortstop, ending the inning.

The Riverside team took their positions for the top of the ninth inning. "Go get 'em, big guy," said Coach Carroll, as Henry Glance left the dugout and walked toward the mound.

Henry looked back at the coach. "I'll give it my best shot."

Riverside's left-hander had struck out the first two Redlands batters and was one out away from a no-hitter when he heard a familiar voice coming from the on-deck circle. "I'm gonna take you deep, Glance."

It was Henry's longtime nemesis, Robert "Big Bob" Power. Ever since Little League, the powerful slugger had been spoiling games for Henry Glance. Known as one of the most dangerous amateur hitters in Southern California, Bob Power was also famous for his lack of civility and penchant for shouting obscenities at the most inappropriate times. Four-letter words flowed from his tobacco-stained lips like water. Bob had once dropped a barbell on his toe during a workout session at Vic Tanny's Gym. So objectionable was his verbal outburst, he was asked to leave and not come back.

As Power burrowed into the left-hander's batter's box, Coach Carroll called time-out and walked to the mound. The entire Riverside infield followed suit and gathered around their pitcher.

"I'm wondering if we shouldn't just put this jerk on," said Carroll. "That foul ball he hit in the fifth inning still hasn't come down."

"Don't worry," said Glance. "I won't give him anything good to hit."

"Okay, but be careful," said Carroll, walking off the mound and heading back to the home-field dugout.

No one could get Bob Power's goat like Larry Jansen. Larry knew how to push all the right buttons—anything to throw the powerful slugger off his game and cause him to strike out or pop up. In his catcher's squat and about to set the target, Jansen looked up at the burley Redlands catcher. "Hey, Bob, did you forget to shave this morning, or are you tryin' ta grow a beard with all that peach fuzz on your chin?"

Power looked back at Jansen and made an unintelligible grunting sound. "Keep it up, Jansen," said Power. "I'll shove this bat up—"

"That's enough," said the umpire. "Let's play ball."

Henry Glance's first pitch to Bob Power was a letter-high fastball that sizzled as it passed over the outside corner of the plate. The resounding *WHOP* of the ball exploding into Jansen's catcher's mitt was heard as far away as the parking lot, evoking a comment from one of the late arrivals. "Hank Glance must be pitching today."

"Hooah," shouted the umpire, pivoting to his right and extending his right arm.

"Wow! That one hurt my hand," said Jansen, standing up and tossing the ball back.

Stepping from the batter's box, Power took two quick practice swings and stepped back in. Glance's second pitch was an off-speed curve that dove downward and off the plate. "Ball," shouted the umpire. "One and one."

Henry began rubbing up the ball as he turned away from home plate and inspected his outfield. All three outfielders had shifted to the right and were positioned with their backs against the fence. Believing that the cagey Riverside pitcher wasn't about to give him anything good to hit, Bob Power inched closer to the plate. Turning to face his opponent, Henry made note of what Power had done. The two fierce competitors were locked in a game of ball-field chess. It was up to Henry to make the next move.

"Hey, Glance, if you're afraid to pitch to me, maybe you guys would like to forfeit right now," shouted Power, squirting a thin stream of tobacco from between his two front teeth.

"That'll be enough, Bob," warned the umpire.

Henry's next pitch was a head-high fastball that missed the powerful batsman by inches and sent him diving to the ground. "Ball," shouted the umpire, pointing his finger at the Riverside pitcher, as if to say *You've been warned*.

Power climbed to his feet, brushed himself off, and gave Henry an angry stare. Before stepping back in the box, he turned to Larry Jansen. "I bet you two don't have the guts to throw me another strike."

"That last one just missed your head," said Jansen, looking the enraged slugger straight in the eye. "You know how wild Hank can be sometimes."

"That's enough, Larry," said the umpire.

Smiling, Jansen dropped to the crouch position and extended two downward-facing fingers. Henry stared in at his lifelong friend and shook his head. Without moving the target, Jansen extended one finger. Again, Henry shook him off. "Time out," said Jansen, running out to the mound. "Whaddaya wanna do, Hank? The last time you threw this beast a changeup, he hit it half a mile."

"Give me an inside target," said Henry. "I'll put a fastball in on his hands. If he swings, he'll either miss it cleanly or hit it on the handle and break his bat."

Glance kicked his right leg in the air and let fly with a fastball directly at Larry Jansen's target. Power turned on the ball, as he'd done so many times before, expecting it to hit the sweet spot on his thirty-five-ounce

Louisville Slugger and rocket over the right-field fence. Instead, the ball came to rest on the bat's handle, breaking it in two and sending a weak ground ball toward the three-four hole between first and second base.

"Shiiit!" shouted Power, flinging his bat against the backstop. Panicked by the thought of making the last out and granting Henry Glance a season-ending no-hitter, the Redlands catcher turned and rumbled down the first-base line.

Glance bolted from the mound and raced to cover first base as Jack Riley fielded the ball. "Jack," shouted Henry, approaching the bag. Failing to get a firm grip on the ball, Riley made an errant throw that sailed three feet over Glance's head. Still running at full speed, the six-foot-one-inch southpaw made the leap of his life, whirled and caught the ball in his right hand, and came down directly in the path of a 265-pound oncoming train. Bob Power slammed into Henry's exposed left side so hard, women in the stands shrieked and looked away. "I think that big sonofabitch killed him," said an elderly gentleman in the back row of the bleachers. "He's not movin'."

"You're out," shouted the first-base umpire, seeing the ball still firmly lodged in Glance's glove. Riverside had won the game, and their star pitcher had finished the season with his second semipro league no-hitter, but for Henry Glance, it was the end of a dream.

After five hours of surgery, the insertion of a metal pin in the carpals of his left wrist, and two months in a cast, the handwriting was clearly on the wall. "Your chances of pitching in college, let alone the major leagues, are slim to none," said Glance's orthopedic surgeon. "If I were you, I'd start making other career plans."

ELEVEN

IT WAS THANKSGIVING DAY 1967 when the telephone rang at the Glance residence in Temecula.

"Hello," said Mary Glance.

"Hi, Mary. This is Larry Jansen. Happy Thanksgiving."

"Hi, Larry. We haven't heard from you in a while."

"I wanted to give Hank a little time to sort things out after his wrist surgery. Has he decided what he's gonna do yet?"

"Well, he's not going to Stanford, but I guess you already knew that."

"Yeah, I heard they recruited Gary Miller after Hank got hurt."

"Things were looking pretty dark around here for a while, but I think Henry's ready to move on with his life now. He finally sent his transfer papers to Chico State and received his acceptance notice about three weeks ago."

"That's great! Wait 'til Hank hears—"

"Next to playing baseball, Henry's always wanted to do something with wildlife," said Mary. "He's loved animals and the outdoors ever since he was a little boy. If there's a bird book Henry hasn't read, I've never heard of it."

"Yeah, he's always pointing out birds to me."

"I'll never forget the time you boys rode up on your bikes with that goose stuffed in Henry's backpack."

"I remember that," said Larry. "Hank named it after his uncle Roscoe, didn't he?"

"Yes, he did. My brother and Henry were close until Roscoe moved to Oregon."

"Whatever happened to that goose, anyway?"

"Roscoe hung around here for three or four years after you boys brought him home. One morning Henry went out back to feed the chickens, and he was gone. Henry looked all over for any sign that a fox or something might have gotten him but never found so much as a feather."

"Do you think he might have flown away?"

"His wing never completely healed, but that old gander could still fly short distances. Henry thinks he might have made it as far as Jaspers' pond and joined up with some of the wild geese."

"I hope so," said Larry.

"Me too. I bet you're waiting to talk to Henry, aren't you? He's out back with his father. I'll get him."

"Nice talking to you, Mary."

"It was good talking to you, Larry. I'm so glad you and Henry have stayed close all these years. He thinks the world of you, you know. It'll be just a minute."

"Hey, Larry," said Henry.

"How have you been, Hank? Are you ready to rejoin the human race? Your mom says you received your acceptance notice from Chico State."

"I did, a couple weeks ago."

"Guess who else is goin' to Chico State?"

"I don't know, who?"

"Me!"

"I thought you were gonna stay around here and play for San Bernardino State."

"I decided I needed a change of scenery. Besides, the more I learn about Chico State, the better I like it. The enrollment is only six thousand, and most of the students walk to class or ride a bike. Since I don't have a car, that suits me just fine."

"How do you plan on getting there?"

"I guess I could take a Greyhound," said Larry, waiting for Henry's response.

"You could probably ride with me, but there's not much room in my Bug," said Henry, laughing. "We could strap your stuff to the roof."

"Gee, that's awfully generous of you."

"Don't mention it."

"Have you found a place to stay yet?"

"As a matter of fact, I have."

"Do you have a roommate?"

"Why? Are you interested?"

"Well, yeah, I might be."

"I don't know," said Henry, laughing again. "I plan on doin' a lot of studying and you're pretty much of a goof-off."

"A goof-off? My grades are just as good as yours."

"Yeah, but you're majoring in PE, and I'm majoring in biology."

"I have some pretty tough classes."

"Like what, advanced badminton? I bet you go to class every day in your gym shorts."

"As a matter of fact, I do. It's great hearing you laugh again, Hank. How'd you know I was gonna call?"

"Mitch Rider told me the other day when I called to get his cousin's phone number."

"So, are we gonna be roommates?"

"Absolutely."

"What did Mitch's cousin tell you?"

"His name's Fred."

"All right, what did Fred tell you?"

"He gave me the phone number of this sweet little old lady named Mrs. Iverson. She owns an old two-story house on Chestnut Street, four blocks from campus. I called her yesterday and asked about renting a room."

"What did she say?"

"She said she has a room available in the basement. The basement has four rooms: three singles and one double. All the single rooms have been rented by male college students. The two guys in the double room are moving out this week."

"What about food?"

"Fred said he bought a meal ticket at the Shasta Dining Hall. It's located on campus, right next to the bookstore."

"That sounds good. How much is a meal ticket?"

"I guess it's pretty reasonable. He suggested that we put our names on the list for a part-time job at the dining halls as soon as we get there. By washing dishes two hours a day, we can earn enough to pay for our meal tickets."

"I'm game. When do we leave?"

"How 'bout next week? Mrs. Iverson said we could pay the rent when we get there. She's not even going to make us pay a cleaning deposit."

"That's great!"

"Yeah, she said I sounded like a nice young man on the phone, so she didn't think it would be necessary."

HENRY'S VOLKSWAGEN BEETLE WAS JAM-PACKED with everything from bedsheets to baseball equipment when Henry and Larry left for Chico at 4:00 a.m. on Sunday, November 26, 1967. They putted through Los Angeles without a hitch but discovered that excess weight was going to be a problem when they began their arduous trek up the Grapevine.

"Are we gonna make it?" said Larry.

"I think so," said Henry, "as long as we keep it in third gear and don't try to go any faster than thirty-five. If this stretch gets any steeper, you may have to get out and walk."

Once Henry and Larry had made it over Tejon Pass, it was smooth sailing up Highway 99 through Bakersfield, Modesto, Stockton, and Sacramento. Just north of Sacramento, the landscape changed from tall buildings, highway interchanges, and overpasses to open space and flooded rice fields. "Boy, is this a breath of fresh air," said Larry.

"I think our adventure is just beginning," said Henry. "Fifteen or twenty miles up the road, Highway 99 forks to the left, toward Yuba City. After that we'll be in Northern California."

"I can't wait. What time did you tell Mrs. Iverson we'd be in Chico?"

"I told her we'd try to make it by 5:00. She said the fog has been rolling in lately, which could slow us down a bit."

"Hank, there's something I wanted to talk to you about."

"What's that?"

"I called the Chico State baseball coach the other day and asked about trying out for the team this spring."

"You did?"

"Yeah, his name is Dave Hall. Coach Hall said the previous varsity coach had just retired and he would be taking over the job."

"Is that a good thing?"

"It could be. With a new coach, it gives me a better chance of making the team."

"Why's that?"

"Being new, he may not have next-year's team already picked out."

"That makes sense. What did you tell him?"

"I told him I played first-string catcher for Riverside City College my freshman and sophomore years and we won the conference title both seasons. I also told him the main reason we won was because of an incredible left-handed pitcher named Hank Glance."

"Why'd ya tell him that? I can't pitch anymore."

"During the conversation, I happened to mention that you were a hell of a first baseman and one of the best hitters I ever played with."

"Larry, you're my best friend and I appreciate what you did, but I'm comin' to Chico to finish my education, not play baseball. I was devastated when I lost my scholarship and my opportunity to pitch for Stanford. For the next two months, I refused to even look at a baseball, let alone play the game."

"I know how you feel, Hank, but I'm not gonna give up on you yet."

The boys were a mile or so north of Live Oak when Henry said, "Look at that!"

"What?" said Larry.

"Out to the west, it looks like that little mountain range just popped up in the middle of all those rice fields."

"Those mountains look surreal," said Larry, "like something you'd see in a fairy-tale book."

"That's exactly what I was thinking," said Henry. "I'd like to take a closer look sometime."

"Maybe someday you will," said Larry. "I'm getting hungry. Let's get something to eat in the next town. I just saw a sign that said GRIDLEY 4 MILES."

"Wait a minute," said Henry. "Isn't Gridley where that game warden disappeared?"

"It's amazing that you would remember that, Hank. It's been seven or eight years since those poachers shot the goose and we talked to the game warden down in Temecula."

"Did I ever tell you that Ned McCullough came by the farm twice after the goose-shooting incident?"

"No, you didn't."

"The first time he came by to check on the goose. The second time he brought me a book and a stack of handy little booklets."

"No kidding?"

"Yeah, the book is called *Wildlife Law Enforcement*."

"What were the booklets?"

"Let's see, there was one on trout, one on waterfowl, one on furbearers, and one on warmwater game fish of California."

"Right now, I'm more interested in hamburgers and milkshakes of

California," said Larry. "How 'bout we try Pearl's Roadside Diner? The sign says it's three miles ahead."

"Sounds good to me," said Henry.

"So, did you read all this stuff Warden McCullough gave you?"

"I not only read them all, cover to cover, I memorized the scientific names of every trout in California. Ask me for the genus and species of any trout."

"Rainbow trout."

"*Salmo gairdnerii*. Ask me another."

"I don't know any others. Are you planning to be a game warden now?"

"You never know."

"I thought you were gonna be a pro baseball player."

"That was one book I read and threw away."

"We'll see about that," said Larry. "I wonder if they ever found out what happened to that game warden who disappeared."

"Why don't we stop and ask?" said Henry. "Here's Pearl's Diner co-min' up on the right. It looks like a respectable place."

Henry and Larry walked in and sat down at the counter, three seats from an elderly gentleman drinking coffee. A curvaceous, middle-aged woman with medium-length blond hair was busy wiping down a table at the far end of the restaurant. "I'll be right with you," she said.

"Hey, Hank, do you have a quarter? I wanna play something on the jukebox."

As Larry flipped through the song selections, Henry reached into his pocket and pulled out a quarter. "What are you gonna play?"

"How 'bout 'Surfin' Safari?' It'll remind us of surfing at Huntington Beach last summer. That's the one thing I'm gonna miss about not going to school down south."

"Me too," said Henry, perusing the menu. "When I left home, my board was hangin' from the barn wall, covered with cobwebs. It almost brought tears to my eyes."

"Don't worry, those good lookin' honeys up in Chico will make you forget all about the beach."

"Welcome to Pearl's," said the waitress. "What can I get for you boys?"

"I'd like a hamburger and a chocolate milkshake," said Larry.

"Would you like fries or coleslaw with that?"

"Fries, please."

"What about your good-looking young friend here?"

"Henry, the waitress asked what you're gonna have."

With the Beach Boys singing in the background, Henry lowered the menu and cracked a smile. "I think I'll have the same thing he's having, with coleslaw instead of fries, please."

"Coming right up."

"Pearl, can I get a refill?" said the elderly man at the counter.

"I'll be with you in a minute, Earl."

Pearl returned with Henry's and Larry's order. "Is there anything else I can do for you boys?"

"No," said Henry, "but I was wondering if I could ask you a question."

"Of course."

"Did you happen to know the game warden who disappeared around here about ten years ago?"

Pearl almost dropped the dishes she was carrying, and Earl choked on his coffee. Regaining her composure, Pearl said, "Why do you ask?"

"We heard the story and wondered if anyone had ever found out what happened to him," said Henry.

"You'll have to excuse me," said Pearl, her hands trembling. "It's been years since anyone around here has even mentioned Norm Bettis's name. The day he disappeared, he raced across this driveway, right past the spot where your car is parked. It was December 13, 1956, and nobody's seen him or his car since."

"It was rainin' like hell that day," said Earl.

"Do you have any idea what might have happened to him?" said Henry.

"Hmm," mumbled Earl.

"Earl, you hush now," said Pearl. "I have my own ideas about what might have happened to Norm, but it's just ideas, and I best keep 'em to myself."

"I understand," said Henry. "Was Warden Bettis married?"

"Yes, he was. Martha Bettis still lives in the same little house at the north end of town. Her neighbors say she walks out on the front porch every evening at 5:00, hoping Norm will drive up the driveway in time for dinner."

"Wow," said Henry, "what a sad story."

"Trouble is, they ain't no closure," said Earl, stepping away from the counter and preparing to leave. "I hope someday they catch the dirty sonsabitches who done Norm in."

"Maybe they will," said Henry, "maybe they will."

"Where you boys headed?" said Pearl.

"We start at Chico State this spring," said Larry. "Hank and I are both transfer students from Riverside City College."

"Well, good luck with your studies. If you're ever in the neighborhood again, please drop by."

"We will," said Henry, leaving a tip on the bar and heading toward the door.

Henry threw Larry the keys as they walked across the gravel parking lot to the car. "You drive," he said. "I suddenly feel like playing my guitar."

"I've always wanted to play the guitar," said Larry, steering Henry's VW Beetle back onto the two-lane highway, "but I've never had the patience to learn."

"It does take patience," said Henry, strumming a tune, "and a tolerance for pain."

"Pain?"

"I practiced for weeks before my fingers were strong enough to play a chord without the strings buzzing. More than once, I thought about taking this old guitar my uncle Roscoe gave me and smashing it against a telephone pole."

"I recognize that tune you're playing. It's on a folk-song album my parents have."

Henry entertained Larry with an instrumental medley of popular folk songs as the boys slowly cruised through Gridley. Impressed by the tree-lined streets of Victorian houses, Craftsman bungalows, and historic brick buildings, Henry said, "It's hard to imagine anything like that happening in a wonderful little town like this."

"Anything like what?" said Larry.

"That game warden disappearing. Everyone seems to think he was murdered. It's been ten or eleven years now. You'd think someone would at least find his car."

TWELVE

Henry Glance would later describe the last twenty-six miles between Gridley and Chico as a feast for his twenty-year-old eyes, unrivaled by any scenic path he'd ever taken before. Just north of Gridley, on Highway 99, he and Larry passed mile after mile of flooded rice fields occupied by flocks of ducks, geese, and magnificent snow-white swans.

"What are those big white birds?" said Larry.

"Those are whistling swans."

"No kidding? They make the geese look small."

"Pull over right here. I want to look at something," said Henry. Reaching behind his seat, Henry pulled out a pair of binoculars. "You aren't gonna believe this, but there's a mature bald eagle perched on top of that old cottonwood snag. Here, take a look."

"Wow! A real, live bald eagle. I can see its white head."

"It's probably a big female. The females are larger than the males."

"I didn't know that, Hank. This is already turning into quite an adventure."

Just south of Chico, Henry and Larry crossed over Butte Creek and remarked how extraordinary it was to have a healthy trout stream flowing on the outskirts of town. Many of Southern California's rivers and streams had been reduced to polluted puddles or cement-lined ditches where people discarded their bottles, cans, old tires, and stolen shopping carts.

"That's Butte Creek," said Henry. "Salmon and steelhead run up that stream during the spawning season. There's another stream called Chico Creek that runs right through the Chico State campus."

"How do you know so much about this place?"

"I've been doing research. I also sent away for a map of Chico. Highway 32 is coming up. Turn west on Highway 32, which will eventually become 8th Street. When we get to Chestnut Street, turn right, and we're there."

"It's a good thing. I feel like a sardine jammed into this tin can for the last twelve hours. I see Chico has no shortage of trees."

"That's what Chico is famous for: tree-lined streets, Chico State College, and Bidwell Park. I read that the original *Robin Hood* was filmed in Bidwell Park."

"Hank, you're a wealth of information."

"I'm curious about life, Larry. We don't have much time on this planet, and I want to learn everything I can while I'm here."

"We'll have time for that philosophical crap when classes begin in January," said Larry, straining his eyes to read street signs in the dark. "Right now, I'm more worried about missing Chestnut Street."

It was 5:15 when Henry knocked on Mrs. Iverson's door. She was eating dinner with her sister at the time, so she handed Henry a key. "Just take the narrow walkway on the south side of the house. When you get to the end, turn left and you'll see a door that leads into the basement. Gary lives in the room at the top of the stairs, next to the bathroom. At the bottom of the stairs, you'll find a hallway with three rooms: two on the right and one on the left. You boys will be at the end, on the left. Make yourselves comfortable. Oh, there's a pay phone in the hallway that you're welcome to use. I'll see you in the morning."

Henry led Larry around the south corner of the house and down the walkway. Larry pointed out a small, half-open window mounted at ground level. "This must be ours," he said. "If anyone comes to visit, we'll see their legs coming down the pathway before they reach the door."

Opening the door into the basement, Henry and Larry were immediately greeted by a husky, twenty-two-year-old man with reddish-blond hair, a bushy mustache, and freckles. Wearing Bermuda shorts and a yellow Hawaiian shirt, he smiled broadly and extended his right hand. "Hi, I'm Gary Lytle. You must be our new neighbors. Welcome to Mrs. Iverson's pit."

"Is that what you call it?" said Henry, chuckling. "I'm Hank Glance, and this is Larry Jansen. Have you lived here long, Gary?"

"Three semesters now. I transferred from Yuba College a year and a half ago. As you can see, this is the luxury suite." Gary stepped back from his doorway and offered Henry and Larry a view of his eight-by-twelve-foot room, furnished with a twin bed, a four-cubic-foot refrigerator, a one-burner gas range, a cupboard, and a table that also served as a desk.

"Do you cook for yourself or eat at the dining hall?" said Larry, curious about Lytle's extremely limited living space.

"I cook for myself," said Lytle. "After spending the last five summers cooking for hungry trout fishermen in the wilds of Colorado, Wyoming, and Montana, I've learned to make do with the essentials."

"That's interesting," said Henry. "I'd like to hear more about that when we get a chance."

"I'll look forward to it," said Gary. "As you can see, my door is always open. By the way, Brad and Dennis, the two guys living in the rooms down the hall, do eat at the campus dining hall."

"Thanks, Gary," said Henry. "It's been a pleasure meeting you." Flipping on the light, Henry and Larry climbed down the stairs, walked to the end of the hallway, and unlocked the door on the left.

"This is actually a pretty nice setup," said Henry. "It's clean, and don't forget, we have our own window." The room contained two twin beds, two dressers, two small desks, and a closet. A ledge ran the length of the south wall, and a small, propped-open window adorned the upper right corner.

Henry and Larry spent the next half hour unloading the car and carrying their belongings to the room. As Larry hung clothes in the closet and Henry put sheets on his bed, Larry said, "Hey, Hank, I hear someone walking past our window."

The basement door opened. "Whaddaya know, it's the village idiot," said Gary. "Where you been all day?"

Brad Foster hurried past Lytle's room and continued down the stairs. "I've been at the library," he shouted back. Unlocking the door to his room, Foster flipped on the light and tossed a stack of books on the bed.

"What were you doing in the library—trying to impress one of your girlfriends?" said Lytle.

The basement door opened for a second time, revealing a thin, dark-haired man wearing black, horn-rimmed glasses. "Hi, Gary. How are you this evening?"

"I couldn't be better. How's my buddy Dennis? You must have left before daylight this morning; I didn't even hear you go out."

"It was pitch dark when I left for my 7:30 tax class. My day continued to get better after that. I had cost accounting at 11:00 and auditing at 4:00. Between classes, I was in the library studying for finals."

"You're a glutton for punishment, my friend."

"You got that right. Sometimes I think I should have stayed a French major."

Dennis walked down the hallway and unlocked the door to his room. Turning on the light, he neatly stacked a loose-leaf notebook and three textbooks on the desk. Bleary-eyed and in need of sleep, he managed a convincing smile and stepped across the hallway to meet his new neighbors. "Hello, I'm your next-door neighbor, Dennis D'Agostino."

"Hi, Dennis. Good to meet you. I'm Hank Glance."

While shaking Henry's hand, Dennis saw Larry emerge from the closet. "Wow! You're a big sonofabitch. Do you play football?"

Before Larry could respond, Brad stepped into the hallway and shouted, "Lytle, what would you know about studying?"

"Sometimes it's like a three-ring circus around here," said Dennis. "Those two never stop bantering with each other, but it's all in fun. They're both nice guys."

"No problem," said Larry, smiling and extending his hand. "To answer your question, I haven't played football since high school. I do play baseball, though."

"What about you, Hank? Do you play baseball?"

Henry shook his head and went back to making his bed.

"That's kind of a sore subject," said Larry. "We'll explain later. Right now, I need to finish hanging these clothes."

"Brad and I were gonna walk up to Denny's on 6th and Main. You guys are welcome to join us," said Dennis.

"We both ate a hamburger a couple hours ago," said Larry, "but I could choke down somethin' else before bedtime. How 'bout you, Hank?"

"Yeah, I'll tag along."

Just then, Brad popped his head in the doorway. "I see our new neighbors have arrived. I'm Brad. How are ya?" Muscularly built, Brad stood about Henry's height and had medium-length, sandy-brown hair, brushed straight back. "Have you guys eaten?"

"I just asked them to walk up to Denny's with us," said Dennis.

"Good. We'll ask Lytle if he wants to go, on our way out."

While polishing off a patty melt, twenty-three-year-old Brad Foster regaled the rest of the group with highlights from his childhood in nearby Orland and the two years he'd spent in the army. "I grew up hunting, fishing, and playing football," said Brad. "We had one of the best small-school football teams in the country. After graduation in 1962, I spent a couple years in the army before taking advantage of the GI Bill and going back to school."

"Were you in Vietnam?" said Larry.

"No, I spent most of my military time as an MP in Germany."

"What do you plan to do when you graduate?" said Henry.

"Probably be a cop. I'm leaning toward law enforcement."

"This guy's a walking girl magnet," said Gary. "He changes girlfriends like the rest of us change our socks."

"You're exaggerating, Lytle. By the way, thanks for ruining my date the other night."

"I think I did you a favor, Brad. Susan didn't have a sense of humor and obviously wasn't your type."

"What about you, Dennis?" said Henry. "What's your story?"

"After three semesters as a French major, I took out a school loan for several thousand dollars and traveled around Europe for a year. As my nest egg dwindled, I gravitated to a small beach town in Spain, where I played ping pong all day and survived on a daily diet of paella."

"You've heard of pool sharks?" said Brad. "This guy's a world-class ping-pong player."

"I was able to make a living at it for over six months," said Dennis. "Returning to Chico State, I figured I'd have a better chance of earning a decent living and paying back my school loan if I changed my major to accounting."

"Now it's your turn, Gary," said Brad. "If you're not gonna eat those fries . . ."

"I was an only child," said Lytle.

"That figures," commented Brad. "I bet you were spoiled rotten."

"Not exactly. My parents split up when I was twelve. I ended up living here in California with my mother while my father moved to Colorado to take over his father's outfitting business."

"What's an outfitting business?" said Larry.

"This one's called Lytle's Big Sky Outfitters and Guide Service. It's one of the biggest and oldest outfitters in the Western United States."

"You still haven't told me what it is."

"They either own or lease ranches in Colorado, Wyoming, and Montana. For a hefty price, they provide hunting and fishing opportunities to people who wouldn't otherwise have access to thousands of acres of unspoiled country inhabited by elk, trophy mule deer, antelope, Rocky Mountain bighorns—you name it. During the summer months, they provide access to some of the finest trout-fishing rivers and streams in the country. Every summer, for the last five years, I've worked for my father as a guide and cook for groups of wealthy fishermen."

"What a great summer job," said Henry. "Do you get to ride horses?"

"Sure do. I've still got the saddle sores to prove it. Sometimes our pack trains go fifteen or twenty miles back into pristine wilderness that would make your eyes pop out."

"What are your clients like?" said Larry. "I bet you've run into some interesting people."

"They all have one thing in common."

"Lots of money?" said Henry.

"That's right. I've led pack trips for movie stars, governors, senators, and all kinds of corporate big shots. Most of 'em have been well behaved, but we've guided our share of drunks and arrogant assholes."

"So, are you going to move back there permanently when you finish school?" said Henry.

"That's the plan. My father wants me to take over the reins from him, like he did for his father. I've been learning the business as I go."

"You two new guys haven't said much," said Dennis.

"We've been friends since the second grade," said Larry. "I'll tell you a little story about something that happened to us about eight years ago. Hank and I had planned to go fishing down in Temecula, where we were living at the time, but our adventure turned out to be much more than we bargained for."

"Now you have us hooked," said Gary.

"You tell 'em the rest, Hank."

"No, you started it, Larry. You finish it."

"Anyway," said Larry, "Hank and I saw these two poachers shoot a goose out of season. Hank didn't want 'em to get away, so he took their keys and threw 'em in the weeds. To make a long story short, the game warden came and busted these guys. Afterwards, he told us about this game warden in Gridley who disappeared, along with his patrol car."

"I remember when that happened," said Brad. "It was on TV and in all the local newspapers. I don't think they ever found the game warden or his car."

THIRTEEN

SHROUDED IN BONE-CHILLING FOG for weeks on end, Chico in December was a new experience for the boys from Temecula. More than once, they questioned their decision to leave Riverside County, where December temperatures averaged in the mid- to upper sixties.

As junior transfers, Henry and Larry were permitted to register for classes ahead of underclassmen. This didn't free them from the pandemonium and confusion of obtaining class cards in a gym filled with hundreds of clamoring students. It did, however, improve their odds of securing the classes they needed.

Henry's rigorous class schedule of lectures, labs, and field trips would be a challenge, and with little financial help from home, a part-time job was essential. By asking around, he learned that a thirty-five-year-old gentleman named Vijay was responsible for hiring student dishwashers for the campus dining halls.

"I will add your name to the waiting list," said Vijay, "but as you can see, over fifty students are ahead of you."

That night, Henry dialed his parents' number from the pay phone in the hallway outside his room. After letting it ring once, he hung up. A few seconds later, the phone rang, and Henry answered. During the conversation with his father, Henry mentioned that he had put his name on a lengthy waiting list for a part-time dishwashing job in the dining halls.

"What are your chances of being hired?" said Will.

"Not good. There's about fifty students ahead of me."

"Here's what you do. At least once a week, go in and ask this B.J. if any job openings have come up. It wouldn't hurt to even contact him twice a week."

"It's Vijay, Dad."

"What?"

"His name's Vijay, not B.J."

"What difference does it make? The point is, a squeaky wheel gets greased. Pretty soon he'll get to know you, and you'll be surprised how well that works."

Henry knocked on Vijay's office door every Monday morning for the next four weeks. Each time, Vijay would tell him there were no job openings. One Thursday morning during the last week of February, Henry was walking through the campus dining hall when he felt a tap on his shoulder.

"Mr. Glance," Vijay said, "one of our noontime dishwashers at Craig Hall has quit. You may have the job if you'll promise to stop bothering me."

"Thank you!" said Henry. "What are the hours?"

"Eleven to one, Monday through Friday."

"That's perfect. I'll have just enough time to get there after my 9:30 ornithology class. When do I start?"

"You may start today, after you fill out and sign a few papers."

Henry repeatedly thanked Vijay for the job offer and couldn't wait to call and tell his father. A few minutes after signing the papers, he was passing through the campus dining hall breakfast line when an attractive young lady with a gorgeous smile said, "Good morning, Henry. Did I see you talking to Vijay a few minutes ago?"

"Yes, you did," said Henry, a puzzled look on his face. *Who is this vision of loveliness, and how does she know my name?* Racking his brain for an answer, Henry remembered having talked to her briefly while on a field trip to Bidwell Park the previous week. He'd been intrigued by her uncanny ability to identify nuthatches, wrens, and warblers simply by listening to their calls. "Oh, you're Anne, from my ornithology class. I didn't recognize you with the apron and that net covering your hair."

"Well?"

"Well what?" said Henry, smiling nervously.

"Did he offer you a job?"

"As a matter of fact, he did. How did—"

Before Henry could finish, the line had moved on and Anne was serving another hungry student. As Henry walked to a table, tray in hand, he glanced back in the direction of the food line and caught Anne watching him. Seeing his glance, she averted her gaze.

The next morning, Henry showed up early for his ornithology lecture in hopes of catching Anne alone and asking for an explanation. It was about ten minutes before class time when Henry heard laughter in the hall. Through the open doorway, he spotted Anne talking to a towering, dark-haired student wearing a red-and-white Chico State letterman's jacket. Fearful that Anne would see him watching, Henry looked away. *I've seen that guy before,* thought Henry, taking another quick peek.

The subject of Henry's consternation was none other than Len Sharp, better known to Chico State basketball fans as "The Sharpshooter." Thoroughly disillusioned, Henry again looked away. *It figures that a beautiful girl like Anne would have a big-time jock like Len Sharp for a boyfriend. What in the world was I thinking?*

Entering the classroom, Anne and her best friend, Sara Nichols, took seats in the front row. As the instructor was about to begin, Anne turned and scanned the room behind her. Spotting Henry in the middle of the back row, she made eye contact, smiled, and directed her attention to the front.

When the lecture was over, Henry picked up his books and, with his head down, traversed the narrow aisle to the door. "Were you going to leave without talking to me?" came a female voice.

"I didn't think—"

"I saw you watching my cousin and me."

"Your cousin? I—"

"I'm Anne Sharp. I don't think we've been formally introduced."

"I'm Hank Glance," said Henry, squeezing her warm hand as if it were a baby robin that had fallen out of the nest.

"Anne, are we still going to the baseball game this afternoon?" said Sara, walking out the classroom door and finding herself engulfed in a stampede of students on their way to the next class.

"I wouldn't miss it," shouted Anne. "I'll meet you at three, like we planned."

"Do you like baseball?" said Henry, as Anne returned her attention to him.

"I do. We have a new catcher who hit the farthest home run I've ever seen, last week against Humboldt State."

"I heard about that," said Henry. He didn't let on that Chico State's new catcher was his longtime friend and roommate Larry Jansen. Larry had begun the baseball season playing second string, but after throwing out two base runners and hitting a towering home run against Humboldt State, the permanent position behind home plate had become his for the taking. "Anne, were you going to explain how you knew I had applied for a job in the dining hall?"

"I'd love to, Hank. Is that your real name?"

"My real name is Henry, but everyone except my mother calls me Hank."

"Would you mind if I call you Henry?"

"Not at all. You can call me anything you want."

"Henry, I only have ten minutes to get to my next class, so we'll have to talk another time."

"No problem. I better head for Craig Hall, anyway."

"That's right!" said Anne, smiling as she walked out the door. "You don't want to be late on your first day at work. Good luck, Henry."

"HOW'D YA DO?" SAID HENRY, as Larry entered their room on a Friday evening after his home game with San Francisco State.

"We lost again in the last inning. Our starter ran out of gas in the eighth, and we don't have a closer who can come in and shut 'em down. Tommy Glazer threw San Francisco's number-four hitter a big round-house curve, and he hit a two-run dinger to win the game."

"How did you do?"

"I just told you."

"No, I mean how did Larry Jansen do?"

"Oh, I hit a line-drive double off the fence and walked twice. You normally don't wanna know about the games. What's up?"

"I know you have a doubleheader tomorrow, but would you mind playing catch with me on Sunday?"

"No problem. Do you mind if I ask what prompted this?"

"I don't know," said Henry, not wanting to divulge the real reason for his change of heart. "Maybe it's the spring-like weather."

Larry arrived back at the room about 5:00 Saturday evening, after the day's doubleheader with San Francisco State. Tossing his catcher's mitt on the bed, he said, "I'll be right back." When Larry returned, Henry was still seated at his desk, agonizing over a quantitative-analysis problem.

"Hey, buddy, we need to talk," said Larry, flopping on the bed and placing his hands behind his head. Henry didn't answer. "Hank! Did you hear what I said?"

"Just a minute, Larry. I'm trying to figure out this last problem."

"Sorry."

"Okay, tell me all about it," said Henry, turning around in his chair. "How'd the games go?"

"We split the doubleheader, but that's not what I wanted to talk to you about."

"What's on your mind?"

"Walking back to the locker room after the second game, I caught up with Coach Hall and asked him about the possibility of your coming out for the team. He remembered what I'd told him earlier about your being a great left-handed pitcher and getting hurt."

"Uh-huh."

"He said at this late date, the only way you could make the team is as a pitcher. He's already got two first basemen and plenty of outfielders, but the team could use a good left-handed relief pitcher. His exact words were, 'If your friend can pitch half as well as you say he could before he got hurt, I'll find a spot for him on the team. If not, tell him not to waste his time or mine by coming out.'"

Deep in thought, Henry sat on the edge of his wooden chair. *Now what do I do? I started all this by asking Larry to play catch with me. Without normal flexibility in my wrist, I may not be able to pitch at all. A week ago, I had finally made peace with myself about not playing baseball. Now I'm just as tormented as ever.*

The northern Sacramento Valley was socked in with a system of low clouds when Henry and Larry walked across the street to the school playground that Sunday morning in mid-February 1968. Henry wore sweatpants and a gray sweatshirt with the words RIVERSIDE CITY COLLEGE BASEBALL stenciled across the front.

"I was wondering if you brought your glove along," said Larry, tossing a baseball in Henry's direction.

"Yeah, I think I threw it in my suitcase out of habit. I've had this old rag for so long, there's not an ounce of padding left in it. Where'd you get this new ball?"

"That's the one I hit out of the park last week. A pretty girl retrieved it and gave it to me after the game."

"Oh, what'd she look like?"

"About five-seven, long brown hair, beautiful smile."

"By any chance, was she wearing a light blue sweater?"

"Yes! How'd you know?"

"A little bird must have told me. How 'bout we move back to sixty feet and see how it goes?"

After fifteen or twenty minutes of playing catch to warm up, Henry decided it was time to test his wrist.

"How's it feel?" said Larry, from the catcher's squat position.

"So far, so good," said Henry. "I'll see if I can put a little more heat on the ball." Throwing three-quarter speed, Henry's arm became fatigued and his wrist began to ache.

"Hank, you look like you're hurting," said Larry. "Maybe we should stop."

"Let me try a curve."

"Go ahead, but with your wrist the way it is, you're probably not gonna be able to put much spin on the ball."

Larry was right. Henry's attempts to throw a curve were met with little success and excruciating pain.

"We're studying pitching and arm movement in my kinesiology class," said Larry. "See how I can bend my wrist backwards almost ninety degrees? The backwards motion in your wrist is zero."

"You're right, Larry, but I had to try."

"I'm your best friend, so I'm finally gonna tell you what you need to hear."

"What's that?" said Henry, tossing Larry the ball.

"First, either forget about this girl you're trying so hard to impress, or ask her out."

"How'd you know about that?"

"You must be kidding! I've known you for twelve years and haven't seen that look on your face since you had the crush on Connie Chase in the fifth grade."

"I didn't know it was that obvious."

"Second, you love nature, and you've wanted to be a game warden ever since we caught those guys shooting the goose. Isn't that why you majored in biology? Once and for all, man, forget about being a baseball player and follow your real dream."

BY LATE FEBRUARY, TEMPERATURES HAD BEGUN to rise, and with them, Henry's spirit. Intermittent rainstorms had turned the bone-dry fields around Chico into landscapes of emerald green. Bright-yellow tidy tips and purple lupines blanketed the hillsides, and all the almond orchards were adorned with magnificent pink-and-white blossoms.

While Henry labored through quantitative analysis and organic chemistry, he embraced ornithology, mammalogy, and ichthyology with the same energy he'd once devoted to baseball. Every field trip into the lands and waters of Butte and Glenn counties was a new adventure for the young man from Temecula. No longer plagued by obsessive thoughts of what might have been, Henry's path was now clear. He would become a California Fish and Game warden and devote his future to the protection of wildlife.

FOURTEEN

Not long after Henry's and Larry's heart-to-heart talk on the Chestnut Street playground, Henry took Larry's advice and conjured up the courage to ask Anne out. He wasn't excited about the movie currently playing at the El Rey Theater, so Henry asked Anne if she'd like to take a drive in the country.

"I've heard that the Sacramento National Wildlife Refuge has lots of waterfowl this time of year," said Henry. "Would you like to check it out Saturday morning? If you don't have other plans, maybe we could make a day of it and have dinner afterwards."

"That sounds like fun," said Anne, not letting on that she'd grown up in Chico and visited the refuge many times with her mother. Anne and June Sharp were avid bird-watchers and proud members of the Altacal Audubon Society.

"Great!" said Henry, relieved and surprised by Anne's quick response. "I'll bring my binoculars."

It was 6:55 a.m. when Henry pulled up in front of a 1920s-era, two-story Dutch Colonial house across the road from Bidwell Park. Peering through the windshield, he marveled at the wooden stairway leading to a covered porch that extended the entire length of the house. At the east end of the porch hung an old-fashioned loveseat, next to two Adirondack chairs. An eye-popping pink dogwood partially obscured Henry's view of the west side of the porch. "I see a light on," Henry mumbled to himself. "Better wait 'til seven before I knock."

Henry climbed out of his VW Beetle and headed up the narrow

cement walkway toward the front porch. He had just reached the first step when Anne opened the front door. "Good morning, Henry," she said, holding a coat in one hand and a wicker basket in the other. "I hope you haven't been waiting too long."

"I just got here," said Henry, his heart skipping a beat. "What a beautiful house. May I carry that basket for you?"

"Thank you. I thought I would bring along a couple sandwiches and something to drink."

"You didn't have to do that."

"It's no problem at all. Maybe we'll have a picnic at the refuge."

"I would really enjoy that," said Henry, opening the passenger door.

"Why thank you, kind sir."

Henry walked around to the driver's side of the car and was about to open his door when he looked up and saw two young ladies dressed in bathrobes, staring at him through the house's picture window. Smiling, he raised his right arm above the roof and waved. The younger of the two giggled and smiled back; the older one shyly turned and walked away.

"How old are your sisters?" said Henry, pulling away from the curb and heading in the direction of 8th Street.

"Joanie is fifteen, and Monica's eleven. How did you know I had sisters?"

"I saw them watching from the window."

"Did they wave to you?"

"Monica did."

"That figures. Joanie's at that age, if you know what I mean. Do you have any brothers or sisters?"

"No, it's just my parents and me. My dad works for the County of Riverside, and my mom's a housewife most of the time. She occasionally acts as a Spanish interpreter for Riverside County Courts. How 'bout your parents?"

"My father's a supervisor with the local power company, and my mother teaches kindergarten. I love watching my mother teach her class. Those kids can be so funny. At the end of every school day, she puts on music and the kids start dancing. It's hilarious. My mother is also very much into nature. She and I have gone on bird walks with the local Audubon group since I was little. If you think I know my birds, you should see her."

For the next several hours, Henry and Anne learned each other's life stories while traveling through some of the most fascinating country

Henry had ever seen. Taking Dayton Road south from Chico, Henry followed Ord Ferry Road to 7 Mile Road before turning south again and traveling through mile after mile of flooded rice fields.

"This is incredible!" said Henry, enthralled by sightings of waterfowl, shorebirds, and various raptors.

"I'm glad you're enjoying yourself, Henry." Anne had seen it all before but found her own love of nature energized by Henry's enthusiasm.

"I'll say!" said Henry, pulling over and training his binoculars on a large, light-colored bird perched at the top of a bare willow tree. "This is a new one for me, Anne. Can you tell what it is?"

Anne had brought along her own binoculars and easily identified Henry's mysterious bird as a female ferruginous hawk. "She just took off and spooked that flock of shorebirds," said Anne. "Isn't she something?"

No longer watching the hawk, Henry had become mesmerized by the wholesome, natural beauty of Anne's face. "She sure is," he replied.

Having arrived at the Sacramento National Wildlife Refuge, Henry and Anne were at the midway point on the auto-tour route when Anne suggested they stop and have a bite to eat. With windows rolled down, they reveled at the sights and sounds of passing waterfowl while talking away much of the afternoon.

"What do you plan to do when you graduate?" said Henry.

"I'll probably teach, like my mother."

"What subject?"

"Science, I guess. I'm majoring in biology, but right now I'm finishing up my general education classes."

"Do you plan on teaching here in Chico?"

"That would be nice, but I wouldn't mind seeing what the rest of California has to offer." Anne handed Henry an apple. "Let's talk about you, Henry. What are your career goals?"

"I've been seriously thinking about wildlife law enforcement."

"You mean like a game warden?"

"Yes, either a state wildlife officer or a federal agent. I've done a lot of research, and a state game warden I met several years ago has given me several books on the subject."

"Really?"

"You sound surprised, Anne. What did you think I'd be interested in?"

"You look like an athlete. I figured you for a future coach or something like that."

"Larry, my roommate, is planning to be a coach. He's the guy who hit that towering home run you were talking about a few weeks ago."

"He's your roommate?"

"Yeah, we've been best friends since the second grade."

"Are you a baseball player too?"

"Not anymore."

"Why not?"

"It's a long story," said Henry, starting the motor. "Right now, I'm enjoying myself too much to spoil it by talking about that subject. I promise to tell you the whole story some other time. Whaddaya say we see what's around this next bend?"

"There should be a peregrine in that row of cottonwoods up ahead."

"Oh, and how would you know that?"

"Uh . . ."

"Never mind," said Henry, laughing. "I already guessed that you'd been here before. How could you and your mom belong to the Audubon Society for all those years and not know about this place?"

It was approaching 4:00 when Henry and Anne headed back across the valley. When they had traveled about twenty miles, Henry began talking about the rapid rate of land development back home in Riverside County. "It used to be mostly farmland and open space south of Riverside," said Henry. "Then developers bought up half the countryside and began building houses and shopping centers. My parents are worried it will spread as far as Temecula."

"Chico has grown too," said Anne.

"Who's this Blake Gastineau? We've seen ten Gastineau Land Company signs since leaving Chico this morning."

"It's interesting that you would ask that," said Anne. "Blake Gastineau has been a concern of the conservation group my mother and I belong to for some time now. Ralph Gastineau, Blake's father, owned several thousand acres of mostly farmland between Chico and Gridley. Before he passed away, Ralph protected much of that land from development by placing it under a recently passed law called the Williamson Act."

"What's the Williamson Act?"

"People call it the Williamson Act, but it's really the California Land Conservation Act. The basic idea is to preserve open space and agricultural land by giving landowners a tax break. As I understand it, the landowner signs a ten-year contract to voluntarily restrict his land use and not develop the land."

"Sounds like a great idea. What happened when Gastineau's father died?"

"When Ralph Gastineau passed away, his two sons, Blake and Chester, inherited all the land and a large sum of money. Chester wanted to continue in his father's footsteps and leave everything pretty much the way their father had intended. Blake, on the other hand, wanted to subdivide the land and get out of the farming business altogether. When he found out that much of the land had been encumbered by the Williamson Act, he split with his brother and started this land-development company."

"What did he use for money?"

"There was this huge court battle. It was in the papers for weeks. When it was finally settled, Blake received several million dollars in cash and sole ownership of all the parcels that hadn't been included under the Williamson Act. Chester got a few thousand acres of farmland, the ranch, and all the farming equipment."

"How much land did this Blake end up with?"

"Apparently, Ralph had been quite an investor. He owned interest in property all over the county, some of it in Chico. It wasn't long before those land-company signs you were asking about showed up in front of property where almond and walnut orchards had been cut down and burned to make room for shopping centers, strip malls, and apartment complexes."

"That's quite a story, Anne. I hope all this depressing talk about land development hasn't affected your appetite."

"Not at all, Henry. It's good to know that you feel the way I do about wildlife and our natural resources."

"I've felt that way for as long as I can remember. Sometime, I'll tell you a story about saving a Canada goose from two poachers when I was eleven years old."

"I'd love to hear about that."

"Right now, we're gonna have dinner at this little barbeque place on Dayton Road."

"You mean Wasney's?"

"Yes. Have you eaten there before?"

"Henry, you're adorable! Everybody in Chico knows about Wasney's. My dad loves the place. He's known the owner for years."

"Is the food good?"

"Yes," said Anne, laughing, "it's very good."

FIFTEEN

FRED RIDER HAD TALKED ABOUT PIONEER WEEK, but Henry had to experience it for himself to appreciate the transformative effect this annual event had on the Chico State campus. The celebration, along with the warmer weather of early May, brought a recognizable change in the appearance and general attitude of the Chico State students. Where they had previously come to class in casual but socially presentable attire, students were now seen walking the halls, classrooms, and courtyards of Chico State in shorts, cut-off jeans, T-shirts, tank tops, Roman sandals, and in some cases, bare feet. For six days in May, students were unofficially absolved from the rigors of daily study and offered a time to relax, enjoy Chico's glorious spring weather, and participate in the festivities.

On campus, fraternities and sororities converted the quad into an authentic Western ghost town. Competition was keen as organizations promoted their candidates for the coveted titles of Sheriff and Little Nell. Off campus, bleary-eyed, semi-inebriated students ventured from one kegger to the next, carrying plastic cups filled with lukewarm beer.

Friday afternoon, the day before the Pioneer Day Parade, Henry returned to Mrs. Iverson's basement early. His last class of the day had been canceled because no one else had shown up.

"Hey, Gary," said Henry, "I figured you'd be down at one of the keggers."

"I would have been, but my friend Enos just showed up from Yuba City. He and I are gonna be in the parade tomorrow." Enos, a short, heavyset man in his mid-twenties, smiled, shook hands with Henry, and handed him his business card.

"I didn't know you belonged to one of the fraternities, Gary."

"I don't. Enos and I are gonna be what you might call last-minute entries."

Just then, Brad and Dennis walked in the door. "Hey, guess who we just saw standing in front of Kendall Hall?" said Brad.

"The Durango Kid?" said Gary.

"How'd you know?"

"I think I read somewhere that he was gonna be grand marshal."

"It was neat," said Dennis. "He was wearing a sombrero and dressed in his cowboy outfit, just like on TV. The only thing different was his gray hair."

"Was Cactus Jack with him?" said Enos.

"If I'm not mistaken, he's up on Boot Hill," said Gary.

"Gary, every time I walk by this room, something interesting is going on," said Henry.

"You ain't seen nothin' yet," said Gary. "Wait 'til tomorrow."

"We're going up to Bear Hole to go swimming," said Brad. "Do you guys wanna go?"

"Sure," said Henry. "That sounds like a lot more fun than sitting around drinking stale beer on a hot afternoon like this. I'll bring my face mask, in case we see some fish. I heard in my ichthyology class that there were a few spring-run salmon in Chico Creek."

"I didn't know there were salmon in Chico Creek," said Dennis.

"Historically, spring-run Chinook salmon would leave the Sacramento River and enter Big Chico Creek sometime between March and June," said Henry. "They'd hold over in the deeper pools of Chico Creek Canyon during the summer months and spawn in the fall when the water had cooled. They're still commonly seen swimming their way upstream through Bidwell Park."

"Thanks for the biology lesson, Professor Glance," said Brad. "Now let's get going."

With Henry bouncing around in the back seat, Brad drove his 1960 Ford Falcon off the pavement and up a bumpy road into upper Bidwell Park. They came to a primitive parking area occupied by one car and a beat-up, gray Ford pickup. "I think this is about as far as we're gonna go," said Brad.

Henry and Dennis followed Brad down a narrow trail, into a canyon of massive basalt cliffs. At the bottom flowed Big Chico Creek. Bordered by a riparian forest of willows, oaks, alders, and Indian rhubarb, the stream tumbled past car-sized boulders into a deep pool of crystal-clear, cerulean-blue water.

"Wow!" said Henry, feasting his Southern California eyes on the most gorgeous stream he'd ever seen. "We don't have anything like this where I come from."

While Henry used his face mask to scan the deeper water for trout and salmon, Dennis paddled around in the shallows and Brad flirted with two college girls sitting on a blanket nearby. The students had delighted in the pleasures of Bear Hole for thirty minutes, when a shotgun blast interrupted the serenity of the moment and reverberated up the canyon wall.

"What was that?" shouted Henry, coming to the surface. "It sounded like something exploded under water." Dennis and Brad pointed upstream.

Henry, who was wearing a pair of old tennis shoes to protect his feet from the jagged rocks, climbed to the top of a boulder to get a better look. Within seconds, Brad and Dennis had joined him. Standing ankle-deep in the water below were two men in their thirties, one of them holding a 12-gauge, double-barreled shotgun. The smaller man, shirtless and wearing suspendered overalls, held a wriggling, three-foot salmon in his left hand. The shooter wore faded blue jeans and a white T-shirt. Lifting the shotgun to his shoulder, he waited for another school of salmon to navigate the shallow riffle between Bear Hole and the diversion dam just upstream.

"Here comes three more," said the man holding the fish. "Shoot!" Two shotgun blasts rocked the stream bottom and sent a wall of water splashing onto the south shore. "Damn! You missed."

Infuriated by what he'd seen, Henry picked up a rock and hurled it at the shooter's feet. The splash caused both salmon poachers to look up. "That's right, we saw what you did," shouted Henry.

The shooter turned and scrambled up the steep trail toward the parking lot, his companion following close behind.

"Henry, where ya going?" said Dennis.

"I'm gonna get their license number," Henry shouted back. "They're probably the ones driving that old pickup." Henry had remembered Warden Ned McCullough's advice from years before: No need to confront the violators. Just get a license number and write down any pertinent information.

Henry reached the parking lot just in time to record the poachers' license number. He watched the pickup rattle down the road towards

Chico until it was almost out of sight. Just before it disappeared below the hill, the brake lights came on and the shirtless passenger stepped out of the truck. Reaching into the pickup bed, he grabbed something and tossed it into the weeds on the north side of the road.

Brad, Dennis, and Henry jumped in Brad's Ford Falcon and rumbled down the hill. When they'd reached the point where the object had been thrown from the pickup, Henry hollered at Brad to stop.

"It had to be the fish," said Henry, climbing from the back seat. "I think it landed right out there somewhere." Henry picked up a discarded beer bottle and placed it upright on the side of the road. He jumped back in the car and urged Brad to drive on.

As luck would have it, a Chico police officer was parked near the entrance to Hooker Oak Park. Henry explained to the officer what had just transpired. "I saw that pickup go by a few minutes ago," said the officer. "I'll call my dispatcher on the radio and ask her to contact the local game warden."

"Warden Austin will 11-98 with the reporting party at the entrance to Hooker Oak Park. ETA ten minutes," said the dispatcher.

The three college students were standing outside Brad's car, admiring the massive valley oak from which Hooker Oak Park had gotten its name. With a characteristic smile on his lean face, Warden Tom Austin pulled up next to Brad's Ford Falcon and climbed from a dark-green, Dodge sedan. Crowned with a mop of graying hair, Austin was tall, willowy, and viewed the world through a pair of navy-blue-and-gold horn-rimmed glasses. "Are you the young fellas who requested a warden?"

"I'm Hank Glance," said Henry, extending his hand. "These are my friends Dennis D'Agostino and Brad Foster. We were swimming up at Bear Hole when we heard a shotgun blast coming from the creek, just upstream. Two men had shot a salmon and took off in an older-model, gray Ford pickup. Here's the license number. On the way down the hill, they threw something out of the bed of the pickup. I think it was the fish they killed. I marked the spot."

"Why don't we go up and see if we can find whatever it was these guys threw from the pickup," said Austin. "Hank, you can ride with me if you'd like."

"Are you sure? My shorts are still a little wet from swimming."

"I'm sure. Go ahead and hop in."

When Austin and Glance were six hundred yards west of the Bear Hole parking area, Henry said, "There's that beer bottle. Stop right here."

Everyone spread out and began searching the area north of the road. Within minutes, Dennis cried out, "I think I've found something. It's a big fish."

Having already run a radio check on the license number, Tom Austin called the boys over and explained his next move. "The license number you gave me comes back to an address in Chapmantown."

"How far away is Chapmantown?" said Henry, believing it was another city.

"About ten minutes."

"In that case, I'd be happy to go with you and identify those guys."

Leaving Brad and Dennis behind, Henry rode with Austin to a heavily shaded neighborhood in south Chico. Slowly cruising down a quiet street, near what Austin described as Dead Horse Slough, Henry spotted a gray Ford pickup parked on the left side of the road ahead. "That's the pickup," he said.

"Are you sure?"

"Positive. The shotgun I told you about is in the gun rack behind the seat."

Austin pulled his patrol car off the pavement, into the shadow of a fruitless mulberry tree. "This house looks familiar," said Austin, watching it from the opposite side of the street. "I'm thinking I may have been here before on a search-warrant detail."

The pickup's registered owner lived in a small, wood-framed house, bordered on three sides by a four-foot-high chain-link fence. Inside the fence were two mixed-breed barking dogs. The open garage at the west end of the house contained an assortment of car parts, a work bench, and an upright freezer. A red Ford sedan, its rear bumper bashed in, sat in the oil-soaked gravel driveway.

"I hear a woman's voice coming from inside the house," said Henry. "Sounds like she's pretty angry."

"Yeah," said Austin. "Somebody's getting quite a tongue lashing."

Just then, a shirtless man wearing suspendered overalls opened the screen door and began walking out to the street. "That's one of them!" said Henry. "He's the one who was holding the salmon."

Spotting Austin's patrol car, the shirtless man did an about-face and started walking back toward the house. "Hello," said Austin, crossing the street. "I'd like to talk to you."

Austin's voice had been heard from inside the house. A slender woman with shoulder-length, bleached-blond hair and a cigarette dangling from her lips opened the screen door and stepped outside. "Blackie," she shouted, "get your ass out here."

"What the hell now?" came a male voice from inside the house. Seconds later, a heavyset man wearing cutoff jeans and a partially torn, dark-blue tank top kicked open the screen door and stormed outside. "Mona, I'm tired of your—"

"We've got company," said Mona. "Shut up and go see what he wants, as if I didn't know."

"That's the shooter," said Henry through the open window of Austin's patrol car. "He changed his clothes."

"I'm Warden Austin. Were you fellas in upper Bidwell Park this afternoon?"

"Why?" said the shooter. "What's this all about?"

There's my answer, thought Austin. "Did you shoot a salmon?"

"We was up at Bear Hole a little while ago," said Blackie, "but we never shot no salmon."

"Do you gentlemen have identification?"

"Both men handed Austin their driver's licenses. The shooter was identified as Orville Blackman. The other man, who lived two houses down the street, was identified as Donald Knox. "Is this your pickup, Mr. Blackman?"

"Yeah, it's my pickup. I told you we ain't shot no salmon. You can search my truck, my house, anything ya want."

"Is your pickup locked?"

"Course it's locked. I don't trust these kids around here."

"Would you please unlock it for me."

Blackman unlocked the pickup and stepped back while Austin checked the shotgun to see if it was loaded. Both barrels were empty. Austin laid the shotgun on the hood of his patrol car then led the two poaching suspects to the trunk, where he revealed the salmon Blackman and Knox had discarded earlier. "I have at least three witnesses who saw you gentlemen shooting at salmon in Big Chico Creek. They also saw you in possession of the salmon you see here. We found it by the side of the road, where you left it. Big Chico Creek is closed to the take of salmon, and at no time can you shoot them with a shotgun."

"So, what's gonna happen?" said Blackman, realizing his goose was cooked.

"I'm going to file a criminal complaint with the Butte County District Attorney, charging you both with the violations I just described. Mr.

Blackman, your shotgun will be held in evidence until the judge determines what to do with it."

"I didn't shoot the salmon. Why are you charging me?" said Knox.

"I'm charging you with possession of an unlawfully taken salmon. You were seen holding the fish while your partner did the shooting, and based on what my witness saw, you were the one who threw it from the truck."

"Do you think this will go to trial?" said Henry, on the ride back to his room on Chestnut Street.

"I doubt it," said Austin. "If it does, I'll need you and your friends to testify."

"I'd be happy to testify, and I'm sure my friends would also. How much will those two salmon poachers be fined?"

"Not nearly enough, but I'm gonna recommend that the shotgun be forfeited."

"Before you drop me off, I'd like to ask you about something."

"What's that?"

"There was this warden down in the Gridley area who disappeared ten or twelve years ago. Based on everything I've been told, they never found him or his patrol car. Do you know anything about that?"

"You bet I do. I was still up in Greenville when Norm Bettis disappeared, but I participated in the search, along with half the Department of Fish and Game and every sheriff's deputy in Butte, Glenn, and Sutter County."

"Do you have any idea what might have happened to him?"

"Everybody seemed to think he got bumped off by the duck draggers. There were some bad hombres down in that Butte Sink area. Some of them felt it was their birthright to kill as many ducks as they wanted and any state game warden or federal agent who got in their way would get what he deserved."

"Did they actually say that?"

"Not in so many words, but that was the general feeling. Most of the people I interviewed clammed up and wouldn't say anything. Mike Prescott and I drove back into some holes you wouldn't believe, down along the river. We'd see these homemade, wooden signs saying NO GAME WARDENS BEYOND THIS POINT and FISH COPS, ENTER AT YOUR OWN RISK—most of 'em misspelled."

"Who is Mike Prescott?"

"He's the warden over in Willows."

"What about the car? Did they ever find Warden Bettis's patrol car?"

"Apparently, someone reported seeing what looked like a Fish and

Game patrol car headed west on Highway 162, near Butte City. It was raining hard the day Norm disappeared, so whoever it was who saw that car couldn't get a good look at the driver."

"What I don't understand is the mentality of these poachers," said Henry. "Do they think these ducks grow on trees and there's no end to them? Look at what happened to the passenger pigeon. At one time, it was the most abundant bird species on Earth. There were billions of them, and those commercial hunters completely wiped 'em out. Sorry, but I get emotional when I think about it."

"No apology necessary, Hank. That's why I became a game warden. Have you thought about taking the warden's exam?"

"It's interesting that you ask that. When I was eleven, I talked to a warden down in Temecula, and he asked me the same question."

"Oh, who was that?"

"Ned McCullough. Do you know him?"

"Ned and I went through the academy together. I haven't seen him in years."

"Warden McCullough even gave me some study material. I plan on taking the exam next fall, when I turn twenty-one."

"How long before you graduate from Chico State?"

"Two more semesters after this one and I should have my degree in biology."

Coming to a stop in front of Mrs. Iverson's boarding house, Austin handed Henry his business card. "Here's my number. Call me if you ever want to go on a ride-along."

"That would be fantastic. I would jump at the chance to ride on patrol with you."

"I tell you what," said Austin. "Next Wednesday, I'm supposed to go up and work the Blairsden area while the district warden is off. It's gonna be a long day, but you're welcome to come along."

"Count me in," said Henry. "Where's Blairsden?"

"It's up off Highway 70, east of Quincy. We'll patrol up the Feather River Canyon. You'll think you've died and gone to heaven when you see the river."

Henry had no idea where Quincy or the Feather River Canyon were located, but he intended to look them up on the map rather than reveal his ignorance to Warden Austin. "I can't wait! What time will you pick me up?"

"Five o'clock."

"I'll be waiting out here in front," said Henry.

SIXTEEN

Henry's alarm clock went off at 4:30, giving him just enough time to shave and brush his teeth before Tom Austin arrived at 5:00. Having notified his supervisor at the Craig Hall Cafeteria that he wouldn't be at work that Wednesday in early May 1968, his conscience was clear. Henry figured an all-day ride-along with a California Fish and Game warden more than justified his skipping classes for the first time since he'd been a student at Chico State.

Driving south from Chico on Highway 99 with Henry in tow, Warden Austin turned east on Highway 70, passing the town of Oroville and reaching the Feather River Canyon as the sun peeked over the mountain.

"This is incredible!" said Henry, looking down at the river below. "Do they catch a lot of fish in the Feather River?"

"That's a sad story," said Austin. "The river you see down there was once a premier salmon- and steelhead-spawning stream. That changed when they built all those dams."

"You can't stop 'em from building dams, but you can play an important role in the protection of our fish and wildlife," said Henry. "That's the great thing about being a Fish and Game warden."

"Where did that come from, Hank? Sounds like you're still trying to make up your mind."

"I've pretty much made up my mind, Tom. This is what I wanna do."

"Smart man," said Austin, smiling. "When we get to Quincy, I'll buy you breakfast."

A mile or so past the tiny outpost of Merlin, Austin pointed out the mouth of Rock Creek. "The water flowing over those granite boulders is so clear, you can see the trout swimming around, ten feet under water."

"I'd like to check that out sometime," said Henry.

"I'm surprised you haven't been up here already. Rock Creek has always been a favorite swimming spot for the college students."

"Until recently, I haven't done much of anything except study and work at the dining hall. A couple months ago, a friend and I spent the day at the wildlife refuge over in Willows."

"Was this one of the guys I met the other day at Bidwell Park?"

"No, it was actually a young lady from my ornithology class."

"Oh . . . a girlfriend?"

"I'd sure like her to be my girlfriend, but so far we're just friends."

"What's her name?"

"Anne Sharp. She and her family live here in Chico. By the way, where do you live, Tom?"

"We have a couple acres out north of town, off Cohasset."

"How long have you lived there?"

"I spent most of my career in Greenville, before transferring to Chico in 1963. We bought the place a month or so after I transferred."

"Chico is such a great town. Why'd you wait so long to transfer?"

"You'll learn the answer to that question when you become a warden yourself. The best warden's districts are hard to come by. Some of these old-timers put down roots and never leave. The warden whose place I took occupied the Chico patrol district for thirty years."

"Don't these wardens want to promote?"

"Would you if you could spend the rest of your career getting paid to patrol beautiful places like this?"

"I'm beginning to understand," said Henry.

"Unless you've got an influential uncle in Sacramento, you'll probably begin your Fish and Game career in one of three places: LA, the Bay Area, or down in the desert somewhere. Nothing wrong with that. Those are great places to learn the ropes."

"It all sounds great to me. I don't care if they send me to Blythe. I've read there's lots of fish and wildlife down along the Colorado River."

"Sounds like you've been doing your homework," said Austin. "Here's one of those hydropower dams I was telling you about."

Continuing southeast on Highway 70, Austin and Glance passed the intersection with Highway 89. Ten miles up Highway 89 was the picturesque mountain village of Greenville, where Tom Austin and his family had lived for many years. During the Greenville years, Austin had frequently patrolled the Portola warden's district when Clyde Mathers was on vacation. On one occasion, Austin had worked with State Park Ranger Ron Travers on a bear-poaching investigation inside Plumas-Eureka State Park. Since then, Austin and Travers had remained good friends.

"Here's what I have in mind for today," said Austin, continuing east from Quincy after a hearty breakfast. "Clyde Mathers called me last night and said there's a bunch of outlaws out of Oroville camped in the little Forest Service campground east of Long Lake. Clyde's gonna be out of commission for a couple weeks with a bad back, so he asked me to go up and check on these guys. I'd like to stop and see a friend of mine on the way."

"Sounds good to me," said Henry.

Arriving at Plumas-Eureka State Park headquarters, Austin introduced Henry to his friend Ranger Ron Travers. A competitive weightlifter, thirty-six-year-old Travers was decked out in his Class A state-park-ranger uniform and Smokey the Bear hat.

"What's the occasion?" said Austin.

"Some bigwigs from Sacramento are supposed to come up today," said Travers. "Jack wants everyone to look sharp."

"Do you have time to explain a little bit about the park to my young friend here? He's a junior down at Chico State and plans to become a Fish and Game warden or a park ranger when he graduates."

Travers explained to Henry that in addition to the park's many natural features, including Jamison Creek, it offered a look back into California's mining history.

Henry focused on the natural beauty that had been preserved in the park, rather than the environmentally destructive gold-mining period. "What a wonderful place to work and spend the summer," he said.

"What are you studying?" said Travers.

"I'm a third-year biology major."

"I graduated from Chico State," said Travers. "Four of the best years of my life."

"I hear that from a lot of people," said Henry.

"As a matter of fact, we just signed up two young ladies from Chico State to work in the visitor center this summer."

"I envy those girls," said Henry. "I guess I'll be bagging groceries in Temecula again."

"We hire three other seasonals to help our maintenance crew during the summer months. Two of 'em live here in the area, and the third one just informed me that he isn't coming back. If you're interested in the job, I'd encourage you to fill out an application while you're here."

"I'll say I'm interested! My only concern would be finding a place to stay. I have to save every penny I can to pay tuition and living expenses at school."

"Follow me, and I'll show you our accommodations for seasonals who don't live in the area." Henry and Tom followed Travers down a path south of the visitor center to two modest, cedar-framed cabins. "The one on the right sleeps two. This is where our two female seasonals will stay. The other cabin is pretty small, as you can see, but it does have a loft where one person can throw a cot and a sleeping bag."

"This is luxurious compared to my room at school," said Henry.

"Make sure you leave your phone number on the application," said Travers. "I'll call you in a week or so and let you know if you got the job. Jack, our head ranger, will have to make the final decision. He's down in Sacramento this week."

"All I have is a pay phone in the hallway," said Henry. "If I'm not there, one of the other guys will take a message. I'll also leave my parents' home phone number in Temecula."

"We usually send out an official notice," said Travers. "The starting date this year is the first Monday in June."

IT WAS APPROACHING 10:00 A.M. when Austin and Glance reached the community of Graeagle and climbed the steep mountain road toward Gold Lake. Halfway up the mountainside, Austin turned off the pavement and headed east on a narrow dirt road fraught with sharp rocks and fallen tree branches.

"When we come to a point where the road drops down into the campground, we're gonna stop before we reach the overlook," said Austin.

"Is trout fishing good in Long Lake?"

"Clyde doesn't think the outlaws out of Oroville are fishing in Long Lake."

"Where are they fishing?"

"It's a well-kept secret, but there's a one-mile hiking trail from the Long Lake Campground past the east shore of Long Lake to Silver Lake. Every year, about this time, trout congregate at the mouth of a stream that runs between Long Lake and Silver Lake. Clyde's informant said these guys from Oroville have been hiking up there early each morning and returning to camp about noon, with stringers of fish."

"How many trout can they have?"

"That reminds me," said Austin, turning off the ignition and reaching into the back seat. "I brought you my old copy of the *California Fish and Game Code*."

"Are you sure you want to give me this?"

"I'm sure. They just sent me a new edition this week."

"Thank you so much," said Henry, thumbing through the book.

"You're welcome. As you read it, you'll learn how the system works. California's fish and game laws are passed by the state legislature and published in the *Fish and Game Code*. The legislature authorizes the Fish and Game Commission to set regulations based on those laws. Regulations set by the commission are published in Title 14 of the *California Administrative Code*; they typically deal with things like hunting and fishing seasons, bag and possession limits, methods of take— things like that. To answer your question, the bag and possession limit for trout here in the Sierras is ten fish per person."

"I can't wait to read this," said Henry.

"It's a real page-turner," said Austin, laughing. "Once you start reading it, you won't be able to put it down. Before we get to the campground, I'm gonna teach you two important rules that every successful game warden must follow."

"What are they?" said Henry.

"Rule number one: When you exit a vehicle, do it quietly and never, I mean never, slam the door behind you. I can't tell you how many times I've had investigations blown by some thoughtless jackass who climbed out of the car and slammed the door. Rule number two: Whisper. Always whisper when you're involved in a situation like the one we're about to tackle. That's especially important up here in the mountains where our voices carry. I've been sitting on one side of a lake and clearly heard conversations over a quarter mile away. It's hard enough to catch some of these hard-core violators without announcing our arrival."

"Those are lessons I'll never forget," said Henry.

"Good. Here's an extra pair of binoculars."

As Clyde's informant had described, the primitive Long Lake Campground was occupied by one large camp. It contained two camp trailers with pickups attached and one light-blue Chevy pickup with a full-sized camper mounted in the bed. The vehicles and trailers had been arranged in a circular fashion, with the Forest Service table and fire pit in the center. "Looks like there's six of 'em," whispered Austin, from a hidden vantage point on the hill above.

"How do you know?" said Henry.

"Count the lawn chairs around the campfire. From the looks of all the beer cans, these guys enjoyed themselves last night. I see a couple tackle boxes, an empty worm box, and what looks like a package of marshmallows on the table."

"Do ya think they roasted marshmallows last night?"

Austin laughed. "My guess is they're using the marshmallows to keep their worms up off the bottom. It's an old bait fisherman's trick. Speaking of bait fishermen, I hear voices."

Six middle-aged men appeared on the trail beyond the campground. All six were carrying fishing gear. "Here's what we're gonna do," whispered Austin, gesturing for Henry to follow him back toward the patrol car. "You're gonna stay right here on this hill and watch every move these guys make for the next hour. I'm gonna drive down the hill and into camp to make a routine contact. If I don't find anything wrong, I'll climb back in my car, head up the hill, and let them see me drive away. When I'm out of earshot, I'll tuck the car back in the trees and wait."

"Then what?" said Henry.

"If my hunch is correct, these gentlemen will have a couple ice chests stashed outside of camp somewhere. It's your job to watch and find out where."

With Henry back in position, Warden Austin drove into the suspects' camp as the six fishermen approached. "How you fellas doin'?" said Austin, flashing a friendly smile. "Looks like you had some luck."

"We did," said a heavyset man carrying a fishing rod in one hand and a stringer of rainbow trout in the other.

"That's a beauty on the end of your stringer," said Austin. "Where you guys from?"

A bearded man carrying a fishing rod and a heavily laden canvas creel answered, "I'm from Palermo, Pete lives in Richvale, and the rest of these hooligans live in Oroville."

"Jimmy doesn't live in Oroville anymore," said Pete, chuckling. "Ever since his wife threw him out, he's been livin' in that silver trailer over there. It's usually parked out behind my barn, plugged into a fifty-foot extension cord."

"Before you fellas settle in for the rest of the day, I'd like to take a look at all your fish and your fishing licenses," said Austin.

"No problem," said a tall, slim gentleman wearing a green fishing vest. "We figured that's what you were here for."

As Henry watched from above, Austin carefully counted sixty freshly gutted rainbow trout, all of them inside creels or hanging from stringers, and checked six valid California fishing licenses. "I see that all of you limited out today. Are there any other fish in camp?"

"No," said Pete. "You're welcome to check our ice boxes, but all you're gonna find is beer, some steaks, a couple cartons of eggs, and two pounds of baloney."

"Okay," said Austin, "I'll take a quick peek and get out of your hair. You fellas are probably hungry."

Escorted by members of the group, Warden Austin examined every ice chest and ice box in camp. When finished, he asked if there were any other fish that he hadn't checked. Some in the group shook their heads, while others replied with a firm "No." Austin thanked the men for their cooperation and disappeared over the horizon in a cloud of powdery, red dust.

"Anyone ready for a sandwich?" came a voice in the crowd.

"Where's that bag of chips?" came another.

Henry's own stomach grumbled as he trained his binoculars on the picnic table where everyone sat for the next hour, drinking beer and eating baloney sandwiches. Finally, the taller man who'd been wearing the green vest stepped from the table and disappeared inside one of the trailers. Seconds later, he reappeared, carrying a large, clear plastic bag. He reached inside his creel, pulled out ten trout, and dropped them into the plastic bag. As he was leaving camp, he was called back by one of the other fishermen. Laying his plastic bag full of trout on the table, the taller fisherman walked back inside his trailer and came out with another plastic bag. The second fisherman took the bag and began filling it with fish from his stringer. When he'd finished, he handed his bag of fish to the taller man. The taller angler carried both plastic bags down a narrow path toward a swampy area overgrown with high grass and stunted willows.

Henry watched as the taller gentleman returned to camp without the fish he'd been carrying. During the next half hour, each of the four remaining fishermen carried plastic bags of trout down the same marshy path and returned empty-handed.

At the stroke of 1:00 p.m., Austin's squeaky shocks announced his return. "How'd it go?" he whispered, stepping from the car.

"It happened just like you said," whispered Henry. "I watched them carry their fish down a path and into that jungle of willows next to the campground."

"Okay, hop in. We'll go down and pay these guys another visit."

Austin pulled into the camp to discover one of the fishermen sitting at the table, drinking beer. He didn't have to ask where the other fishermen were. He could hear them snoring from ten yards away.

"Wha'd ya do, forget somethin'?" shouted the glassy-eyed old codger wearing overalls and a straw hat.

"What's your name?" said Austin, looking back over his shoulder.

"Barney."

"Well, Barney, please tell your friends I'll be back in a few minutes. Ask everyone not to leave camp."

Austin locked his car and followed Henry across the road toward the adjacent wetland. Just before entering a grove of stunted old-growth willows, Henry glanced back at the camp and saw Barney watching from his lawn chair, his neck outstretched and his mouth agape.

"Looks like an army has marched through here," mumbled Austin, ducking under an overhanging tree limb.

"The path forks here," said Henry, "but most of the boot tracks continue this way. It's getting squishier as we approach the creek."

Reaching the stream bank, Henry saw that the footprints made a sharp right turn and continued upstream for another ten yards before stopping at a three-foot-high pile of branches. "Here's something," he said.

"Wha'd ya find?" said Austin.

"I think there's something hidden under these branches. It looks like a tarp of some kind."

Breathing heavily, hands resting on his hips, Austin approached his young protégé. "Look," he said, pointing to a nearby willow tree. "They must have brought along a chainsaw to cut all these branches."

"Do you want me to remove them?"

"Before you do, let me walk back and see if there's any film in my camera. It's been a while since I've used it."

When Austin returned to his patrol car, all six fishermen were awake and milling around the picnic table.

"What ya up to?" said Virgil, a slightly built, baldheaded man smoking a pipe. "Barney said ya wanted ta talk to us."

Reaching into the trunk of his patrol car, Austin pulled out an Argus C3 camera enclosed in a leather case. He closed the trunk and raced back down the trail.

"Before you remove the branches, let me take a few photographs," said Austin. "I wanna show the lengths these characters have gone to in an effort to hide their fish." He photographed not only the pile of limbs but the chainsaw cuts on the surrounding trees.

When Austin had finished taking photographs, Henry pulled back a tattered shower curtain to reveal three large aluminum ice chests: two silver and one red and white.

"Okay, pop the lids, and we'll see what these guys have been up to," said Austin. All three ice chests were filled to the brim with iced-down trout packed in plastic bags. After taking several more photographs, Austin and Henry carried the three ice chests back to the fishing camp.

The six anglers had gathered around the picnic table. "Which of you put your fish in this red-and-white ice chest?" said Austin.

"None a them ice chests belong to us," said Barney. "They musta been left here by somebody else."

Henry signaled Austin from the car and pointed to the chainsaw sitting on the tailgate of one of the pickups.

"Who does the chainsaw belong to?" asked Austin.

"It's mine," said Jimmy, identified as James Cameron.

"Mr. Cameron, I'm afraid I'm gonna have to confiscate it."

"What for?"

"You used it to cut all those tree branches by the creek. Then you used the branches to hide your fish."

Jimmy was a woodcutter by trade. It suddenly dawned on Pete, identified as Peter Smith, that if Jimmy were to lose his chainsaw, he might be living out behind Smith's barn and burning his electricity forever. "No need for that," said Smith. "All those ice chests belong to us."

With Henry tallying their findings on a notepad, Austin counted a total of 132 rainbow trout inside the three ice chests. Warden Austin explained to the fishermen that he would file a formal complaint with the Plumas County District Attorney's office. Each of the six men would be charged with joint possession of seventy-two trout over the legal possession limit. Henry had looked forward to testifying in court, but all six fishermen forfeited bail, each paying $300.

SEVENTEEN

"**H**EY, SAD SACK, WHY ALL THE GLOOM?" said Larry, climbing into Henry's VW Beetle.

Henry's first semester at Chico State had ended in late May 1968. He should have been ecstatic, having received A's in ornithology, mammalogy, ichthyology, and organic chemistry, and a hard-earned B in quantitative analysis.

"It's nothing," said Henry.

"Nothing, my ass. I've been around you long enough to know when something's troubling you. What is it—that girl you've been seeing?" Henry made a U-turn in the middle of Chestnut Street and headed east toward Highway 99. "Come on, I'm gonna bug ya all the way to Temecula unless you tell me what's wrong."

"I've called Anne three times this week. Every time I call, her little sister answers and says she's not home."

"Did you ask where she is?"

"I don't get the chance. She always hangs up the phone. I've thought about going over there, but I've never met Anne's parents, and I don't want them to think I'm some lovesick kid who can't live without their daughter."

"Have you heard from the state park?"

"That's another thing. The ranger I spoke with said he'd let me know if I got the job by this week. I'm supposed to go back to work at Dale's Market on Monday. I can't go to work in the grocery store on Monday and, a couple days later, tell the store manager I just got a call from

Smokey the Bear so I'm leaving to work in the mountains of Northern California for the summer."

"I see your point," said Larry. "I'll probably stay in Temecula and work in my uncle's hardware store like I did last summer."

"I know what that's all about," said Henry, bursting into a belly laugh.

"I'm sure I don't know what you mean."

"Could her name be Jeanette Rogers? You thought I was sleeping, but I heard you talking in the hallway last night. How many quarters did you put in that phone? Every time I started to nod off, I'd hear *ka-ching-ka-ching*. 'Jeanette, sweetie, are you still there?'"

"If this is what it takes to hear you laugh again, it's worth it," said Larry. "When are we gonna stop and get something to eat?"

Henry and Larry arrived in Temecula just after midnight. Everyone was in bed at the Glance farmhouse. Weary from the ten-hour drive, Henry flipped on the study lamp in his bedroom and found a pile of mail sitting on his desk. At the top of the pile was a light-blue envelope with a Chico postmark stamped in the upper right-hand corner. About to rip open the envelope, Henry was interrupted when the bedroom door opened and a dear friend walked in with her tail wagging. "Daisy!" whispered Henry, dropping to his knees and giving her a hug. "I've missed you so much."

With Daisy now lying at his feet, Henry sat at his desk and began reading from a greeting card with a photograph of Yosemite Falls on the front cover.

Dear Henry,

I'm sorry I didn't get a chance to see you before Sara and I left on our trip. My last final exam was a few days before yours, and Sara was eager to get going. She's driving, so I didn't have much to say about it. I called your Chico number before we left. No one answered, so I thought I'd write you at your home address. Remember? You gave it to me the day we visited the wildlife refuge. You wrote it on a napkin at Wasney's restaurant and said I might need it sometime.

Sara and I have wanted to visit Yosemite National Park since the sixth grade. We figured this was a good time to go, since our summer jobs begin next Monday. We'll be working in the Plumas-Eureka State Park visitor center. They even have a little cabin for us to stay in. I'm so excited!

It looks like we won't see each other again until classes begin in late August, so have a great summer, and I'll look forward to seeing you then.

Love,
Anne

Henry rummaged through the remaining mail, searching for any correspondence from Plumas-Eureka State Park. Finding none, he folded his arms, closed his eyes, and laid his head down on the desk. Sensing Henry's disappointment, Daisy sat up and nudged Henry's bare leg with her wet nose. "Daisy," said Henry, lifting his head and smiling. "I can always count on you to make me feel better. Let's go to bed."

It was 8:10 Friday morning when Henry awoke to the sound of the kitchen phone ringing. "Hello," said Mary Glance. "Henry's still sleeping, Mr. Travers. May he call you back?"

"Mom, I'm awake," shouted Henry, jumping out of bed and putting his pants on. "Don't hang up. I'll be right there."

"Henry's on his way to the phone, Mr. Travers. Nice talking to you. Here he is."

"Mr. Travers," said Henry, catching his breath. "Sorry about that. I didn't get home until late last night."

"I understand," said Travers. "I know this is kinda late notice. Are you still interested in working at the park this summer?"

"You bet I am!"

"When can we expect you?"

"When would you like me there?"

"All of the other seasonals start on Monday. Can you be here by then?"

Henry started to answer then remembered his commitment to George Brennan at the market. "Mr. Travers, can I call you back in an hour? There's something I need to take care of before I can give you a definite answer."

"Sure, Hank. I'll be here in the office for the next hour."

"I'll call you right back. Thanks so much."

"Mom, I have to go down to the market and see George Brennan."

"Can't you call him on the phone?"

"No. I think it would be better if I see him in person."

"Well, you might want to put on a shirt and some shoes."

George Brennan was the manager of Dale's Market. He'd also been Henry's Little League baseball coach and had followed Henry's remarkable baseball career all the way through high school and junior college. As desperately as Henry wanted the state-park job, he wasn't about to leave his mentor and longtime friend in the lurch.

"Good morning, Thelma," said Henry to the veteran grocery clerk who was about to wait on a customer.

"Well if it isn't Hank Glance. Are you back from that college up north?"

"That's what I need to talk to George about. Is he around?"

"He's in his office. You know where it is."

"There's a sight for sore eyes," said George, seeing Henry walk through the swinging green doors. "The last time I saw you, you were just comin' outta surgery at the hospital in Riverside."

"A lot's happened since then," said Henry.

"Hank, I'm so sorry about what happened with your pitching arm. Every time I think about that big sonofabitch slamming into you, it makes me sick."

"It was disappointing for a while, but I've moved on now."

"That's good. I'm afraid I've got some bad news for you."

"What's that?"

"Business has been real slow since that subdivision went in across the highway and they built the new shopping center. Dale told me this morning that we can't afford to hire any extra help this summer. I argued with him for twenty minutes, but he wouldn't budge."

"I appreciate your trying to save my job, George, and everything else you've done for me over the years."

"It's been a pleasure," said George, shaking Henry's hand. "You were a hell of a ballplayer, but I'm even more proud of the young man you've become."

"That means a lot coming from you, George. I'll keep in touch," said Henry, bolting for the swinging doors, waving to Thelma, and dashing toward the open storefront.

"Where ya goin' in such a hurry?" said Thelma.

"To the High Sierras," Henry shouted back.

"Don't forget to write."

"I won't. Yahoo!"

EIGHTEEN

Averaging sixty miles an hour, it took Henry almost twelve hours to make the trip up Highway 395 to the mountain village of Graeagle. It was just after dark on a moonlit Sunday evening when he entered Plumas-Eureka State Park. Ron Travers had told Henry to make himself comfortable in the cabin on the left. The refrigerator would be operating, and a porch light would be left on above the door.

Henry's VW Beetle putted past the visitor center and down a narrow, unpaved path before it chugged to a stop between the two cabins. It was the first week in June, but at 7400 feet, there was a nip in the air when Henry stepped from the car in his OP shorts, Mexican sandals, and T-shirt. Stretching his tired back, he noticed a 1965 Chevy sedan parked near the cabin next door. All the lights were off in the cabin, so Henry figured Anne and Sara had already gone to bed.

"Something about him looks familiar," said Sara, peeking from the window.

"Sara, go to bed," said Anne, tucked in her warm sleeping bag.

"Looks like he's gonna unload his stuff."

"Sara, we have to get up early tomorrow."

Henry had begun to open the cabin door when the overhead porch light lit up his face. "Anne, it's Henry!"

"What?"

"Our new neighbor is Henry."

"Sara, please stop joking around. I'm tired, and I need to get some sleep."

"I'm not joking, Anne. Doesn't Henry drive a VW Bug? I tell you, it's

Henry." Anne climbed out of her sleeping bag and hurried to the window. "He just went inside," said Sara. "He'll be back out in a minute."

Anne's heart raced as she and Sara waited for their new neighbor to reappear. "My God, it is Henry!" said Anne.

"How do you know? He hasn't come out yet."

"His car. He left the passenger door open, and the dome light is on."

"What difference does that make?"

"Henry puts sweatshirts over the vinyl seatbacks to keep from burning his back in the summertime. I recognize that old gray sweatshirt."

"Here he comes," said Sara.

Henry walked to his car, leaned in, and pulled a cooler from the back seat. Pushing the door closed with his foot, he returned to his cabin.

"Hello, Henry," came a soft voice from the wooden deck next door. Setting the heavy cooler down on the front-porch step, Henry turned to find Anne staring at him. She was dressed in her bedroom slippers and a bathrobe.

"I bet you're surprised to see me," said Henry, hopping up next to her.

"That's an understatement," said Anne, extending her arms and inviting a hug. "Did you get my letter?"

"Yes," said Henry. "That's how I knew you and Sara were here." Henry noticed Sara watching them from the doorway. "Hi," he said, a euphoric smile on his face. "Do you remember me from ornithology class?"

"How could I forget? You're the one who kept me from getting an A."

"I did?"

"Yeah, you and Anne set the grading curve so high, I missed out by one point."

"Why don't we all go inside," said Anne. "It's chilly out here."

"Just for a couple minutes," said Henry. "I'll explain why I'm here and say goodnight. Tomorrow's gonna come early."

The entire summer crew had already assembled in the visitor center when Henry walked in on Monday morning at 8:00. Ron Travers introduced Henry to head ranger Jack Ketchum, a stern, gray-haired veteran who ran the park like a finely tuned instrument. Then he described the duties each seasonal was expected to perform. Anne Sharp and Sara Nichols would meet and greet visitors, answer questions in the visitor center, and conduct interpretive presentations. George Cooper, Merlin Reams, and Henry Glance would work for maintenance supervisor Harry Craddock, cleaning antique mining machinery, hosing down restrooms, hauling garbage, and clearing trails.

Off work at 5:00, Henry would clean up and meet the girls for dinner at 6:00. Both excellent cooks, Anne and Sara offered Henry a deal he couldn't pass up: Henry would chip in on the groceries and wash dishes in return for a homecooked meal every evening. So pleased was Henry with this arrangement, he used part of his first paycheck to buy fishing licenses for Anne and Sara.

One morning near the end of June, Henry was reading a large map on the visitor-center wall. Finding a tiny blue dot near the eastern park boundary, he said, "This looks interesting."

"What looks interesting?" said a female employee standing behind the counter.

"Madora Lake. I wonder if it contains fish."

Overhearing the conversation, Ranger Jack Ketchum walked out of his office. "The fishing's no good in Madora Lake. It's overgrown with weeds, and the mosquitoes will eat you alive," he said.

"That's good to know," said Henry. "Thanks for telling me, Jack."

Suspecting something fishy about Ranger Ketchum's unsolicited advice, Henry questioned Harry Craddock about it that afternoon. "Is that what he told you?" said Craddock, a smile on his face.

That evening after dinner, Henry asked Anne and Sara if they'd like to take a hike into Madora Lake. Usually eager to go along on outings, Sara claimed she had some reading to do and declined the offer. "I'll go," said Anne. "What do I need to bring?"

"Better wear long pants," said Henry. "There might be mosquitoes. Don't forget your fishing license."

"Are we going fishing?"

"I thought we'd take along a rod and reel, just in case the lake looks fishable."

"This should be fun," said Anne.

Once at the trailhead, Henry reached into the back seat of his VW Beetle and pulled out a backpack, a two-piece fishing rod, and a Mitchell 300 spinning reel. Piecing the rod and reel together, he handed it to Anne and placed the backpack on his back.

"Is this everything?" said Anne.

"Not quite," said Henry, popping open the trunk at the front of his car. Reaching inside, he pulled out a deflated, one-man raft rolled in a tight ball.

"Are you planning to use that, Henry?"

"I might. Depends on what we find."

"Where's the paddle?"

"Don't have one," said Henry, laughing. "I just lay the fishing rod in my lap and hang my arms over the side."

"Do you have a life jacket?"

"A life jacket. What's that?"

"Henry, I hope you don't plan on paddling out in the lake without a life jacket."

"Why, Anne, I didn't know you cared."

"I care very much," said Anne, taking Henry's hand as they began the three-quarter-mile walk to the lake.

As Henry and Anne strolled side by side, Anne pointed out the incredible wildflower display along the trail: purple asters, penstemon, lupine, and paintbrush. The buckbrush was in bloom, exuding a sickening-sweet aroma the native bees seemed to love.

"You wouldn't think there'd be so many beautiful wildflowers at this elevation," said Henry. "And look at all the butterflies around that puddle up ahead. I see painted ladies, California sisters, checkerspots . . . over there is a tiger swallowtail. Anne, I feel like a kid in a candy store."

"How do you know so much about butterflies, Henry?"

"When I was a kid, I was always playing baseball, exploring the hills near our home, or reading books about animals. My grandmother gave me a butterfly book when I was eight or nine years old. I read it so many times, the cover fell off."

"Speaking of your home, I thought you had a summer job lined up in Temecula."

"I did, but ever since they built that huge subdivision and shopping center, the mom-and-pop market where I worked has lost business. The owner said he couldn't afford to hire extra help this summer. I felt sorry for my friends who work there but practically did summersaults when I found out I was gonna be able to come up here and be with you."

Anne stopped suddenly, reached up, and gave Henry a soft kiss on the cheek. Blushing from ear to ear and overcome with a sensation he'd never felt before, Henry reached out and gently pulled Anne close. "May I kiss you back?" he said.

"You're so sweet, Henry," said Anne, staring into his eyes.

Henry wrapped his right arm around the base of Anne's neck and tenderly kissed her. Not knowing what to say when he released Anne from his embrace, Henry mumbled, "Anne, do you still wanna go fishing?"

"I think we'd better. We still have a month and a half before school starts and I think it's best we don't let on how we feel about each other."

Still overcome with emotion, Henry took a deep breath. "Anne, I think you're right, but it's not going to be easy for me."

"Me either," said Anne. "I have a confession to make."

"What's that?"

"The reason Sara didn't come with us this evening is because I asked her to give us some time alone together." Arm in arm, Henry and Anne continued down the trail toward the lake.

"I think this is it," said Henry. "It looks pretty shallow and overgrown with weeds, but I see a few open spots where we can drop a fly." From his backpack Henry pulled a small box containing several plastic bubbles and an assortment of well-worn flies his uncle Roscoe had given him years before. "First, we tie this plastic bubble to the end of our line, then we tie three feet of number-four monofilament leader to the other end of the bubble."

"Fascinating," said Anne. "So, which fly are we gonna use?"

"How about this one?"

"What's it supposed to be?"

"It's supposed to resemble a mosquito. I'm not so sure about that, but, hopefully, it will fool the trout."

When everything was ready, Henry handed Anne the fishing rod and pointed to a circle of open water fifteen yards from shore. Much to Henry's surprise, Anne hit the target with pinpoint accuracy, bringing a fourteen-inch rainbow to the surface.

"You've got one, Anne. Keep your rod tip up, and don't let him get away."

Anne's trout finally tired, allowing her to pull the brightly colored fish to shore. Henry grabbed it by the lower jaw and gently removed the hook. "What would you like to do, Anne?"

"Release him, Henry."

"Are you sure?"

"I'm sure."

"Good for you. This one will live to fight another day. Anne, I'm impressed."

"Why, Henry? My dad and I used to fish up at Butte Meadows every opening day. I once caught a six-pound German brown in DeSabla Reservoir. Did you think because I'm a girl I didn't know how to fish?"

"That thought did cross my mind, but I'm more impressed with your kind heart and concern for the resource. I think you and I may be kindred spirits."

"That's so sweet of you to say, Henry. Now I want to see you catch a fish."

Eager to try his luck near the north shore, Henry began the arduous chore of blowing up the one-man raft. When he'd finished, he waded knee-deep in the lake, straddled the raft, and sat down. Reaching back over his shoulder, he asked Anne to hand him his fishing rod.

"Henry, I'm concerned about your going out on the lake without a life jacket or a paddle."

"Don't worry, Anne. I used to do this all the time when I was a kid."

"You were smaller then, Henry. Now you make that raft look like a postage stamp."

"I'll just make a couple casts over there by that fallen log and head back. The mosquitoes are starting to get worse, so we don't wanna stay too long."

Paddling backwards, Henry came to within fifty feet of the north shore and cast his fly into a six-foot circle of dark water next to a partially submerged log. While slowly working his bubble back toward the raft, Henry felt a mighty tug. "I think I've got a good one, Anne."

The trout swam toward the deepest part of the lake then turned and passed directly under the raft, bending Henry's bargain-basement JC Higgins rod in half. Holding the rod in his right hand while paddling frantically with his left, Henry tried to keep the determined fish from reaching a morass of sunken logs and tangled branches. Believing his opponent had finally tired, Henry leaned to his left and reached down to grab its lower jaw.

"Henry, be careful," came a shout from the shore, just as the fish bolted for the bottom. Losing his balance, Henry fell headfirst into the drink. Scrambling to the surface with the rod still clenched in his right hand, Henry dog-paddled to a half-submerged log, grabbed a limb with his left hand, and pulled himself up. "Henry, are you all right?"

"I'm okay, Anne. He's still on the line."

With water streaming from his hair and into his eyes, Henry continued to play the trophy-sized trout until it finally tired. "This must be the granddaddy of the lake," said Henry, holding the five-pound trout up for Anne to see. "What a gorgeous fish!" Gently removing the hook, Henry reached down and released his prize.

"How are you gonna get back?"

"That may be a challenge," mumbled Henry, dressed in Levis, a T-shirt, and low-top Converse All Star tennis shoes. Removing the fly and bubble from the end of his line, Henry shoved the butt end of the rod, with the reel still attached, through the neck hole of his wet T-shirt and down his back. Sitting down on the log, he slid into the water and swam freestyle to the raft. After removing the rod and reel and tossing them into the raft, Henry held on and kicked his feet toward the south shore until he touched bottom.

"Was it worth it?" said Anne, wading out to give Henry a hand.

"Are you kidding?" said Henry, wiping water from his eyes. "I haven't had this much fun since I was a kid."

"I've got news for you, Henry. You're still very much a kid."

Henry laughed. "Anne, there's a mosquito buzzing around your ear. Maybe we should head back before they get worse. I'll take the raft and the backpack if you'll carry the rod and reel. Boy, was that fun!"

The next morning everyone was standing around the entrance to the visitor center when Harry Craddock asked Henry if he'd made the trip to Madora Lake yet. Jack Ketchum happened to be nearby and cocked his ear in Henry's direction. "We did," said Henry. "Anne and I hiked to the lake yesterday evening."

"Did you catch any fish?" said Craddock.

"Jack was right. The lake was overgrown with vegetation, and the mosquitoes practically ate us alive."

ONE EVENING IN MID-AUGUST, before Henry and the girls returned to school, Harry Craddock invited Henry, Anne, Sara, Ron Travers, and Ron's wife, Brenda, to a barbeque at his home. A bachelor, Harry lived with his mother and two aunts in a Victorian mansion on a hill overlooking what Henry described as a "glorious" mountain meadow. "Harry, how fortunate you are to live in a place like this," said Henry, sitting in a lawn chair around a 1920s-era, Olympic-sized swimming pool.

"I guess somebody has to do it," said Craddock.

"Hank," said Ron Travers, "have you thought anymore about becoming a state-park ranger?"

"That would be my second choice," said Henry. "Right now, I have my heart set on becoming a Fish and Game warden."

"You may want to reconsider," said Travers. "Park rangers work in some pretty interesting places."

"I've always loved nature," said Henry. "As a Fish and Game warden,

I'll be able to have a positive, tangible effect on our natural resources."

"You could do that as a park ranger."

"Yes, but park rangers are restricted to a single park. As a game warden, I would have the entire state to protect, including the ocean."

"Isn't a game warden's job dangerous?" said Brenda. "Everybody you contact is carrying a gun."

"Henry, tell Ron and Brenda about that game warden who disappeared," said Anne. "The one you told me about."

"Anne, they may not be interested."

"I'm interested," said Travers.

"So am I," said Craddock.

NINETEEN

T HE WEEK AFTER TURNING TWENTY-ONE in November of 1968, Henry skipped his classes at Chico State and drove down to the State Personnel Board in Sacramento. Eager to avoid the crowds, he was standing in front of the building when the doors opened at 8:00. Tacked to the bulletin boards inside were announcements for various state exams, each one listing the education and/or experience needed to qualify. Unable to find what he was looking for, Henry asked a female clerk for assistance.

"If it's not on the wall, it will be in one of these books," said the clerk. "What is it you're looking for?"

"Information about the Fish and Game warden's exam. I called earlier and was told it was coming up in March."

The clerk handed Henry a copy of the Fish and Game warden's exam announcement and an application form. "You might be interested in this one also," she said.

"What is it?"

"It's called the State Service Entrance Exam. Several of the departments, including State Parks, use it to screen applicants."

"No kidding?" said Henry, thinking about State Park Ranger Ron Travers and the encouragement he'd given him the previous summer.

"If I were you, I'd get your application in right away," said the clerk. "The filing period ends soon."

THE TELEPHONE RANG IN THE HALLWAY of Mrs. Iverson's basement at 9:05 on Wednesday evening, December 11, 1968. "Somebody get that," shouted Gary Lytle, "I'm watching my show." Henry knew that Gary always watched the *Beverly Hillbillies* on Wednesday nights, so he broke away from his homework, walked into the hallway, and answered the phone. It was Warden Tom Austin. Austin apologized for calling so late, explaining that he had just come in from the field and wanted to know if Henry would be interested in a ride-along on Saturday.

"Saturday's the first day of winter break and I was gonna head home for a couple weeks," said Henry.

"I understand. I'm gonna be working ducks down in Willows this Saturday, and I thought you might like to get your feet wet."

"That would probably be the case," said Henry. "I don't have rubber hip boots."

"What size do you wear?"

"Twelve."

"That's the same size I wear. I'll loan you a pair of mine if you want to postpone your trip for a day."

"It's a deal," said Henry. "I'm taking the warden's written exam in March, so I need all the experience I can get. What time will you be picking me up?"

"How's five o'clock sound? You better get used to waking up with the chickens if you're gonna be a game warden."

A STRONG SOUTH WIND WAS WHISTLING through the trees out front when Austin pulled his patrol car into Mrs. Iverson's driveway. His headlights lit up the covered front porch where Henry was waiting. "How ya doin'?" said Tom, as Henry climbed into the passenger seat. "It's been a while."

"I've been doing pretty well," said Henry. "A lot has happened since I saw you last spring."

Austin and Glance headed west on Highway 32. "How's that workin' out with the young lady you mentioned last time we worked together?"

"Very well, thank you."

"What are ya gonna do when you graduate and become a warden? Is she gonna be able to live in Los Angeles or some hellhole like Barstow or Brawley?"

"We've talked about that. I guess we'll have to make a decision when the time comes. Anne's getting her teaching credential, so I think she could get a job just about anywhere."

Reaching Hamilton City, Austin turned left onto Highway 45 and headed south for twenty-four miles to the riverside village of Princeton.

With a glimmer of light in the eastern sky, Austin and Glance followed Norman Road through ten miles of flooded rice fields.

"Down at the end of this road is the Sacramento National Wildlife Refuge Hunting Area," said Austin. "That's where people who can't afford to belong to a duck club go to hunt ducks and geese. Shoot days are Saturdays, Sundays, and Wednesdays."

"How do we fit in?"

"It'll be getting light soon, so I'm gonna hide the car behind this shack over here and bring you up to speed on today's detail."

Austin explained that waterfowl nesting grounds in the prairie pothole regions of Canada and the United States had been dry that year. With less habitat, there was less opportunity for ducks to nest and successfully raise their broods. Mallard and canvasback numbers were dangerously low, so the daily bag limit for mallards was set at three and the daily bag limit for canvasbacks was set at two. The overall daily bag limit was five ducks. Reaching into the back seat, Austin grabbed a canvas bag containing a battery-powered, portable radio.

"This is a heavy damn thing, but it's all we've got," said Austin. "The dial is set on car-to-car, which is what we'll be using. Don't move the dial from this setting or you'll activate the repeater and everyone from here to Fresno will be listening in on our conversation."

"I won't," said Henry.

"Good. Here's the on-off switch. This thing uses a lot of juice, so I suggest you leave it off unless you have something to report. My call number is 251. Yours will be Portable One. If you're gonna call me, push down on the mic, say 'Two-five-one, Portable One,' and release the mic. I'll respond, 'Two-five-one, go ahead.' Then you push down on the mic again and state your business."

"I understand."

"Up the road a few miles we'll come to an S turn. After that, the refuge hunting area will be on the left. I'm going to drop you off near a willow thicket that grows at the top of a levee. Find yourself a good place to hide, and wait for something to happen. Here's a pair of binoculars."

"Where will you be?"

"I'll be a half mile east of you. We've been getting reports of hunters throwing ducks and geese to their friends on the other side of the canal, outside the hunting area."

"What's that all about?"

"That way they don't have to stop hunting when they reach the legal limit. Hunters are required to present their birds at the check station when they leave the hunting area at the end of the day."

"I get it," said Henry.

"When you see their friends driving away with the illegal birds, radio me with a description of the vehicle and their direction of travel. They'll either be heading west, toward Highway 99, or east, toward me. If we work it right, the hunters won't see me stop the car and we'll be waiting for them when they show up at the check station later. Shooting time is over at 4:45 p.m., so I'll pick you up where I dropped you off, at 4:30."

"Sounds good," said Henry.

"Here's a backpack that should contain everything you'll need for the stakeout. My wife added a sandwich and a jug of water."

"Please thank her for me," said Henry.

Wearing hip boots and a camouflage raincoat, Henry climbed to the top of the levee that bordered Norman Road and found a place to hide. It was a minute or two before the 6:45 legal shoot time, but he could already hear gunfire in the distance. Checking out his surroundings, Henry found a twenty-foot-wide canal to his left that ran parallel to the road. On the opposite side of the canal was another levee. Beyond that levee was the refuge hunting area—a vast expanse of ponds, high grass, and tules.

Henry watched from his hiding place as hunters assumed their positions in various duck blinds and spread their decoys. With a thirty-mile-per-hour south wind blowing throughout the morning, ducks and geese from the 11,000-acre closed area to the north frequently took to the air and ventured into the hunting zone. Some of the more skilled hunters allowed birds to come within range, while novices and so-called sky-riders shot at anything that flew over. At one point, Henry heard a hunter shout, "What were you shooting at, you jackass? Those ducks were a mile high."

While enjoying the peanut-butter-and-jelly sandwich Mary Austin had made for him, Henry noticed two hunters leaving their blind a few minutes before noon. They began wading across an expanse of shallow water, in Henry's direction. Reaching the shore, the hunters fought their way through another two hundred yards of tules and high grass before coming to the levee on the opposite side of the canal from Henry's hidden position. Each man had a leather duck strap containing three ducks slung over his shoulder. With the aid of binoculars and the brilliant afternoon sunshine that had just broken through the clouds, Henry easily identified the contents of each duck strap: the bearded man's strap contained three drake mallards while his hunting partner's strap held one drake and two hen mallards.

Henry quickly jotted down detailed descriptions of each hunter. The first displayed a scruffy, three-day-old beard and had smeared his face with black and green paint. Dressed in full camo, he wore suspendered chest waders and a black stocking cap. His 12-gauge pump shotgun was decorated with camouflage paint. Five different duck calls hung from his neck.

The second hunter was slightly taller than the first and had a slender build. He wore brown chest waders and a waist-length camo rain jacket. His face was also splattered with black and green paint, and a camo baseball cap covered his head. Henry watched him unzip his rain jacket, exposing a black-and-red, plaid flannel shirt.

At 12:58 p.m., a black, 1960 Chevy pickup approached from the west. It stopped at the south side of Norman Road, directly across from where the two duck hunters were waiting. Henry wondered how the driver of the pickup knew where to stop, then spotted a ten-foot-high willow growing at the top of the north levee, clearly visible from the road and from inside the shooting area.

Turning his portable radio to the on position, Henry pressed the mic and whispered, "Two-five-one, Portable One."

"Two-five-one, go ahead."

"A transfer is about to take place. The vehicle is a black Chevy pickup, occupied by a single adult male. Stand by."

"Ten-four."

Henry watched as a slender young man wearing Levi jeans and a dark-blue sweatshirt ran from his pickup to the top of the north levee. Seeing him, the hunters began tossing ducks over the twenty-foot-wide canal.

"How many are there, Josh?" shouted the young man.

"Six."

"I only see five here."

"One of 'em fell in that clump of high weeds next to the water."

"I see it."

"Be careful you don't fall in."

"I got it. Do you still want to meet at Dwight's?"

"Yeah, we should be there by 6:30."

With three ducks in each hand, the young man raced back to his pickup, threw the ducks in the bed, and took off.

"Two-five-one, Portable One," said Henry.

"Two-five-one, go ahead."

"The black pickup is headed east, in your direction. Disregard that; he just made a U-turn and is headed west, toward the highway. There should be six mallards in the bed of the pickup."

Warden Austin raced past Glance with his red spotlight in the on position. Watching with his binoculars, Henry saw the black pickup and Austin's patrol car come to a stop several hundred yards down the road. Thirty minutes later, Austin radioed Henry. "Portable One, Two-five-one."

"Portable One, go ahead."

"I made contact, and your description of items transferred was correct. Are you able to see the suspects from your vantage point?"

"Affirmative."

"Continue surveillance and leave your radio turned on."

"Ten-four."

The wind calmed to a gentle breeze that afternoon, and hunter success dwindled with it. Instead of non-stop shooting, as was the case in the morning, only occasional volleys were heard. At 3:10 p.m., Henry watched a flock of five mallards set their wings and swoop in on the suspects' decoys. Only one duck flew away.

Austin returned and picked up Henry at 4:30. While Austin checked hunters leaving the hunting area, Henry sat in the patrol car and waited for the violators to appear. It was 5:35 when the suspects stopped at the check station in a mud-splattered, 1968 Jeep Wagoneer. Recognizing the driver, Henry signaled Austin.

"How'd you boys do?" said Austin.

"We popped a couple birds, but it was pretty slow today," said Josh, the driver.

"May I please see your licenses and duck stamps?" Both men complied, revealing their identities as Josh Colton and Dwight Lynch, both from the nearby town of Willows. "Could I get you to pull your car over here?" said Austin, pointing to his patrol car. "I'll take a quick look at your birds."

After moving his car, Colton climbed out of his Jeep and dropped the tailgate. "We shot six ducks," he said, pointing to six ducks lying next to a mesh bag filled with plastic decoys.

"Are these all of the birds you killed today?" said Austin, examining four mallards, a hen wigeon, and a drake gadwall.

"That's it," said Colton. "I told ya the hunting was slow."

"Please dump out your decoy bag," said Austin.

"What for?" said Colton. "I didn't see you do that to the hunters in front of us."

"Would you like to do it, or shall I?" said Austin.

"I'll do it," said Colton, emptying the bag out on the gravel parking lot. Noticing that the bag had not been completely emptied, Austin reached inside, felt around with his hand, and pulled out a rooster pheasant.

"Looks like you forgot something," said Austin, proceeding to search the car from front to back while Colton and Lynch stood by silently. When Austin had finished searching the vehicle, he requested driver's licenses from Colton and Lynch.

"So how much is that pheasant gonna cost me?" said Colton.

"I'm afraid there's a little more involved here than taking a pheasant out of season," said Austin.

"What?" said Colton.

"Are you familiar with a young man named Jake Colton?"

"He's my kid brother. What about it?"

"You gentlemen were seen transferring six mallards to him earlier in the day. The mallard limit is three per person. By my count, you killed ten between the two of you."

Passenger Dwight Lynch had been quiet up to that point, but no longer. "Nobody saw me transferring any mallards!"

Austin calmly walked over to his patrol car and asked Henry for clarification. "Ask him to unzip his jacket," said Henry. "If you see a black-and-red plaid, flannel shirt, that's our man." Returning to the jeep, Austin instructed Lynch to unzip his jacket. Lynch complied, revealing the shirt Henry had described.

A formal criminal complaint would be filed with the Glenn County District Attorney, Austin explained. "Mr. Lynch, you will be charged with take and possession of an overlimit of mallards, take and possession of an overlimit of ducks in general, and violation of hunting-area regulations. Mr. Colton, you will be charged with unlawful take and possession of a pheasant during closed season, take and possession of an overlimit of mallards, take and possession of an overlimit of ducks in general, and violation of hunting-area regulations. Your eighteen-year-old brother, Jake, will be charged as an accomplice in the taking of an overlimit of mallards and an overlimit of ducks in general."

"Why involve my brother?" said Colton. "He ain't done nothin'. Me and Dwight killed the ducks."

"When the three of you planned this event, you created a criminal conspiracy," said Austin. "Your brother helped you carry it out by meeting you out on the road and taking the ducks so you two could continue to kill more birds. Remember when I asked if you had killed any other birds today? You told me these six ducks were it. The only reason I'm not taking your shotguns is because you gentlemen have good identification. Would you like me to continue or move on to these other hunters patiently waiting behind you?"

"Josh, let's get outta here before he changes his mind," said Lynch.

It was just after 7:00 when Austin and Henry left the hunting area and headed east, toward Chico. "How 'bout I buy you dinner?" said Austin. "That's the least I can do after you made those cases for me."

"I had a good time," said Henry. "Those guys seemed pretty angry. I thought I might have to help you arrest them."

"They were just blowing off steam. The trick is to stay calm and not let them trap you into an argument or some type of altercation."

WITH THE WARDEN'S EXAM IN MARCH and graduation looming in June, Henry decided to case his aces. Beginning in early February, he took exams every Saturday morning for seven weeks straight. The positions he applied for included Chico police officer, City of Sacramento fireman, state insurance investigator, state narcotics enforcement agent, fisheries biologist, state park ranger, and Fish and Game warden.

"How many exams are you gonna take?" said Larry, as Henry Glance, Larry Jansen, Gary Lytle, Brad Foster, and Dennis D'Agostino sat around their usual corner table at Denny's on a rainy Sunday evening in late March 1969.

"Yeah, Hank. Don't tell me you're planning to be a narc," said Foster.

"No, Brad, I'm not planning to be a narc."

"Then why'd ya sign up to take the exam?"

"For the same reason Larry takes batting practice before every game. I wanted to get a feel for civil-service exams before taking the one I was interested in."

"How'd ya do?" said Dennis.

"Knowing Hank, he aced every damn one of 'em," said Larry.

"Why do you say that?" said Dennis.

"Because the guy's got a photographic memory. Back in high school, the teachers stopped correcting his papers. They'd just write a big A across the top and save themselves the time and trouble."

"That's enough, Larry," said Henry. "Don't forget I got a B in quantitative analysis last semester."

"I think I know why that happened," said Larry.

"Why?" said Dennis.

"He was in love, and his mind was on something other than figures," said Larry.

"Will you guys knock it off?" said Henry. "Dennis, you haven't said what you're gonna do."

"Didn't I tell you? I've been offered an auditor's position by Sacramento County. I start the first of June, right after I graduate. They said if I get my CPA, it won't take long to move up the ladder."

"Congratulations!" said Henry, standing up and snatching Dennis's dinner tab from the table. "You're the first one in Mrs. Iverson's pit to be offered a real job."

PART THREE

TWENTY

Tom Austin called again the last week in April 1969. "How'd you like to work the opening day of trout season?"

"I'd love to!" said Henry.

"Then I'll see you Saturday morning at five o'clock. We'll grab a bite at Ruby's before heading up the mountain."

When Austin pulled into the driveway at Mrs. Iverson's pit, Henry was waiting with a backpack in one hand and a pair of new hip waders in the other. "What's with the boots?" said Austin. "You're always welcome to borrow mine."

"I know," said Henry, "but I think I'm gonna need my own pair soon."

"Why? Did you hear the results of your warden's exam?"

"I did."

"Let me guess. You received the highest score in the history of the department and came out number one on the list."

"How'd you know?"

"You can't keep something like that a secret in this department. Congratulations, my friend. Well deserved."

"Thanks, Tom. I owe it all to you and Ned McCullough."

"I doubt that, but we have a lot to talk about," said Austin, parking in front of Ruby's, a converted train car located just five blocks from the Chico State campus.

"I think it's my turn to buy you breakfast," said Henry, following Austin up the steps.

"Maybe next time we work together you'll be wearin' a badge and a gun. Then you can buy me breakfast," said Austin. "Ruby, how the hell are ya? I swear, you look more ravishing every time I see you."

"Tom, you rascal. Flattery will get you everywhere. Find yourselves a seat. Let me guess—coffee for you and water for your young friend."

"Promise me you won't breathe a word about this to anyone," said Austin.

"I promise."

"After leaving the Gridley warden's position vacant for the thirteen years since Norm Bettis's disappearance, the department has finally advertised it."

"What does that have to do with me?"

"It has a great deal to do with you, since no warden in the entire state has put in for it."

"Nobody?"

"Not a soul. And Gridley is one of the best warden's positions in the state. It has everything: waterfowl, pheasants, deer, quail, salmon, steelhead—"

"I still don't get it," said Henry

"It means they're gonna have to fill the Gridley warden's position from the list."

"And if I'm number one on the list?"

"Bingo!"

"Wow! My head is spinning. Do you really think I have a chance at the Gridley position?"

"I do, but don't count your chickens just yet. Better wait 'til you receive official word from Sacramento. Meanwhile, they'll be sending you a stack of papers to fill out. Don't hesitate to put me down as a reference. One of the captains will do a background check on you. It'll probably be some desk jockey out of Sacramento, but it could be Chuck Odom."

"Who's Chuck Odom?"

"He's my captain. He'll be yours too, if you get the job. Chuck's captain's squad includes the Portola, Chico, Quincy, Oroville, Orland, Willows, and Gridley warden's districts."

"I've learned a lot from you, Tom, and I want you to know how much I appreciate everything you've done for me."

"You'll learn even more when they send you to the POST academy," said Austin.

"POST?" said Henry.

"Peace Officers Standards and Training. You'll have to go through the training course before you become a California peace officer. I think it's eight or ten weeks now, maybe longer."

"Where do I go for that—Sacramento?"

"No, I think the department is still using the Riverside Sheriff's Academy."

"That'll be nice. Riverside is only forty miles from home."

"You'll probably get to go home on weekends, but I think you stay in the barracks during the week. This is a military-style boot camp, just like the army. You'll have to cut your hair and wear a uniform."

"What are some of the courses?"

"You'll spend half the day in the classroom, learning about search and seizure, the California Penal Code, the Vehicle Code, ethics, and things like that. The other half will be outside, doing firearms training, cuffing techniques, hand-to-hand drills, and lots of physical exercise. I hear the instructors like to torture everyone by making them run up Mount Rubidoux and back."

"I've run up Mount Rubidoux before."

"No kidding?"

"Yeah, it was for a fund-raising event when I was a junior in high school."

"How long has your family lived in the Riverside area?"

"My parents originally came from San Diego and bought the farm in Temecula when I was in second grade."

"I heard Temecula is growing."

"Way too fast for my taste. Developers are buying up all the land and building subdivisions."

"Well, if things work out the way we talked earlier, you may be living in Gridley before long."

"Do you know how strange that sounds to me?"

"What's strange about it?"

"Remember when I told you about meeting Ned McCullough when I was eleven and him telling my friend Larry and me about a Fish and Game warden who mysteriously disappeared?"

"Yeah."

"When Norm Bettis disappeared in 1956, I was nine years old and living 500 miles away. What are the odds of me becoming a game warden myself and taking over Warden Bettis's patrol district?"

"That does seem like quite a coincidence."

"If you think that's a coincidence, wait 'til you hear the rest. At the end of November 1967, Larry and I were on our way to Chico for the first time when we passed a sign that said GRIDLEY 4 MILES. Ned McCullough's story about the game warden who disappeared immediately popped into my head. Larry was amazed that I remembered the name of the town where it happened. He was hungry, so we stopped at the first restaurant we came to. It was a little coffee shop just south of Gridley called—"

"Don't tell me," said Austin. "Pearl's Roadside Diner?"

"You guessed it!"

"I'd forgotten that Pearl's was Norm's favorite place to eat. He insisted on going there for breakfast every time I came down to work ducks."

"This is getting spookier all the time," said Henry. "Larry and I were finishing our hamburgers when I asked the waitress if she'd mind my asking her a question."

"What did this waitress look like?"

"I remember her being in good shape for a woman in her early fifties, if that's what you mean."

"That had to be Pearl. It wasn't just the food that Norm liked about that place. Anyway, wha'd ya ask her?"

"I asked if she knew anything about the game warden who had disappeared ten or eleven years before."

"And?"

"She didn't say anything at first. In fact, she almost dropped the stack of plates she was carrying. I remember this old man sitting at the bar choking on his coffee and spraying it all over the counter. After regaining her composure, Pearl wanted to know why I would ask such a thing."

"Wha'd you tell her?"

"I told her we had heard the story and were curious if anyone had ever found out what happened to the game warden. She told me that Norm, as she called him, had disappeared on December 13, 1956. She remembered him racing across the driveway where my car was parked. The old man sitting at the bar said it was raining like hell that day."

"Did they tell you anything else?"

"I asked if she had any ideas about what might have happened to the warden. That's when the old man at the bar started grumbling and making noises. Pearl told him to keep quiet and mind his own business. She said she had her own theories but thought it best to keep them to herself."

"Ya know, that investigation continued for over a year before they finally gave up," said Austin. "The sheriff's department, state police, Fish

and Game, . . . I think even the FBI was involved at one time or another.
I wonder if anyone bothered to interview Pearl."

"If they did, she didn't say anything about it to me."

"Did she tell you anything else?"

"I asked her if the warden who disappeared had been married. She said
he was and his wife still lived in the same little house at the end of town."

"That would be Martha. I need to go by and see how she's doing.
What about the old guy? Did he say anything else?"

"Yes. Larry and I were walking out the restaurant door when the old man
said, 'I hope they catch the dirty sonsabitches that done old Norm in.'"

After a long day of counting trout and checking fishing licenses, Tom
Austin dropped Henry off at Mrs. Iverson's house. "Well, good luck with
your finals," said Austin. "Not that you'll need any. Be sure to call me as
soon as you hear from Sacramento."

"I will," said Henry. "I'm trying not to think about it too much because I don't want to jinx it."

"If they assign you the Gridley position, you and I are gonna have
adjoining patrol districts. That means we can work on the Bettis murder
investigation together."

"Is it still considered an investigation after thirteen years?"

"Murder investigations are never over until they're solved. I have a
feeling with your brain and my experience, we have a good chance of
finally cracking the case."

"I hope you're right, Tom."

"You bet I'm right, but we have to do it in the next three years."

"Why's that?"

"Because that's when I park my patrol car at the Sacramento office,
turn in my badge, and spend the rest of my life fly-fishing in those mountains up there."

"I'll call you as soon as I hear. Thanks for everything, Tom. See you
soon."

MONDAY MORNING, APRIL 28, 1969, AT 8:35, Henry had just walked out
the door of Mrs. Iverson's basement when he heard the phone ringing in
the hallway.

"Hello," said Brad Foster. "Who is it you want to talk to? He just
walked out the door. Just a minute, I'll see if I can catch him." Seconds
later, the door at the head of the hallway flew open and Henry came running down the stairs.

"Is it for me?"

"Here he is," said Foster, handing Henry the phone.

"Hello," said Henry, catching his breath.

"Is this Henry Glance?"

"Yes, it is."

"This is Lloyd Frailey, at Fish and Game headquarters, in Sacramento."

"Yes, Mr. Frailey?"

"Are you still interested in becoming a Fish and Game warden?"

"Absolutely!"

"Well, young man, it looks like we've got a position for you in Gridley. How does that suit you?"

"Are you kidding? When do I start?"

"First you're gonna have to go through the law enforcement academy down in Riverside. The next cycle begins the first of June."

Later that day, Henry caught Anne coming out of her last class. Together, they walked past the bookstore to the nearby amphitheater. The stage of the amphitheater was on one side of Chico Creek and the seats were on the other. Henry and Anne sat in the top row so they could watch the stream flow by.

"What would you like to hear first," said Henry, "the good news or the bad news?"

"Tell me the bad news first," said Anne. "Let's get it out of the way."

"The bad news is I'm going to be attending the law enforcement academy in Riverside for two and a half months, beginning the first of June. The good news is I got the Gridley warden's position."

"Henry, that's wonderful!" said Anne, kissing Henry and giving him a big hug.

"Since you and Sara will be working at the state park again this summer, you won't even miss me."

"Of course I'll miss you, Henry. I'll miss you more than you know." Distracted by a school of spring-run salmon swimming upstream, Henry didn't respond. "Henry, here I am pouring my heart out to you and you're paying more attention to those fish."

Henry laughed. "I'm sorry, Anne. I'll think about you every day while I'm learning about search and seizure and running up Mount Rubidoux."

HENRY GRADUATED FROM CHICO STATE at the end of May 1969. Before leaving for Riverside, he and the men of Mrs. Iverson's pit met at Denny's for the last time. While sitting around their corner table, everyone discussed his future plans. Dennis D'Agostino would marry his girl-friend, move to Sacramento, and work as an accountant. Brad Foster was waiting to hear from Glenn County about a deputy sheriff's position. Gary Lytle had made up his mind to move to Montana and take over his father's outfitting and guide-service business. Larry Jansen's dream of becoming a major-league baseball catcher hadn't worked out; he would settle for a job teaching PE and coaching baseball in Lake Elsinore.

As for Henry, he would spend the next two and a half months down on Box Springs Road in Riverside. After completing his required law-enforcement training, he would return to Northern California and begin what was to be the greatest adventure of his life.

TWENTY-ONE

HENRY BREEZED THROUGH THE ACADEMY, finishing first in a class of thirty Riverside County sheriff's deputies, eight City of Riverside police officers, two Inglewood police officers, six Corona police officers, and four California Fish and Game wardens. With two weeks off at the end of August 1969, he had time to find a place to live and get reacquainted with Anne. Anne was beginning her senior year at Chico State. She would spend another year student teaching before being eligible for her teaching credential.

A rundown farmhouse northwest of Gridley would serve Henry well for the time being. The rent was cheap, and the neighbors were quiet. Soon after moving in, Henry noticed two older-model pickups driving by the house at odd hours of the day and night. Determined to prevent any would-be outlaws from learning his work routine, he parked his patrol truck in the barn when he was off duty and did his best to work unpredictable hours.

The first major event on Warden Glance's rookie-year calendar was the September 1, 1969, dove opener. Most of the valley wardens in Chuck Odom's captain's squad planned to work the foothills west of Orland and Willows, where a healthy crop of turkey mullein was attracting record numbers of mourning doves. As Willows warden Mike Prescott put it, "If a cold snap doesn't chase the birds south a week before the opener, those dove hunters are gonna have a field day."

Young Warden Glance had spent the last week of August scouting his own valley district for potential hotspots. Late Sunday afternoon, August

31, he hit avian pay dirt. "I've never seen so many doves," Henry told Anne over the telephone. "They were flying in and out of that harvested safflower field like a swarm of bees."

"Do the hunters know about it?" said Anne.

"I suspect some of 'em do. You can't keep something like that a secret for long. I found a good place to hide my truck back in the trees, along Butte Creek. I'm gonna be there before daylight tomorrow morning and see who shows up."

"Henry, you be careful. One of my cousins was hit in the eye with a shotgun pellet on opening day of dove season a couple years ago."

"I'll be careful, Anne. How are your classes going? Did you get the ones you wanted?"

"My classes are going well, Henry. I'm looking forward to seeing you on Wednesday, when you come up for the barbeque."

PUSHING THE SCREEN DOOR OPEN with his boot and stepping out onto the rickety, wooden front porch, Henry carefully placed his cereal bowl, a banana, and a glass of orange juice on a wooden table built by the farm's original owner in 1938. It was 4:30 a.m. when the neighbor's prize-winning Rhode Island red cut loose with a series of cock-a-doodle-doos and the lights came on in Glenn Darby's barn down the road. Serenaded by the bellowing of hungry cows waiting to be milked, Henry reveled in the cool morning breeze that flowed from the nearby alfalfa field. He finished his Cheerios just in time to greet Darby's black Lab as she pranced up the porch steps with her tail wagging. "Hello, Molly," said Henry, patting his canine friend on the head and stroking her silky-smooth ears. "No time to throw the ball this morning, so I'll get you a dog biscuit and send you back home."

Long before the sun came up on opening morning, Warden Glance's patrol truck was tucked behind a row of mature cottonwoods, east of the Butte Creek levee. With binoculars in hand and a look of exhilaration on his face, Henry was hiding next to a cement irrigation outflow pipe, a quarter mile from the harvested safflower field he had described to Anne the night before.

Official shooting time was 6:06 a.m. At 6:01, three newer-model pickups entered the field, drove past Henry's hidden position, and stopped. Glance removed a notepad from his shirt pocket and recorded descriptions of each truck: a white-over-lime-green Chevy, a black Ford, and a red Dodge. As Henry watched and listened, six dove hunters climbed from the pickups, loaded their shotguns, and fanned out across the field, fifty yards apart. By 6:30, the morning temperature had risen to seventy degrees.

Henry sat and listened to the characteristic whistle of dove wings as the evasive birds zipped and darted in and out of harm's way. A barrage of shotgun blasts had begun at 6:43, reached a crescendo by 8:00, and subsided by 10:30. He listened to the hunters laughing and shouting back and forth as they retrieved whatever birds they could find and returned to their respective pickups.

Minutes later, Henry's attention was diverted to two elderly hunters who'd come walking down the levee road in his direction. "How'd you fellas do?" said Glance, stepping from his hiding place behind the cement water pipe.

"We each shot six or seven birds," said the taller of the two gentlemen. "We didn't do nearly as well as that bunch out in the safflower field. That one guy must have dropped nineteen or twenty doves. I don't think he found half of 'em."

"There they go now, in those three pickups," said the second hunter. "They'll be back this afternoon. You can bet on it."

After counting the elderly hunters' doves and examining their hunting licenses, Henry questioned his earlier decision. *Why didn't I go over and check out those hunters in the safflower field before they left? They may come back this afternoon, but I have no way of knowing how many birds they killed this morning.*

It was almost noon when Glance raced back home, parked his patrol truck in the barn, and closed the wooden doors behind him. He climbed the back stairs and entered the spacious farmhouse kitchen. Tromping across the linoleum floor, Henry continued down the hallway and entered the largest of three bedrooms.

Tossing his gun belt on the bed, Henry quickly changed from his uniform into OP shorts, a gray T-shirt, and leather sandals. Washing down a peanut butter sandwich with a glass of ice-cold well water, he grabbed the keys to his VW Beetle and ran out the back door.

It took Henry ten minutes to reach Highway 99, head south, and arrive at the only motel in town: a twelve-unit, single-story establishment called the Peach Blossom Inn. Parked on the opposite side of the highway, Henry recognized two of the three pickups he was looking for. The white-over-lime-green Chevy and the black Ford were parked near the far north end of the motel. The parking space next to them was empty.

Hearing laughter, he directed his attention to a wooden gazebo in the middle of the lawn out front. Four thirty-plus-year-old men were sitting around a table, eating sandwiches and drinking beer. With an industrial-sized Rain Bird sprinkler operating back and forth across the lawn, Henry found it difficult to make out what the motel guests were saying.

"I had a hunch you guys would be here," Henry said to himself as he drove across the highway and up the gravel driveway to the office. A bell jingled overhead as he stepped inside and walked up to the desk.

"Sorry, we're full up," came a female voice from the living quarters in back.

"I wanted to ask a question," said Henry.

"Just a minute," she said, turning down the TV. "How can I help you?"

"I have a large group of friends coming up from the Bay Area tomorrow, and I was wondering if any of the rooms near the north end of the motel will be available. My friends like to stay at that end because it's quieter."

"Let's see," said the clerk, examining the registration book. "Depending on how fast our cleaning lady works, the three rooms on the end should be available after four o'clock. Normally they'd be available after three o'clock, but the gentlemen in those rooms have requested a one o'clock checkout."

"Thank you very much," said Henry. "I'll take one of your cards and have my friends call to make a reservation." Stepping outside, Henry noticed that the red Dodge pickup had returned and two more men were walking across the lawn toward the gazebo, each carrying a six-pack of beer and a bag of groceries. Henry drove out of the motel parking lot the opposite way he'd come in so he could discretely record the license numbers of the hunters' pickups. Two of the registered owners were from Concord, California, the other from nearby Walnut Creek.

Warden Glance was sitting in his hiding place behind the irrigation pipe, when the same three pickups returned to the safflower field that afternoon. By 4:30, the doves had begun flying back and forth across the field, and by 6:00, it sounded like a war zone. Henry watched as one bird after another folded its wings and tumbled to the ground. The last bird of the evening was killed at 7:45 p.m.—ten minutes after legal shooting time. When all three pickups had left the scene, Henry drove out to the county road and headed home.

Tom Austin's phone rang at 9:10 p.m. "Hello."

"Hi, Tom. This is Hank. How did your day go?"

"It was actually kinda slow for an opener. How 'bout you?"

"I have a group of six hunters from the Bay Area I'd like to talk to you about."

"Are they the ones you ran the radio check on?"

"Yes. They slaughtered the doves this morning and again this evening. They're staying at the Peach Blossom Motel on Highway 99, and they asked for a late checkout tomorrow afternoon, so—"

"They're planning on hunting in the morning before they head home," interrupted Austin.

"Exactly. They keep their ice chests in the motel rooms, so I'm thinking about hitting them just after they load up and are ready to leave. Since there's three vehicles and six hunters, I was hoping you'd be available to come down and give me a hand."

"What time do you want me there, Hank?"

"I'm gonna be watching these guys again in the morning. As soon as they leave the field and head back to the motel, I'll radio you. How 'bout meeting me across from the cemetery at the north end of town and we go from there?"

"Sounds good. I'll make sure to be on your end of the valley in the morning."

Henry radioed Austin Tuesday morning at 10:45. After meeting Glance across from the cemetery at 11:40, Austin followed Henry south on Highway 99. The two wardens passed through downtown Gridley before turning east for two blocks, turning south for three more blocks, and turning west again, toward the highway. Fifty yards from Highway 99, Henry stopped on the south side of the road, in front of a weed-strewn vacant lot. While Austin waited in his patrol car, Henry ran across the lot to the rear of a boarded-up auto repair shop. Able to clearly see the north end of the motel from his hidden vantage point, Henry watched until the hunters had finished loading their pickups and were preparing to leave.

At 12:45, Henry signaled for Austin to move in. Austin raced across the highway and entered the motel parking lot from the north end, just as the white-over-lime-green Chevy pickup and the red Dodge pickup were backing out of their parking spaces. The black Ford pickup had pulled away a few seconds earlier and was driving past the office and out to the highway when Henry entered from the south side and met it head-on. Henry climbed from his patrol truck and walked up to the driver's window. "Would you gentlemen please park over there next to your friends. We'd like to check your birds and your hunting licenses before you leave."

"Look," said the driver, later identified as Lawrence Vogel, a forty-three-year-old dentist from Concord, California, "I have a business to run, and I'm in a hurry to get home."

Pointing to the parking spot next to Vogel's hunting companions, Henry repeated, "Please park over there next to your friends."

Vogel and his passenger were already in Austin's face by the time Henry had parked his truck and joined the group. "How long is this going to take?" said Vogel. "My son and I need to get going. I have patients scheduled in the morning, and he has classes to attend."

"If you gentlemen will hand me your hunting licenses, we'll get you on your way as soon as possible," said Austin.

Expecting the young rookie to grab the ball and run with it, Austin looked at Henry and handed him the six hunting licenses he'd collected. Taking Austin's cue, Glance said, "You gentlemen have done a lot of hunting for the last two days. We'd like to inspect any game you have in your possession. We'll begin with Mr. Shipley and Mr. Metzger, in the white-and-green Chevy pickup. Mr. Shipley, does this vehicle belong to you?"

"It's mine," said Shipley, kicking the gravel under his feet and pounding the back of the tailgate with his fist.

"This is probably gonna to take a while," said Austin. "Why don't the rest of you fellas grab a couple lawn chairs outta your pickups and relax."

At Henry's request, Harold Shipley, a forty-three-year-old insurance broker from Concord, opened his camper shell and pulled two large ice chests out onto the tailgate. The first ice chest contained drinks and various food items. The second contained several iced-down plastic bags stuffed with dove breasts. While Henry counted, Austin tallied the results. Henry counted a total of sixty dove breasts—twenty over the legal possession limit for two hunters. The twenty illegal dove breasts were seized into evidence and tagged. Glance and Austin proceeded to the red Dodge pickup.

Raymond Brooks, a forty-three-year-old pharmaceutical salesman from Pleasant Hill, stood up. "How much is this going to—"

"Is there a way we can speed this up?" interrupted Lawrence Vogel.

"Larry, you need to be quiet and let these officers do their job," said Shipley.

"Since when do you tell me to shut up?" said Vogel.

"Since right now, Mr. Big Shot. Just because you drive a Mercedes and live on the hill with all the millionaires, you don't have the right to screw things up for the rest of us. We want to get out of here just as badly as you do."

"Looks like we've got a few more birds here," said Henry, prompting Austin to get out his notepad. Brooks and Rumsey also possessed sixty dove breasts—twenty over the legal possession limit for two hunters.

After recording Brooks's and Rumsey's driver's license information, Glance and Austin continued to the black Ford pickup. Lawrence Vogel and his twenty-year-old son, Scott, were waiting with two ice chests sitting on the tailgate. The first ice chest contained beer and soft drinks. The second held plastic bags filled with dove breasts. Henry counted a total of seventy-six dove breasts—thirty-six over the legal possession limit for two hunters. Immediately after Glance and Austin seized the Vogels' unlawfully possessed doves, Scott Vogel closed the lids on the two ice chests, slid them against the cab of the pickup, and secured them with a bungee cord.

Henry was about to move on to the next step in the investigation when he remembered something he'd seen earlier that morning, just as the sun was coming up. A bird had fallen victim to the hunters' shotguns, but it didn't look quite right. The same size as a mourning dove, it flew at a distinctively different cadence. Playing a hunch, Henry asked Scott Vogel to release the bungee cord and slide the ice chest containing beer and soft drinks back onto the pickup bed.

"What for?" said the curly-haired spitting image of his father. "You already looked in that ice chest."

"Scott, let him do his thing so we can get the hell out of here," said the elder Vogel.

"But he already looked in that cooler," said Scott. "All it contains are beer and sodas."

Scott Vogel's reluctance to surrender the ice chest gave Henry even more reason to suspect there was something illegal inside. Henry climbed into the bed of the pickup, walked to the ice chest in question, and opened the lid. Removing several beer and soft-drink containers, he reached under a layer of ice and felt yet another plastic bag. "Oh, no!" mumbled Henry, pulling the plastic bag from the ice and holding it up for everyone to see. The small, multicolored falcon inside looked nothing like a gray mourning dove. "It's a kestrel," said Glance.

"What?" said Lawrence Vogel. "Scott! I told you to get rid of that damn thing."

Disgusted by what he'd discovered, the young rookie requested identification from the two violators and seized each of their shotguns into evidence. Placing the shotguns inside his patrol truck, Henry turned to Austin and whispered, "If it were up to me, these two would spend the next sixty days in the Butte County Jail."

"You're doing great," said Austin. "When we're done here, I'll buy you lunch at Pearl's."

"Oh no you don't," whispered Glance. "It's my turn this time." Henry returned his attention to the six hunters. "I'd appreciate you gentlemen listening carefully while I explain what's going to happen."

"HOW DOES IT FEEL TO FINALLY BE A GAME WARDEN?" said Austin, as he and Henry walked into Pearl's Roadside Diner and sat down.

"I feel badly about all those doves," said Henry. "And that beautiful little kestrel. What kind of lowlife scum would shoot a bird like that?"

"You're gonna see a lot of that kind of thing over the next thirty years," explained Austin.

"If it isn't Tom Austin."

"Hello, Pearl," said Tom, standing up and giving her a hug. "It's been a while."

"I'll say it has. I think it's been ten or fifteen years."

"Pearl, this is the new Gridley Fish and Game warden, Hank Glance."

"You don't have to get up," said Pearl, shaking Henry's hand. "Have you been in here before? You look familiar, and I never forget a face. Especially a nice-looking one like yours."

"My friend and I came in here a couple years ago on our way to Chico State," said Henry.

"Wait a minute. I think I've got it. Your friend was a great big guy, and one of you asked me about Norm Bettis."

"That was me."

"Pearl, we'd like to talk to you about that if you've got a minute," said Austin.

"Let me take your order and as soon as these other folks leave, I'll come back and sit down with you gentlemen."

As Henry and Tom were finishing their afternoon meal, Pearl walked over and sat down at the end of the table. "Pearl, did I tell you how good you look?" said Austin. "You haven't aged a bit."

"Tom, you always were a charmer. How can I help you boys?"

"You may not remember this," said Henry. "The last time I was in here you said you had your own thoughts about what might have happened to Norm Bettis but preferred to keep them to yourself. An old-timer was sitting at the bar, and you told him to keep quiet."

"You've got quite a memory," said Pearl.

"You don't know the half of it," said Austin.

"That old-timer must have been Earl Glenn," said Pearl. "You know, he passed away last month, at ninety-six. Earl would come in every morning for his cup of coffee and a slice of apple pie. I didn't mean to be unfriendly, Hank, but I didn't know you from Adam at the time. How was I to know that this young man who walked into my restaurant would end up taking Norm's place?"

"That is a little hard to believe," said Austin.

"You can't keep a secret in a small town like this," said Pearl. "Nobody really knows what happened to Norm, but everyone has a theory or two. Trouble is, if you mention somebody's name, next thing you know, that person is ticked off and saying bad things about you. In my business, you can't afford to have that happen."

"Just between the three of us, what do you think happened?" said Austin. "Hank and I plan to break this case wide open before I retire in three years."

"Oh you do, do you?" said Pearl, chuckling. "You two are gonna accomplish what all those detectives couldn't? It's been thirteen years since Norm disappeared, and nobody's even found his car."

"Please tell us what you think," said Henry.

"This might not be anything, but I remembered it a couple days after that detective from Sacramento interviewed me."

"Anything you can tell us would be helpful," said Austin. "We're starting from scratch, with nothing to go on."

"The summer before Norm disappeared, I remember overhearing him talking to Earl about workin' over in the hills west of Willows and running into a couple poachers he knew. It was near some lake."

"East Park?" said Austin.

"No, that's not it."

"Black Butte?"

"No."

"Stony Gorge?"

"That's it—Stony Gorge Reservoir. Apparently, these two no-goods were up there deer huntin' outta season, but they heard Norm coming and hid their rifle. Norm told Earl he ended up finding the rifle after the poachers drove away and left his business card in the rifle's place. He'd written on his card that in exchange for the rifle, he'd give 'em each a citation for huntin' deer outta season."

"That's funny," said Henry.

"Norm and Earl thought so too. They got to laughing one day here in the restaurant and couldn't stop. I asked what was so funny. That's when Norm started laughing again and said, 'I wish I could have seen the look on that smartass little punk's face when he found my card.'"

"Did Norm mention any names?" said Henry.

"He may have to Earl, but that won't do you any good now."

"By any chance, did Earl have a wife? If so, is she still living?" said Henry, taking notes.

"He did," said Pearl. "Her name is Thelma Glenn, and she lives in that trailer park up the road."

"First chance we get, we'll go over and talk to Thelma," said Austin.

"Earl would grab that old homemade cane of his and walk over here every morning from the trailer park," said Pearl, standing from the table as two customers walked in. "Unless it was raining, of course. That reminds me. It was raining cats and dogs the day Norm disappeared. I don't think I've seen it rain that hard since."

"Is there anything else you can think of?" said Henry, coming to his feet and placing a twenty-dollar bill on the table.

"Not at the moment, but if anything else comes to mind, I'll give one a you boys a call. Do you have a card or somethin'?"

"I have a brand-new one," said Henry, handing it to Pearl with his left hand. "I just received a box of these in the mail."

"I don't see a ring on your finger," said Pearl. "Aren't you married?"

"Not yet," said Austin, laughing and giving Pearl a hug. "Give him a year or two."

"Who's the lucky girl?" said Pearl. "Anyone I know?"

"I don't think you know her," said Henry. "Anne lives in Chico. She and I met at Chico State. We're not actually engaged, but I'm hoping to change that tomorrow evening."

"Oh?" said Austin. "What's happening tomorrow evening?"

"I've been invited to Anne's parents' house for a barbeque. I'm hoping for an opportunity to get Anne alone so I can pop the question."

"Do you have a ring?" said Pearl.

"Yes. It's not exactly the Hope Diamond, but it's all I could afford."

"It's the meaning that counts," said Pearl. "Good luck, Hank. I hope it works out for you."

"Thanks so much, Pearl," said Henry, following Austin out the door. "I do too."

TWENTY-TWO

T HE NEXT DAY, AFTER HENRY'S BIG dove case, wardens Glance and
Austin stopped for breakfast at Pearl's Roadside Diner.

"That was quick," said Pearl, pouring Austin a cup of coffee. "I
haven't seen you two since yesterday. To what do I owe this unexpected
pleasure?"

"We're taking yesterday's evidence down to Sacramento headquarters," said Austin.

"None for me, thanks," said Henry.

"I forgot. You don't drink coffee, do you?"

"I asked him how he planned to be a game warden if he doesn't drink
coffee," said Austin.

"Before you gentlemen leave, there's something else I'd like to tell you."

"No time like the present," said Austin.

"Four young men used to come in here for breakfast about once a
week during the winter months. I remember 'em because they'd always
leave mud tracks across the floor and under that table over there by the
window."

"Sounds like duck hunters to me," said Austin.

"These guys would be jabbering away, but every time I came near
their table, they'd clam up. I was about to take their order one morning
when Norm Bettis drove past the window in his patrol car. He had a
green Ford sedan like yours, Tom. Anyway, when they saw Norm walking from the parking lot to the back door, all four of 'em stood up and
said they'd changed their minds."

"Do you know who these men were?" said Henry.

"I didn't at the time, and they never came back to the restaurant after Norm disappeared."

"Did you tell any of this to the investigators?" said Austin.

"No, because it never crossed my mind. Not until last night, when I saw one of 'em on TV."

"Who was that?" said Henry.

"He looks older now, and he's lost most of his hair, but it was him all right. I recognized his voice and those pock marks on his cheeks."

"Who?" said Austin.

"That big land developer who's buying up property all over the county. They interviewed him last night about a gas station and a speedy mart he's building out west of Chico. The film showed 'em bulldozing an almond orchard to clear the land."

"What's this guy's name?" said Henry.

"The news reporter called him Blake Gastineau."

Henry wrote down what he'd just heard on a notepad he removed from his shirt pocket. He remembered Anne talking about Gastineau a couple years before—the day of their picnic at the Sacramento National Wildlife Refuge. "Anything else you can think of?" he said.

"No, but I'll keep my eyes and ears open. If you boys start asking questions around here, it'll get back to me, as sure as there's a ketchup stain on your shirt."

"Oh, no!" said Henry. "This is a brand-new uniform shirt."

"Don't worry, Hank. This will get it out."

"Thanks so much, Pearl."

"My pleasure. You make sure Tom gets you back from Sacramento in plenty of time for the barbeque tonight. You don't wanna be late for that."

THE REGION 2 FISH AND GAME OFFICE was located next to the Sacramento State College campus, off Highway 50, along the south shore of the American River. Austin led Henry down the hall to meet Captain Russ Gifford. Gifford oversaw the evidence locker and several evidence freezers. The freezers were filled with everything from salmon and steelhead to waterfowl, venison, doves, and bobcat hides. The walk-in locker was a spacious room lined with shelves containing hundreds of rifles, shotguns, rods, reels, and assorted tools of the poacher's trade: spears, pitchforks, fish nets, snares, and steel leghold traps.

"What did you guys bring me?" said Gifford.

"Two shotguns, some dove breasts, and a kestrel," said Henry.

"Here's where you log everything in. When you're finished, I'll show you where to put it."

After logging and securing their evidence, Henry asked Captain Gifford about a rifle that would have been logged by Warden Norman Bettis back in 1956. "Any rifles or shotguns placed in the locker more than ten years ago would have been adjudicated and returned to their rightful owners," said Gifford. "Either that or forfeited by the court and sold at auction."

"Would you still have a record of them?" said Glance.

"We usually save the old evidence tags and store them in the cage at the back of the office," said Gifford. "I'll unlock the cage and you can search to your heart's content." Opening the door to the walk-in cage, Gifford pointed to several rows of shoeboxes, all containing old evidence tags. Henry located the box labeled 1956 and found one evidence tag issued by Warden Norman Bettis. It involved a Winchester, lever-action .30-30 rifle, owner unknown. Fortunately, Bettis had written the rifle's serial number on the tag.

"Would you mind if I take this with me?" said Henry.

"Sure," said Gifford. "I'll put a dated notecard in its place."

It was approaching 2:00 p.m. when Glance and Austin returned to Gridley. "Do we have time to contact Thelma Glenn and Martha Bettis today?" said Austin. "We can always do it next week. You don't want to be late for your barbeque."

"I think we can fit it in," said Henry, "as long as I have enough time to take a shower and get to Chico by 6:00."

Tom's and Henry's first stop was the trailer park where Thelma Glenn lived. Thelma was a sweet little old lady of eighty-seven who refused to let Henry and Tom leave before trying a slice of her blackberry pie. "I picked the berries myself, down by the slough," said Thelma. "Earl and I used to do it every year."

"Did Earl ever talk about any conversations he'd had with Norm Bettis?" said Austin.

"He talked about Norm all the time," said Thelma. "I think Norm was in that restaurant down the road almost as often as Earl. He'd park in back so nobody'd know he was there. A lot of good that did."

"Did Earl ever mention any names?" said Henry. "People that Norm might have talked about?"

"I'm sure he did, but it's been thirteen or fourteen years since Norm disappeared. Come to think of it, Earl did mention a couple young guys who came in the restaurant a year or two ago. He said they were askin' about Norm."

"That was probably my friend Larry and me," said Henry.

"I'm sorry I can't be of more help," said Thelma. "My memory isn't what it used to be. Have you talked to Martha Bettis?"

"That's where we're going next," said Austin.

"She helps out at the library on Mondays and Fridays. What's today—Thursday?"

"Yes, it is," said Henry.

"Then she should be home. Do you know where she lives?"

"I do," said Austin.

Martha Bettis's heart skipped a beat when she turned from watering her zinnias and saw Tom Austin's patrol car roll up the driveway. A petite woman in her late seventies, she wore blue tennis shoes, shorts, a light-colored blouse, and a straw hat. "Hello, Martha," said Austin, closing the driver's door behind him. "How ya been?"

"You startled me, Tom. For a second I thought—"

"I know, Martha. I'd like you to meet Hank Glance."

Henry walked over and shook Martha's hand. "A pleasure to meet you, Mrs. Bettis. Your zinnias are beautiful. I especially like the orange ones."

"Thank you," said Martha, reaching down to turn off the faucet. "My, they're hiring them young these days."

"Hank just graduated from Chico State," said Austin. "He came out number one on the warden's list."

"That's wonderful. Why don't you two come inside and I'll pour you a glass of iced tea."

As they entered the house, Glance and Austin heard a voice coming from the large birdcage hanging at the corner of Martha Bettis's shaded front porch. "The captain's an asshole. The captain's an asshole."

"I see you still have your parrot," said Austin, laughing.

"Oscar can be embarrassing at times. Norman taught him to say that twenty years ago."

"Is Oscar an African grey?" said Henry. "They're supposed to be incredibly smart."

"He's too smart for his own good," said Martha. "I usually put him in the back room when I know company's coming."

Entering the small, carpeted living room, Henry examined several framed photographs of the man Martha Bettis identified as her husband. An 8 by 10, black-and-white photo hanging near the doorway showed a young and slender Norman Bettis standing on the deck of a battleship with a row of shipmates. Sitting on the hearth was an enlarged black-and-white photo of Martha and Norman on their wedding day. "And I took this one in 1924, the year Norman was hired by Fish and Game," said Martha, handing Henry a glass of iced tea. "He only wore that Stetson when the captain was around."

"The captain Oscar mentioned?" said Henry.

"No, that captain came along twenty years later," said Martha, smiling. "Please sit down and make yourselves comfortable. What can I do for you gentlemen?"

"Martha, Henry and I would like to ask you a few questions about Norm and his disappearance." Martha began to tear up. Mindful of her feelings, Tom and Henry waited until she regained her composure.

"Why the renewed interest?" said Martha, rubbing her eyes. "It's been years since those detectives came to the house."

"Hank and I have been kicking over a few rocks lately, and we think we may have something to go on." Glance and Austin spent the next half hour questioning Martha about her husband's disappearance on Thursday, December 13, 1956.

"I was asked those same questions every day for a week," said Martha. "Norm never talked about people he'd had run-ins with because he didn't want to worry me."

"You mentioned Norm's office a few minutes ago," said Henry.

"I know what you're thinking," said Martha. "Those detectives went through his desk with a fine-toothed comb and couldn't find anything."

"What about a diary?" said Austin. "The department always provided us with those hardbound *Daily Reminders*."

"I'm so glad you brought that up," said Martha. "I was cleaning out the backyard shed the other day and found a cardboard box under the work bench. It was filled with those green diaries you're talking about."

"You mean the detectives didn't go through Norm's diaries?" said Henry.

"They couldn't find 'em, so I figured Norm must have thrown them away. He was such a neatnik. Everything had to be in its place. If something was lyin' around, Norman would throw it out."

"He wouldn't have thrown away his current diary," said Austin.

"No, his 1956 diary is probably still in his patrol car. Wherever that is."

"Would you mind if we looked through the ones you found?" said Henry.

"Not at all. Take the whole box."

ANNE WAS READING ON THE FRONT PORCH swing when Henry arrived at the Sharp residence at 6:00. "Hi, Anne," said Henry, carrying a box of apples across the sidewalk and up the narrow cement walkway.

"I'm so happy to see you, Henry. Where did you get those beautiful apples?"

"I drove up to Paradise to meet with the captain the other day and saw this little stand on the side of the road. These are the best apples I've ever eaten. Even better than the ones we used to buy in Oak Glen down south."

"My parents will love you for it," said Anne. "Come over here and sit down on the swing with me."

Sycamores, bigleaf maples, and a giant valley oak shaded half of the Sharp family's one-acre backyard. The other half contained a variety of mature fruit trees and scattered residuals from June Sharp's once-thriving vegetable garden. "Henry, would you like to walk out and pick a couple tomatoes with me?" said June, a forty-four-year-old version of Anne with shorter hair and strikingly attractive in her own right.

"I'd love to," said Henry. "I'm surprised you still have tomatoes in September."

"A few tomatoes and some butternut squash," said June. "About this time every year, the deer come across the road from the park and glean what's left of the garden."

"I see that."

"We don't mind sharing with the deer, as long as they leave Dave's fruit trees alone."

"Those trees look pretty healthy to me. Looks like peach, nectarine, cherry, and . . . is that an apricot?"

"You seem to know your fruit trees, Henry."

"My parents have a small farm in Temecula."

"Anne told me that. You're the subject of a lot of her conversations."

"I hope that's a good thing. I think the world of your daughter."

"Mom," shouted Monica, Anne's youngest sister, "Dad wants to know if he should start the barbeque."

"She feels the same way about you, Henry."

"Mom!"

"I heard you, Monica. Tell your father to go ahead. The chicken is in the refrigerator. I'll be there in a minute."

While June and Anne prepared the salad, Dave Sharp, a tall, thin man in his late forties, peppered Henry with questions about everything from Henry's ultimate career goals to fishing. An avid fly fisherman, Dave owned a drift boat, a skiff, and two canoes. He used the drift boat on the Sacramento River while maintaining the skiff and both canoes at the family's Lake Almanor cabin. "People like Almanor for its trout fishing," said Dave, "but I've caught some nice smallmouth bass in that lake."

"I haven't had the opportunity to get up to Almanor yet," said Henry, "but I've heard a lot about it."

"Do you like to fish, Henry? I bet being a game warden, you know where most of the good fishing spots are. I remember one time I was about to release a nice steelhead over on the Sacramento River, downstream from Scotty's Landing. I was hangin' over the gunnel of my drift boat, when I looked up and saw that old game warden who used to be around here. He was hidin' in the bushes above the riverbank, watching me with binoculars."

"Wha'd ya do?" said Henry, laughing.

"I waved to him."

"How did he react?"

"I must have embarrassed him, because he ducked out of sight and I never saw him again."

"I think I know who you're talking about. He retired seven or eight years ago. Tom Austin is the current Chico district warden. He's a great guy and a good friend of mine."

When the dinner dishes had been washed and put away, Henry and Anne took a stroll across the road to Bidwell Park. Coming to a bench on the shore of Big Chico Creek, Henry asked Anne if she'd like to sit and watch the sun go down.

"This looks like a great spot," said Anne.

"Anne, there's something I wanted to ask you."

"What's that, Henry?"

"Have you thought about where you'd like to teach after you get your credential?"

"Why do you ask?"

"I was wondering if you'd thought about Gridley. It's a wonderful little town, and they have a good school system. I've done some research."

"Gridley is thirty miles from Chico," said Anne, a coy smile on her face. "That would require a lot of driving."

"Well, not if you—"

"Henry, what is it you're trying to say?"

"If you lived in Gridley, you wouldn't have to drive so far."

"By any chance, is this a marriage proposal?"

"Yes!" said Henry, pulling a tiny box from his pocket. "I know this isn't the biggest diamond you've ever seen, but—"

"It's beautiful, Henry. I accept!"

Henry and Anne had both been blessed with an extra helping of common sense. Before walking back to Anne's house and telling her parents the news, they sat on the park bench for the next hour and discussed plans for what was to be a lengthy engagement. Since Anne was still almost two years away from earning her teaching credential, they decided that she would continue to live at home until the big day came.

TWENTY-THREE

W ARDEN HENRY GLANCE'S FIRST FULL YEAR on the job went by quickly. Between deer season, waterfowl season, pheasant season, trout season, salmon season, out-of-district assignments, and required training, he found little time to conduct a murder investigation. Glance did, however, set aside certain evenings every month for reading the thirty-one years of daily diaries Martha Bettis had given him. Beginning with the journal from 1924, the year Bettis was hired, Henry examined page after page, searching for clues to Norman Bettis's disappearance.

On the evening of April 26, 1970, Henry arrived home from an out-of-district assignment working the high lakes northeast of Stirling City. After showering and calling Anne, he sat down at his desk, turned on the reading lamp, and opened Norman Bettis's 1938 diary. Glance continued to read into the early morning hours, progressing through November and December of that year. That's when he noticed that Bettis's normally vague, unintelligible notes had become increasingly astute and easier to understand. According to Warden Bettis, federal wildlife agents had been conducting an undercover market-hunting investigation in and around the rice fields and wetlands of Butte, Glenn, and Colusa counties. He had been meeting weekly with the federal agents, keeping them abreast of the local gossip.

On Wednesday, December 14, 1938, Bettis wrote that he had received an anonymous telephone call. The caller said a Gridley resident named Dud Bogar was selling wild ducks to a turkey farm somewhere near Lincoln, California. Bettis indicated in his writings that he was familiar with Bogar and had suspected him of being a duck poacher since the first time he'd encountered him, in the early 1930s.

On Thursday, December 15, 1938, Bettis provided the information he'd learned about Dud Bogar to Federal Agent Walt Fletcher. On Thursday, December 22, 1938—three days before Christmas—Bettis wrote that he and Martha were coming out of King's Market in Gridley when he saw Dud Bogar talking to the Butler Farms delivery-truck driver. When Bogar spotted Bettis watching him, he abruptly ended the conversation and walked away.

After reading until almost daylight, Henry slept until 10:00 a.m. and awoke with a renewed confidence that he would eventually solve the mystery of Norman Bettis's disappearance. Later that day, April 27, 1970, he drove to the Butte County Sheriff's Office in Oroville. "See where the sign above the door says RECORDS?" said the sheriff's-office receptionist, pointing down the hallway. "Walk through that door and ask to speak with Lois Reed."

Henry introduced himself to Reed, who was working at the information counter when he entered the room. A gracious, middle-aged woman with short, dark hair, Lois had begun working for the sheriff's office just out of high school. During her twenty-five-year career in the records department, she had developed close working relationships with national, state, and local enforcement agencies throughout the United States.

"I have the serial number of a .30-30 rifle that was logged into the Sacramento Fish and Game office by Warden Norman Bettis in 1956," said Henry. "Any information you could come up with about this rifle and its original owner could prove helpful to the investigation I'm working on."

"Isn't Norm Bettis the warden who disappeared?" said Lois, continuing to thumb through a stack of files. "I remember all the commotion in the sheriff's office when that investigation was going on. Newspaper and television reporters were in here every day, asking for the latest scoop."

"Yes," said Henry. "Bettis's warden position has been left open all these years. Since I'm the warden who finally took his place, I feel compelled to find some answers to his disappearance."

"I see," said Lois, staring at the fledgling wildlife officer in his crisp new uniform. "And you're going to crack the case that every detective in Northern California couldn't?"

"I'm just trying to tie up a few loose ends," said Henry. "Ya never know where they might lead."

"Are you having any success?"

"A little."

"I remember Norm Bettis coming in here about once a week. The first words out of his mouth were, 'Is the coffee hot?' He and the previous sheriff were fishing buddies."

"Interesting."

"By the way, over in Archives, we have a file cabinet full of information about that investigation. Any time you want to go through it, let me know. Meanwhile, I'll see what I can do with this serial number you gave me. Where can I reach you?"

"Today's actually my day off, so you'll be able to reach me at home. I should be there for the rest of the day."

AFTER MEETING WITH LOIS at the sheriff's office, Henry sat on his shaded front porch and slogged through ten more years of Norm Bettis's diaries. Bettis had become considerably less productive during most of the 1940s, with few items of interest to write about.

"Here's something," said Henry, coming to the page labeled November 14, 1948:

> Today I caught Dud Bogar's kid and two others in Jeb
> Riddle's packing shed with an overlimit of pheasants.
> Hollis is as big as his old man, and, from the looks of it,
> just as dumb.

Dud Bogar was mentioned in Bettis's diaries for the last time on December 12, 1954:

> I read in this morning's paper that Ardis "Dud" Bogar
> passed away.

The phone on Henry Glance's kitchen wall rang at 2:00 p.m. "Hello," said Henry.

"Is this Warden Glance?"

"Yes, it is."

"This is Lois at the Butte County Sheriff's Office."

"Yes, Lois. Thank you for getting back to me. Were you able to come up with anything?"

"The rifle was reported stolen in 1957, by its owner, Tucker Clement Stillwell."

"Really?" said Henry.

"If Mr. Stillwell is still living, he's ninety-two years old. His date of birth is July 13, 1877. The only address given for him is General Delivery, Kingfisher, Oklahoma."

"That's strange."

"Why is it strange?"

"Norm Bettis logged the rifle into our Sacramento office in 1956. It stayed there until it was sold at auction in 1966. Why would it be reported stolen in 1957?"

"Your guess is as good as mine. The record shows that the rifle was a special edition, lever-action Winchester with special engraving. That's all I could come up with."

"It gives me a place to start," said Henry. "Thanks so much for the help."

"Any time. Drop in and see me if you want to look at the investigation files over in Archives."

Henry telephoned the Kingfisher, Oklahoma, post office. He learned that Stillwell was a familiar name in Kingfisher. The postmaster refused to tell Henry anything else over the phone. After hanging up, Henry telephoned the Oklahoma Department of Wildlife Conservation and asked to speak with the game warden whose patrol district covered Kingfisher. "That would be Luke Haskins in Blaine," said the dispatcher. "If you give me your number, I'll have Warden Haskins call you."

Tuesday morning at 6:00, Henry's phone rang. Normally, he would have been up and around, but it was his day off and he had stayed up reading Bettis's diaries until after midnight. "Good morning, Beverly," he said, rubbing his eyes.

"Uh, this isn't Beverly," came a male voice on the other end of the line. "This is Warden Luke Haskins in Oklahoma. Is this Warden Hank Glance?"

"Yes," said Henry, now wide awake. "If anyone calls at this hour, it's usually the sheriff's graveyard-shift dispatcher."

"A likely story," said Haskins, laughing. "I forgot y'all were in a different time zone."

"No problem. I'm just glad you called."

"What can I do for ya?"

"Do you have a few minutes? This may take a while."

"I can't think of anything I'd rather be doin' right now. You talk, and I'll listen."

Kindred spirits, Henry Glance and Luke Haskins carried on their conversation for over an hour. Before getting down to the business at hand, Henry asked Haskins about his background and how he liked being an Oklahoma wildlife officer.

Twenty-three-year-old Haskins had entered the University of Oklahoma on a partial baseball scholarship, intending to become a pharmacist, like his father. "I couldn't handle all those chemistry classes and play baseball at the same time," said Haskins, "so I switched my major to liberal studies, with an emphasis on criminal justice. About three years ago, I took the warden's exam, and here I am."

"What position did you play?"

"Game warden."

"No, I mean on the baseball field."

"I knew what you meant," said Haskins, laughing. "I played catcher."

"Did you start for U of O?"

"No. I was good enough to make the team but spent most of my college baseball career warming up pitchers in the bullpen. What about you?"

"I pitched two years for Riverside City College and was offered a scholarship to play for Stanford but ended up breaking my left wrist. That was the end of my baseball career."

"That's too bad. I bet you were pretty disappointed."

"I was devastated at the time, but things turned out better than I expected."

"How's that?"

"I ended up graduating from a great four-year school in Northern California, meeting the love of my life, and becoming a Fish and Game warden. Knowing what I know now, I wouldn't change a thing."

Getting down to business, Glance told Haskins the story of Warden Norman Bettis's mysterious disappearance. It was Haskins's assignment, should he decide to accept it, to go to Kingfisher, find out if Tucker Stillwell or any of his relatives were still around, and learn as much as he could about the person who stole the .30-30 rifle.

Haskins snickered.

"Why are you laughing?" said Henry.

"Do you have any other names you'd like me to check out?"

"Two others. Why?"

"Would either of them be Bogar?" Haskins heard Henry drop the phone.

"Luke, is there something you'd like to tell me?"

"The Stillwells and the Bogars have been poaching deer, bear, ducks, quail, squirrels, rabbits, paddlefish, and every other critter in these parts since way before I was born."

"Are the Stillwells and the Bogars related?"

"They're related all right. A bunch of 'em live over in Kingfisher. Another part of the clan lives in Watonga. And a few live up here in Blaine, where I am. Every time I get a call about somebody jacklightin' deer in the middle of the night, it turns out to be a Stillwell, a Bogar, or both. There must be fifty of 'em, and they're all related."

"Well, just so you know, the other two folks I'd like you to check out are Ardis Bogar and his son, Hollis Bogar. Ardis apparently went by the nickname of Dud."

"That figures," said Haskins. "I'll do some nosin' around and see what I can come up with. I might take Sam Turner with me. He's a veteran warden who's chased these outlaws around for years and may know one or two of 'em willing to talk to us."

Henry heard back from Luke Haskins three days later, on Friday evening, May 1, 1970. "Hank, buddy, I got some information for ya."

"That's great, Luke. I can't wait to hear it."

"This afternoon, Sam Turner and I drove to Kingfisher and spoke with Grandma Stillwell. Sam said she was the matriarch of the Stillwell clan and the only one likely to tell us anything. Those folks do not like law enforcement, especially game wardens. We drove down a dirt road, passed a couple keep-out signs, and came to a half-dozen shacks out in the pucker brush. It was just like on *Hee Haw*: chickens runnin' around and a hound dog sleepin' on the front porch. Grandma Stillwell was out there on the porch with the dog, sittin' in a rockin' chair."

"Was she willing to talk to you?"

"Grandma Stillwell, whose name is Emma, turned out to be the sweetest little thing you'd ever wanna meet. She told us everything we wanted to know, and more."

"I'm anxious to hear all about it."

"Okay," said Haskins. "Stop me if I go too fast. Tucker Stillwell was Emma's husband for over seventy years. He passed away two years ago, at the age of ninety. One of Tucker's prized possessions was a Winchester .30-30 rifle that he kept in a leather case, hidden under the bed."

"The one I told you about, with the fancy engraving?"

"That's the one. Revis Stillwell was Tucker's and Emma's second son. He married Loretta Bogar. Revis and Loretta had a son they named Ferlin, after their favorite country singer, Ferlin Husky. Small for his age, Ferlin grew up fightin', stealin', and gettin' in trouble. He hated being called Ferlin, so everyone called him Richie, seein' that his middle name was Richard."

"I'm following you so far."

"Good," said Haskins. "Ardis Bogar, known to friends and family as Dud, was Loretta Stillwell's older brother. At the age of twenty-five, he was workin' on a chain gang over in Guthrie when he escaped and ran off to California. Dud would later marry a woman named Virginia, who left him two years later with a stack of bills and a son named Hollis."

"What about the rifle?"

"I'm gettin' to that. Richie Stillwell had always admired his grandpa's fancy rifle. One day, Tucker reached under the bed to get his rifle, and it was gone."

"Did she say when that was?"

"I asked her, and she said it was either 1954 or 1955, but Tucker never reported it stolen until two or three years later."

"Why did he wait so long to report it?"

"I asked her that too. She said a Stillwell would never snitch on another Stillwell. Apparently, ol' Tucker felt that enough time had passed and Richie had probably sold the rifle or lost it somehow. Just in case the law ended up with it, Tucker wanted it back."

"Any idea where Richie Stillwell is now?"

"Grandma said Richie came back from California just before Christmas, in 1956. When he showed up at the house without the rifle, Tucker told Emma to send him away. A week later, they heard that Richie had robbed a gas station in Oklahoma City and killed the attendant. Emma said her grandson Richie died in the electric chair two years later. I checked on that and found out Ferlin Richard Stillwell was executed at Oklahoma State Prison in 1958."

"Luke, were you able to find out anything about Hollis Bogar?"

"Jeb and I talked to Loretta Stillwell about her nephew Hollis. She said nobody's heard anything about him since Dud passed away."

"I can't thank you enough," said Henry. "If there's anything I can ever do for you, please give me a call."

"I will," said Luke. "Please let me know if you crack that case. You have my phone number. I'll be sure to mail you the documentation on Stillwell."

TWENTY-FOUR

IT WAS MID-AUGUST 1970 WHEN ANNE RETURNED from Plumas-Eureka State Park, where she and her friend Sara had spent their third summer working as seasonal employees. Excited to see her future husband, she dropped Sara off in Chico and raced down Highway 99 to Henry's rented farmhouse outside Gridley.

Henry and Anne spent a couple of hours getting reacquainted and had dinner in town before venturing out on Henry's front porch to watch the sun go down. "This is where I spend most of my time when I'm not working," said Henry. "That noisy old swamp cooler doesn't work so well when it's this hot and humid."

"It's nice out here," said Anne. "I can feel a breeze coming from that alfalfa field."

"That's because they just irrigated. I slept out here on the porch most of July, thinking about you up there in the mountains."

"Wasn't it uncomfortable sleeping on this splintery old porch?"

"Not at all. I just blew up my air mattress, covered it with a sheet, and brought out my pillow. Next thing I knew, it was daylight and Molly was licking my face."

"Molly? Who's Molly?"

"Molly is the neighbor's black Lab. She trots down here every morning about the time Glen Darby turns on the barn lights and begins milking his cows. She visits for a while, then I give her a treat and send her back home."

"Will she be here in the morning, before I leave?"

"What time are you leaving?"

"I have a meeting with my teaching supervisor at 10:00, so I'll have to leave for Chico by 7:30. I want to go home first and change clothes."

"Anne, are you going to mind living here for a while after we get married? I know this old farmhouse is pretty run down, but will it do until we can afford a place of our own?"

"Henry, as long as I'm with you, I can live anywhere. Besides, I like being out here in the country. It's so peaceful."

"You might think differently when Darby's rooster starts crowing at four o'clock in the morning."

"I want our life together to be one big adventure, Henry."

"I have a feeling it will be, Anne."

ANNE HAD LEFT FOR CHICO AT 7:30, and Henry was about to open the barn door when the phone rang. "That's probably the captain," said Henry. "He calls like clockwork, every Monday morning. Come on, Molly. I'll give you a dog biscuit, then you have to go home." Running up the back steps and into the kitchen, Henry answered, "Good morning, Chuck. I think it's gonna be another hot one today."

"Not where I am," said the familiar voice on the other end of the line. "It's colder than a well-driller's ass in December here in Bozeman."

"Is this Gary?" said Henry, laughing.

"It sure as hell is," said Gary Lytle, Henry's college friend from Mrs. Iverson's basement.

"Anne and I were just talking about you last night, Gary. How do you like living in Montana?"

"The wind blows all the time, but I'm getting used to it. Speaking of Anne, did you guys tie the knot yet?"

"We're leaning toward next May, when she gets her teaching credential."

"Are you gonna have a wedding?"

"If we do, you'll be one of the first people we invite."

"I'll look forward to that, Hank. You and Anne are two of my favorite people. I don't know anyone I trust more than you. That's one of the reasons I'm calling."

"I appreciate your saying that, Gary. Is your outfitter business going well?"

"My dad has had some health problems, so he turned it completely over to me."

"Nothing like jumping right into the fire. What does that involve?"

"I book clients, arrange trips, buy supplies, and make sure everyone gets paid, while our three foremen take care of the dudes."

"Dudes?"

"That's what our horse handlers call clients. Hank, do you have a few minutes? There's something serious I'd like to talk to you about."

"I've got all day, Gary."

"If anything comes of this, after you hear what I have to say, I want it understood that I'll only deal with you."

"I guess you better tell me what's on your mind. This does sound serious."

"Last season, we took this wealthy oil executive from Piedmont, Oklahoma, and his twenty-two-year-old son on a Rocky Mountain bighorn hunt in Colorado. The oil executive's name is Winthrop Thaddeus Burnside, if you can believe that. He told us to call him Thad."

"What is it about Oklahoma?"

"Excuse me?"

"It's a long story, Gary. I'll tell you about it some other time. Was the bighorn hunt successful?"

"It was. Our client bagged a Boone and Crockett class trophy ram. Mr. Burnside had previously killed a stone sheep in British Columbia and a Dall sheep in Alaska. After killing that big Rocky Mountain ram in Colorado, he became obsessed with the idea of killing a desert bighorn and completing what they call a grand slam."

"I'm familiar with that," said Henry.

"That's all this guy and his son talked about all the way back down the mountain. They must have asked five times if we could arrange a desert bighorn hunt."

"What did you tell 'em?"

"I told 'em we weren't licensed in Arizona or Nevada and I didn't think California allowed desert bighorn hunts. That's when Beau Burnside, Thad's son, started whining about how difficult it was to get drawn for a sheep hunt and couldn't we pull a few strings. Some of these wealthy clients are used to getting their way and don't like taking no for an answer."

"So, did you pull a few strings?"

"I didn't, but I found out later that my foreman Ray Sutton had given Beau the name and phone number of a guide he knew in Arizona."

"What's this guide's name?"

"His name is Porter Sledge, but Ray says he goes by Sonny."

"Is Sledge a legitimate licensed guide or just an outlaw friend of your foreman's?"

"I suspect the latter."

"I'm all ears, Gary."

"This morning, I received a phone call from Beau Burnside. Beau tells me his father turns sixty in September and he's arranged a desert bighorn hunt with this Sledge character as a surprise birthday gift."

"Sounds like trouble to me."

"I'm thinkin', I hope you didn't send him any money."

"Did he?"

"What do you think? Sledge wanted a five-thousand-dollar deposit, so Beau sent him a check. The hunt is scheduled for the third week in September."

"Did Sledge ask Beau who had referred him? That's usually a clue as to whether or not this guy is a legitimate guide."

"Sledge did ask, and Beau told him he got his name and number from Ray Sutton. After hearing Ray's name, Sledge became quite accommodating."

"This is becoming more interesting all the time. What happened next?"

"As it turns out, Thad Burnside has been working on this big oil deal in Saudi Arabia and will be out of the country the third week in September."

"Did Beau ask for his deposit back?"

"He did, and what do you think Sledge's answer was?"

"Sledge told him his deposit was nonrefundable."

"You guessed it. Sledge said Beau was welcome to come in his father's place but the check had already been cashed and the money spent."

"Did Beau press the issue?"

"He did, and Sledge essentially told him to pound sand down a rat hole. According to Beau, Sledge sounded like he was drunk."

"What does this Beau expect you to do?"

"Since Ray Sutton works for Big Sky Outfitters and Guide Service and he turned Beau onto Sledge, Beau thinks it's our responsibility to somehow get his money back. I thought about hanging up on him, then I remembered you were a game warden and might be interested in this."

"Arizona and Nevada are out of my jurisdiction, Gary."

"I figured that, but you may feel differently when you hear the rest of the story."

"You mean there's more?"

"A lot more. I asked Beau to give me a day or two to try to come up with something. Then I called Ray Sutton and told him to meet me in my office."

"What kind of person is Ray Sutton?"

"Ray's a decent, hardworking cowboy who hasn't always used the best judgment. I told him if he wanted to keep his job, he'd better come clean and tell me everything he knows about Sonny Sledge. Ray got married recently and his wife is pregnant, so the prospect of losing his job got his immediate attention."

"I bet it did."

"About a year and a half ago, Ray met Sledge in Las Vegas for a weekend of gambling, drinking, and who knows what else. They got drunk one night and Sledge spilled his guts about this little side business he's been running. Sledge is a part-time mechanic and lives in Bullhead City, Arizona; Bullhead City is twenty miles from Needles, California. Every chance Sledge gets, he goes exploring in the mountains outside of Needles. Ray gave me the names of the mountains, and I wrote them down. There's the Providence Mountains, the Old Woman Mountains, and the Turtle Mountains. All of them contain bighorn sheep. Sledge knows where the springs and water holes in these mountains are located. During the hot summers, the sheep must come to water, and that's when they're easy pickings. Those were Sledge's words, according to Ray."

"Interesting," said Henry.

"There's more," said Lytle. "Sledge has an associate who lives two blocks from the Needles game warden and monitors his every move. The warden is an older man who maintains a predictable schedule. His days off are Mondays and Tuesdays so that's when Sledge and his partner conduct their dirty business."

"What about taxidermy work? Does Sledge arrange to have his clients' trophies mounted?"

"I asked Ray about that. He said Sledge's partner is an expert skinner. He capes the rams in nothing flat, and they drag the carcasses out in the creosote for the buzzards to feast on. Sledge is apparently in cahoots with an outlaw taxidermist in Las Vegas named Kurt Schuler. Schuler has a shop in Las Vegas but apparently does his real work in an old warehouse. Sledge didn't tell Ray where the warehouse was but hinted that it was north of the city. He also told Ray he's seen everything from polar bears to Siberian tigers in Schuler's warehouse. Schuler has five or six Mexican laborers doing the skinning and grunt work for him. Since they're in the country illegally, he pays them next to nothing."

"Sounds like Ray is a wealth of information, but can we trust him?"

"I told Ray if this thing goes sideways, we'll know why and he can count on being fired. He said Sledge already called to ask about Burnside. Ray said he recommended him, that's all. He assured me that he wouldn't spill the beans. If Sledge calls again, he'll play along with whatever I tell him to say. Ray's wife doesn't want him to have anything to do with Sledge, anyway."

"I have an idea," said Henry. "Why don't you call Beau back and ask if he'd be willing to speak with me. Go ahead and tell him I'm a California game warden."

"I can do that," said Lytle. "Come to think of it, you two have something in common."

"What's that?"

"Baseball. Beau played for the University of Oklahoma. I think he said he was a pitcher."

That afternoon, Henry dialed the Oklahoma phone number Gary Lytle had given him.

"Burnside Oil," said a female receptionist.

"Yes, may I speak to Mr. Burnside, please?"

"Winthrop or Beauregard?"

"Excuse me?"

"Would you like to speak with Winthrop Burnside or Beauregard Burnside?"

"Beauregard, please."

"I'll see if he's in."

"Mr. Burnside's office, Jeanie speaking," said a young woman with a soft Southern accent.

"Hello, this is Henry Glance. May I please speak with Mr. Burnside?"

"Yes, Mr. Glance. One moment please."

"This is Beau."

"Hello, Mr. Burnside. This is Warden Hank Glance from California. Gary Lytle said you were willing to talk to me about a hunting guide named Sonny Sledge."

"Yeah, that sonofabitch took my five-thousand-dollar deposit and refuses to return it."

Rather than jump right into the crux of the mater, Henry attempted to break the ice with a little friendly chitchat. "Gary tells me you played baseball for the University of Oklahoma."

"I did. How are you gonna get my money back from that drunken thief in Arizona?"

"What years did you play there?"

"What difference does it make? Sixty-six and sixty-seven."

"What position did you play?"

"Pitcher. Can we get on with this?"

"No kidding?" said Henry. "I was a pitcher too."

"Where, in Little League?"

"That's funny," said Henry, laughing.

"Look, Warden whatever-your-name-is. I'm a busy—"

"Hank Glance."

"I have an important meeting in a few minutes."

"Would you like me to call you back when you have more time?"

"Just a minute. Jeanie, call Jack and tell him I'm gonna be a few minutes late."

"Should I tell them to tee off without you?" said Jeanie.

"Just tell 'em something came up."

"Yes, Mr. Burnside."

"All right, Warden Hank Glance. I've canceled my meeting, so you have my complete attention."

"This Sledge character is bad news. Had your father gotten caught up in his dirty business, he could have been arrested and charged with some serious crimes. I can't promise to get your money back, but if you agree to help us, this could turn out to be one of the most exciting and worthwhile things you ever do."

"What would this involve?"

While Burnside listened, Henry spent the next twenty minutes explaining his plan for an undercover sting, using Burnside as a civilian operative.

"Normally, I would turn you down flat," said Burnside, "but the prospect of getting out of town for a while next month appeals to me. I just broke up with my girlfriend, and she won't leave me alone. Last night she showed up at my pad during a party and embarrassed the hell out of me. Have ya ever had that problem? Just a second. Jeanie, hold all my calls."

"No, can't say that I have."

"Sorry, what was I saying? I always lose my train of thought when she comes in the room."

"That's all right," said Glance. "You were saying that the thought of getting out of town in September appealed to you."

"Yeah. Why don't you give me a day or two to think about this."

"By the way, Mr. Burnside—"

"You can call me Beau. I was just being an asshole before."

"Beau, do you remember playing baseball with a catcher named Luke Haskins while you were at the University of Oklahoma?"

"Are you kidding? Luke and I were buddies. I was the fifth reliever on the team, and he was the second-string catcher. We spent a lot of time together, watching games from the bullpen. How do you know Luke?"

"He's a warden with the Oklahoma Department of Wildlife Conservation. I just spoke with him the other day."

"We haven't seen each other since graduation. If you talk to Luke again, please give him my best. Meanwhile, I guess you can count me in on this undercover scheme of yours."

Beau Burnside agreed to call Sledge and tell him he would take his father's place on the bighorn-sheep hunt. Accompanying Beau would be his twenty-two-year-old "cousin," Hank. "Don't call Sledge until I work things out with my supervisors," said Henry. "I'll call you back in a day or two."

Henry telephoned Captain Chuck Odom. After hearing what Henry had to say, Odom set up a meeting in Sacramento with California Department of Fish and Game (DFG) Region 2 Inspector Bill Matson and U.S. Fish and Wildlife Service (USFWS) Special Agent in Charge Roy Campbell. Intrigued by Henry's story, Agent Campbell contacted the Southern California USFWS special agent in charge, Gene Parnell. When asked if he knew anything about a Las Vegas taxidermist named Kurt Schuler, Parnell said his agents had been trying to find an opening into Schuler's illegal taxidermy operation for several years.

"This could be the break we've been looking for," said Parnell. "How soon can we set up a meeting with Warden Glance?"

Bill Matson arranged for Henry to be flown to Southern California the following morning by Region 2 Warden Pilot Lance "Snap Roll" Heinrich. The meeting was held in the Department of Fish and Game's Region 5 Office on Golden Shore Drive in Long Beach. Attending were DFG Region 5 Inspector John Stackhouse, DFG Patrol Captain Jim Granger, USFWS Special Agent in Charge Gene Parnell, USFWS Special Agent Eric Norris, and DFG Warden Henry Glance. Glance presented a detailed explanation of the situation, describing everything he'd learned about Sonny Sledge, taxidermist Kurt Schuler, and civilian undercover operative Beau Burnside.

"I'm impressed with the way you've taken the bull by the horns and run with this investigation so far," said Inspector Stackhouse, a forty-eight-year-old veteran of the Department of Fish and Game. How long have you been on the job, Henry? Is it Henry or Hank? I heard someone call you Hank."

"My name is Henry, but most of my friends call me Hank. If you count my time at the academy, I've been on the job a little over a year."

"Working undercover can be difficult and extremely dangerous. Do you think you can handle it?" said Stackhouse.

"I was wondering the same thing," said Captain Granger. "He's just a kid. How old are you, anyway?"

"I'll be twenty-three in November."

"I rest my case," said Granger. "Do we want to commit this much time, money, and personnel to an investigation run by a twenty-two-year-old kid with a year on the job?"

"Let him answer the question," said Stackhouse. "Go ahead, Hank."

"I'm confident I can handle it," said Henry. "The success of this investigation may depend on Beau Burnside. He and I have developed a pretty good rapport over the phone, and I'm not sure he would be willing to work with anyone else. The original informant is a friend of mine, whom I've known since college. He said right from the start that he and his foreman, Ray Sutton, would only deal with me. If Sutton were to tip off Sledge, the case would go south in a hurry."

The room was quiet. Finally, Agent Parnell spoke up. "We've been trying to get something on Kurt Schuler for several years now. Based on the uncorroborated information we have, this man is doing business with illegal operators all over the world. Who knows when another opportunity like this will come along? I say we put our money on Hank here and go for it. We're willing to put up the money for the hunt and allocate as many officers as we need. You California boys are deputized to enforce federal wildlife laws, but you're still going to need us if this investigation leads into Arizona and Nevada."

Inspector Stackhouse instructed Henry to set up the hunt and report back to him as soon as possible. Fortunately, Beau Burnside had learned the art of bullshitting from his oil-executive father. Minutes into a phone conversation with Sonny Sledge, Beau had Sledge eating out of his hand. "Give me a call when you and your cousin get into Bullhead City," said Sledge. "Don't worry about motel reservations. I'll take care a that for ya."

"We're not used to staying in fleabag motels," said Burnside, "so don't book us into some dump."

"Oh, no," said Sledge, sounding tipsy. "This is a real nice place, right on the river."

The hunt was scheduled to take place on Monday, September 14 and Tuesday, September 15, 1970. Burnside agreed to bring his own rifle. Water and other provisions would be supplied by Sledge and the man Sledge described as his associate.

"My cousin lives in San Bernardino, so I'll be flying into Ontario Airport and riding with him to Bullhead City," said Burnside. "We should be there by seven o'clock on Sunday evening."

"One more thing," said Sledge.

"What's that?"

"I'm gonna need another five thousand ta complete the deal and arrange for the taxidermy work."

"I'll bring the money," said Burnside, "but I better kill a trophy ram, or you're not getting another penny. That's what you promised the first time I called, and I'm gonna hold you to it."

"Don't worry," said Sledge. "If you can hit the broad side of a barn at fifty yards, you'll get your trophy ram. I've got one all picked out for ya."

Burnside telephoned Henry after ending his conversation with Sledge. "Everything is set up," he said. "I was skeptical about this idea at first, but I'm becoming more excited about it all the time."

"I'll work out the logistics and get back to you," said Henry.

With the trap set, Henry contacted Inspector Stackhouse. Stackhouse advised the federal agents and set in motion legal provisions for Beau Burnside or Warden Henry Glance to take one fully protected California desert bighorn sheep during the undercover investigation.

A coordination meeting was scheduled for Saturday afternoon, September 12, at the Long Beach Fish and Game office. Henry arranged for Beau Burnside to fly into Orange County Airport early that afternoon. Flying from Sacramento, Henry arrived ahead of Burnside and met him at baggage claim.

"How was your trip?" said Henry.

"I had to change planes once, but I got to see the Pacific Ocean before we landed."

"That makes it all worthwhile. A warden is waiting outside to take us to the Long Beach Fish and Game office."

TWENTY-FIVE

"THIS IS INCREDIBLE," said Inspector Stackhouse, as Henry Glance and Beau Burnside walked through the conference-room door. "You two look so much alike, you could be brothers."

Born six months apart, Henry and Beau were remarkably similar in appearance: both six-feet-one, athletically built, with dishwater-blond hair trimmed just over the tops of their ears.

It took three hours to review all the details of the investigation and make sure everyone was on the same page. Since the hunt would take place in an isolated desert location, it was going to be impossible to provide immediate backup. Glance and Burnside would have to rely on quick wits and good judgment to carry off their ruse.

Captain Granger handed Henry the keys to a jet-black, 1970 Chevrolet Chevelle that had been seized by the Los Angeles County drug task force, forfeited by the court, and signed over to the Department of Fish and Game for undercover use. It was equipped with a radio hidden inside the locked glove box and a set of civilian license plates.

"It's a good thing this air conditioner works," said Henry, as they passed through Barstow and headed east on Interstate 40 toward Needles.

"Have you ever been to Oklahoma in the summertime?" said Beau. "Temperatures can be in the eighties and you're so hot you can't breathe."

Just beyond Ludlow, Henry pointed out a road that led south from I-40. "Do you remember a TV show called *Route 66*?"

"Are you kidding? I never missed an episode. When I turned sixteen, my daddy bought me a Corvette convertible just like the one Martin Milner and George Maharis drove on the show."

"The original Route 66 runs south on that road up ahead and passes an old ghost town called Danby. South of Danby are the Old Woman Mountains, where we may be hunting tomorrow."

"You're a regular walking encyclopedia, Hank."

"I've been told that before."

Glance and Burnside had traveled east for another fifty miles when they came to the intersection of Highway 40 and Essex Road. "If we were to go north on that road," said Glance, "we'd eventually come to the Providence Mountains. That's another place where we may be hunting tomorrow."

"Didn't you mention a third mountain range at the meeting yesterday?"

"I did. The Turtle Mountains are about forty miles south of Needles, off Highway 95. We don't know which mountain range Sledge plans to hunt, so our department will have backup officers staged somewhere near all of them."

"What about the federal agents? How do they fit in?"

"Here's how it works. California Fish and Game wardens are state peace officers, authorized to enforce any state law or local ordinance in the state of California. We are also commissioned by the U.S. Fish and Wildlife Service to enforce federal fish and wildlife laws listed in Title 50 of the *Code of Federal Regulations*. We can cross state lines under certain circumstances, but it's not a common practice. Bottom line, the feds will take over as the investigation extends into Arizona and Nevada."

"I'm glad I asked," said Beau, laughing. "Are you as hungry as I am?"

"You sound like my friend Larry. We'll be in Needles in another half hour. Why don't we eat there before heading up to Bullhead City?"

After grabbing a bite to eat in Needles, Glance and Burnside crossed the Colorado River bridge into Arizona and drove north to Bullhead City. Arriving shortly after 7:00 p.m., Henry gassed up the car while Beau dropped a dime in the pay phone and called Sledge.

"I was wonderin' when you was gonna get here," said Sledge, his words slurred.

"I told you we'd arrive about 7:00," said Beau. "It's 7:15 now."

"Stay where you are. I'll be down after I throw on a shirt and some shoes."

Driving a light-gray, 1965 Ford Bronco blanketed in dust, Sledge met Glance and Burnside at the gas station and led them to a fifties-era motor inn on the eastern shore of the Colorado River. "This here's where you'll be spendin' the night," said Sledge, a beady-eyed little man in his mid-forties wearing cutoff jeans, a dirt-stained tank top, and leather sandals. Sledge dropped the tailgate, reached into an ice chest, and pulled out three cold beers. He and his would-be clients stood in the shade of a mesquite tree and discussed the next day's hunt. "What part of Oklahoma is you boys from?"

"I live near Oklahoma City," said Beau.

"I haven't lived in Oklahoma since I was a kid," said Henry. "San Bernardino's where I live now."

"Did ya remember ta bring your rifle?" said Sledge. "These big rams are hard ta bring down, so ya need somethin' with a punch."

"I brought my daddy's 30.06, like I told ya I would," said Beau.

"That's good," said Sledge. "I'll bring along my rife, just in case."

"Just in case what?"

"Just in case ya don't kill him on the first shot. We don't want no wounded sheep runnin' around the desert. It's bad for business, if ya know what I mean."

"Where we gonna be huntin'?" said Henry, hoping to alert the back-up team.

"I'll tell ya that in the mornin'," said Sledge, "after we meet up with my partner." Sledge pulled another beer from the ice chest, closed the tailgate, and hopped into his Bronco. "Get a good night's sleep, gentlemen. Five o'clock comes early."

That night, Henry called his contact, U.S. Fish and Wildlife Special Agent Eric Norris, and provided the description and license number of Sonny Sledge's Ford Bronco. He also gave Norris the name and location of the Bullhead City motel where he and Burnside would be staying.

When the sun came up on the morning of September 14, 1970, Palo Verde Warden Andy Howard and Needles Warden Dave Finch were in position off old Route 66, near Danby. They had chosen this location in case Sledge planned to hunt the Old Woman Mountains. Long Beach Marine Warden Jack Mayberry and Baker Warden Jeff Mitchell were staked out north of Interstate 40, with a clear view of Essex Road, should Sledge plan to hunt the Providence Mountains. Forty miles south of Needles, near the four-wheel-drive road into Mopah Springs and the Turtle Mountains, sat Blythe Warden Rich Calloway and Parker Dam Warden Mark Rollins.

Sledge picked up Glance and Burnside at 5:00 a.m. and drove to a coffee shop in Needles. Pushing open the fingerprint-smudged glass door, Henry and Beau were greeted by a blast of cigarette smoke and a forty-nine-year-old beanpole, introduced by Sledge as his partner, Clem Beasley.

"What do you do when you're not traipsing around the desert?" said Glance, sitting at the breakfast table across from Sledge and Beasley.

"I sell Indian crafts to the snowbirds during the winter months," said Beasley. "I'm half Chemehuevi, ya know."

"No kidding?" said Beau, holding back a chuckle. Although Beasley's skin was the color and texture of boot leather, and his shoulder-length gray hair was tied in a ponytail, Beau suspected that their garrulous guide had no more Native American blood flowing through his veins than the customers he swindled with his Taiwanese trinkets and doodads. Beasley chattered nonstop during breakfast and all the way to the Highway 95 Turtle Mountains turnoff.

"Wow!" said Henry, marveling at a pair of imposing, rocky spires in the distance.

"The far one is Mopah Peak," said Beasley, sitting in the back seat next to Glance. "Some people call it Mexican Hat. It's a thousand feet high and straight up. There's a spring near the base, and that's where we're headed."

Sledge's Bronco rumbled through three miles of rocks, soft sand, and ancient creosotes before coming to a stop near the mouth of a desert wash. "We walk from here," said Sledge.

Henry kept his eyes open and his mouth shut for most of the three-mile hike up the sandy, rock-strewn wash to Mopah Springs. Having read extensively about Sonoran Desert flora and fauna, he silently celebrated sightings of palo verde, barrel cactus, mesquite, and smoke tree. As the morning progressed and sunshine peeked over the adjacent hillsides, reptiles began to appear. Lightning-fast zebra-tailed lizards darted from one prickly bush to another, while whiptails slinked slowly across the sand like miniature dinosaurs. At one point, Henry stopped to admire a horned lizard sunning itself on a nearby rock.

"Better keep movin' if we're gonna get there before the sheep come down from the mountain," said Sledge.

"How do you know they'll come down from the mountain?" said Beau.

"They gotta come down for water," said Beasley. "And we'll be a-waitin' for 'em."

Approaching the base of the mountain, Sledge cautioned Glance and Burnside to keep quiet and follow his lead. He led them to a group of smaller crags overlooking a well-traveled sheep trail. The trail extended from the treacherously steep mountainside to a grove of desert fan palms. "Sometime during the next three hours, a band of desert bighorns will climb down from that mountain and come to the spring for water," whispered Sledge. "The other day we saw three young rams and a full-curl granddaddy with 'em."

"The spring is at the base of those palm trees," whispered Beasley. "It's no bigger than a washtub, but every critter within five miles comes here to drink at one time or another."

It was a few minutes after 10:00 when Sledge scanned the sunlit east face of the magnificent volcanic peak and noticed movement amongst the jagged, gray-and-red-colored rocks. "Here they come," he whispered. "It's almost impossible to see 'em way up in those rocks unless ya know what you're lookin' for."

An hour after Sledge had first spotted the band of sheep climbing down the sheer spire, seven sheep appeared in the open and made their way to the spring. "Looks like they're all ewes," whispered Beau.

"Don't worry," whispered Beasley, "the rams won't be far behind."

"I think I see one now," said Henry. "He just walked out onto that lowest ledge."

"Sure is," said Beasley, focusing his binoculars. "That's the granddaddy Sonny was talkin' about. Don't he look proud, posin' there like he's king a the world?"

"I see three smaller rams in the shade, just below him," said Sledge. "Beau, I want you to quietly rack a cartridge into the chamber and lock the bolt in place. Stay low, and don't even think about shootin' until I give you the word. I'll tell you when it's time. We're downwind, so they shouldn't be able to smell us."

All seven ewes had drunk their fill and were heading back up the mountain when the rams walked out of the rocks and ventured toward the spring. The younger rams stepped aside and let the dominant, full-curled ram drink first. Kicking and butting, the others jostled for position behind him. When the big ram had finished drinking, he turned and slowly walked up the trail from which he'd come. "He'll stop in a minute to smell the air," whispered Sledge. "That's when you'll take him. Put the crosshairs right behind his shoulder."

Resting his left shoulder on the large rock he hid behind, Beau

Burnside took a deep breath, let it out slowly, and gently squeezed off the trigger. *KA-BOOOOM* came a resounding blast that could be heard by Warden Rollins, three miles away. Beau hit his mark and the ram dropped dead in his tracks. Before Henry could compliment Burnside on his marksmanship, Beasley and Sledge were dragging the carcass into the shade of some nearby rocks. "The sooner we get this big boy caped out, the cleaner the mount is gonna be," said Beasley. "It don't take long in this heat for the hair to start slippin' and the hide to go bad."

Henry and Beau watched as Beasley took a razor-sharp skinning knife from his canvas backpack and began cutting through the ram's hide. Almost sickened by the sight, Henry reminded himself that by taking this single bighorn and building a case against these two money-grubbing criminals, he and fellow officers would save countless other animals. Should they find and arrest Kurt Schuler, the Las Vegas taxidermist, the investigation would be a resounding success.

Like a surgeon, Beasley completed the process by sawing through the ram's eye sockets and disconnecting a set of twenty-pound horns from the skull. When he'd finished, Sledge instructed Henry and Beau to help him drag the carcass away from the spring and into a nearby wash. "In a week, this carcass will be completely eaten by the critters," said Sledge. "Nobody will be the wiser."

By 2:15, Sledge's Bronco was back on Highway 95 and headed north toward Needles. Warden Rollins watched them pass from a hidden location on the east side of Highway 95. When the Bronco was out of sight, Rollins signaled Calloway to pick him up. Calloway radioed Agent Norris that the subjects were headed north, toward Needles, and a shot had been fired. Together, Calloway and Rollins drove across the highway and followed Sledge's Bronco tracks.

Reaching the wash where Sledge and the others had parked, Calloway grabbed his camera and both wardens began the arduous hike to Mopah Springs. They were a quarter mile from their destination when Rollins spotted the first turkey vulture. Soon, more than a dozen birds circled the carcass. After chasing a coyote away, Calloway photographed the sheep while Rollins took tissue samples.

Meanwhile, Sledge dropped Beasley off at the restaurant parking lot in Needles. With the cape safely stashed inside a cooler and the horns wrapped in a black plastic garbage bag, Sledge, Glance, and Burnside headed back to Bullhead City. Sledge had no way of knowing that the minute he crossed over the Colorado River into Arizona—with an unlawfully taken bighorn sheep, for which he had already been paid $5,000—he'd violated the federal Lacey Act and committed what could be classified as a felony.

Arriving at the motel, Sledge pressed Beau Burnside for the other $5,000. Beau paid him in cash with investigation money provided by Agent Parnell.

"How soon are you going to get my ram to the taxidermist?" said Beau. "I don't want it to spoil."

"I'll have it to him today," said Sledge. "He's the best in the business, so I'm sure you'll be happy with his work. It's my understandin' that you want the mount shipped to your business address in Oklahoma?"

"That's right," said Beau. "Ship it to the address I wrote on the back of my card. How long will it take?"

"It may be a year or so before you get your mount."

"Who do I call to check on it?"

"Call me," said Sledge. "You have my number."

As Sledge drove away from the motel, Warden Glance quickly unlocked the Chevy Chevelle glove compartment and radioed Agent Norris. "The items you're looking for are in the rear of the Bronco," said Glance. "You'll find a cape in the ice chest and the horns in a black garbage bag."

"Ten-four," said Norris. "We'll take it from here."

U.S. Fish and Wildlife agents followed Sledge to his residence, a singlewide mobile home located in a shaded trailer park upriver from the motel. Sledge climbed back into his Bronco ten minutes later and drove across the river into Nevada. A team of federal agents, leapfrogging back and forth in unmarked cars, followed Sledge to Las Vegas. Sledge continued to the northern outskirts of Las Vegas before turning east from Highway 95, driving 300 yards up a paved access road, and disappearing behind a fabricated steel warehouse building.

Sledge's Bronco reappeared thirty minutes later, traveled back to Highway 95, and was stopped at the intersection by six federal agents in three unmarked cars. "Are you Porter Sledge?" said Agent Norris, displaying his badge and identification.

"Yeah," said Sledge. "What's this all about?"

"Please turn off the ignition and step out of the car."

As agents searched the Bronco, Sledge was cuffed, frisked for weapons, and placed under arrest. The ice chest in back contained nothing but ice, and the black plastic bag Henry had previously described was gone. Minutes later, a federal marshal arrived in a caged patrol unit and transported Sledge to a Las Vegas jail. All six agents jumped back into their cars and descended upon the warehouse from which Sledge had just come.

Agent Norris and his team rounded the north end of the warehouse and drove south past a dumpster and two ten-by-ten, roll-up doors—both closed. The officers came to a stop next to an older-model Pontiac Tempest station wagon parked in front of the entrance.

Agent Norris was about to knock on the entrance door, when he and the rest of his crew heard chains rattling. Frozen in position, they watched one of the roll-up doors slowly rise. When it stopped, a twenty-plus-year-old Hispanic laborer pushed a cart outside, in the direction of the dumpster.

"Hello," said Norris, "We'd like to speak with the owner of the warehouse."

"No entiendo," said the young man.

"The owner is not here," came a voice from inside the building. All six agents quickly positioned themselves, shoulder-to-shoulder, in the open doorway. "You must come back later," said a middle-aged Hispanic gentleman.

"We are federal wildlife agents," said Norris, displaying his badge and identification. "These men will remain here in the doorway until a search warrant arrives. I suggest you and your workers stop what you're doing and relax. If we see anyone attempting to remove or destroy evidence, they will be arrested."

From their vantage point in the doorway, agents saw the head of an African eland, a standing ten-foot polar bear, a mountain lion posed in the crouch position, and a perched golden eagle. They continued to secure the premises while Agent Norris drove to a nearby pay phone and telephoned another agent waiting at the federal prosecutor's office in Las Vegas. Much of the necessary probable cause statement had already been written. Norris provided the agent in Las Vegas with additional information, including what Warden Glance had witnessed, what Norris and his agents had witnessed, a detailed description of the premises to be searched, and a list of items to be searched for.

The search warrant arrived at 6:35 p.m., ten minutes before Kurt Schuler. While Schuler and his employees sat and watched, federal agents conducted a methodical search of the building, its dumpsters, seven large freezers, and all of Schuler's business records. Within the first half hour, agents found the bighorn-sheep horns and cape that had recently been delivered by Sonny Sledge. They also found two other sets of bighorn-sheep horns and capes, both tagged by Sonny Sledge.

By daylight the next morning, agents had seized into evidence three desert bighorn sheep, a bald eagle, two golden eagles, an Alaskan brown bear, a polar bear, a Siberian tiger, two mountain lions, a leopard, a sable antelope, and an African eland.

All of Shuler's records were seized into evidence and examined over the next several days, allowing agents to build substantial criminal cases against Kurt Schuler, Sonny Sledge, and nine wealthy big-game hunters.

Sonny Sledge was later convicted of felony conspiracy and several Lacey Act violations. He was ordered by the federal court to return $5,000 to Beau Burnside, return $5,000 to the U.S. Fish and Wildlife Service, and pay a fine of $100,000. Sledge was sentenced to one year in federal prison, and his hunting and guiding privileges were revoked for life. He was also forbidden from possessing a firearm or being in the field with anyone else who was hunting, guiding, or in possession of a firearm.

Kurt Schuler was convicted of numerous Lacey Act violations involving the importation and possession of wildlife unlawfully taken in the United States, Africa, and the Soviet Union. He was also convicted of violating the Bald and Golden Eagle Protection Act. For his wildlife-related crimes, Schuler was sentenced to one year in federal prison and ordered to pay a fine and civil penalties in the amount of $450,000. His records were turned over to the Internal Revenue Service, after which the IRS charged Schuler with tax evasion and sent him to prison for an additional three years.

For his part in the unlawful take and possession of a fully protected California desert bighorn sheep, Clem Beasley was charged in state court and convicted of felony conspiracy. Since he was already a convicted felon at the time of sentencing, Beasley was sent back to prison for a period of five years.

All nine wealthy hunters convicted in the case plea-bargained through their attorneys and paid substantial fines. None of them received jail or prison sentences.

HENRY TELEPHONED GARY LYTLE IN LATE SEPTEMBER to thank him for his part in the investigation. "Without your help, none of those people would have been caught," said Henry.

"I'm glad I could help," said Lytle. "How are you coming on your murder investigation? Or have you forgotten about that?"

"I was working a couple good leads when this bighorn-sheep investigation came up. Unless I get sidetracked again, I'm going to devote serious time to that investigation this coming year."

"If anyone can solve that case, you can, Hank."

TWENTY-SIX

W ARDEN GLANCE HAD RACKED UP over 200 hours of overtime planning and conducting the undercover bighorn-sheep investigation in Southern California. Because of Henry's significant, but justified, breach of department policy, Captain Odom ordered him to take the entire month of October 1970 off. When November finally rolled around, Henry was biting at the bit to go back to work and check out information he'd gleaned from Norman Bettis's diaries.

By mid-morning on Monday, November 2, 1970, Henry had tracked the last official documentation of Hollis Bogar's whereabouts to July 4, 1956, at the City of Chico's One Mile swimming pool. According to Butte County Sheriff's Department records, Bogar had been arrested by officers of the Chico Police Department for disturbing the peace and public drunkenness. Bogar's personal information sheet provided the following:

Name: Hollis DeWayne Bogar
Date of Birth: 11/21/30
Birthplace: Chico, California
Height: 6'4"   Weight: 265
Hair Color: Brown   Eye Color: Brown
Description of Marks, Scars, and Tattoos: Chipped upper front tooth
Home Address: Shady Rest Trailer Park, Space 106, Gridley, CA 95948

Henry was about to close Bogar's criminal file folder and return it to Records Clerk Lois Reed when he noticed a familiar name handwritten at the bottom of a release-from-custody form inside. According to the form, Bogar had been bailed out of jail by Blake R. Gastineau.

"Did you find what you were looking for?" said Reed, sensing a positive change in Henry's normally stoic demeanor.

"I did, Lois. Would you mind checking out one more name for me?"

"Sure. What's the name?"

"Stillwell, Ferlin Richard."

"Why does Stillwell ring a bell?"

"Back in April, you checked out the serial number of a .30-30 rifle for me. That afternoon, you called and said the rifle had been reported stolen by a man named Tucker Stillwell in Kingfisher, Oklahoma."

"I remember now."

"Ferlin Stillwell was Tucker Stillwell's grandson. He was also the person who stole the rifle."

"How did you find that out?"

"A friend of mine in Oklahoma did some detective work for me."

"Let me see if I can find something on Mr. Stillwell. I'll be right back."

Minutes later, Reed returned with Stillwell's criminal file folder. Perusing the folder's contents, Henry learned that Ferlin Richard Stillwell—aka Richie Stillwell—was born in Kingfisher, Oklahoma, on June 9, 1932. He was five-feet-six-inches tall and weighed 155 pounds. Stillwell's only distinguishing mark was the tattoo of a dagger on his right forearm. His home address was listed as Shady Rest Trailer Park, Space 106, Gridley, CA 95948.

"Just as I suspected," mumbled Henry.

"What did you suspect?" said Reed.

"Thanks for all the help, Lois. I left the folders on the counter. I'll see you later."

"Wait a minute, Hank. You didn't answer my question."

"If I told you, it would spoil the story," said Henry, walking toward the door. "You'll have to wait and read about it in the paper."

"Don't get too cocky, young man. And be careful."

That evening, Henry telephoned his friend and working partner, Tom Austin, to tell him what he'd learned.

"Norm Bettis wasn't much of a writer, and most of his entries were chicken scratch," said Henry, "but I was able to read between the lines and come up with a few possible leads."

"I'm listening," said Austin.

"Norm suspected that a local man named Dud Bogar was selling ducks to an outfit called Butler Farms. Dud Bogar died in 1954, but his son, Hollis, may have carried on the tradition. I ran a record check on Hollis today and found out he was arrested on the fourth of July 1956, for disturbing the peace. Guess who bailed him out of jail?"

"I don't know. Who?"

"Remember that big land developer Pearl told us about?"

"You mean Blake Gastineau?"

"You guessed it."

"Whad ya find out about that .30-30 rifle?"

"It belonged to a guy named Richie Stillwell, who turned out to be Hollis Bogar's cousin and Dud Bogar's nephew. Stillwell stole the rifle from his grandfather, in Kingfisher, Oklahoma, and brought it with him when he came out to California. Stillwell was arrested with Hollis Bogar on the fourth of July 1956 and was also bailed out of jail by Blake Gastineau."

"I'm still here," said Austin.

"According to Bogar's and Stillwell's rap sheets, they lived together at the Shady Rest Trailer Park, Space 106, here in Gridley. I'm going there first thing tomorrow morning. Would you like to join me?"

"What time do you want me there?"

"Why don't you meet me here at the house about 8:00? After we check out the trailer park, we'll pay a surprise visit to Mr. Gastineau, in Chico."

"Sounds good."

Tuesday morning, November 3, 1970, Henry Glance and Tom Austin drove into the Shady Rest Trailer Park. Driving past the office, they followed a path through the park to Space 106. When Glance and Austin arrived, they found an older-model, silver trailer with a blue, 1952 Plymouth sedan parked out front. A heavyset, elderly gentleman wearing brown slacks, a sleeveless undershirt, and suspenders answered the door.

"Hello. I'm Warden Hank Glance, and this is Warden Tom Austin. Would you mind if we ask you a few questions?"

"No, go right ahead. My name's Bill Thompson. I'd invite you fellas inside, but my wife and I don't have a lot of room."

"That's okay," said Glance.

"This is a great-looking vintage trailer," said Austin.

"It didn't look that great when we moved in," said Thompson. "Dorothy and I spent a couple months making repairs and cleanin' it up."

"When did you move in?" said Glance.

"Dode, when did we move here?"

"First of February 1958," came a female voice from inside the trailer. "Right after we sold the butcher shop."

"Do you own this trailer?" said Austin.

"Not really. Hal Craven and I made a business arrangement."

"Who is Hal Craven?"

"Hal is the owner of the trailer park. Dode and I mind the office when he's not around, and all we have to pay are the utilities and the space rental fee."

"That sounds like a good deal," said Glance.

"It is for us," said Thompson. "We couldn't afford much else, livin' on Social Security and what little we got for the shop."

"Where was your shop?"

"Ya know where King's Market used to be, before they went out of business?"

"I think so. Isn't the old building still on Magnolia Street?"

"Yes. Our shop was inside King's Market. We bought it in 1942, when we moved up here from Escondido."

"Do you remember dealing with a business called Butler Farms?"

"You bet," said Thompson. "That's who we bought all our turkeys from. I think they went outta business about the same time we sold the shop."

"Did they ever deliver anything besides turkeys?"

"I don't think so. Like what?"

"Never mind," said Glance. "Do you happen to know who lived in this trailer space before you and your wife?"

"I don't, but Hal Craven, down at the office, should be able to help you. He's owned this park for over thirty years."

"Mr. Thompson, it's been nice talking to you. Thanks so much, and please give our best to Dorothy," said Glance.

"I will," said Thompson, smiling. "Dode, the game wardens said to give you their best."

"That's nice."

"You boys be careful," said Thompson.

Hal Craven was waiting outside when Glance and Austin pulled up in front of the office. "I saw your truck go by a few minutes ago," said Craven. "Did one of my tenants poach a deer or somethin'?"

"No," said Glance, introducing himself and Warden Austin. "We were hoping you could answer a few questions for us."

"I'll do my best."

"Did a couple young men live in trailer Space 106 before Mr. and Mrs. Thompson?"

"Yes, they did. I'll have to pull out my records to give you the details. This may take a while, so you gentlemen better come in the office and sit down. Would either of you like a cup of coffee?"

"I just had one, and my partner doesn't drink coffee," said Austin, taking a seat next to Henry in front of Craven's desk.

"It's been thirteen or fourteen years since those bums lived here," said Craven, thumbing through a loose-leaf binder. "Here's what I was looking for. The trailer in Space 106 originally belonged to a man named Ardis Bogar."

"Did he go by Dud?" said Glance.

"He did," said Craven. "Dud lived here in Space 106 until he passed away on December tenth—"

"1954?" said Glance.

"That's right," said Craven. "The trailer sat vacant for about a year, until Dud's son showed up. I forgot his name. Let me look here in the book."

"Was it Hollis?" said Glance.

"Right again," said Craven. "Maybe I should be asking you questions."

"Don't feel like the Lone Ranger," said Austin. "He usually answers my questions before I ask them."

"I knew Hollis was gonna be trouble, but what could I do?" said Craven. "The trailer belonged to his old man, and I needed rent money for the trailer space. Before I knew it, Hollis's cousin was livin' in the trailer with him."

"Tell him, Hank," said Austin, laughing.

"Would his cousin have been Richie Stillwell?"

"Yup. What a foul-mouthed little punk he was," said Craven.

"I've heard that before," said Glance.

"My phone was ringing off the hook with complaints about those two drinkin' and raisin' hell at all hours of the day and night."

"How long did this go on?" said Austin.

"It went on for an entire year, until both of 'em up and left."

"When did they leave?" said Glance.

"They paid their last space rental fee on December 5, 1956. Sometime around the middle of December, I started hearin' comments about how quiet and peaceful it was at the back of the park without those two troublemakers around. I walked back to investigate. Stillwell's old pickup was gone, and the trailer door was wide open. 'Is anybody home?' I said. No one answered, so I closed the door and went about my business. With Christmas comin' up, I plum forgot about it until January's rent came due."

"Did they ever show up?" said Austin.

"No, we never saw either one of 'em again."

"Did you notify the police?" said Glance.

"I mentioned it to a Gridley police officer who drove through here once in a while. He checked and found out Bogar and Stillwell had warrants out for their arrests. Apparently, they had failed to show up in court for some drunken brawl they got into in Bidwell Park. The officer said Bogar and Stillwell probably skipped town. That trailer sat there empty for almost two years, until I slapped a lien on it, took legal possession, and rented it to the Thompsons."

Glance and Austin thanked Craven for the information and drove away. "Where do you think they ended up?" said Austin, as he and Henry headed north, toward Chico.

"Who?" said Henry, deep in thought.

"Bogar and Stillwell."

"I know where Stillwell ended up."

"You do?"

"Didn't I tell you last night on the phone?"

"No, you left that out."

"Richie Stillwell was electrocuted."

"Wha'd he do, stick his finger in a light socket?"

"No, he was executed in Oklahoma for murdering a gas-station attendant during a holdup. I have no idea where Hollis Bogar is, but I find it curious that he disappeared about the same time as Norm Bettis."

"How do you know all this?"

"I've been busy, Tom."

"I'll say you have. When ya gonna slow down?"

"When we find out who killed Norm Bettis. I'll tell you everything else I know on the way to Chico."

Forty-five minutes after leaving the trailer park in Gridley, Glance and Austin entered the Gastineau Development Company parking lot, on Park Avenue, in Chico. Parked in front of the office were a fire-engine-red Corvette Stingray convertible and a light-green, 1962 Ford Falcon. As Glance and Austin climbed from the patrol truck, a tall, potbellied man wearing a tweed cabbie cap opened the office door and began walking toward the red convertible.

"Excuse me, Mr. Gastineau?" said Glance.

The subject of Henry's attention turned around and looked back at the approaching uniformed officers. "Uh, I'm in a hurry," he said.

"We didn't mean to startle you," said Glance.

"You'll have to make an appointment with my secretary."

"We'd just like to ask you a couple quick questions," said Glance. "Then we'll get out of your hair."

"What's this all about?" said Gastineau, his pockmarked cheeks turning red and the car keys jingling in his hand.

"When was the last time you saw Hollis Bogar or Richie Stillwell?"

"I don't know anyone by that name," snapped Gastineau.

"Sheriff's-office records show that you bailed them out of jail on July 4, 1956," said Glance. "Are you sure you don't know them?"

"I don't like where this is going," said Gastineau. He climbed into his Corvette and drove out of the parking lot. Reaching Park Avenue, he turned right, burned rubber, and sped away.

"Whaddaya think?" said Henry, as he and Austin watched Gastineau's car disappear into the distance.

"I think we've got a tiger by the tail," said Austin. "He seems awfully worried about something."

That evening, Henry and Tom Austin sat in the tules, binoculars in hand, watching a pair of hunters fire away at passing ducks until there was just a glimmer of reddish-yellow light in the western sky.

"Aren't you gonna miss this when you retire?" said Henry.

"You bet I am," said Austin. "I've thought about staying on a couple more years, but I've got my thirty years in, and I don't want to end up like Norm Bettis. If he had retired when he should have, he'd be home with Martha right now, watching TV."

"I hear 'em coming back to their car," whispered Henry.

Glance and Austin seized evidence and issued citations to the two hunters for taking ducks after legal shooting hours. During the drive back to Gridley, Austin asked Henry what the captain thought about him spending so much time on the Bettis investigation.

"What do you think?" said Henry.

"He told you to stop wasting time on a murder case you're never gonna solve."

"You know Chuck pretty well, Tom. Now that we got that outta the way, Norm Bettis suspected Dud Bogar of selling ducks to an outfit called Butler Farms."

"Didn't you ask Mr. Thompson about Butler Farms this morning at the trailer park?"

"Yes. I did some digging and found out Butler Farms is a defunct turkey ranch, located a few miles north of Lincoln. According to the Placer County deputy I spoke with on the phone, they mysteriously went out of business about a dozen years ago. How would you like to take a drive down there on Thursday?"

"Why wait until Thursday?" said Austin. "Let's go tomorrow."

"I would, but Anne and I have plans for tomorrow evening. If you and I were to get involved in something . . . you know what I mean."

"Say no more," said Austin. "I'll pick you up Thursday morning at 6:00."

TWENTY-SEVEN

Early Thursday morning, November 5, 1970, Henry Glance and Tom Austin found themselves twenty miles south of Marysville. "The deputy said Coon Creek Road will be on our left, after we cross Coon Creek," said Henry. "It's supposed to be poorly marked and easy to miss."

"Is it paved?" said Austin.

"I think he said it was all gravel. We drive about two miles on Coon Creek Road before coming to a wooden archway that says BUTLER FARMS. We go through a gate and drive another half mile to what's left of the old turkey farm."

"Does anyone live there?"

"I asked the resident deputy about that. He said the house is boarded up, but a man named Hector Campos lives in the bunkhouse at the end of one of the old turkey sheds. Campos was the last remaining employee when Tina Butler sold the place to a group of investors. The investors asked Campos to stay on and act as caretaker until they decide what to do with the property."

It was 7:30 when Henry opened the gate under the archway, allowing Austin to pass through in his patrol car. Five minutes later, Glance and Austin approached a 200-square-foot, stucco-sided office, two rows of ventilated corrugated metal buildings, and a smaller corrugated metal building.

"Those must be the turkey sheds," said Austin, coming to a stop and turning off the ignition.

"Here comes someone," said Henry, pointing to a dark-skinned, gray-haired man wearing a long-sleeved cotton shirt, brown pants, and a white cowboy hat.

"Buenos días, caballeros. Soy el capataz de este rancho. ¿En qué puedo servirles?"

"Wha'd he say?" said Austin.

"He said he's the ranch caretaker and asked if he could help us."

"Bueno!" said the caretaker. "Many policemen have come to this place. You are the first who speaks Spanish."

"Un poco," said Henry, extending his hand. "Hace muchos años que no hablo español."

"I am Hector Campos. To what do I owe this unexpected pleasure?"

"I'm Warden Hank Glance, and this is Warden Tom Austin. We're here because we received information that someone at this turkey farm was illegally buying and selling wild ducks."

"I am sorry, gentlemen, but you are thirteen years too late. The federales came with a search warrant and left with many boxes of records, papers, and at least ten large bags of feathers. They were looking for the names of restaurants Señor Pinky was selling ducks to."

"When you said, 'federales,' whom were you referring to?" said Glance.

"Game wardens like you but from the federal government."

"I thought that's what you meant but wanted to make sure. Would you mind telling us who Señor Pinky is?"

"Why don't we go inside the office, out of the cold wind, and I will tell you everything I know," said Campos.

Campos unlocked the door and led the officers inside. The office was completely bare, except for an old-fashioned oak desk, an oak banker's chair, and two rickety Windsor chairs. With every spoken word came an echo across the dented linoleum floor. "Warden Glance, please sit in that desk chair. It is more comfortable."

"Are you sure?" said Henry.

"Of course. You and Warden Austin have kind faces. I will tell you a story I did not tell the federal game wardens. It has been bothering me for many years, and I still have nightmares about it."

"We're happy to listen," said Henry.

"Pinky Butler was a very bad man," said Campos. "You asked about the sale of wild ducks. He bought and sold thousands of wild ducks brought here by hunters."

"Do you remember the names of any of the hunters who sold ducks to Pinky Butler?" said Henry.

"Only one," said Campos. "He drove an ugly green car and Señor Pinky called him Dud."

"That would be Dud Bogar," said Glance.

"That's right!" said Campos. "His name was Dud Bogar. A few years before the federal game wardens raided the farm, Dud Bogar arrived one morning with a younger man. Señor Bogar quit delivering ducks after that, and the younger man took his place."

"Do you remember anything about this younger man?" said Austin.

"He was tall and . . ."

"And what?" said Glance.

"I am not sure how to say it in English. Tenía marcas de viruela en la cara."

"He had pockmarks on his face?"

"Sí," said Campos. "Pockmarks on his face. This man brought ducks here for two or three seasons, then he did not come anymore."

"Because of the federal game wardens?" said Austin.

"No, the federal game wardens did not come until a year after the tall young man quit coming. Señor Pinky had other hunters who sold him ducks; some of them came from Oregon. I saw their license plates."

"Do you remember what year it was when the young man quit coming?" said Henry.

"The federal game wardens came in 1957, so it had to be 1956. I wrote down the license number of the young man's car. I will give it to you before you leave."

"How did you happen to write down his license number?" said Glance.

"For many years, I have kept a small notebook under my mattress," said Campos. "Like you, I write things down."

"This is getting more interesting all the time," mumbled Austin.

"Pardon me, Warden Austin. I did not hear what you said."

"Please tell us more about Señor Pinky," said Austin.

"When Señor Pinky was angry, he took it out on other people. Once, he beat me half to death for talking to the other workers about asking for more money. We worked hard, and because we did not have papers, Señor Pinky paid us very little."

"Please go on," said Austin. While Campos talked, Henry gently opened and closed each desk drawer, finding them all empty.

"Señor Pinky was furious after the game wardens left with all his records. That night, my friend Pedro and I heard terrible screaming coming from the house. We ran to see what was going on. When we got there, Señora Butler was outside, lying on the ground with her nose bleeding and her eye black and blue. Señor Pinky saw us trying to help her and began hitting me. Pedro told him to stop, but Señor Pinky kept it up. That's when Pedro picked up a rake and hit Señor Pinky across the back with the handle. Señor Pinky was bent over, trying to catch his breath, when Pedro said to take Señora Butler away. I asked Pedro if he was sure. He said he was sure and we should go."

"What happened after that?" said Austin.

"The next day, when the federal game wardens returned to arrest Señor Pinky, he and Pedro were both gone. I told them Senor Pinky must have run away to avoid being arrested. I did not mention anything about Pedro."

"What about Pedro?" said Austin.

"I received a letter from Pedro a month later. He had gone back to Mexico."

"Did he mention anything in the letter about what had happened to Pinky?" said Glance.

"No. Pedro said he was going to Tampico to get a job. That was the last time I heard from my friend."

"Did they ever find Pinky?" said Austin.

"No. Señor Pinky was never seen or heard from again. I should probably not be telling you this, but I showed Señora Butler where I had seen Señor Pinky hiding his money. Señor Pinky kept his money in coffee cans, buried in the woods beside the creek. That money is what Señora Butler lived on until she could sell the farm. It took her over two years."

"That's quite a story," said Henry. "Would you mind if we looked around the place?"

"I would be happy to show you anything you want to see," said Campos, standing up and leading Austin out the door. "Turkeys were kept in the two larger buildings. The smaller one, over there, contains the turkey-plucking machine and Señor Pinky's gigante meat grinder."

While Campos and Austin talked outside, Henry slid a pull-out writing board out from the top-right corner of the desk and examined it for phone numbers or any other useful information. Finding nothing of interest, he pulled the board completely out and turned it over. He discovered a sheet of tablet paper taped to the underside of the board. A list of three phone numbers was handwritten in pencil on the paper. Henry jotted down the numbers and returned the shelf to its original position. Having heard Campos's story about the federal wardens showing up unannounced several years before, Henry speculated that Pinky might have quickly pulled the shelf out and turned it over to prevent the investigators from finding the numbers.

After a cursory peek into the two turkey buildings, Campos led Glance and Austin into the smaller corrugated metal building where the plucking machine and Pinky Butler's meat grinder were housed. "This is where all the birds were plucked and prepared," said Campos. "These machines could pluck a bird clean in just a few minutes. We'd wrap the ducks in cellophane and stuff them inside the turkeys."

"Pretty slick," said Austin.

"Mr. Campos, would you mind telling us about that contraption over there," said Henry, pointing to a massive, stainless-steel machine with a bathtub-sized hopper at the top and a series of frightening-looking blades visible through an opening in the front.

"That was Señor Pinky's meat grinder," said Campos. "I saw him throw chunks of turkeys, pigs, and other animals into the hopper. Nothing larger than a noodle came out the other end. Señor Pinky would laugh and say he was supplementing his turkeys' diet with extra protein."

"Does it still work?" said Austin.

"I don't know," said Campos. "The last time I heard it running was . . ."

"What were you going to say?" said Henry.

"Nothing," said Campos. "The new owners are planning to haul it away when they tear down all the buildings. Is there anything else you gentlemen would like to see?"

"No," said Henry. "Thanks so much for showing us around and telling us about the place. What will you do if they tear all this down?"

"I will probably go back to Mexico. Maybe I'll go to Tampico and try to find my friend Pedro."

"If we should ever need to get in touch with you, is there a number we could call?" said Henry.

"I will give you my brother Raul's phone number. He is a successful businessman in Mexico City. Raul always knows where to find me. And here is the license number I promised you earlier."

"Thanks so much," said Henry. "Hasta la vista."

"Adiós, mis amigos," said Campos, waving. "Buena suerte."

"What a nice guy," said Henry.

"Do you think he told us everything?" said Austin.

"About what?"

"You know what."

"Do you believe in karma, Tom?"

"That's what I thought," said Austin.

"How 'bout we stop in Marysville and get a sandwich?" said Henry. "I'm buying."

While Glance and Austin sat outside a Marysville hamburger stand— Henry munching on a turkey sandwich and Tom enjoying a lumberjack burger—Austin said, "What were you doing in the office while Hector and I were talking outside?"

"I found three phone numbers I'd like to check out. One of 'em has a Biggs area code and prefix. I'm guessing the Biggs phone number and the vehicle license number Hector gave us are connected to the same person."

"And who would that be, Sherlock?"

"Think about it, Watson," said Henry, laughing. "It's as plain as the mustard on your face."

TWENTY-EIGHT

TUESDAY MORNING, NOVEMBER 10, 1970, HENRY placed a notepad and a freshly sharpened pencil next to his phone. He then picked up the receiver and called the operator. The young warden had found area code 503 in front of the first phone number he'd discovered under the pullout shelf in Pinky Butler's office desk. "Area code 503 covers the entire state of Oregon," said the operator.

"What about this prefix?" said Glance, providing the first three digits he'd found next to area code 503.

"That would be Klamath Falls. If you give me the entire number, I would be happy to dial it for you."

"Thanks so much," said Henry, giving the operator the ten-digit number. Before Glance had thought of something to say, the phone rang once and a woman answered.

"Hello."

"Uh, may I please speak to . . . Joe."

"Who?"

"Joe."

"Nobody here by that name." The woman hung up.

Henry wrote in his notes that the first number was still in service and dialed the second number. This number contained Henry's own area code and a recognizable Willows, California, prefix. After listening to the phone ring seven or eight times, he hung up and made a note that the number was also in service but no one had answered.

The third and final number Henry had uncovered in Pinky Butler's desk contained a Biggs, California, prefix. Dialing the number, Henry heard the phone ring twice, followed by a recorded message: "The number you have dialed is no longer in service."

Having conducted his initial investigation, Glance called his friend Lois Reed at the Butte County Sheriff's Records Division. He provided Lois with the three phone numbers.

"I know you're busy," said Henry, "but if you could put some names and addresses with those numbers, I would be eternally grateful. I also have one vehicle license number."

"I'll see what I can find out and call you back," said Lois.

Twenty minutes later, Henry's phone rang. "Hank, this is Lois. Do you have a pencil ready?"

"I do."

"The first number is currently listed to Homer and Blanch Leadbetter, 40832 Dry Creek Road, Klamath Falls, Oregon. The second number is listed to Melvin Cobb, 5689 Pine Street, Willows, California."

"Go ahead with the third one . . . Lois, are you still there?"

"Hank, is this the same investigation you were working on the last time I saw you?"

"Yes."

"Are you ready for this?" Lois's voice was now barely audible.

"I am."

"The phone number was previously listed to Blake R. Gastineau, 39680 County Road E, Number 2, Biggs, California. The vehicle license number you gave me comes back to a 1949 Ford coupe. The car was formerly registered to Blake R. Gastineau, at the Biggs address I just gave you. Gastineau sold the car and transferred ownership on December 20, 1956."

"Exactly one week after Norm Bettis disappeared," mumbled Henry.

"What? I didn't quite catch that."

"That's all very interesting, Lois."

"Hank, Blake Gastineau is a very powerful man, with friends in high places. May I give you some advice?"

"Of course."

"Be careful."

"What makes you say that, Lois?"

"When you work in the sheriff's office as long as I have, you hear things."

"Lois, you sound like my mother. I'll be careful. Thanks so much for your help and your concern."

Mike Prescott was next on Henry's list. The longtime Willows Patrol District warden had been on the job for thirty years and was scheduled to retire in February.

"Hi, Mike. This is Hank Glance. How does it feel to be a few months from retirement?"

"Pretty damn good, Hank. Pretty damn good. I had a lot a good years workin' for this outfit, but I'm tired of all those phone calls in the middle of the night: 'There's somebody out here late shootin' ducks.' 'There's somebody spotlighting deer.' 'A bear keeps knocking over my garbage can.' 'A mountain lion's after my goats.' You know what I'm talkin' about?"

"Sure do," said Henry. "I wanted to ask about someone who lives in the Willows area."

"Anything I can do to help."

"Have you ever heard of a man named Melvin Cobb?"

"Hank, I can probably tell you anything you want to know about Mel Cobb. At one time, he was the biggest duck poacher in Glenn County. He got busted pretty good by the feds about thirty years ago but was back to his old tricks a year later. That's all some of these guys know how to do—kill ducks. It's in their blood, and I don't think they can stop."

"Where is Cobb now?"

"One night about twenty years ago, Mel was driving lickety-split down a canal bank. I guess he missed the turn, because they found him and his car plowed into the bank on the other side of the canal the next morning. He's been in a wheelchair ever since, paralyzed from the neck down."

"Well, I guess you answered my question."

"How's that?"

"I found his phone number hidden in the desk of a guy named Pinky Butler, who ran a turkey farm near Lincoln."

"I remember him," said Prescott. "Wasn't he stuffing his turkeys with ducks and delivering 'em to customers? I was tickled to read that several upscale restaurants in the Bay Area got busted by the feds."

"I don't suppose you still have that article?"

"I just might. If I can find it, I'll send it to you. Give me your mailing address, Hank."

Encouraged by what he'd learned from Mike Prescott, Henry's next call was to the Oregon State Police. He was told that Trooper Lance Kirby, of the Fish and Wildlife Division, was responsible for the area in and around Klamath Falls.

"I'll have Trooper Kirby call you," said the receptionist.

Kirby returned Glance's call one hour later. "Are you familiar with a man named Homer Leadbetter?" said Glance.

"I haven't heard that name mentioned in five or six years," said Kirby. "Leadbetter has been arrested two or three times for taking overlimits of ducks. We heard rumors that he was selling ducks to someone down around Sacramento but never could corroborate it."

At age twenty-three, Warden Glance had already perfected most of the skills necessary to be an outstanding investigator. The one skill he hadn't yet mastered was patience. Henry couldn't wait to question Blake Gastineau about his association with Pinky Butler. That afternoon, he put on his uniform, jumped in his patrol truck, and drove straight to Gastineau's office.

"Mr. Gastineau, there's a Fish and Game officer out here who would like to speak with you," said the receptionist, over the intercom.

"What's he want?" said Gastineau.

"He said it's a private matter and he'd prefer to speak to you directly about it."

"Go ahead and send him in, Glenda."

"Aren't you the same game warden who accosted me the other day?" said Gastineau, leaning back in his chair, lighting a cigar, and showing off the heels of his alligator-skin boots.

"I did ask you a couple questions," said Glance.

"And I gave you my answer. I don't know the people you mentioned, and that's it. Is there anything else I can help you with Warden . . . what did you say your name was?"

"Glance, Warden Hank Glance." Henry watched Gastineau write his name on a piece of paper. "Mr. Gastineau, what was your relationship with Pinky Butler and the Butler turkey farm?"

Removing his boots from the desk, Gastineau stood up, walked to his office door, and opened it. "Glenda, he said, "show Warden Glance out, and don't let him back in unless he has a warrant."

That afternoon, Henry was patrolling west, toward the Gray Lodge Wildlife Area, when he received a radio call from the Sacramento dispatcher.

"Two-five-three, Sacramento," the dispatcher said.

"Two-five-three, go ahead."

"Two-five-three, Two-five-zero requests a landline ASAP."

"Ten-four. Two-five-three."

His stomach churning, Henry turned his patrol truck around and made a beeline for home. He dialed Captain Odom's number and was greeted by an angry voice in the middle of the first ring. "Hello."

"Hi, Chuck. This is Hank. The dispatcher said you wanted to talk to me."

"Hank, do you remember me telling you the other day that I didn't want to receive any irate calls from the director?"

"Yes."

"The director just spent the last fifteen minutes chewing my ass out."

"I'm sorry, Chuck. What did he say?"

"He said he just received a call from Assemblyman Dell Kickbusch, who spent ten minutes chewing his ass about some overzealous young game warden named Hank Glance, who's been harassing a prominent businessman in Chico."

"I was just doing my job, Chuck."

"Let me remind you that your job is enforcing fish and game laws, not solving fourteen-year-old murder cases. You're a game warden, Hank, not a homicide detective."

"But I think I've almost got this thing figured out."

"I don't want to hear it," said Odom. "Here's what you're gonna do. You're gonna forget about this murder investigation and go back to bein' the crackerjack game warden I know you to be. And that goes for your sidekick, Tom Austin. Yes, I heard about him too. He's gonna hear from me as soon as I hang up the phone. Have I made myself clear, Warden Glance?"

"Yes."

"Good! Now go back to work."

TWENTY-NINE

Although HE DIDN'T SHOW IT at the time, Henry reacted to the captain's cease-and-desist order like a spirited racehorse left kicking and neighing at the starting gate. To make matters worse, Tom Austin called twenty minutes later to say he was retiring. "Why now?" said Henry. "I thought you were gonna stay on a couple more years."

"I was only going to stay on to help you solve the Bettis murder case. If the captain and those pinheads in Sacramento weren't so worried about stepping on some bigshot developer's toes, we would have done it."

"I tried to tell that to Chuck, but he didn't want to hear it."

"Chuck is a good supervisor, but he's also a company man. He quit being one of us when he pinned those bars on his collar."

"I guess you're right, Tom."

"You bet I'm right. Everything boils down to money and politics. It's great to be idealistic, but reality always bites dreamers like us in the ass."

"Thanks for setting me straight," said Henry, laughing. "I feel better now."

"Glad I could help. On the brighter side, when's the wedding?"

"Saturday, May 22, right after Anne finishes her student teaching and applies for her teaching credential. We're counting on you and Mary being there, so please put it on your calendar."

"I'll do that as soon as I hang up."

"Speaking of calendars, what's your retirement date?"

"June 30, 1971."

"I think that's the same day Mike Prescott is retiring over in Willows."

"It is. Mike and I were both hired in 1941, and it looks like we'll go out together. He wants to have a retirement party. I'm leaving through the back door."

"At least we have another six months to work together, unless the captain said to knock that off too."

"He didn't say anything about it to me."

"Good. A storm is rolling in, and tomorrow's a shoot day at Gray Lodge. Why don't you meet me here at 4:30. We'll leave your patrol car in the barn, grab a bite at Pearl's, and spend the day working ducks."

"Looking forward to it, Hank. I'll see you in the morning."

MONDAY AFTERNOON, FEBRUARY 22, 1971, ANNE came rolling up the driveway after a long day of student teaching in Gridley. Henry was out front painting the trim on the farmhouse that was to be their home until they could afford a place of their own.

"Henry, I'm so excited! Wait 'til you hear the news."

Placing his brush on the edge of the paint can, Henry walked over to greet his future wife. "I'd give you a hug, but as you can see, there's more paint on me than on the house. Let's sit on the porch and you can tell me all about it."

"Are you doing all this work for me, Henry?"

"I would have painted sooner, but I was waiting for a stretch of warmer weather. Would you like some iced tea? I made some for you."

"First let me tell you my surprise."

"Go ahead, Anne. I'm anxious to hear it."

"Mom and I arranged for you and me to be married at the college amphitheater on the banks of Chico Creek. What do you think about that?"

"I think it's fantastic. What a great idea!"

"It was actually my mom's idea. She knows how you and I cherish nature, especially streams."

"Please tell your mom how grateful I am."

"That's not all, Henry. We're going to have the reception in our backyard. Mom has already rented a big tent, in case it's too hot in late May. Sometime soon, I hope you and I can sit down and decide on guests to invite. The amphitheater accommodates up to 300 people."

Henry laughed. "I can give you my list right now, Anne. Let's see, there's my parents, Tom and Mary Austin, Larry Jansen, Gary Lytle, Brad Foster, Dennis D'Agostino, Ron and Brenda Travers, Harry

Craddock, and maybe a few players from my Riverside City College baseball team. If everyone brings a wife or a girlfriend, that might bring it up to about twenty."

"What about aunts, uncles, and cousins?" said Anne.

"I only had my uncle Roscoe, and he passed away several years ago. I don't have any cousins. We could invite Captain Odom and his wife, but Chuck is probably still mad at me about the Bettis investigation."

"Henry, your captain isn't still mad at you. You did the right thing, and I have a feeling you'll solve that case someday."

"Do you think so, Anne?"

"Mark my words, something will happen and you will break that case wide open."

"You always make me feel better. Hey, I just thought of two more people to invite."

"Who?"

"Martha Bettis and Pearl at the diner. That leaves about 275 guests for you and your mom to invite, Anne."

"Don't laugh, Henry. My parents both grew up here in Chico and graduated from Chico State. We have enough friends and relatives living within twenty miles of Chico to fill the amphitheater."

"I bet you do. How was school today?"

"It went well. I found out there's going to be an opening for a seventh-grade science teacher at the end of this school year."

"Wouldn't it be great if you could snag that position and teach right here in Gridley?"

"I should have a pretty good chance. I'm doing my student teaching at the school where the opening's going to be, and they seem to appreciate my work."

"To know you is to love you, Anne."

"You're a little bit biased, Henry."

"Maybe I'll drop by once in a while with an orphaned hawk or an injured owl to show your students."

"I'm sure they'd love that. I would too. You always look so handsome in your uniform."

HENRY'S AND ANNE'S WEDDING WENT OFF without a hitch. Although late May temperatures ranged from the high eighties to the low nineties, Big Chico Creek provided a cooling effect and all the guests remained comfortable throughout the short ceremony. It didn't hurt that most of the ninety-four attendees showed up in casual summer attire, as per the bride's and groom's invitation instructions.

Sara Nichols was Anne's obvious choice for maid of honor, and Larry Jansen drove all the way from Lake Elsinore to be Henry's best man. Sara, who had just signed a contract to teach second grade in nearby Hamilton City, arrived looking radiant. Her appearance didn't go unnoticed. Larry, who'd been teaching PE and coaching baseball for the past two years, couldn't have been more smitten.

"What happened to Jeanette Rogers?" mumbled Henry, as he and Larry stood side by side on the cement stage, watching Chico Creek flow by.

"She took one look at Lake Elsinore and said adiós."

"Well, good luck with Sara. She's a nice girl. With her being six feet tall and you six-four, your kids are a cinch to make the high-school basketball team."

"That thought did cross my mind," said Larry, chuckling.

"Look!" said Henry, pointing to a school of spring-run salmon swimming upstream.

"Only you would notice a school of fish at a time like this, Hank."

"Larry, I really appreciate your coming all this way to be my best man."

"I wouldn't have missed it for the world." Larry's eyes were glued to Sara as she walked up the cement pathway and assembled at Henry's right. As the music began to play, everyone returned their attention to the pathway, where Anne and her father approached. "Good luck, Hank. We've come a long way since second grade."

Henry could almost hear his own heart beating as he smiled and bumped elbows with his lifelong friend. "Here we go."

After the wedding, it was time to meet and greet guests at the reception. Henry spent the first hour hugging and shaking hands with Anne's friends and relatives. Looking over Anne's shoulder, he spotted Gary Lytle, Brad Foster, and Dennis D'Agostino standing near the bar—each with a beer in his hand.

Gary Lytle had flown all the way from Montana to attend the wedding. Henry would have invited him to stay at the farmhouse, but Henry's parents and Larry Jansen were already occupying the available beds. Brad Foster took up the slack and invited Gary to stay with him and his wife at their home in Willows. Finally catching Henry alone, Brad couldn't wait to tell him what had happened the previous afternoon.

"This guy rents a car at the Sacramento Airport and drives up to our house," said Brad. "You know where we live, Hank."

"I do."

"Gary pulls up in our driveway, walks to the door, and rings the bell. I had just finished my shift and was on my way home. Did I tell you I made detective?"

"No, you didn't," said Henry. "Congratulations!"

"Yeah, it's almost unheard of to make detective after only two years in uniform."

"Cut the bull and finish your story so I can go get another beer," said Gary.

"See what I have to put up with?" said Brad. "Nothing's changed with this guy. He's just as cantankerous as ever."

"So, what happened?" said Dennis.

"Anyway, Gary rings the bell, Susan comes to the door, and Mr. Personality says, 'You look familiar. Have I seen you somewhere before?'"

"You mean Gary didn't know that you and Susan had gotten married?" said Henry.

"The same Susan that Gary had embarrassed on her first date with Brad," said Dennis, laughing.

"Now that Dennis has ruined the rest of my story, Gary might as well go get his beer," said Brad.

"Thanks, Brad. Does anyone else want one?"

"I do," said Dennis.

"Dennis, how have you been?" said Henry. "Did Janet come with you?"

"She's over at the table, talking to Anne and Susan. That was the nicest wedding I've ever been to, Hank. Short and sweet, just the way I like 'em. You couldn't have picked a better location. I saw you pointing at those fish that swam by."

"It was Anne's mother's idea. She and Anne's father were married on that same spot, twenty-five years ago."

Working their way from table to table, Henry and Anne found Ron and Brenda Travers sitting at a table with Tom and Mary Austin. Ron said he'd been promoted to Ranger 2 at Plumas-Eureka State Park. Henry asked about Harry Craddock and learned that he had retired to help his mother and two aunts run a bed-and-breakfast business at the ranch. "Harry said to give you both his best and tell you he's sorry he couldn't make the wedding," said Travers.

"Speaking of bed and breakfasts," said Anne, "Henry and I are spending the next three nights at a bed and breakfast in Pacific Grove. After Pacific Grove, we're going to drive down the coast and spend a few days with Henry's parents in Temecula."

"Then what?" said Mary Austin.

"Then I become a permanent Gridley resident," said Anne. "You should see how nice the outside of that old farmhouse looks after Henry painted it."

"I think the inside of that old house could use a woman's touch," said Tom.

"I plan to spend June and July working on the inside," said Anne. "If it's not too late, Henry and I also want to plant a garden."

"Anne just signed a contract to teach seventh-grade science in Gridley," said Henry.

"That's wonderful, Anne," said Mary Austin.

"Thanks, Mary. I start the second week of August, with staff meetings and in-service training. What about you, Tom? Henry tells me you're retiring next month. Are you excited?"

"I wanted to stay on and help Hank solve the Bettis murder case, but we all know how that turned out."

"Tom, your captain is right over there," whispered Mary. "He's gonna hear you."

"I don't care. What's he gonna do—fire me?"

"No more wine for you. And I'm driving home," said Mary.

"Tell us about the Bettis case," said Ron Travers, sitting across the table.

"Hank can tell it better than I," said Tom. "In a way, he's been working on it since he was eleven years old."

"Tom," said Mary, "Hank doesn't want to tell that sad story on his wedding day."

THIRTY

SINCE MIKE PRESCOTT AND TOM AUSTIN had retired, Warden Glance was temporarily left with the southern half of Glenn County and the northern half of Butte County to patrol, in addition to his own sizeable district. Having studied a Mendocino National Forest map the night before, Henry decided to spend opening morning of archery deer season patrolling an area of southern Glenn County known as Sheetiron Mountain. It was August 21, 1971.

Glance had never been to Sheetiron Mountain and didn't know what to expect when he got there. What he found was a tangle of Forest Service roads and logging spurs that led in a hundred different directions. All the roads and adjacent trees were engulfed in a fine, powdery dust from the procession of logging trucks that had rumbled through the forest all summer. To make matters worse, the temperature had reached ninety degrees by noon and the enthusiastic young warden had yet to encounter a single hunter.

Not willing to give up, Henry headed north in the afternoon and eventually came to an intersection. According to the wooden Forest Service sign, he had four choices: turn around and go back the way he'd come, continue on his present course and eventually reach Alder Springs, turn right toward Highway 162, or turn left and eventually reach Bald Mountain. Henry would later write in his daily diary:

> Due to the absence of hunting activity, my initial decision was to turn right and head toward Highway 162. I had driven a mile or so toward 162 and home when

my gut said to turn around and go the other direction.
So I did.

Henry had driven three or four miles up the long, winding road to
Bald Mountain when he came to a light-blue, World-War-II-era Willys
Jeep. The jeep was parked next to an iron gate with a metal sign read-
ing ROAD WASHED OUT—OFFICIAL VEHICLES ONLY BEYOND
THIS POINT.

Stepping from his patrol truck, Henry peered into the jeep and noticed a broken arrow lying on the back floorboard. A broadhead was
attached to the business end of the arrow, indicating that the operator of
the jeep was probably a deer hunter. "He must have walked out this logging spur," mumbled Glance. "I've been up here in these woods all day
and haven't contacted a single hunter. There's no way I'm going home
without checking this guy out."

Henry rummaged through a box on the front seat of his patrol truck
until he found his only Forest Service key. The key fit, so he swung open
the gate, drove through, and locked the gate behind him. Judging from
the abundance of weeds growing in the middle of the narrow dirt road,
Glance figured his pathway hadn't been graded or maintained in years.
With a jungle of chamise and manzanita on his right and a sheer cliff on
his left, Henry shoved the truck into low gear and crept up the mountainside. The road eventually leveled out at the top and continued another two miles before coming to a wooden barrier and another sign,
this one reading DANGER—ROAD WASHED OUT.

Climbing from the truck, Glance walked around the barrier and approached the cliff's edge. Looking out over the canyon, he saw what remained of an old clear-cut on the opposite side. To his right and directly below was a massive abyss, filled with dirt, rubble, fallen rocks, and
dead trees. "My God!" said Henry. "It looks like half the mountainside
sloughed off and fell into this canyon."

"Hello," came a voice from the canyon below.

Looking to his left, Henry watched a tall, thin, blond-haired man,
who looked to be in his mid-twenties, climb the edge of the canyon on a
sixteen-inch-wide deer trail. Strapped to the man's back was a king-sized
backpack, a quiver full of arrows, and a hunting bow.

"Hello, yourself," said Glance. "That's a long way down. Did you go all
the way to the bottom?"

The hunter removed his cumbersome backpack and sat down on a nearby rock. "I stuck a little forky about ten o'clock this morning," he said, still trying to catch his breath.

"Did you find him?"

Coming to his feet, the hunter turned and pointed into the canyon. "I wasn't about to quit until I did. See that patch of live oaks at the bottom-left?"

"Yes."

"I followed his blood trail through those trees and another half mile before I found him lying dead in the dry streambed. I didn't want the meat to spoil, so I gutted him, hung him in the shade, and skinned him out."

"Sounds like you've done this before."

"Many times, and I've never let a deer go to waste."

"I'm impressed. What about yellow jackets?"

"They were all over the carcass in seconds, so I boned him out, packed the meat in that big backpack over there, and hiked up here."

"May I see the antlers and your deer tag?"

"You bet. I have a handy-dandy little meat saw I use to remove the skullcap and the antlers."

"What's your name?"

"Dana Adler. What's yours?"

"Hank Glance. Glad to meet you, Dana. I wish every hunter were as conscientious as you seem to be."

"Thanks for saying that," said Adler, handing Glance a small set of forked antlers with a filled-out deer tag attached. "I respect the sport of hunting and the game I hunt."

"Is your hunting license handy?"

As Adler unzipped the side pocket on his backpack and reached inside for his hunting license, an orange styrofoam ball fell out and rolled across the ground at Henry's feet.

"What's this?" said Henry, reaching down and picking it up.

"I was wondering the same thing myself. See that pile of slash and dead trees near the bottom of the canyon?"

"Yes."

"I was about forty yards from there when I spotted that orange ball you have in your hand."

"You must have good eyes if you spotted this on the ground from forty yards away."

"It wasn't on the ground; it was dangling in the air. I knew it had to be attached to something, so I walked over to investigate. What I found was a heavy-duty wire sticking up out of the ground. The ball you have in your hand was attached to the end."

"That's strange," said Glance.

"I'd like to stay and talk, but I'd better take care of that deer meat before it spoils."

"Throw your gear in the back of the pickup. I'll give you a ride to your jeep."

HENRY AND ANNE WERE SITTING on the front porch, watching the sun go down. "Henry, you look like you have the whole world on your shoulders. What's on your mind?"

"Huh?"

"Henry, what are you thinking about?"

"Something that happened today. What time is it, Anne?"

"It's 8:15."

"I'm gonna make a quick phone call to Tom Austin."

"Take your time. I need to work on some lesson plans anyway."

"Hello," said Austin.

"Tom, this is Hank. How's retirement treating you?"

"Great, Hank. How did the archery opener go?"

"I decided to work the west side of the valley, in Mike's old district."

"Let me guess. It was hot, dusty, and you didn't check a single hunter all day."

"You're close, but I did check one hunter."

"Archery deer opener is usually a big waste of time. Don't feel like the Lone Ranger."

"Something happened that I wanted to talk to you about."

"I like that. It means you haven't forgotten about me."

"I found this old logging spur behind a locked gate. The road is closed because half the mountain came down at some point and washed it out. To make a long story short, this hunter I contacted showed me an orange ball he found at the bottom of the canyon. It was attached to some kind of heavy wire that was sticking up out of the ground. I know it's a long shot, but—"

"It could be an antenna, like the one attached to the rear bumper of Norm Bettis's patrol car?"

"Exactly! By any chance, do you feel like taking a hike tomorrow? Since you don't have a patrol car anymore, I'll be happy to drive up to Chico and pick you up."

"What time will you be here?"

"How's 7:00 sound?"

"I'll be waiting."

It was 9:30 when Glance and Austin passed through the gate and headed up the logging spur toward the washout. The temperature had already reached eighty-four degrees on the mountain, with an expected high of 103 in the valley.

"I was awake half the night trying to think of possible scenarios," said Henry. "Could it be that Norm Bettis was just in the wrong place at the wrong time when the mountain caved in? I remember the old man at the diner saying it was raining like hell the day Bettis disappeared."

"That's a possibility," said Austin, "but why would Norm be way up here, forty miles from his own district, in the middle of December?"

"This could turn out to be a waste of time, but it's worth checking out," said Glance. "We'll bring a shovel in case we have to do some digging."

At age sixty, Tom Austin was still in good shape. He and Henry easily traversed the deer trail that Dana Adler had used the day before. Glance and Austin reached the bottom of the canyon and made their way across the fallen rubble to the south end of the slash heap. "I see what your hunter must have been talking about," said Austin. "It does look like an antenna."

"It sure does. I guess I'll start digging here and hope I hit something."

"What if the car is facing the other direction? You could dig all the way to China and not find anything."

"I don't think it's gonna make any difference anyway, Tom. The ground is like dried cement. What we need is a crew of workers with picks and digging bars."

"You could check with CDF and see if they have a con crew available."

"Today's Sunday, so I'll check with them first thing tomorrow morning. I'm sorry I got you all the way up here for nothing."

"I needed the exercise. If we end up finding Norm's car, it'll be worth it."

As LUCK WOULD HAVE IT, the local con crew was in between jobs when Henry contacted California Department of Forestry Captain Bob Schafer Monday morning. Arrangements were made to meet at the washout site Wednesday morning at 8:00. Henry had promised Tom that he wouldn't go back down the canyon without him, so at 6:30 Wednesday morning, he picked Austin up at his home in Chico.

A crew of twelve prisoners from the Glenn County Jail conservation camp began digging with picks, shovels, and digging bars at 9:15. At 12:30, a crew member nicknamed Jinx shouted, "Captain Bob, my bar just hit something hard, and I don't think it was a rock."

"What did it sound like?" said Schafer.

"It sounded like the roof of a car."

"Are you sure?"

"I'm pretty sure. I've wrecked enough cars to know what that sounds like." The rest of the crew laughed.

Captain Schafer instructed three other inmates to begin digging around the bar, in hopes of clearing enough dirt and debris to make an identification. When they had completed their task, the captain pulled a small flashlight from his belt and shined it into the hole. "Whatever's down there is painted dark green," he said.

Shivers ran down Henry's spine as he hurried to see for himself. *Have we found Norm Bettis?* he wondered. *How will I break it to Martha?*

"Not many other cars are painted that color," said Austin. "A lot of it is rusted, but I definitely see game-warden green down there."

It was 4:00 p.m. before the car was completely exposed. As anticipated, it turned out to be a dark-green Ford sedan with Fish and Game insignias on the doors. The windshield, back window, and all the side windows were broken out. The inside of the car was caked with dried mud, from floorboard to roof.

"I wonder if anyone's inside," said one of the inmates. Seconds later, the driver's-side door fell open, a slab of dried mud fell away, and the skeletal remains of a hand and partially clothed left arm were exposed.

"Looks like you found your missing game warden," said Captain Schafer.

"Not necessarily," said Austin. "Norm was only five-eight. Look at the length of this man's arm. It hangs clear to the floorboard. And he's not wearing a wedding ring. Norm never took off his wedding ring."

"The ring could have fallen off," said Schafer. "What's left of his shirt is the same khaki color as the uniform shirt Hank is wearin.'"

"But it doesn't fit him," said Henry. "Look, the cuff is hanging barely past his elbow. I think what we need to do right now is secure the possible crime scene and not touch another thing."

"What about the door?" said Austin. "Should we leave it hanging open like that?"

"No, let's push it closed and prop one of these branches against it," said Glance.

"Hank, I need to get this bunch back to camp before 6:00," said Schafer. "If you need us tomorrow, give me a call. You have my card."

"Bob, may I ask one more favor?" said Henry.

"Absolutely."

"When you get back to camp, would you please telephone the Glenn County Sheriff's Office and ask them to send out their homicide investigators. You can explain how to get here better than I can, and I'd rather not put this out over the radio."

"No problem. It will probably take me an hour and a half to get to a phone. Is that all right?"

"Yes. Thanks so much for everything."

"Don't mention it. I'm glad we could help."

Three hours after Schafer and his crew had left, an unmarked sheriff's unit and a marked sheriff's unit arrived at the wooden barrier where Henry's patrol truck was parked. The first officer to step out of the unmarked unit was Detective Brad Foster.

"Hello, Hank," said Foster. "Did you finally find your missing fish cop?"

"How did you know about that, Brad?"

"Don't you remember? You told me about the game warden who disappeared four years ago, when we were living in Mrs. Iverson's pit."

"That's right. I forgot about that. Brad Foster, this is Tom Austin. He just retired from Fish and Game a month ago and has been working this case with me, off and on, for the last two years."

"I met Tom at your wedding," said Foster, shaking Austin's hand. "These are my evidence experts, Sergeant Jack Weaver and his assistant, Deputy Holly Ward. Our uniformed officer, over there talking on the radio, is Deputy Bill Jennings. What are we looking at, Hank?"

"As soon as we determined that it wasn't Norm Bettis in the front seat of that car down there, the scene changed from a possible accident to a homicide. We didn't want to contaminate any evidence, so we secured the area and I asked the CDF captain to telephone your office. I'm glad they chose you to respond, Brad."

"They didn't exactly choose me. Our veteran detective is on vacation in Hawaii. The captain caught me in the hallway, told me about the call, and said to grab the evidence-collection crew and get up here as quickly as possible. He said the sheriff knew Norm Bettis personally and wants to be kept abreast of anything we find."

"I'll point the car out from the edge of the cliff," said Henry. "It's getting dark, but you should still be able to see it from here."

"Wow! That's a long way down," said Foster. "How do we get there?"

"The only way down is that narrow deer trail, and I'm not sure it would be safe carrying all your evidence-collection gear down there and back in the dark."

"That's why we brought Officer Jennings along," said Foster.

"To use as a pack horse?" said Austin, laughing.

"No, to guard the scene until tomorrow morning. He's on duty to-night, so he can sit here in the comfort of his patrol unit until we return."

"I think that's a wise decision," said Glance, pointing into the canyon. "The man sitting in the front seat of that car has been there for fifteen years. One more night shouldn't make any difference."

"Are you sure it's not your game warden?" said Foster.

"Tom and I don't think so."

"Who do you think it is?"

"I have a good idea. Unless you're in a hurry to leave, I'll share my thoughts with you."

Brad Foster and the rest of the sheriff's investigators stood at the hood of Glance's patrol truck for the next hour while Glance and Austin briefed them on what they'd learned so far. "Hank, are you absolutely sure it's Hollis Bogar in that car down there and not Norm Bettis?" said Foster.

"Let me put it this way, Brad. I'm positive it's not Norm Bettis, and I'm ninety-nine percent sure it's Hollis Bogar."

"If you're right, we've got a murder investigation on our hands," said Foster. "How 'bout we meet here at 8:00 tomorrow morning and get busy?"

"Ha!" scoffed Austin.

"Is there a problem?" said Foster.

"Tell 'em, Hank."

"I was ordered by my captain not to spend any more time on the Bettis murder investigation. He also told me to stay away from Blake Gastineau."

"Why?" said Foster. "As much as you already know about this case, I'd be a fool not to have you investigate it with me."

"I questioned Blake Gastineau twice about his association with Hollis Bogar and Richie Stillwell. Gastineau complained about me to Assemblyman Dell Kickbusch, Kickbusch complained to the head of our department, the head of our department complained to my cap-tain, and—"

"And you got an ass chewin', is that it, Hank?" said Foster.

"That's about it. I'm learning about politics the hard way."

"Kickbusch is an asshole," said Austin. "A couple years ago, the warden up in Susanville caught him and two of his rich friends comin' out of a private ranch with three untagged deer. Kickbusch has never let us forget it."

"Don't give up yet," said Foster. "I'll call the sheriff when I get back to the office and ask him to make a few phone calls."

"It's kinda late," said Henry. "Do you think it'll do any good?"

"Bob Carlson has been Glenn County sheriff since before you or I were born, Hank. During his time in office, he's made a few friends in high places. Higher than Mr. Kickbusch. Be sure to stay close to the phone when you get home tonight."

It was 11:15 p.m. when the telephone rang at the Glance residence. Henry was in the bathroom brushing his teeth, so Anne answered.

"Hello, Anne. This is Chuck Odom. Is Hank available?"

"Yes, Chuck. I'll get him."

"Henry, Chuck is on the phone."

"How'd he sound?"

"Not too happy."

"Hello, Chuck."

"Hank, I'll make this short. You have my permission to assist the Glenn County Sheriff's homicide investigators with the Bettis murder investigation."

"Are there any restrictions?"

"If you stay within the state of California, there are no restrictions. Keep track of your expenses, and turn in your paperwork on time."

"Thank you, Chuck."

"Good night," said Odom, hanging up the phone.

"What did he say?" said Anne, as Henry climbed into bed.

"He said I have his permission to work the Bettis investigation with the Glenn County Sheriff's Office. Chuck is used to going to bed with the chickens. For him to be up this late, he must have just received a call from somebody upstairs."

"Henry, you're doing the right thing, and that's all that matters. When you finally catch the scoundrels responsible for Norm Bettis's murder, all will be forgiven."

"I hope so, Anne. I sure hope so."

THIRTY-ONE

IT WAS THURSDAY MORNING, AUGUST 26, 1971, when Warden Henry Glance and the Glenn County Sheriff's homicide investigation team arrived at the site where Norman Bettis's patrol car was found. Sergeant Weaver and Deputy Ward stepped off a perimeter around the car and marked it with yellow crime-scene tape. As if they were paleontologists searching for ancient fossils, Weaver and Ward donned plastic gloves and began chipping sections of dried mud from inside the vehicle.

"This guy was at least six-three or six-four," said Sergeant Weaver, having removed enough dried mud from the skeleton to make a reasonable assertion. "It looks like he tried to wear the uniform shirt, but it was too small."

"He's also wearing blue jeans," said Foster. "I guess it's safe to assume this guy isn't your game warden, huh, Hank?"

Deep in thought, Henry nodded. "He was probably wearing Bettis's hat too. I bet we find it in the car somewhere."

"What do you think caused the mountain to cave in?" said Deputy Ward.

"It looks like much of the mountain was clear-cut at some point," said Henry. "By removing all the vegetation that anchors the soil, it makes steep hillsides, like this, vulnerable to erosion. All it takes is a couple gully washers, and down it comes."

"Do you think it was raining when the mountain came down?" said Foster.

"According to the man I spoke with in Pearl's Diner, it was raining like hell the day Bettis disappeared," said Glance.

"What day was that?"

"December 13, 1956."

"Jack, can we pull this guy out of the car and search him for identification?" said Foster.

"As soon as Holly takes a couple more photographs, we'll lay him on that tarp over there," said Weaver.

"There's the hat you were talking about," said Ward, as Weaver and Foster lifted the body from the car.

"Believe it or not, that flattened piece of cloth was a Stetson at one time," said Henry.

While Weaver and Ward gently rolled the body to one side, Detective Foster reached into the driver's back pocket and pulled out a brown leather wallet. "Looks like he just got paid, Hank. There's four twenties, a ten, and a five in here."

"That's a lot of cash for this guy to have on him," said Glance. "Does he have a driver's license?"

"No driver's license," said Foster, "but there's something here with his name on it. Looks like a 1955 hunting license. Okay, Hank. Last night you were ninety-nine percent sure the man in the car was Hollis Bogar. How sure are you now?"

Henry leaned over and examined the dead man's exposed, upper front teeth. "Now I'm a hundred percent sure," he said.

"What convinced you?" said Deputy Ward.

"I already had a good idea it was Bogar, based on the process of elimination," said Glance, "but it was that grin that confirmed my suspicion. Hollis Bogar's rap sheet listed a badly chipped upper front tooth."

"Jack, would you bring me an evidence envelope for Mr. Bogar's items?" said Foster.

"I'll be right there, Brad," shouted Weaver from inside the car. "I just found the keys."

"Where were they?" Foster shouted back.

"In the ignition."

"Give it a turn and see if she starts."

"I already did," said Weaver, laughing. "I think the battery's dead. Do you wanna look in the trunk?"

"I guess we'd better," said Foster. "Hank, would you like to do the honors?"

"You go ahead, Brad," said Glance. "There's nobody in there."

"I should know better than to disagree with you, Hank, but this time you're mistaken."

"What makes you think so?"

"This Bogar character hit Warden Bettis over the head with something. His plan was to drive to the edge of the cliff, place Bettis in the driver's seat, and push him over the side. If someone finds the car, it looks like Bettis accidentally drove off the cliff. Unfortunately for Bogar, the mountain caved in before he could carry out his plan."

"You've got this case wrapped in a nice, neat bow already, huh, Brad?" said Henry, smiling.

"Yup! I think we're gonna find your game warden and solve the murder in one day. Sometimes the simplest explanation is the best explanation."

"I agree with your theory, Brad, except for one important detail."

"What's that?"

"Warden Bettis isn't inside the trunk."

"If he's not in the trunk, where is he?" said Deputy Ward, listening to Glance and Foster banter back and forth.

"I don't know where he is now," said Glance, "but at the time this car went off the cliff, Bettis was probably in the trunk of a second car."

"A second car?" said Foster "What second car?"

"Think about it, Brad. Do you think Bogar intended to walk all the way back to Gridley after pushing Bettis and this car off the cliff?"

"I have an idea," said Deputy Ward. "How 'bout we open the trunk and find out which of you is right? It's almost noon, and we still have a lot of work to do."

Despite being severely damaged, the trunk popped open easily. The only items inside were a set of jumper cables, a handyman jack, and a wooden box containing C-rations and two rolls of toilet paper.

"You were right again, Hank," said Foster. "Why aren't you smiling?"

"Because there's no shovel."

"No shovel?"

"The department issues a handyman jack and a shovel to every warden, in case he gets stuck in the mud. I've learned a lot about Norm Bettis during the last two years. He was fastidious to the extreme, and it wasn't like him to go on patrol without a shovel in his car."

"Brad," shouted Weaver, "I found a little green book. I think it's a diary of some kind."

"That must be his 1956 diary," said Glance. "It's the only one missing from the box Norm's wife gave me."

"All the pages are stuck together, and it looks like an envelope is sticking out from between the last fifteen or twenty pages," said Weaver.

"We don't want to tear the pages or smear any information that might be inside," said Foster. "Let's wait until we get back to the office before we try to open it."

"Here's something else," said Weaver. "It's an aluminum paper case."

"Secure that too, Jack," said Foster. "We'll open it back at the office."

"Okay," said Weaver. "The only other things I've been able to find are a bunch of scattered keys and a pair of smashed sunglasses."

"I see that the coroner has arrived to take charge of the body," said Foster. "Let's pack up what we have and head back to the cars."

NORM BETTIS'S 1956 DIARY was a four-by-seven-inch, hardbound, dark-green book with the title *Daily Reminder* embossed on the cover. Stuffed between the pages marked December 13 and December 14 was a grease-stained envelope with a partial license number handwritten in pencil across the front. The first few characters on the envelope read WDO 8. The last two numerals had rotted away, along with the other half of the envelope. Detective Foster instructed Deputy Ward to run all the numerical possibilities and combinations until she came up with a plausible suspect vehicle. "By plausible, I mean any vehicle registered to a Northern California address," said Foster.

"This may take some time," said Ward. "And some of these cars may no longer be in service."

"I know, Holly," said Foster. "Just do the best you can, and stay on it until you come up with something."

Norm Bettis's 1956 diary turned out to be badly damaged by a combination of mud, moisture, and age. Most of the pages were stuck together and fell apart when an attempt was made to separate them. "I forgot to tell you that Bettis wasn't much of a report writer," said Henry. "I learned that after going through thirty years of his previous diaries. Most of his pages were empty, and what he did write was usually chicken scratch."

"What do you think this is?" said Foster, looking at the page marked December 13. Bettis had scribbled four entries, one per line, in the middle of the page.

"Whatever he wrote is illegible," said Glance. "But the fact that he made four separate entries may be a clue."

"A clue to what?" said Foster.

"A clue to the number of possible suspects."

"And how many would that be?"

"Four."

"Remind me again who these possible suspects are."

"Hollis Bogar is the first," said Glance.

"In golf, we call that a gimme," said Foster. "What else ya got?"

"Richie Stillwell is the second."

"Didn't you tell me he was executed in Oklahoma for killing a gas-station attendant?"

"Yes, I did."

"When did that happen?"

"He murdered the attendant on December 22, 1956, and was executed in December 1958."

"Bogar and Stillwell are mentioned in the diary," said Ward, listening in on the conversation between Glance and Foster.

"On what page?" said Foster.

"August 12," said Ward. "That's one of the few pages in the diary that wasn't destroyed. I read Warden Bettis's entry before you gentlemen came in this morning."

"Please tell us what it said, Holly," said Foster.

"I'll do better than that. Here's a xeroxed copy."

> Contacted Hollis Bogar and Richie Stillwell behind locked Forest Service gate off Bald Mountain Road. Subjects claimed they weren't hunting. After confiscating their key and locking them out of the property, I returned to the contact site and found where they'd hidden a .30-30 rifle, a buck knife, and a canvas bag containing a rag and six .30-30 rounds. Expecting them to return for their rifle, I left my business card and a note in the rifle's place. Stillwell was hostile and uncooperative throughout the contact.

"Now we have a motive and a prime suspect," said Foster. "If Stillwell murdered the Oklahoma gas-station attendant nine days after Bettis disappeared, I think there's pretty good odds he killed Bettis too."

"Stillwell may have had a motive," said Glance, "but I'm convinced there were more people involved in this conspiracy than just he and Bogar."

"So now we have a conspiracy on our hands?" said Foster.

"I believe so," said Glance.

"Who's your third suspect—that bigshot developer over in Butte County? Wha'd you say his name was?"

"Blake Gastineau. Let's forget about him for now and see what's inside that aluminum paper case."

"Good idea," said Foster. "Holly, what did you find in the aluminum paper case? I saw you looking at it earlier."

"I found a stack of nineteen gas-station receipts," said Ward.

"Was there one dated December 13?" said Glance.

"Yes, there was, and it was issued by Bill's Friendly Service in Gridley. You'll be interested in knowing that the slip was signed by Norman Bettis. The initials EK were written at the bottom-right corner."

"Bill's Friendly Service is now a TV repair shop," said Glance, "but if Bill is still around, he may be able to shed some light on the subject."

"What's Bill's last name?" said Foster.

"I have no idea. He was out of business long before I moved to Gridley. I shouldn't have any trouble finding out and contacting him if he's still in the area."

"What do you think about this?" said Foster. "This afternoon I'll take the diary down to the DOJ lab in Sacramento. Maybe they can decipher whatever it was that Warden Bettis wrote on December 13, 1956. Holly, when Jack gets back, I'd like the two of you to work that partial license-plate number until you come up with something we can use. Hank, I'll leave it up to you to find Bill of Bill's Friendly Service. Good luck."

THIRTY-TWO

Henry returned to Gridley about four o'clock, after having spent all morning and most of the afternoon working the Bettis murder case with Brad Foster and members of the Glenn County homicide investigation team. Rolling into town on the Colusa Highway, he continued east on Sycamore Street and stopped at the post office. "Hello, Lucille," said Henry, to the middle-aged clerk at the counter. "I wonder if you could help me with something."

"I will if I can, Hank."

"Do you happen to know the former owner of Bill's Friendly Service?"

"I guess I should know him," said Lucille, a friendly smile on her face. "He lives across the street from me."

"May I ask his last name?"

"Wha'd he do—catch too many fish?"

"No," said Glance, returning her smile. "I'd just like to ask him a few questions."

"It's Oliver."

"Would you mind giving me his address?"

"Just a minute," she said, dialing the telephone on the desk behind her. "Millie, this is Lucille. No, I'm not calling to give you that recipe you asked for. There's a nice-looking young man here at the post office, wearin' a badge and a gun. No, he's not comin' to arrest Bill, but he would like to talk to him. Do you mind if I send him over? Okay, thanks." Hanging up the phone, Lucille grabbed a piece of scratch paper.

"I really appreciate your help," said Henry. "Thanks so much."

"You're welcome. Here, I drew you a little map. Go west on Sycamore until you come to Oregon Street. Turn right, go three blocks, and it's the green house with the white trim."

"What side of the street is it on?"

"It'll be on your left. Bill will be out on the front porch waiting for you. More than likely, he'll be wearin' one of those sleeveless white undershirts so he can show off his tattoos."

Henry found Bill Oliver sitting on his front porch, drinking a beer. As Lucille had predicted, the seventy-five-year-old former chief petty officer was wearing a sleeveless white undershirt. Oliver proudly displayed an anchor on his left shoulder and a hula dancer on his right.

"Mr. Oliver?"

"Yes," said Oliver, standing and extending his hand. "Lucille said you wanted to talk to me. You're welcome to call me Bill. Most of my friends call me Chief."

"Bill, I'm Warden Hank Glance, with the Department of Fish and Game. I've been working with the Glenn County Sheriff's Department on the recently reopened Norman Bettis murder investigation."

"I haven't heard Norm Bettis's name mentioned in years. Would you like a beer?"

"No thanks."

"How 'bout a glass of iced tea?"

"Sure, that would be great."

"Millie," Oliver shouted through the screen door, "bring our guest a glass of iced tea."

"Aye aye, sir."

"How many times have I told you not to call me sir?"

"I know, I know," said Millie. "You worked for a living."

"Did you know that Warden Bettis bought gas at your station on the day he disappeared?" said Glance.

"I didn't know that," said Oliver. "My bookkeeper used to keep track of all the gas receipts."

"I have a copy of that particular receipt, and the initials EK are at the bottom right-hand corner. I was hoping you could tell me who that is," said Glance.

"Of course. That would have been Elwood Keane. Nice kid."

"Do you happen to know where I might find Mr. Keane?"

"You aren't gonna believe this, but Elwood was in the Seabees and shipped out for Antarctica about the time that gas receipt was signed."

"Antarctica? You mean the South Pole?"

"That's what I mean. He was attached to a naval construction battalion that was building a scientific research station down there."

"Have you heard from him since then?"

"Yes, I got a letter from Elwood four or five years later. He said he had finished his stint in the navy, married a girl in New Zealand, and settled down in some little fishing village."

"Did he happen to give you his address or phone number?"

"I think he included a phone number in his letter. Come on in. I'll see if I can find it for ya."

"Here's your tea," said Millie.

"Thank you very much."

"Millie, this is Warden Hank Glance."

"Good to meet you," said Millie. "They must be making game wardens younger and better looking these days."

"I remember putting it in my desk," said Bill. "Here it is. I never did try to call Elwood, considerin' the price of a long-distance call to New Zealand."

Henry sat and visited until he'd finished his iced tea. "Thanks for the information," he said. "It's been great meeting you both."

"Let me know if there's anything else I can do to help," said Bill. "And please give my best to Elwood."

THAT EVENING, HENRY EXPLAINED TO ANNE that he would be staying up until midnight to call Elwood Keane.

"Why would you call someone at midnight?" said Anne.

"Because he's a possible witness in the Bettis murder investigation. And because he lives in Riverton, New Zealand. If my calculations are correct, it will be seven o'clock tomorrow evening where he lives."

"I hope you're right. I've had a long day, so I'm going to bed."

At the stroke of midnight, Henry dialed the New Zealand phone number Bill Oliver had given him.

"Hello," said a female voice.

"Hello, this is Fish and Game Warden Hank Glance in California. I'm trying to reach Elwood Keane. By any chance, is he at this number?"

"I can barely hear you," said the woman. "Who do you want to speak to?"

"Elwood Keane."

"Just a minute, please. Elwood, there's someone in California who would like to talk to you."

"Hello, this is Elwood."

"Mr. Keane, this is Fish and Game Warden Hank Glance. I'm calling from Gridley, California. Bill Oliver, one of your former employers, gave me your number."

"I remember Bill. How's he doing?"

"He's retired now and doing well. He said to give you his best. The reason I called is I'm investigating the murder of a game warden you may have known named Norman Bettis."

"A murder! When did this happen?"

"Warden Bettis disappeared on December 13, 1956. We're investigating the case now because we recently discovered his patrol car and some possible clues to his disappearance. One of those clues is a gas receipt from Bill's Friendly Service dated December 13, 1956, with your initials on it . . . Mr. Keane, are you still there?"

"Warden Glance, this is Matilda Keane. My husband has begun to hyperventilate. I think he's going to be all right, but he's going to need a few minutes to recover. May he call you back?"

"I don't want you to have to pay for the call," said Glance, "so please ask Mr. Keane to call collect. I'll be waiting by the phone."

Henry was reading at the kitchen table when the phone rang five minutes later. "Hello."

"This is the overseas operator. Will you accept a collect call from Elwood Keane in New Zealand?"

"Yes, operator."

"Go ahead, Mr. Keane."

"Warden Glance, I'm so sorry about what happened. When you said Warden Bettis disappeared on December 13, 1956, it was like being hit with a bolt of lightning. After all these years in Antarctica and New Zealand, I had no idea. If I had, I would have contacted the police years ago."

"It sounds like you have something to tell me," said Henry.

"I remember it like it was yesterday. Those four duck poachers drove into the station just after daylight, demanding that I serve them first."

"Did you know these guys?"

"I went all the way through school with three of 'em. We were in the same grade and graduated from high school together."

"Do you remember their names?"

"Blake Gastineau was the ringleader. Hollis Bogar was the class bully. He did whatever Gastineau told him to do, including beating up on other kids. Jimmy Riddle was driving the car. The fourth guy was a cocky little squirt with a big mouth. I think he was Bogar's younger cousin. Warden Bettis may have mentioned his name to me, but I don't remember."

"Does the name Richie Stillwell ring a bell?"

"That's it!" said Keane. "The others called him Richie."

"Would you mind telling me whatever details you can remember about that morning?"

"The sun wasn't even up yet when they drove into the station. I told Warden Bettis about 'em when he came in a couple hours later."

"Mr. Keane, are you still there?" said Glance, after a thirty-second pause.

"I'm sorry, Warden Glance."

"Please call me Hank."

"Hank, it just dawned on me that if I hadn't given this information to Warden Bettis, he might still be alive. I had debated whether to tell him what I'd seen and was shipping out the next day, so I was reluctant to get involved in anything."

"What had you seen?" said Glance.

"It was almost an hour before shooting time and these guys came in the station with blood and feathers all over the rear bumper of their car. Bogar had fresh mud on his pantlegs."

"Being a game warden myself, I can honestly say you did the right thing by telling Warden Bettis about it. Most of our important cases result from information provided by the public. What happened next?"

"I told Warden Bettis about my suspicions and even gave him the license number of the car Riddle was driving."

"By any chance, was the license number you gave Bettis written on an envelope?"

"I believe it was. I also suggested he check out the packing shed on Old Man Riddle's property."

"Tell me more about this packing shed. I think I read something about it in Bettis's diaries."

"I had informed on them back in high school."

"Who's them?"

"Blake Gastineau, Hollis Bogar, and Jimmy Riddle. They had killed a bunch of pheasants on Riddle's grandfather's farm. Warden Bettis caught them in the act of picking and cleaning the birds in Old Man Riddle's packing shed. I think Bogar had to spend some time in reform school for that."

"Do you remember the make of the car they were driving when they pulled into the station?"

"Not really. I think it was large, maybe a Buick or an Oldsmobile. Bogar got out of the car at one point and threatened me. I remember that."

"If things work out and we're able to put together a case against these guys, would you be willing to come back to the states and testify?"

"Absolutely! I feel terrible about what happened to Warden Bettis. The least I can do is testify at the trial. I can just see the looks on Gastineau's and Bogar's faces when they see me on the witness stand."

"Gastineau, but not Bogar."

"Why not Bogar?"

"Because Bogar's dead. We found him at the bottom of a canyon in Warden Bettis's patrol car."

"Was Warden Bettis in the car also?"

"No, we haven't found him yet. Do you have any idea where I might find Jimmy Riddle?"

"All I remember is he lived with his mother out west of Gridley, on his grandfather's farm. It's the same farm where the packing shed is located."

"That's okay," said Henry. "I should be able to find it."

"Riddle wasn't really such a bad guy," said Keane. "I think he just got mixed up with the wrong crowd. I don't know anything about Bogar's cousin."

"Stillwell is dead too," said Glance. "He was executed for murdering a gas-station attendant in Oklahoma."

"I guess that leaves Gastineau and Riddle, doesn't it?" said Keane. "Good luck with your investigation, and be sure to let me know if I can help."

"You've been a huge help, and I really appreciate it," said Henry. "I'll definitely be in touch as this investigation progresses."

THIRTY-THREE

Warden Glance called Detective Foster on the morning of August 30, 1971, to tell him what he'd learned about Bill's Friendly Service gas station and the attendant with the initials EK. "I located the previous owner of the station," said Henry. "He's a retired navy chief named Bill Oliver. Oliver said the initials EK were those of a man named Elwood Keane, who happened to be filling in at the station on December 13, 1956. Keane belonged to a U.S Navy construction battalion called the Seabees and was scheduled to ship out for Antarctica the next day."

"Antarctica?" said Foster.

"You heard correctly. Keane wrote a letter to Oliver, dated January 14, 1961, telling him that he had finished his stint in the navy, gotten married, and settled down in a little fishing village called Riverton. Riverton is on the southern coast of New Zealand, where Keane spent most of his leave time while he was stationed in Antarctica. Fortunately, the phone number Keane provided at the end of his letter to Bill Oliver is still good."

"You called him in New Zealand?"

"I did. Since New Zealand is nineteen hours ahead of us, I called him at twelve o'clock last night. When I told Keane about Warden Bettis's disappearance, the poor man practically went into shock."

"Why?"

"He blamed himself for Bettis's death. Keane said if he hadn't told Bettis about the four duck poachers who drove into the station early that morning, Bettis might still be alive."

"Before you go any further, let me guess who those four duck poachers were."

"Sure. Give it your best shot."

"Blake Gastineau, Hollis Bogar, Jimmy Riddle, and Richie Stillwell."

"That's right! How'd you know?"

"I just received a call from the DOJ lab in Sacramento. They were able to decipher the blurred names on Bettis's December 13, 1956, diary page. Some numbers and two more obscure words were scribbled in pencil at the bottom of the page. The numbers were probably Bettis's odometer reading at the time."

"What were the two words?"

"The technician at the lab said she's pretty confident about the second word but not at all sure about the first."

"What was the second word?"

"Shed."

"What letter does the first word begin with?"

"Either a P or an R."

"I'll bet Bettis wrote the words 'packing shed,'" said Henry. "It fits perfectly with the story Keane told me last night. Keane had informed Warden Bettis about Blake Gastineau, Hollis Bogar, Jimmy Riddle, and Richie Stillwell driving into the station before shooting time on December 13, 1956. The rear bumper of Jimmy Riddle's car was smeared with fresh blood and down feathers. Bogar's pantlegs were lathered in mud, indicating he'd been out all night tromping through some wet rice field."

"What's this have to do with a packing shed?"

"Keane had grown up with Gastineau, Bogar, and Riddle. They all graduated from Gridley High School together. According to Keane, he had once turned these guys in to Bettis for taking overlimits of pheasants. Bettis caught them in the act of picking and cleaning the pheasants in a packing shed belonging to Jimmy Riddle's grandfather. On the day Bettis disappeared, Keane had suggested to him that the poachers—Gastineau, Bogar, Riddle, and Stillwell—might have taken their ducks to the same packing shed."

"I think I know where that shed is," said Brad. "Jack and Holly were able to put a name and address with that partial license number we found on the envelope stuck in Bettis's 1956 diary."

"Incidentally, that license number was written on the envelope by Elwood Keane," said Henry.

"I figured as much," said Brad. "The registered owner of the car was James Jebediah Riddle, and he lived at 58723 Road 29, Gridley, California."

"How soon can you be here?"

"I'll be at your place in an hour, Hank. We'll take my car, so be sure to wear civvies."

It was 10:15 a.m. when Glance and Foster arrived at the farm on County Road 29 where Jimmy Riddle had lived for most of his life. "Look at this old, two-story brick house," said Foster, as he and Glance cruised up the gravel drive leading to the residence. "It must be a hundred years old."

"They don't make 'em like that anymore," said Henry. "Let's knock at the door and see if anyone's home."

"Good morning," said Detective Foster, displaying his identification. "Are you Mrs. Riddle?"

"No," said a slightly overweight, middle-aged woman wearing a cloth apron. "I'm Margie Palmer. My husband and I bought this place from James Riddle six months ago."

"Would you happen to know where we can find Mr. Riddle?"

"No, but my husband, Lyle, may be able to help you. He's down at the shed."

"How do we get to the shed?" said Foster.

"Just follow the driveway around the house and down the road. You'll run right into it."

Near the packing shed, Henry noticed a rusted-out Oldsmobile up on blocks, with all of its tires missing. "Stop right here," he said.

"What's up?" said Brad.

"I wanna check out that old yard car." Seeing no license plate on the front bumper, Henry led Brad to the rear of the car. "Does this license number look familiar?" The plate read WDO 876.

"You're lucky you got here when you did," said a voice coming from the shed. "The auto wreckers are coming to haul it away tomorrow. Ten bucks, and that fine automobile is yours."

"You drive a hard bargain," said Foster, laughing. "Are you Lyle Palmer?"

"I am. What can I do for you gentlemen?"

"I'm Detective Brad Foster, and this is Warden Hank Glance. We're here investigating a possible murder."

"A murder! What murder?"

"It happened almost fifteen years ago and may have occurred in this packing shed," said Foster.

"Are you kidding?"

"I wish we were. Your wife said you might be able to help us find the former owner, James Riddle."

"I have his address," said Palmer. "Last I heard, he was still living in a run-down apartment in Live Oak."

"Would you mind if we look around your shed?" said Glance.

"It's a mess, but help yourselves. We've been hauling moth-eaten old furniture and junk away since the day Margie and I moved in."

"Did you happen to find anything unusual or out of place?" said Glance.

"No, not really," said Palmer, his voice quavering.

"Mr. Palmer, you seem nervous," said Foster. "Is there something you'd like to tell us?"

"I didn't know a murder was committed here." Glance and Foster patiently waited for Palmer to continue. "A couple weeks ago, I removed an old Morris chair from the back of the shed over there."

"And?" said Foster

"And I found a gun lying under it."

"A gun?" said Glance. "What kind of gun?"

"A Smith and Wesson .38 revolver. My brother was here at the time and saw me pick it up."

"Was it loaded?" said Glance.

"It contained five live rounds and one expended shell casing."

"Did you think to contact the police?" said Foster.

"I did at first, but my brother offered me a hundred bucks for the gun, so I sold it to him. Maybe that wasn't such a good idea."

"What's your brother's name?" said Glance.

"Look, I don't want to get him in trouble. How 'bout I make a quick phone call and see if he'll bring the gun back?"

"Okay," said Foster. "We'll follow you to your house and wait outside while you make the call."

"I guess that would be all right. I don't want to alarm my wife. She can get pretty excited."

While Glance and Foster stood outside the screen door, they heard Palmer talking to his brother on the kitchen telephone. "Tim, this is Lyle. Do you still have that gun I sold you? Good. I need it back . . . because two officers are here and the gun may have been involved in a murder."

"A murder?" blurted Margie Palmer. "Lyle, what's this about a murder? I knew there was something fishy about this place when you bought it so cheaply."

"Margie, would you please lower your voice? The officers are right outside. Tim, are you still there? You need to bring the gun back right now, or I'll give the officers your address and they can come and get it . . . yes, I'll give you back your hundred dollars." Palmer hung up the phone and walked outside. "He's on his way over and bringing the gun."

When Tim Palmer arrived, he demanded to know why the gun was being taken by the officers. "We'll run the serial number and be right back," said Foster.

According to the radio dispatcher, the revolver had been registered, in 1954, to a man named Lloyd Frailey. Henry immediately recognized Frailey as the Department of Fish and Game's longtime training inspector. Further inquiry revealed that all the duty weapons issued to wardens in 1954 were registered under Frailey's name. The revolver Foster held in his hand had been issued to Warden Norman Bettis.

Foster advised the Palmer brothers that the revolver belonged to the Department of Fish and Game and would be seized into evidence. Lyle understood, but his brother wanted his money back. "I guess you guys will have to work that out," said Foster. "We never did look around inside the shed. Would you mind if we do that before we leave?"

"Sure, go ahead," said Lyle. "I'm gonna run back to the house and give my brother his hundred bucks so he'll quit whining. I'll be right back."

While Foster inspected the inside perimeter of the building, Henry walked across the shed's cement floor, looking upward. "What are you looking for?" said Brad.

"The gun contained one expended shell casing," said Glance. "That means Norm got off a shot. If there was a tussle, there might be a bullet hole in the ceiling."

"I'm back," said Palmer.

"Mr. Palmer," said Glance, "would you please show us where you found the Morris chair and the gun."

Palmer took several strides toward the south wall and stopped. "It was right about here," he said. "Keep in mind that I had to move a lot of other furniture that was piled in front of the chair. This place was a mess."

"Does this look like a bullet hole to you?" said Glance, pointing toward a tiny, round hole at the center of the metal roof.

"It sure does," said Foster. "I can see the sun shining through."

"Where do we go from here?" said Glance, as he and Foster drove away from the packing shed and past the Palmers' house.

"We've added a few more pieces to the puzzle," said Brad, "but we're still a long way from filing a murder complaint."

"We have two living suspects," said Henry. "I'd like to save Gastineau for last, so that leaves Jimmy Riddle."

"I have to meet a man in Hamilton City about a stolen car this afternoon," said Brad. "How 'bout we pay Mr. Riddle a surprise visit tomorrow morning?"

"What about Mr. Palmer? Are you sure he won't call Riddle and let him know we're coming?"

"While you were checking out the inside of that Oldsmobile, I had a little talk with Palmer. I read him the riot act about not reporting that gun. I also made it clear that he wasn't to contact Riddle until we've had a chance to talk to him."

"How'd he react?"

"He said he hasn't seen Riddle in six months and didn't think he had a phone. Besides, I've got a feeling there's hard feelings between Riddle and Palmer."

"What makes you say that?"

"Remember when we overheard Palmer's wife sayin' that Lyle bought the property for half what it was worth?"

"Yeah."

"He didn't come out and say it, but I surmised from my conversation with ol' Lyle, back there, that Jimmy Riddle is in poor health."

"So ya think Riddle was in desperate need of money and Palmer swindled him?"

"That might explain why Palmer didn't wanna go to the police when he found that gun," said Foster.

AT 9:00 A.M. ON THE MORNING of August 31, 1971, Henry Glance knocked twice on Jimmy Riddle's apartment door. Hearing someone hacking his guts out inside, Glance knocked again.

"If you're a bill collector, go away," came a shout from inside. "I already gave you bloodsuckers everything I have."

"We're law enforcement officers," Foster shouted back. "We'd like a few minutes of your time."

"It's not locked. Come on in." Foster opened the door and peeked inside. "I'm in here."

Following a trail of clothes, towels, cigarette butts, and pill containers, Glance and Foster made their way down the hallway to the bedroom. The pungent odor of tobacco-stained walls permeated the room where forty-year-old Jimmy Riddle lay propped up on the bed.

"Mr. Riddle, I'm Detective Brad Foster, and this is Fish and Game Warden Hank Glance. We were out at your former property on Road 29 yesterday. The new owner told us we might find you here."

"Did he tell you I have stage-four lung cancer and had to sell my place for half what it's worth to pay my medical bills?"

"No, he didn't mention that. We realize this is probably not a good time, but we'd like to talk to you about another Fish and Game warden who disappeared fifteen years ago. His name was Norman Bettis."

As Glance and Foster waited for a response, the expression on Riddle's pasty-white face morphed from anger to a pleasant smile.

"Mr. Riddle, are you all right?" said Henry.

"I had a dream that you guys would come. You have no idea how long I've waited to shed this burden."

"Does that mean you're willing to talk to us?" said Foster.

"If you'll call me Jimmy, instead of Mr. Riddle, I'll tell you everything you want to know."

Riddle gave Detective Foster permission to record his statement. Although he was not in custody and had volunteered to discuss Norm Bettis's disappearance, officers Foster and Glance decided to avoid any legal challenges later and read Riddle his Miranda rights. Riddle waived his rights and eagerly began.

PART FOUR

THIRTY-FOUR

GLANCE AND FOSTER DROVE STRAIGHT to the Glenn County District Attorney's office after leaving Jimmy Riddle's apartment. Foster had called from Gridley and arranged for Sheriff Bob Carlson and District Attorney Frank Braden to meet with them at one o'clock. During the meeting, Foster and Glance took turns detailing all the evidence and information they had gathered so far, including Warden Bettis's patrol car, Warden Bettis's duty weapon, Hollis Bogar's body, Elwood Keane's statement, Richie Stillwell's involvement, and most importantly, Jimmy Riddle's recorded eyewitness account of Norman Bettis's demise.

"Does your witness know he can be charged as an accomplice?" said Braden.

"He's aware of that," said Foster. "Mr. Riddle has stage-four lung cancer and is not expected to live much longer. He said he wanted to get this off his chest before he dies."

"Let's hope he lives long enough to testify," said Braden. "I don't suppose this Stillwell character would be a reliable witness."

"Stillwell was executed for murder in 1958," said Glance.

"Here in California?"

"No, in Oklahoma. He robbed a gas station and killed the attendant."

"These are model citizens we're dealing with," scoffed Braden. "I'm pleased with everything you officers have come up with, but we need a body or some type of physical evidence to prove that Warden Bettis is dead."

"James Riddle has described to us where the body is buried," said

Foster. "It's close to the location where we found Warden Bettis's patrol car. Warden Glance and I plan to take a crew up there in the morning."

"I hope you're successful," said Braden. "Before I take this to the grand jury, we'll need something other than Riddle's testimony."

"We're going the grand-jury route?" said Sheriff Carlson.

"Absolutely," said Braden. "We don't want our key witness to die on us before going to trial. I'll expect a detailed narrative of the information Detective Foster and Warden Glance just provided on my desk by 8:00 tomorrow morning. As soon as I hear from you officers after your dig tomorrow, I'll prepare an indictment proposal and summon the grand jury. Keep in mind that once the media gets wind of this, it will be all over the local and national news. Bob, you and I will need to prepare a unified statement."

"Brad, did you and Hank say that our witness is living in some seedy apartment in Live Oak?" said Carlson.

"Yes," said Foster.

"As sick as Riddle is, all it would take is a pillow and a little pressure to put him out of his misery," said Carlson. "Let's find him a safe place to live between now and the trial. I'll make a few phone calls."

Bob Carlson had been sheriff of Glenn County for so long, he knew just about every voting-age adult by his or her first name. By the end of the day, August 31, 1971, Carlson had arranged for Jimmy Riddle to be moved to an immaculately clean Victorian boarding house in Willows. A qualified nurse would check on Riddle and provide for his health-related needs every day until the trial was over.

Henry telephoned Anne to tell her he would be working on a preliminary report for the district attorney until the wee hours of the morning. "Henry, are you saying that you've solved the murder of Norman Bettis and you're about to arrest the person responsible?" said Anne.

"It looks that way, but we still have to find Bettis's body. It may be another week or so before we slap the cuffs on this guy. Meanwhile, don't tell anybody about this."

"I understand, Henry. I'm so proud of you."

"For what?"

"For being such a good person and sticking with this case when everyone else had given up."

"Maybe I'm just stubborn," said Henry, laughing. "I love you, and I'll be home as soon as possible."

Henry's next call was to Captain Chuck Odom. He would tell Odom that he could not work the next morning's dove opener because he would be in the final stages of the Norm Bettis murder investigation. After a thirty-second pause, Odom said, "Are you telling me you've found Bettis's murderer?"

"It may be another week or so before we make an arrest, but we know who did it," said Glance. "We've also found Bettis's patrol car and have a good idea where Bettis is buried."

"Hank, I owe you an apology. I admit that I thought this whole thing was a boondoggle and you were wasting the department's time and money. I hope you'll forgive me."

"Nothing to forgive. If I had been in your shoes, I probably would have thought the same thing. I'm looking forward to chasing duck poachers again when this is finally over."

"You're one hell of an investigator, Hank."

"Thanks, Chuck. I'll talk to you again soon."

At 8:00 a.m. on the morning of September 1, 1971, Brad Foster and Henry Glance handed their professionally prepared narrative to District Attorney Frank Braden and walked out the door.

"Where are you guys going in such a hurry?" said Sheriff Carlson, just arriving.

"We're going up into the mountains to see if we can find Norm Bettis's body," said Foster.

"That's right," said Carlson. "Good luck, and don't come back until you do."

Because the Bettis murder case had been given top priority by the Glenn County sheriff and the Glenn County district attorney, the chief deputy coroner was instructed to participate in the search for Norm Bettis's remains. Warden Glance and Detective Foster led the way in Glance's Dodge Power Wagon, while Chief Deputy Coroner Roy Giles, Evidence Sergeant Jack Weaver, and Deputy Holly Ward followed in a fully equipped van assigned to the coroner's division of the sheriff's office.

"What do you think, Hank?" said Foster, as the search vehicles passed through the iron gate and headed up the hill. "Are we gonna find Bettis?"

"We'll find him," said Glance.

"How can you be so sure?"

"It's bigger than the both of us, Brad. You can call it superstition, intuition, confidence, or whatever you want, but we're going to find Norm Bettis today, and we're going to find him right where Jimmy Riddle said he'd be."

"I hope you're right, Hank. The success of our case depends on it."

Members of the search detail noticed that several basketball-sized boulders had rolled down from the mountain and covered the area directly beneath the rock formation Riddle had described. After the group rolled the boulders aside, Glance grabbed a pick and began loosening the hard clay surface. Jack Weaver and Brad Foster were next, shoveling the loosened dirt. This process continued for almost an hour, until Holly Ward shouted, "Stop! I think I see a rib cage."

Ward immediately went to work with a four-inch pointing trowel, a small hand pick, and a three-and-a-half-inch, soft bristle brush. As more bones were uncovered, she graduated to smaller tools, including a standard toothbrush. "Holly, you're pretty good at that," said Giles.

"I should be," said Ward. "I majored in archaeology at USC."

"And became a deputy sheriff?" said Foster. "What happened?"

"I ran out of money and needed a job. Here's something that looks like . . . yup, we have a skull."

One look at the left side of the victim's skull confirmed what Jimmy Riddle had said. Henry envisioned the assailant grabbing a shovel handle, as if he were going to swing a baseball bat, and walloping Norm Bettis across the side of his head with the metal blade.

"Do you think it's worth trying to find the murder weapon?" said Foster, breaking Henry's concentration.

"Let's go see," said Glance, leading Foster across the narrow dirt road to the cliff on the other side. "It has to be down there somewhere, if what Riddle told us is true."

"Everything he's told us has been right on the money so far," said Foster.

"I'm gonna edge my way down this embankment and see what I can find," said Henry. Being careful not to lose his balance and slide all the way to the bottom, Glance skidded his way down the mountainside until he was beyond a jungle of stunted black oaks and out of sight.

"Hank, are you all right?" shouted Foster.

"I'm okay," said Henry.

An hour had passed when Foster again heard rustling in the vegetation below. He watched with great anticipation as his partner reappeared, covered with oak duff and dead leaves. Glance held a rusted shovel in his left hand.

"You found it!" said Brad.

"It was lying half buried in oak leaves, about fifty yards down," said

Henry. "This has to be the one they took out of Bettis's patrol car. It's a standard-issue Fish and Game shovel, just like the one in my truck."

Returning to the excavation site, Glance and Foster found Deputy Ward photographing the victim's left hand. Still clinging to the proximal phalanx bone of the ring finger was a badly tarnished wedding band. "If there's an inscription on the inside of that band, our job is done," said Henry, recalling a comment Tom Austin had once made about Norm Bettis never taking off his wedding ring.

"We'll find out soon enough," said Giles. "We're about finished here, so if you gentlemen are ready, I'd like to get back to the lab. The DA is eagerly waiting for our results."

When the Glenn County Grand Jury convened on Tuesday, September 7, 1971, District Attorney Frank Braden's proposed indictment charged Blake Ralph Gastineau with one count of murder in the first degree, with the special circumstance that the homicide was committed for the purpose of avoiding or preventing a lawful arrest. The indictment was granted, after which a warrant was issued for Gastineau's arrest. On the morning of Wednesday, September 8, 1971, Warden Henry Glance, Detective Bradley Foster, and two uniformed officers from the Chico Police Department entered the Chico land office of Blake R. Gastineau.

"Mr. Gastineau, Warden Glance and three other officers are here to see you," said Gastineau's receptionist over the intercom.

"Glenda, I thought I told you not to allow Warden Glance in my office unless he had a warrant."

"He does have a warrant, Mr. Gastineau. He says if you don't come out, they will come in after you."

When Gastineau failed to comply, Glance and the other officers walked into Gastineau's office and found him on the telephone, trying to reach his attorney. "Mr. Blake Gastineau," said Glance, "you're under arrest for the murder of Warden Norman Bettis. Please put your hands behind your back."

The local newspaper and TV stations had somehow gotten word that Blake Gastineau was about to be arrested. When Gastineau walked out of his office wearing handcuffs and was driven away in the rear of a caged police car, it set off a statewide media frenzy. After fifteen years, the mystery of Warden Norman Bettis's disappearance had finally been solved, and one of the lead investigators was a young Fish and Game warden with two years on the job, named Henry William Glance.

Blake Gastineau was arraigned on the afternoon of September 8, 1971, in Glenn County Superior Court. When asked by Superior Court Judge Nelson A. Rhodes if he would like to enter a plea, Gastineau, with attorney Gerald M. Burke standing by his side, entered a plea of not guilty. Judge Rhodes set bail at two million dollars. Coming up with ten percent to pay the bail bondsman was an impossible task for Gastineau, since most of his capital was tied up in land deals and construction projects. Brother Chet refused to talk to Blake, let alone loan him money, so the elder Gastineau was forced to take out a second on one of his newly constructed buildings.

Blake Gastineau and attorney Gerald Burke had been wheeling and dealing in real estate since Blake inherited his fortune years earlier. Also in his forties, Burke was a slick-talking lady's man who wore expensive suits and drove around Chico in a Mercedes convertible. Shortage of available cash and arrogance dictated Gastineau's decision to rely on Burke for legal representation, rather than hiring an experienced criminal attorney.

Due to Jimmy Riddle's rapidly deteriorating health, the district attorney made every effort to honor the defendant's Sixth Amendment right. Trouble was, Blake Gastineau was out on bail and the last thing Gerald Burke wanted was a speedy trial. He worked the system for all it was worth, stalling and asking for a continuance every time he came before Judge Rhodes. Had Burke known that the prosecution's primary witness had less than a year to live, his stalling tactics would have been even more relentless. Judge Rhodes set a trial date of Monday, April 3, 1972.

One week after the trial date was set, District Attorney Frank Braden announced that, due to the egregious circumstances surrounding this case, including the torture and brutal slaying of a peace officer to prevent Gastineau's arrest, the prosecution would seek the death penalty.

THIRTY-FIVE

T HE TRIAL BEGAN ON MONDAY, APRIL 3, 1972, in Glenn County
Superior Court. Constructed in 1894, the Glenn County Courthouse
was located in the county seat of Willows, California. Graced with fine,
handcrafted woodwork throughout, the courthouse hosted an elegant
courtroom on the second floor, at the top of a stately wooden staircase.
Emblazoned in glass above the doorway were the words SUPERIOR
COURT JUDGE NELSON B. RHODES.

Judge Rhodes was a sixty-two-year-old former prosecutor with fourteen years on the bench. A large, gray-haired man with a booming voice,
His Honor was well known amongst fellow barristers for being firm, but
fair, and displaying little tolerance for theatrics or courtroom shenanigans.

At the time of the trial, Glenn County boasted a population of 17,500
residents, with most of them living in Willows or Orland. Just about
everyone else in the county called Hamilton City, Elk Creek, Butte City,
or Artois home. Politically conservative and economically dependent on
agriculture—particularly almonds and rice—Glenn County's citizenry
was overwhelmingly white.

It took two full days to voir dire and finally seat a jury of seven men
and five women. Except for a Hispanic gentleman who worked at the
Holly Sugar plant in Hamilton City, the entire jury was white. Members
of the jury ranged in age from thirty-five to seventy-two, two of them
four-year college graduates and one a PhD.

District Attorney Frank Braden's opening statement was brief and to
the point. "The prosecution will show, beyond a reasonable doubt, that

on December 13, 1956, the defendant, Blake R. Gastineau, tortured and brutally murdered California Fish and Game Warden Norman Bettis— and that he committed this heinous crime for the purpose of avoiding or preventing a lawful arrest. The defense will try to convince you that this is a case of one man's word against another's. I urge you to carefully consider the evidence and make your ultimate decision accordingly. If you do, you'll find the defendant guilty as charged and give Warden Norman Bettis, at long last, the justice he deserves."

After making his introduction and trying to endear himself to the jury, defense attorney Gerald Burke eyeballed each of the twelve jurors and suggested that some of them, particularly the gentlemen, might have been hunters at some point in their lives. "Did you ever toss an extra duck or pheasant in your game bag? Perhaps you lost count, or maybe the hunting was so good you got carried away. The point I'm making is, we all did things we probably shouldn't have when we were young and foolish. What's important is whether we matured and eventually became responsible, productive members of society."

Burke continued. "The prosecution's so-called eyewitness is going to tell you that fifteen years ago, he saw Blake Gastineau kill Warden Norman Bettis. While you're listening, ask yourselves this: If that's true, why did he wait fifteen years to tell someone about it? Somebody killed Warden Bettis, it's clear, but how do we know it wasn't the witness himself? My money is on a convicted thief and murderer named Richie Stillwell, whom you'll no doubt learn about as the prosecution presents its tangled web of confusion and inuendo. One thing Mr. Braden said is true: This case may very well come down to whom you believe. Knowing what an intelligent, responsible group you are, I'm confident you'll make the right decision and find Blake Gastineau not guilty."

"All of the witnesses shall remain outside the courtroom until they're called to testify," said Judge Rhodes. "Mr. Braden, would you like to call your first witness?"

The prosecution's first witness was Glenn County Sheriff's Deputy Holly Ward, who testified that she discovered the remains of Warden Norman Bettis on the morning of September 1, 1971. Identification was confirmed through dental records and a wedding band identified by the victim's wife, Martha Bettis. When Gerald Burke had finished cross-examining Deputy Ward, Mrs. Bettis was called to the stand.

"Mrs. Bettis, would you please state your full name for the record," said the judge.

"My name is Martha Abigail Bettis."

"Mrs. Bettis, were you the wife of Norman John Bettis?" said the district attorney.

"Yes."

"How long were you married?"

"Forty-three years."

"Would you please describe your husband's occupation."

"Norman was a California Fish and Game warden."

"When was the last time you saw your husband?"

"The morning of December 13, 1956."

"Would you please describe, to the best of your ability, the sequence of events that occurred on the morning of December 13, 1956."

"Well, Norman got up around 6:30, like he always did. I was out of eggs that morning, so he drank a cup of coffee, ate a bowl of corn flakes, and drove off to work. That's about all I can remember—except for one thing."

"And what's that?" said Braden.

"While Norman sat at the kitchen table, drinking his coffee, he asked me if I thought he should retire. I found that strange because he usually avoided the subject of retirement like the plague."

"What did you tell him?"

"I'm not sure what came over me," said Martha. "Normally, I would have shrugged my shoulders and told Norman to do whatever he thought best. Instead, I became emotional and reminded him of the early years, when he'd be called out in the middle of the night because shots were fired down in Butte Sink or some deer poacher was shining a spotlight around in the foothills south of Oroville. I started sobbing and told him every time he threw on his uniform and rushed out the door, I worried myself sick that he wouldn't come back."

"How did your husband respond?"

"He said I was being silly. Then he climbed up out of that old wooden chair at the end of the kitchen table, gave me a kiss on the forehead, and walked out the door."

"Mrs. Bettis, I would like you to look at this ring and tell the jury if you recognize it." Braden handed Martha Bettis the wedding band that Deputy Ward had found on the finger of the victim's left hand.

"Yes, I recognize it," said Martha, holding back tears. "It's the same one I gave to Norman on our wedding day."

"What is it about this ring that you recognize?"

"Engraved on the inside are the words Norm and Martha."

"Thank you, Mrs. Bettis," said Braden. "That's all I have, Your Honor."

"Mr. Burke, your witness," said the judge.

"I have no questions for this witness," said Burke.

"Thank you, Mrs. Bettis," said the judge. "If Mr. Braden or Mr. Burke don't intend to call you again, you are welcome to remain in the court-room." Martha took a seat in the spectator section, next to Tom Austin.

The district attorney called Elwood Keene to the witness stand. "Mr. Keane," said Braden, "do you know the defendant, Blake Gastineau? If so, how long have you known him?"

"I've known Blake Gastineau since elementary school," said Keane. "We were in the same grade and graduated from Gridley High School together."

"Is Mr. Gastineau in the courtroom today? If so, would you please point him out to the jury."

"That's him," said Keane, pointing to the defendant, who was sitting at the defendant's table, next to his attorney.

"On the morning of December 13, 1956, did you encounter the de-fendant, Blake Gastineau?"

"I did."

"Would you please describe the sequence of events that took place."

"I was about to open up the station when—"

"What station was that?"

"Bill's Friendly Service in Gridley."

"Please continue."

"Like I said, I was about to open the station when these four duck poachers drove in before daylight, demanding that I serve them first."

"Objection!" said Burke, requesting a sidebar.

Burke and Braden approached the bench. "Referring to my client as a duck poacher is clearly an inflammatory statement that could unjustly prejudice the jury," Burke said.

"Sustained," said the judge. "Mr. Keane, please refrain from express-ing your personal opinions and making prejudicial statements. Just an-swer the question." Keane nodded.

"Please explain what you meant by serving them first," said Braden.

"Two men in a pickup, with a dog in back, had driven into the station earlier. They were already waiting for me to open when Gastineau and his friends pulled up to the pumps."

"Mr. Keane, who else was in the car with Blake Gastineau?"

"Jimmy Riddle was driving the car. Blake Gastineau was in the passen-ger seat next to him. Sitting in back were Hollis Bogar and Richie Stillwell."

"How old were the defendant and his companions when this happened?"

"Gastineau, Bogar, and Riddle must have been twenty-five, like me. Stillwell was probably a year or two younger."

"Had you had a problem with Gastineau, Bogar, and Riddle in the past?"

"Yes. When we were seniors in high school, I turned them in to Warden Bettis for poaching pheasants."

"Objection," said Burke, requesting a private conference with the judge. Judge Rhodes called a recess and instructed Burke and Braden to follow him into his chambers.

"Mr. Burke, state your case," said Judge Rhodes.

"This is not only inflammatory, it is completely unrelated to the murder charge before this court," said Burke. "So what if my client shot a few extra pheasants or ducks when he was young and stupid? Those were misdemeanors, and the statutes of limitations for any misdemeanors he might have committed have long since passed. Blake Gastineau has become a successful businessman and a pillar of his community. Mr. Braden is trying to portray him to the jury as nothing more than a common poacher."

"Mr. Braden?" said the judge.

"I'm simply establishing motive, Your Honor. Mr. Gastineau was much more than a common poacher. He was engaged in the lucrative black-market business of killing, selling, and distributing waterfowl to restaurants all over California. Had Ralph Gastineau, Blakes' father, learned that his son had been arrested for this serious crime, Blake stood to forfeit his inheritance. We're talking about millions of dollars in cash and thousands of acres of valuable land. People have been murdered for a lot less."

"You have no idea what Blake's father would have done," said Burke.

"On the contrary," said Braden. "We do know what Blake's father would have done, and we intend to prove it as the trial continues."

"Let's go back in the courtroom," said the judge. "I'll give you my decision there."

Judge Rhodes allowed the district attorney to continue his present line of questioning, as long as he didn't stray too far. Elwood Keene testified that he had seen fresh blood and duck feathers on the rear bumper of Riddle's car and fresh mud on Hollis Bogar's pantlegs nearly an hour before legal shooting time. He'd given this information to Warden Bettis and suggested that the suspected duck poachers might have taken the ducks to Riddle's grandfather's packing shed—the same place where Bettis had caught them with a substantial overlimit of pheasants eight years before.

"Mr. Burke, your witness," said the judge.

"Mr. Keane, did Blake Gastineau ever threaten you or retaliate in any way for your having snitched on him to Warden Bettis about the pheasants?"

"No."

"Doesn't that say something about Mr. Gastineau?"

"I'm not sure what you're getting at," said Keane. "Blake never—"

"Oh come now, Mr. Keane!" said Burke, raising his arms in the air. "You know as well as I do that Blake Gastineau is a kind man, without a vindictive bone in his body."

"Objection," said Braden. "Mr. Burke should be asking questions, not making statements."

"Sustained," said the judge. "Mr. Braden, would you like to redirect?"

"Yes, Your Honor. Mr. Keane, you had begun to respond to Mr. Burke's comment. What were you going to say?"

"Blake Gastineau never did any of his own dirty work," said Keane, "even back in school."

"Why was that?" said Braden.

"Because Hollis Bogar always did it for him. That big bully threatened me clear up until graduation. He did it again that morning, when they came into the station."

"Objection," said Burke.

"Overruled," said the judge. "Mr. Burke, you were the one who opened this can of worms. If you don't have any more questions, let's continue."

"The prosecution would like to excuse Mr. Keane and call Warden Henry Glance to the stand," said the district attorney.

"Warden Glance," said Braden, "when was the first time you suspected that Blake Gastineau might have had something to do with the disappearance of Warden Norman Bettis?"

"Before I knew anything about Blake Gastineau, I began investigating two individuals named Hollis Bogar and Richie Stillwell," said Glance. "Bogar and Stillwell had a run-in with Warden Bettis during the summer of 1956, a few months before Bettis disappeared."

"How do you know that?"

"That information was given to me by Pearl Malloy, the owner and operator of Pearl's Roadside Diner in Gridley."

"Objection," said Burke. "Hearsay."

"Your Honor, Mrs. Pearl Malloy is listed as a witness and is outside the courtroom now," said Braden.

"Then let's call her in," said the judge.

Pearl Malloy testified to having overheard Norman Bettis tell Earl Glenn about his run-in with Hollis Bogar and Richie Stillwell during the summer of 1956. She had also heard Bettis tell Glenn about seizing a rifle belonging to Stillwell. When Burke had finished cross-examining Mrs. Malloy with a barrage of accusations and poorly thought-out questions, Henry Glance returned to the stand.

"Warden Glance, what else did you learn about Hollis Bogar and Richie Stillwell that led you to suspect the defendant, Blake Gastineau?" said District Attorney Braden.

"Hollis Bogar was the son of a man known as Dud Bogar, whom Warden Bettis suspected of unlawfully killing and selling wild ducks. I learned about Dud Bogar by reading thirty-two years of Norman Bettis's daily diaries."

"Objection," said Burke.

"Your Honor," said Braden, "all thirty-two of Warden Bettis's diaries have been made available to Mr. Burke. He was welcome to read them himself, had he chosen to do so."

"I'm going to overrule your objection," said the judge. "Please continue, Warden Glance."

"Warden Bettis had contacted Hollis Bogar and Richie Stillwell while they were hunting somewhere out west of Stony Gorge Reservoir. As a result of that contact, Bettis ended up seizing a rifle owned by Richie Stillwell. The rifle was later logged into the California Department of Fish and Game's Region 2 evidence locker, in Sacramento. Stillwell never claimed the rifle, so it remained in the evidence locker until it was eventually sold at auction. I ran a check on the rifle's serial number and traced it to a man named Tucker Stillwell, in Kingfisher, Oklahoma. Tucker was Richie Stillwell's grandfather. Richie Stillwell had stolen the rifle from him and run off to California."

"Your Honor, where is Mr. Braden going with this cock-and-bull story?" said Burke.

"Mr. Braden, my patience is running thin," said the judge. "I hope there's a point to this line of questioning."

"There is, Your Honor," said Braden. "Please continue, Warden Glance."

"I began asking around about Hollis Bogar and Richie Stillwell," said Glance. "No one, including the manager of the trailer park where Bogar and Stillwell lived, had seen either one of them since the middle of December 1956."

"In other words, they disappeared approximately the same time as Warden Bettis. Is that true, Warden Glance?"

"It sure looked that way to me."

"I'd like you to look at these two rap sheets obtained from the Butte County Sheriff's Department and tell me if you've seen them before," said Braden.

"Yes, I've seen them before," said Glance. "The last official records I could find of Hollis Bogar or Richie Stillwell were in these documents. On July 4, 1956, Hollis DeWayne Bogar and Ferlin Richard Stillwell were arrested at the City of Chico's One Mile swimming pool, for disturbing the peace and public drunkenness."

"What was it about these records that caught your eye?" said Braden.

"On that same day, July 4, 1956, Bogar and Stillwell were bailed out of jail by Blake R. Gastineau."

"Did you confront the defendant with this information?"

"Yes. Warden Tom Austin and I contacted Mr. Gastineau on November 3, 1970. Gastineau was leaving his office and walking out to his car when I called out to him."

"And how did he react?"

"When he turned around and saw the two of us walking toward him in our Fish and Game uniforms, he looked like he'd seen a ghost. His face turned red, and his hands were trembling."

"Did you say anything to him?"

"Yes. My exact words were, 'When was the last time you saw Hollis Bogar or Richie Stillwell?'"

"How did Mr. Gastineau react?"

"He became angry and said he didn't know anyone by that name."

"Did you question Mr. Gastineau on another occasion?" said Braden.

"Yes," said Glance.

"Please explain what happened."

"I had found a list of three phone numbers at what had been the Butler Farms office. Butler Farms, located a few miles north of Lincoln, was previously owned and operated by a man named Clarence "Pinky" Butler, who was the middleman for a once-thriving black-market duck-selling operation."

"Objection," said Burke. "What proof does the prosecution have that Butler Farms or this Pinky character even existed, let alone that my client was in any way associated with them?"

"Mr. Braden?" said the judge.

"Your Honor, if Mr. Burke had examined the witness document I gave him during discovery, he would have seen the names Hector Campos, Lance Kirby, Mike Prescott, and Roy Campbell listed. Those gentlemen are all here to corroborate Warden Glance's testimony and be cross-examined."

"Warden Glance, please continue," said the judge.

"Two of those phone numbers belonged to well-known duck poachers," said Glance, "Homer Leadbetter, in Klamath Falls, Oregon, and Melvin Cobb, in Willows, California. The third phone number was no longer in service, but it had previously been listed to Blake R. Gastineau, at 39680 County Road E, Biggs, California. On November 10, 1970, I contacted Blake Gastineau at his office and asked about his relationship with Pinky Butler and the Butler turkey farm."

"What was Mr. Gastineau's response?"

"He threw me out of his office and said not to come back unless I had a warrant."

"That's all for now," said Braden.

"Mr. Burke, your witness."

THIRTY-SIX

"I'LL TELL YOU WHAT I THINK, Warden Glance. I think you're providing exaggerated, if not false, testimony about my client selling ducks to some character named Pinky," said defense attorney Burke during cross-examination.

The prosecution countered Burke's claims by calling Oregon State Police Officer Lance Kirby, retired California Fish and Game Warden Mike Prescott, Mr. Hector Campos, and U.S. Fish and Wildlife Special Agent in Charge Roy Campbell to the witness stand over the next three days.

Trooper Lance Kirby testified that he had received a call from Warden Henry Glance, asking about a Klamath Falls-area resident named Homer Leadbetter. Kirby had told Glance that Leadbetter was a well-known duck poacher who had been arrested on at least two occasions for taking overlimits of ducks. Leadbetter had been suspected of selling ducks to someone in California, but that information had never been corroborated.

Retired California Fish and Game Warden Mike Prescott testified that he had received a call from Warden Glance, asking about a Willows-area resident named Melvin Cobb. "Mel Cobb was the closest thing to a professional outlaw I ever knew," said Prescott. "He was arrested for selling ducks to an undercover U.S. Fish and Wildlife agent in 1939. That didn't stop him, though. Mel continued to illegally kill and sell ducks right up until the time of his accident."

Hector Campos testified that he had been a longtime employee of Clarence "Pinky" Butler's during the 1950s. That continued until Butler

mysteriously disappeared in 1957. Since that time, Campos had remained on the farm as caretaker for Tina Butler, Pinky Butler's wife, and
the eventual buyers of the property.

"Did you actually witness Pinky Butler purchasing wild ducks from
hunters?" said the district attorney.

"Many times," said Campos. "Over the years, I watched him buy
thousands of wild ducks from hunters who delivered their birds to the
farm."

"What did Mr. Butler do with the ducks he bought from these
hunters?"

"We processed them," said Campos.

"Please explain what you mean by processing them," said Braden.

"The ducks were already gutted, so we'd run them through the plucking machine. The machine would remove all the feathers."

"Then what?"

"Then we'd wrap the ducks in cellophane and stuff them inside the
turkey carcasses. Señor Pinky's drivers delivered turkeys to restaurants
all over California."

"Do you recognize the defendant, Blake Gastineau, as one of the
hunters who delivered ducks to Pinky Butler?"

"Yes. He looks older now, but he's definitely one of the hunters who
sold ducks to Señor Pinky."

"How many wild ducks would you say Blake Gastineau sold to Mr.
Butler?"

"I'm not sure of the exact number, but over a two-year period between 1954 and 1956, Señor Gastineau brought over a thousand wild
ducks to the farm. He quit coming sometime in December 1956, a year
before the federales arrived."

"What do you mean, the federales arrived?" said Braden.

"In 1957, federal game wardens came to the farm with a search warrant," said Campos. "They left with many boxes of records, papers, and
at least ten large bags of feathers."

When defense attorney Burke had finished cross-examining Hector
Campos, District Attorney Braden called U.S. Fish and Wildlife Special
Agent in Charge Roy Campbell to the witness stand. Agent Campbell testi-
fied that he had supervised the 1957 search-warrant detail at Butler Farms.

"When you seized Pinky Butler's records, did you find evidence that
Blake Gastineau or other hunters had come to the farm and sold ducks?"
said Braden.

"We were unable to find any specific information about hunters who had come to the farm and sold ducks to Clarence 'Pinky' Butler," said Campbell.

"What did you find?"

"We did find records of over fifty thousand ducks being sold to restaurants in California and the Western U.S, going back to the 1930s, when Pinky Butler's father operated the business. A list of Butler's regular customers led us to a number of restaurants where arrests were made."

"Were any of these restaurants in Glenn County or Butte County?"

"I don't believe so. It's been fifteen years since that detail went down, but I do remember one particular restaurant in San Francisco called Vannucci's. I walked in the kitchen waving a search warrant, with five more federal officers right behind me. All of us were wearing blue, federal-agent windbreakers. The head chef, who was basting two ducks in wine and butter when we entered, dropped his spoon, began whimpering, and ran out the back door. We later obtained arrest warrants for the owner, the manager, and the head chef. They each paid several thousand dollars in fines and spent six months in jail."

"What about Pinky Butler? What happened to him?"

"Mr. Butler weighed almost 300 pounds. One would think a man that large would be easy to find. When we returned with an arrest warrant the day after our search, he was nowhere to be found. No one has seen hide nor hair of him since."

By the afternoon of April 6, after listening to four days of testimony and cross-examination, Blake Gastineau concluded that his business partner and attorney, Gerald Burke, was overmatched and out of his league. The judge agreed to excuse the jury until Tuesday, April 11, giving Gastineau four days to secure additional counsel. On Tuesday morning, April 11, attorney Marvin W. Spratt, of the San Francisco firm Paddock, Mahill, and Spratt, introduced himself as Gerald Burke's co-counsel. A portly man in his early fifties, Spratt wore glasses, spit-shined wingtip shoes, and a dark-gray continental suit.

District Attorney Braden returned Henry Glance to the witness stand. Glance testified that on August 21, 1971, while patrolling behind a locked Forest Service gate—on Logging Spur A-26, off Bald Mountain Road—he discovered where a timber harvesting clear-cut had caused part of the mountainside to cave in.

"A deer hunter at the scene told me about finding a heavy-duty wire sticking up out of the fallen debris at the bottom of the canyon," said

Glance. "An orange styrofoam ball, which was slightly larger than a golf ball, was attached to the end of the wire."

"Was this heavy-duty wire attached to something?" said Braden.

"Yes. The wire, which turned out to be a radio antenna, was attached to the rear bumper of Warden Bettis's patrol car," said Glance. "On Wednesday, August 25, 1971, we found the car buried directly under that orange styrofoam ball."

"When was the patrol car reported to have disappeared?"

"On December 13, 1956—the same day Warden Bettis disappeared."

Warden Henry Glance, Detective Bradley Foster, Sergeant Jack Weaver, and Deputy Holly Ward each testified to details related to the discovery of Hollis Bogar's body in the front seat of Bettis's patrol car. Bogar had identification on him and was identified through dental records. Also found in the patrol car were a 1956 diary belonging to Norman Bettis and a gas receipt, dated December 13, 1956, that Bettis had signed.

"Evidence found in Warden Bettis's patrol car led Detective Foster and me to the former home of James J. Riddle," said Glance. "The property had been sold, six months earlier, to Mr. Lyle Palmer. While cleaning out the shed and removing old furniture, Palmer found a .38 caliber revolver that had been issued to Warden Norman Bettis by the California Department of Fish and Game. The six-shot revolver was still loaded, with one cartridge having been fired. Palmer provided Detective Foster and me with the current address of the former owner of the farm, James Riddle."

"Did you contact Mr. Riddle?" said Braden.

"Yes. At 9:00 a.m., on August 31, 1971, Detective Foster and I conducted a taped interview of James Riddle at his apartment in Live Oak. Information provided by Mr. Riddle enabled Detective Foster, Chief Deputy Coroner Roy Giles, Sergeant Jack Weaver, Deputy Holly Ward, and me to locate and uncover the remains of Warden Norman Bettis. Bettis's remains were discovered within fifty yards of the cliff on Logging Spur A-26, at the bottom of which Bettis's patrol car and Hollis Bogar's body had been found."

Deputy Coroner Roy Giles testified that extensive damage to the left side of the victim's skull likely resulted from a powerful blow. Based on measurements, the blow could have come from a blunt instrument, such as the blade of a shovel. Found on the side of the canyon, approximately sixty yards from Norman Bettis's remains, was a Department of Fish and Game-issued, long-handled shovel. The shovel was identified by Department of Justice forensics expert Russell Gibbons as the possible murder weapon.

On Friday, April 28, 1972, after sixteen days of testimony and cross-examination involving eleven prosecution witnesses, James Riddle was called to testify. The spectator section stirred with excitement as a uniformed nurse and a bailiff helped the prosecution's star witness navigate his way across the courtroom to the witness stand—a straight-backed wooden chair with a microphone in front of it. Ashen and with most of his hair missing, Riddle was dressed in dark-colored slacks, a white dress shirt, tie, and a sportscoat that hung from his bony frame like a wet sheet over a clothesline.

"This guy looks like he's ready to die," whispered attorney Spratt to his client.

"I barely recognize him," Gastineau whispered.

BAM-BAM-BAM. The courtroom was called to order. "Please state your full name for the record," said the judge.

"James Jebediah Riddle."

"Mr. Riddle, I understand that your voice is weak, but please try to speak up so the jury can hear you."

"Yes, sir."

"Mr. Riddle," said the district attorney, "how long have you known the defendant, Blake Gastineau?"

"Since the first grade," said Riddle. "We grew up in Gridley together."

"At what point did you and Mr. Gastineau begin killing and selling wild ducks for profit?"

"Objection!" bellowed attorney Spratt, slamming his fist on the defense table and coming to his feet. "This line of questioning is inflammatory."

"Sit down, Mr. Spratt," said the judge. "Mr. Burke and Mr. Braden debated that issue earlier in the trial, and I made my decision. Your objection is overruled. Please repeat your question, Mr. Braden."

"Mr. Riddle, at what point did you and Mr. Gastineau begin killing wild ducks for profit?"

"I guess we were about sixteen when the three of us started workin' for Hollis Bogar's old man," said Riddle.

"When you said the three of us, who were you referring to?"

"Blake Gastineau, Hollis Bogar, and me."

"What was Hollis Bogar's father's name?"

"I never knew his real name. Everyone called him Dud."

"And the three of you worked for Dud Bogar, killing ducks? Is that correct?"

"That's right, but we only pulled drags occasionally while we were still in high school. After graduation, we started doin' it full time."

"Please explain to the jury what you mean by pulling a drag," said Braden. Riddle began coughing heavily. "Mr. Riddle, would you like a drink of water?"

"It'll pass in a minute," said Riddle, sipping on a glass of water. "About one or two o'clock in the morning, we'd sneak up on huge flocks of feedin' ducks and empty our shotguns on 'em. All three of us used semiautomatic shotguns with extenders so we could fire as many as eleven shots without reloading. By the time we finished shootin', there'd be ducks lyin' dead all over the field."

"How often was full time?"

"During the winter months, when the ducks were in, we'd pull a drag once or twice a week."

"On average, how many ducks would you kill each time you pulled a so-called drag?"

"We'd kill at least a hundred, sometimes more," said Riddle. "If the shootin' was extra good, we'd pick up the mallards and sprig and leave the others lay."

"When you said you'd leave the others lay, what were you talking about?"

"All the smaller and less desirable ducks, like teal, gadwalls, wigeons, and spoonies."

"You mean you'd just leave them in the field to rot and go to waste?"

"Objection, Your Honor. Where is Mr. Braden headed with this?" said Spratt.

"I'm establishing motive, Your Honor," said the district attorney.

"Objection overruled. Mr. Braden, make your point."

"Yes, Your Honor. Please continue, Mr. Riddle."

"Yeah, we couldn't carry 'em all, and we didn't have time to chase down the wounded ones, so we'd just pick up the dead mallards and sprig."

"What is a sprig?"

"That's what we called pintails."

"And you got paid for the ducks you killed?"

"Yeah," said Riddle. "Dud would run 'em down to his buyer. The buyer would pay him, and Dud would pay us."

"When did Blake Gastineau become the leader of this commercial operation?"

Riddle coughed briefly, took another drink of water, then continued. "I think it was during the summer of 1954 that Dud turned the business over to Blake."

"Please explain."

"Dud was gettin' sicker by the day. He had lung cancer, like me, and couldn't cut the mustard anymore."

BAM-BAM-BAM. "There will be order in this court," said Judge Rhodes.

"Your Honor," said Braden, "may we request a short recess?"

A ten-minute recess was granted, during which District Attorney Braden, Warden Glance, Detective Foster, and James Riddle held a short conference in a sectioned-off space behind the law library at the back of the courtroom. As diplomatically as possible, Braden explained to Riddle that they had tried to keep his medical condition a secret.

"The cat's outta the bag now," said Foster.

"Don't be surprised if the defense starts using delaying tactics," said Braden. "Mr. Spratt has a reputation for dirty tricks."

"Now I get it!" said Riddle. "You guys are afraid I'll kick the bucket before the trial's over. Don't you worry. I ain't goin' nowhere any time soon."

Braden patted his star witness on the back, as Glance and Foster helped Riddle return to the witness stand.

"Mr. Riddle, you were telling the jury about Mr. Gastineau taking over the operation," said Braden.

"Yeah," said Riddle. "It was that summer, in 1954, that Dud introduced Blake to his buyer and told Hollis and me that we'd be takin' orders from Blake from then on."

"Why Blake and not Hollis? Wasn't Hollis Dud's son?"

"Hollis was Dud's son, all right, but he was dumber 'n a rock. Blake was a pretty slick operator, even in those days. I think Dud recognized the businessman in him."

"What kind of changes were made?"

"Blake was the new boss, and he would run the ducks down to the buyer every week."

"Did you know who the buyer was?"

"Dud never would tell us, and Blake kept it a secret for a while. One day, Blake let it slip that his buyer was a guy named Pinky, who ran a turkey farm near Lincoln."

"What other changes were made?"

"I became the driver and lookout. We brought in Richie Stillwell to take my place as one of the shooters."

"Did the four of you have a place to hide all the ducks you killed?"

"We did," said Riddle, coughing again. "My grandpa had this old packing shed at the back of the property. After he died, we began using the shed to draw and hang our ducks before Blake took 'em down to his buyer."

"It's three o'clock," said the judge, "so we're going to adjourn until Monday morning at 8:00. Jurors are instructed not to discuss this trial with anyone. You're excused."

Sheriff Carlson, who had been watching the trial from the spectators' gallery, stood up and walked toward the prosecution's table. Waiting for everyone else to leave the courtroom, Carlson advised Glance and Foster that two uniformed officers were waiting to return James Riddle to his temporary residence at the boarding house. "Your man is doin' a damn good job so far," said Carlson. "I'm gonna make sure he stays safe and sound between now and the time he resumes his testimony on Monday."

Henry couldn't wait to get home and spend the weekend with Anne. It had been almost a month since he'd said anything to her besides hello and goodbye. When he parked his patrol truck in the barn and closed the double doors behind him, Anne was standing on the back porch, waiting with open arms. "Hello, handsome stranger," she said. "How'd you like to come inside and get better acquainted?"

It was almost 7:00 p.m. when Henry and Anne awakened from their impromptu afternoon nap. Anne had planned to prepare Henry's favorite dinner, fried chicken and corn fritters, but Henry said it was too late for her to go to all that trouble. Instead, they jumped in Henry's Beetle and zipped down to Pearl's Diner. Pearl stayed open until 8:00 on Friday nights, and Henry wanted to tell her what a great job she'd done testifying at the trial.

"I was glad to do it," said Pearl, handing Henry and Anne each a menu.

"I didn't get to see your testimony, since I was a witness also," said Henry, "but the DA told me he loved the way you stood up to the defense attorney's badgering."

"Do ya think we're gonna win?" said Pearl.

"If the jury makes their decision based on the evidence and isn't fooled by that dog-and-pony-show the defense is putting on, I think we have a good chance," said Henry. "The jury foreman is a retired constitutional law professor from Chico State. Hopefully, he'll see through all the theatrics and steer 'em in the right direction."

"What's his name?" said Anne

"I think it's Carr."

"My dad used to talk about him," said Anne. "He said students loved sitting in on Professor Carr's lectures. Many of them weren't even registered in his class."

"What was the attraction?" said Pearl.

"Every court case he talked about was a fascinating story. The students wanted to find out how they ended."

"I'm anxious to find out how this one ends," said Henry. "It seems like I've been working on it forever."

"Henry, you've done your best, no matter how it ends," said Anne.

Before leaving the restaurant, Henry and Anne invited Pearl and her husband to a barbeque they planned to host on Sunday afternoon.

THIRTY-SEVEN

"**W**HAT A GORGEOUS AFTERNOON," said Henry, pouring charcoal briquettes into the barbeque while waiting for the guests to arrive.

"It's too bad Pearl and her husband can't make it," said Anne, covering the front-porch table with a multicolored vinyl tablecloth.

"Pearl said she'd try to come by if business was slow at the diner. I guess her husband is out on the road. He's a long-haul truck driver."

"Is everyone else coming?"

"I think so. Tom and Mary Austin, Brad and Susan Foster, and Martha Bettis all said they'd be here. Martha was determined to bring a cake or something. I told her we had everything covered and to just bring herself."

"That's good," said Anne. "Here comes somebody up the driveway now. It looks like Martha."

It was approaching 6:00 p.m. when everyone had finished eating and was sitting around the wooden front deck sipping on a glass of wine. "It's been a wonderful afternoon," said Martha. "Henry and Anne, I'm so glad you invited me. I haven't enjoyed myself this much in years."

"Maybe now you'll have some closure," said Tom.

"I hope so," said Martha. "But before I move on with my life, I must do two things for Norman."

"What are they?" said Mary Austin.

"I need to give him a proper burial and a send-off of some kind."

"You mean a church service?" said Susan.

"Not necessarily a church service. Heaven knows, Norman wasn't the most religious man in the world. He cussed like a sailor and left that obnoxious parrot of his with quite a vocabulary."

"Yeah," said Tom, chuckling. "Hank met Oscar the day we came by to see you."

"What do they call it when a group of friends gathers to pay their respects?" said Martha.

"A celebration of life?" said Anne.

"Yes, that's it. A celebration of life."

"Maybe Hank could play his guitar and sing something," suggested Brad. "He used to entertain the rest of us down in Mrs. Iverson's pit."

"I don't think that's what Martha had in mind," said Henry. "Besides, I only know the words to a few folk songs."

"Henry, I'd love to have you play something at the celebration," said Martha. "Norman loved folk music. He was always singing in the shower. The neighbors could hear him from clear across the street."

"Then it's settled," said Tom. "As soon as the trial's over, we'll start making arrangements."

THE TRIAL RESUMED ON MONDAY MORNING, May 1, 1972, with defense attorney Gerald Burke pleading with Judge Rhodes for a continuance.

"What kind of problem?" said Rhodes. "Is he hurt? Is he in the hospital?"

"I'm not sure," said Burke. "Mr. Spratt's secretary spoke with my secretary and said Mr. Spratt would be delayed."

"You're not sure?" roared the judge. "Do you expect me to keep the jury waiting indefinitely?"

"Well," said Burke, having already awakened the sleeping bear, "I was hoping for a continuance until I'm able to find out more."

"It's against my better judgment, but I'll give you until eleven o'clock this morning," grumbled the judge. "Unless Mr. Spratt is lying in a hospital bed somewhere, I'll expect him to be here. If he's not here, I'll expect you to take over."

"Yes, Your Honor."

"One more thing," said Judge Rhodes, as Burke turned and slinked away. "I didn't just fall off the turnip truck, you know. If I find out this is a stunt to prolong the trial, I'll not only hold you and Mr. Spratt in contempt, I'll see to it that you're both disbarred. Is that clear?"

"But what if I can't reach Mr. Spratt?"

"You're wasting valuable time, Mr. Burke."

At 10:55 a.m., Marvin Spratt arrived at the courthouse behind the wheel of a 1952, turquoise-blue Cadillac. At 11:00 a.m., court was back in session.

"Mr. Riddle, please tell the jury what happened on the morning of December 13, 1956—the day Warden Bettis disappeared," said District Attorney Braden.

"I remember it was cold and rainy," said Riddle. "Me and Hollis were busy guttin' and hangin' ducks in the packing shed while Blake was sittin' on an old couch, writin' figures on his notepad."

"Where was Richie Stillwell while this was going on?"

"I'm not sure. He was probably snoozin' somewhere. Richie loved to kill things, but he was worthless when it came to doin' any work. The rest of us were workin' away, when I heard this strange voice. At first, I thought it was Hollis foolin' around. When Hollis said it wasn't him, I looked up and saw the game warden standin' there watchin' us."

"Did he say anything?"

"I remember him sayin' somethin' like, 'You guys never learn, do ya?' Then he started tellin' us to put our car keys and identification on the table in front of him. I figured we were screwed, so I started doin' what the man with the badge and the gun said."

"Please continue," said Braden.

"That's when the three of us saw Richie sneakin' up behind the game warden, with a shotgun in his hand. When the game warden realized we weren't lookin' at him, he turned around and saw Richie."

"Did Warden Bettis say anything?"

"Yeah, he started yellin' at Richie to put the gun down. When Richie refused and kept on comin', the game warden drew his pistol. He was pointin' it at Richie and tellin' him to stop, when Richie slammed the butt of his shotgun into the game warden's forehead. The game warden fell backward, hit his head on the cement floor, and his gun went off, blowin' a hole in the roof."

"What happened then?" said Braden.

"Me and Hollis ran over to check on the game warden. Richie just stood there mumblin'."

"Do you remember what he said?"

"Somethin' about payback for takin' his rifle."

"Would this have been the .30-30 rifle that Stillwell stole from his grandfather?"

"That's right," said Riddle. "The one with the fancy engravin'. Richie was real fond a that rifle and wouldn't let the rest of us even touch it."

"Please tell the jury what happened next," said Braden.

"I was down on my knees, checkin' ta see if the game warden was breathin', when Hollis said, 'He's deader 'n a doornail. I can tell by the way his eyes are rolled back in his head.'"

"And where was Mr. Gastineau while this was going on?"

"He was walking up and down the floor, whinin' about losin' his inheritance. Blake couldn't a cared less about what happened to the game warden."

"Objection!" shouted Spratt. "This witness doesn't know what Mr. Gastineau was thinking."

"Sustained," said the judge. "The jury is instructed to disregard the witness's last statement."

"Did Mr. Gastineau actually say that he was worried about losing his inheritance?" said Braden.

"Several times," said Riddle.

"Do you remember his words?"

"It was somethin' like, 'If we go down for this, Chet will get it all— the money, the land, everything.' He just kept repeatin' that, over and over again."

"Who is Chet?"

"Chet is Blake's brother."

"What happened next?"

"Nobody knew what to do. Blake began to panic and said we had to get rid of the body."

"How did you react to that?"

"I reminded Blake that it wasn't gonna be easy. It was pouring down rain outside, and we'd also have to get rid of the game warden's car. I wanted to turn ourselves in and claim it was an accident."

"Did you suggest that?"

"I practically begged 'em. We were standin' there arguin', when Hollis said he knew how to get rid of the game warden and the car—both at the same time. He took the keys from the game warden's pocket and made Richie help him remove the game warden's uniform shirt. The shirt was three sizes too small, but Hollis put it on anyway. I told him he looked ridiculous and wouldn't fool anybody. That's when Blake told Hollis and Richie to throw the game warden in the trunk of my car."

"What did you say to that?"

"I said, 'Nothin' doin'. You ain't puttin' no dead body in my car.' Blake kept tryin' ta talk me into it. I told him he was waistin' his breath and they'd better come up with somethin' else soon because my mom might have heard the shot and would be comin' down to investigate."

"What did the four of you end up doing?"

"We used Blake's hot rod. You should have heard him complainin' about all the mud."

"Speaking of cars," said Braden, "where did you find Warden Bettis's patrol car?"

"It was sittin' out by the county road. The plan was for Hollis to drive the game warden's car and for the three of us to follow in Blake's hot rod. When we got to a steep canyon over in Glenn County, where Hollis and Richie said the road was washed out, we'd put the uniform shirt back on the game warden, strap him into the driver's seat of his patrol car, and roll him off the cliff. If anybody found him, they'd think he accidentally drove off the cliff and killed himself."

"What time of day was this?"

"It musta been about ten o'clock in the morning. I remember the rain comin' down in buckets."

"And you followed Bogar all the way to Glenn County?"

"Yeah, we drove up Highway 99 to Highway 162 and took 162 the rest of the way. When we reached Stony Gorge Reservoir, we left the pavement and drove up a muddy Forest Service road to a locked gate. Hollis got out and unlocked the gate with a key he found in the game warden's car. I remember we closed the gate after goin' through but didn't relock it. A couple miles up that slippery road is where things got crazy."

"What do you mean, things got crazy?"

"Richie was sittin' in the back seat and he heard it first."

"Heard what?"

"A thumping sound comin' from the trunk. Blake flashed his headlights for Hollis to stop. Then we slowed down, and Blake turned off his engine. That's when we heard the game warden moanin'."

"Please continue," said Braden.

Coughing again, Riddle requested a glass of water. "Blake climbed out of his car and trudged through the mud up to the driver's window of the game warden's car. I could see him tellin' Hollis somethin' and pointin' toward the trunk."

"Where were you while this was going on?"

"I was sittin' in the front seat of Blake's hot rod."

"Then what happened?"

"Blake headed back our way while Hollis climbed outta the game warden's car and opened the trunk." Overtaken by another coughing spell, Riddle apologized and continued to cough until he began spitting up blood.

"I suggest we take a fifteen-minute break," said the judge. "Bailiff, please ask the nurse to step in."

With the jury out of the courtroom, Judge Rhodes asked the district attorney if he'd like to adjourn until the next day. Hearing the judge's question, Riddle said he would be all right if they'd just give him a few more minutes. "This has happened before," he said.

Once the jury was reseated, Judge Rhodes asked the court reporter to read back James Riddle's last statement. "Blake headed back our way while Hollis climbed outta the game warden's car and opened the trunk," said the court reporter.

"Mr. Riddle, please tell the jury what happened next," said Braden.

"When Blake made it back to the hot rod, he opened the driver's door and grabbed his keys outta the ignition. That's when I saw Hollis headin' our way with a shovel in his hand. I knew what he planned to do, so I got outta the car and tried to stop him."

"Were you successful?"

"No. He swatted me aside, causing me to slip and fall in the mud. When I climbed to my feet, I saw that Blake was about to open the trunk of the hot rod and Hollis was waitin' ta clobber the game warden with the shovel."

"Did you say anything?"

"I started shoutin', 'Blake, he's alive. We can't do this.'"

"Please describe to the jury what happened next."

"Blake and Hollis were standin' at the back of Blake's car, soaked to the gills and lookin' like drowned rats. Blake shouted back at me, 'I'm not goin' ta prison because this sonofabitch is too stubborn ta die.'"

"And those were his exact words?" said Braden.

"Yes," said Riddle. "A person doesn't forget somethin' like that."

"What happened next?"

"Did you ever have a jack-in-the-box toy when you were a kid?"

"I did."

"What happened next was kinda like that. As soon as Blake turned the key and raised the lid, allowin' the light and the rain to pour in, the game warden sat up in the trunk. I can still see him sittin' there in his white T-shirt, starin' at Blake."

"Did Warden Bettis say anything?"

"Not a word, but it musta scared the hell outta Blake because he started yellin', at the top of his lungs, 'Kill him, kill him!' I shouted at Hollis not to do it. When Hollis hesitated, Blake grabbed the shovel outta his hands and bashed the side of the game warden's head in."

BAM-BAM-BAM. "There will be order in the courtroom," warned Rhodes. "I will not tolerate any more outbursts."

Braden waited for the spectator section to quiet down. "Then what happened?" he said.

"Next thing I knew, Hollis was runnin' through the pourin' rain back to the game warden's car and Blake was closin' the trunk on his hot rod. Blake yelled at me to get in or he'd leave me behind. Richie was already in the front seat, so I climbed in back. We followed Hollis another mile or so before Richie piped up and said we were gettin' close to the place where the road was washed out. Hearin' that, Blake took his foot off the gas and we dropped back to about fifty yards behind Hollis. We saw Hollis stop at the end of the road, seconds before half the mountain caved in and took him and the car with it."

"What did you end up doing with Warden Bettis's body?" said Braden.

"We weren't about to go anywhere near the mudslide, and Blake couldn't wait to get the game warden out of his car, so we dug a hole right there."

"Can you be a little more specific?"

"Just above us was a rock formation sticking out from the side a the mountain. We buried the game warden next to the road, directly beneath that big rock."

"Who did all the digging?"

"We only had one shovel, so we took turns. I wasn't gonna have anything to do with it, until Blake said I was just as much to blame as the rest of 'em. 'If we go down, you go down,' he said. That's when Richie chimed in and said, 'Yeah, we'll tell the cops it was you that killed the game warden.' Just before we all got back in Blake's car, I saw Blake walk over to the other side of the road and fling the shovel into the canyon."

"Where did the three of you go from there?"

"After that, we went slippin' and slidin' back down the hill. We were lucky to get outta there without slidin' off the cliff ourselves or gettin' stuck in the mud. Before Blake dropped me off at my house, he told Richie and me that he never wanted to see either one of us again. He said, as far as he was concerned, our duck-killin' days were over."

"What about all the ducks you guys had left in the packing shed earlier that day?"

"That afternoon, I dug a big hole out in the orchard and buried 'em," said Riddle.

"Mr. Braden," said the judge, "if you have no more questions for this witness, we'll adjourn until eight o'clock tomorrow morning. At that time, Mr. Spratt and Mr. Burke will begin cross-examination. Mr. Spratt, may I expect you to be here on time?"

"Yes, Your Honor."

"Good." *BAM-BAM-BAM*. "Court is adjourned."

THIRTY-EIGHT

Attorney Marvin Spratt fired a barrage of confusing questions at Jimmy Riddle for two and a half hours on the morning of May 2, 1972.

"Mr. Riddle," said Spratt, "during your earlier testimony, you quoted Richie Stillwell as saying, 'Yeah, we'll tell the cops it was you that killed the game warden.' Do you remember saying that?"

"Yes," said Riddle.

"How long have you known that Richie Stillwell is dead?"

"I didn't know he was dead."

"I remind you that you're under oath, Mr. Riddle. You know as well as I do that Richie Stillwell was executed by the State of Oklahoma for robbing a gas station and murdering the attendant."

"Objection," said Braden. "Mr. Spratt intentionally injected that statement to sway the jury."

"I'm going to overrule," said the judge. "Mr. Riddle is instructed to answer the question."

"I didn't know Richie was dead," repeated Riddle. "I figured he musta gone back to Oklahoma, but I haven't heard anything about him for fifteen years."

Spratt ignored Riddle's response. "Isn't it true that when you found out Stillwell was dead and no one was left to dispute your story, you made a deal with the district attorney to testify against my client?"

"I didn't make a deal with the district attorney or anybody else," said Riddle, coughing. "When Warden Glance and Detective Foster knocked on my door and asked me about Warden Bettis's disappearance, I saw it as an opportunity to finally get this weight off my chest. The story I told is true. Every word of it."

"That will be all," said Spratt.

"I've carried this—"

"I said, that will be all," repeated Spratt.

"Objection," said Braden. "Mr. Spratt asked the question. Mr. Riddle should be allowed to finish his answer."

"Mr. Riddle, please continue with what you were saying," said the judge.

"Thank you," said Riddle, trying to control his coughing and reaching for a glass of water. "I've carried this guilt around with me for fifteen years, feelin' sick every time I thought about that game warden sittin' up in the trunk of Blake's car and Blake crushing his head with a shovel."

The courtroom was deathly quiet. "Mr. Spratt, do you have any more questions for this witness?" said the judge. Busy consulting with Burke at the end of the defendant's table, Spratt did not answer. "Mr. Spratt, you're stretching my patience."

"No more questions at this time," said Spratt.

"Mr. Braden?"

"The prosecution rests, Your Honor."

"It's five o'clock, so we'll adjourn until tomorrow morning at 8:00," said Judge Rhodes. "Mr. Spratt and Mr. Burke, you may begin your defense at that time. I remind the jurors not to speak to anyone about this case."

That night, Burke, Spratt, and Gastineau sat in Burke's Chico office, deliberating over ways to extricate Gastineau from his life-threatening predicament. "Blake's best chance," said Burke, "is for us to come up with a plausible alternative to Riddle's story."

Gastineau directed his attention to Spratt, waiting for an explanation. "You see, Blake," said Spratt, "Mr. Burke and I are not particularly interested in who's telling the truth—you or Riddle. Our job is to make sure the jury finds you not guilty."

"Either that or they're unable to reach a unanimous decision," said Burke. "All we need is one juror who believes your word is better than the word of that burned-out, drunken loser, and we have a hung jury."

"How do we do that?" said Gastineau, lighting a cigar and resting his alligator-skin cowboy boots on the top of Burke's desk.

"Blake, the last time you did that, it took me a month to get rid of the smell," said Burke.

"Did what?"

"Lit up one of those giant cigars of yours. Where do you get those damn things, anyway?"

"Same place I get my boots," said Gastineau, snuffing out his cigar and continuing to chew on the end.

"What about this?" said Spratt. "If Richie Stillwell hit Warden Bettis in the head once, who's to say that he didn't hit him again?"

"I like it!" said Burke. "By the way, that was a stroke of genius today, mentioning to the jury that Stillwell had been executed for murder."

"I thought so," said Spratt. "If Blake answers my questions exactly the way I tell him to, we'll have that hick jury eatin' out of our hands tomorrow."

"RICHIE HIT THE GAME WARDEN TWICE with the butt of his shotgun," testified Blake Gastineau on the morning of May 3, 1972. "The first time he hit him in the forehead, like Jimmy said. After the game warden fell to the floor, Richie hit him again—this time on the side of his face. I yelled at him to stop, but it was too late."

"Why did Mr. Stillwell hit the game warden?" said Spratt.

"Richie was crazy and unpredictable. When the game warden pointed his pistol at him, he probably reacted in self-defense."

"Are you saying that Warden Bettis never regained consciousness after Richie hit him?"

"Yes," said Gastineau. "Maybe all the drugs and alcohol had something to do with the way Jimmy remembers it. All I know is, Warden Bettis never moved a muscle from the time Richie hit him until the time Richie and Jimmy buried him on that hillside."

"Mr. Riddle testified that your car was used to transport the body and all three of you took turns burying Warden Bettis," said Spratt. "Was that an accurate account of what happened on December 13, 1956?"

"No," said Gastineau. "There's no way I would've driven my prized possession up that muddy mountain road, and I was so upset about what Richie had done, I refused to help 'em bury Warden Bettis."

"Please explain to the jury what you meant by your prized possession."

"That would be my 1949 Ford coupe with chrome rims and whitewall tires," said Gastineau, watching the jury out of the corner of his eye. "My father gave me that car as a high-school graduation present."

As Spratt and Gastineau performed their rehearsed Q and A for the jury, Warden Glance began shuffling through a pile of papers in his file folder. Finding what he was looking for, he nudged Braden with his elbow. Braden acknowledged Henry's discovery with a nod and continued to follow Gastineau's testimony.

"Whose car did you use to transport Warden Bettis's body?" said Spratt.

"Jimmy's Oldsmobile, of course. I only went along with this gig because they made me."

"What do you mean, they made you?"

"It was three against one. If I hadn't gone along with them, they were gonna say I killed the game warden."

"Did you kill the game warden?"

"Absolutely not! Richie killed the game warden, and Jimmy knows it. Like you said, Jimmy's just goin' along with the district attorney to keep from bein' sent to prison himself."

"Do you have anything else you'd like to say?"

"Huh?" mumbled Gastineau.

"Mr. Gastineau," repeated Spratt, "is there anything else you'd like to say to the jury?"

"Uh . . . yeah, there is," said Gastineau, shifting to his left and facing the jury, tears welling up in his eyes. "I'm sorry about what happened. We were all young, foolish, and . . . really scared. Richie killed the game warden, and there was nothing I could do about it."

"Thank you, Mr. Gastineau," said Spratt. "The defense rests."

"Mr. Braden, are you ready to cross-examine the witness?" said Judge Rhodes.

"Your Honor, may I request a fifteen-minute recess to confer with my officers?"

"I'll do better than that. It's 11:30 now. We'll take a ninety-minute lunch break. Everyone be back at one o'clock sharp. The jury is advised not to talk to anyone about this case."

"How did you happened to have this?" said Braden, as he, Glance, and Detective Foster huddled in the sectioned-off space behind the court's law library.

"When Hector Campos gave me the license number of Gastineau's car," said Henry, "I ran a check through DMV. The record showed that Gastineau sold it on December 20, 1956. I found it curious that the car had been sold exactly one week after Warden Bettis's disappearance."

"I'd say that was a little more than a coincidence," said Foster.

With court back in session, District Attorney Braden entered a certified California Department of Motor Vehicles document into evidence. He argued that this previously undisclosed record was being used to refute Blake Gastineau's recent testimony.

"Mr. Gastineau, two hours ago, you testified that your 1949 Ford coupe was, if I may use your words, 'your prized possession.' Your father had given it to you as a high-school graduation present, and there was no way you were going to drive it up that muddy mountain road. Is that a fair characterization of what you said?"

"Yeah, I guess so," said Gastineau.

"You loved that car, didn't you? Mr. Gastineau, please answer the question."

"I wouldn't say that I loved it. It did mean a lot to me."

"I'd like you to look at this California Department of Motor Vehicles document, signed by you and dated December 20, 1956." Braden placed the document in Gastineau's hand. "Do you recognize it, Mr. Gastineau?"

"Huh?"

"Let me help you," said Braden, taking the document back from Gastineau. "This document shows that on December 20, 1956—exactly one week after Warden Bettis was brutally murdered—you sold your prized possession, a 1949 Ford coupe, license number QBL 408, to a man named Wilbur Knox, in Stockton, California. If this automobile meant so much to you, why did you sell it so soon after the incident?"

"I don't know," mumbled Gastineau.

"You don't know?" bellowed Braden, turning and facing the jury. "I'll tell you why you sold it. You sold it because it reminded you of the terrible thing you'd done. When Warden Bettis sat up in the trunk of that car that you loved so much, you bashed his head in with a shovel."

"Objection!" shouted Spratt.

"Sustained," said the judge. "The jury will disregard Mr. Braden's last statement."

The prosecution returned James Riddle to the stand, in rebuttal to Blake Gastineau's recent testimony.

"Mr. Riddle," said Braden, "you earlier described how Warden Glance and Detective Foster had knocked at your door. Did you have any idea they were coming?"

"No."

"And you allowed them to record your statement, without any previous preparation or an attorney present?"

"Yes."

"Why would you do such a thing? Weren't you afraid of incriminating yourself?"

"Like I said before, I saw it as an opportunity to ease my conscience. It was because of that horrible incident that I started drinking. I lost my job at the body shop and, for several years, lived off the money my mom left me when she died. When I got sick, I had to sell my Grandpa's farm to pay my medical bills. In case anyone's wonderin' why I cough so much, I have stage-four lung cancer. They can throw me in prison, strap me to the electric chair, or do whatever they want. I'm gonna be dead soon anyway, so it won't matter. What matters is doin' the right thing for once in my miserable life before I die."

"Who killed Warden Bettis, Mr. Riddle?"

"That man right over there," said Riddle, pointing toward the defense table. "Blake Gastineau."

EPILOGUE

W HEN ALL WAS SAID AND DONE, the verdict came down to whom the
jury believed—Blake Gastineau or Jimmy Riddle. On the afternoon
of May 4, 1972, after only four hours of deliberation, jury foreman Roland L.
Carr, PhD, announced that the jury had found Blake R. Gastineau guilty of
murder in the first degree. District Attorney Braden had originally intended
to seek the death penalty, however, on April 24, 1972, while the Gastineau
trial was in progress, the California Supreme Court ruled, in the case of
People v. Anderson, that California's death penalty was unconstitutional.

On May 16, 1972, Blake R. Gastineau was sentenced to life in prison
without the possibility of parole. On May 17, 1972, James Riddle passed
away. Capital punishment was reinstated in California the following year
with the passage of Proposition 17.

Norman Bettis was finally laid to rest on Saturday morning, May 20,
1972, a half mile from Norman's and Martha's home in Gridley. Martha
Bettis, Tom and Mary Austin, and Henry and Anne Glance quietly, and
without ceremony, paid their last respects.

That same afternoon, a gathering of over two hundred Gridley residents,
current and retired law enforcement officers, and Sacramento dignitaries
attended a celebration of life in Norman Bettis's honor. At the end of the
program, Henry Glance walked to the stage and inspired the crowd with a
rendition of Ian Tyson's *Four Strong Winds*. Martha Bettis gave Henry a big
hug, after which she asked the ladies and gentlemen present to stand and
hold up the cold bottle of Olympia beer each of them had been given.

"Here's to you, Norman," she said with tears in her eyes. "I'll love you forever."

STEVEN T. CALLAN IS THE AWARD-WINNING author of *The Game Warden's Son*, named the "Best Outdoor Book of 2016" by the Outdoor Writers Association of California and published by Coffeetown Press of Seattle. His debut book, *Badges, Bears, and Eagles—The True-Life Adventures of a California Fish and Game Warden*, was a 2013 "Book of the Year" award finalist (*ForeWord Reviews*). Callan is the recipient of the 2014, 2015, and 2016 "Best Outdoor Magazine Column" awards from the Outdoor Writers Association of California. The author is an active member of Mystery Writers of America, Western Writers of America, Outdoor Writers Association of California, and Redding Writers Forum. He is currently writing his next novel in the Henry Glance series.

Steve grew up in the small Northern California farm town of Orland, where he spent his high-school years playing baseball, basketball, hunting, and fishing. With an insatiable interest in wildlife, he never missed an opportunity to ride along on patrol with his father, a California Fish and Game warden. Steve went on to graduate from CSU, Chico, and attended graduate school at CSU, Sacramento. Hired by the California Department of Fish and Game in 1974, he began his career as a game warden near the Colorado River, promoted to patrol lieutenant in the Riverside/San Bernardino area, and spent the remainder of his thirty-year enforcement career in Shasta County. Callan earned numerous awards for his work in wildlife protection.

Passionate about the environment, Steve and his wife, Kathy, are avid anglers, kayakers, bird-watchers, and scuba divers. They live in the Redding area.

Learn more about the author and his books at steventcallan.com.

CPSIA information can be obtained
at www.ICGtesting.com
Printed in the USA
LVHW020908120122
708205LV00017B/1929

9 781603 813068